I0781175

N
MOUNT BRENNE
FIORAN
THE KEEP
FIORAN CASTLE
FORGOTTEN FOREST
WEST MARKET SQUARE
DOVENEER
JACKLANDS
RACINE

THE KINGDOM OF ELARIA
NORTHERN PORT
MORANA
KENDALL
EAST MARKET SQUARE
SOLUME
AGRONA SEA
SYNAN
MINES
ISSLOTS
T. MUNRO 2021

Other books by Emilee King

Arie's Story:

Surviving on a Whisper
Surviving through the Night
Surviving to the End
Surviving the After

Elarian Chronicles:

Pieces in the Cinders
Cracks in the Tower

LOST IN THE MADNESS

EMILEE KING

ISBN-10: 1966173076
ISBN-13: 978-1966173076

Cover designed by MiblArt
Map designed by Tiffany Munro

To every lost soul trying to find their way in the dark

CHAPTER 1

A BOOK WITH NO PICTURES

Ally liked to bury things.

Crusty earth gave way under her cracked fingertips as mounds of grainy dirt lodged underneath her nails. The soft scratching sound settled her into a steady rhythm, relaxing her as much as she ever relaxed. Digging had been her favorite thing to do as long as she could remember. Even *before*. She could remember clutching little rocks in her small fist, shaking them triumphantly in the air as her mother pretended to scold her for all the holes in their backyard.

Now, though, it was a way to spend time, a way to combat against the raging boredom of her life. She had already buried over six sticks. She had to do at least two more to reach her goal for the day. Not that it really mattered—nothing mattered in this wasteland.

The muggy air clung thick in her throat, but the tightness in her chest didn't bother her. She'd been breathing the decaying air her whole life and had gotten used to the humid stench. Her mother used to worry it would ruin her lungs; her father used to grunt back that they had to stay.

What's done is done, he would growl, effectively shutting down the conversation.

On that point, Ally could admit, he was right. The damage he'd done to Ally's life was irreversible.

Ignoring the taste of rot that came with each breath, she gave a huff, blowing a piece of stringy blonde hair out of her face. Her kneecaps whined against the hard earth; her shoulders ached with the strain of leaning over for so long. But she had a goal to accomplish. So she disregarded the pain in her bones, the tightness in her chest, the blanket of dread that seemed to follow her everywhere.

And kept digging.

The sun rose as she worked, the light filtering through the smog. Tiny beads of sweat began to form on the back of her neck, dripping down the collar of her cloak. In the distance, someone screamed, then a stray dog howled. Ally hardly noticed. She dug until the hole was as deep as the length of her arm, then she reached into her pocket and pulled out the next stick. She tossed it into the hole without ceremony. A grunt escaped her as she reached across the opening to slide the excavated dirt back in, effectively burying the stick.

The broken branch hadn't been anything special—just a piece of dry wood she'd found the day before, part of yesterday's collection quest. Small. Insignificant. And now buried, never to be seen again, never to be acknowledged or missed.

Just like people. Just like her mother. Just like Ally.

Ally got to her feet and brushed her hands on her dirty pants, admiring her work. A scream sounded again, long and drawn out, until it abruptly cut off.

Just another day in the Molds.

For a moment, she watched the horizon through the hazy air, looking across the vast empty land and past the cluster of shacks beyond. For a moment, she let herself wonder what life was like outside this place. For a moment, she considered walking on and on until she found somewhere better. Anywhere.

But then that moment passed, and she remembered she could never leave. The Molds had marked her, the stench permanently etched into her skin in a way that she could never hope to wash off. There was nowhere else for a rat of the Molds. Definitely not for the child of Monty the Merciless and a dead mother nobody talked about. Her father had damned her to this years ago, ensuring Ally would always be a worthless stick and someday would be buried too. And that would be the end of it.

What's done is done.

Lip curling in disgust, she stared at the sun rising over the land she hated so much. It burned her eyes, but she held her gaze, challenging the sun to give her something more than the fate of a stick.

I'd make you proud, she thought. *I'd make everyone proud, if only you'd just let me.*

Seconds passed and her eyes stung worse and worse. Finally, she growled and blinked away, pressing her palms into her eyes.

"Fine," she muttered as colored spots danced along her vision. "You win." The words burned her grainy, dirt coated mouth. "But someday," she promised, "someday I will stare you down and I will win." Win what, she didn't know. Just *something.*

Brush rustled next to her. She jumped and turned, a shape moving out of the corner of her eye. Or was it still a sunspot? She wasn't sure, but she did know one thing.

Out in the Molds, everything counted as a threat.

Muscles rigid, Ally clenched her teeth and jumped back, expecting the worst: a rabid stray dog, a ruthless neighbor, her drunken father. Instead, she found herself staring at a rabbit. A small, white rabbit, streaked with lines of dirt.

The creature stared at her, as if just as surprised as she was to find it wasn't alone out here.

Once her surprise faded, Ally slowly reached inside her cloak pocket and pawed through her stowed rock collection. Her fist closed around the sharpest one, and she stared at the rabbit, imagining the best way to kill it.

She and Jesper would eat tonight. Actually *eat*, not just slurp up the mushed grains her brother mashed with water every day or get sick off of rancid meat from an old dog carcass they'd once found. They'd learned long ago that trying to trade for actual food themselves in the Molds could only be a death sentence—Jesper had nearly lost his hand the last time they tried— and Monty was only interested in stocking their cupboards with ale.

But this…this rabbit was a gift from the sky. She just had to kill it and somehow skin it. Her brother wouldn't go near the animal while it was bloody, but she could figure out how to skin it herself. Couldn't be much harder than the rotting dog. The rabbit was smaller, sure, but it would be fresh and untouched by decay. A rare miracle.

At the thought of something warm—of meat—Ally's mouth started watering and her stomach grumbled painfully. She could practically smell it now, feel the first bite of meat sliding down her scratchy throat and spreading warmth throughout her bony limbs. She imagined her brother's look of surprised pride at what she was able to do, all on her own.

It was an effort to keep from licking her lips as she took a hesitant step forward. The rabbit cocked its head, black eyes unblinking.

And took off.

Shouting a curse, Ally lurched after it, her worn boots skidding along the uneven ground. The rabbit leapt quick and fast, effortlessly dodging dips and rocks that made Ally stumble. She hissed through her teeth as the distance between her and the rabbit grew larger and larger, her hope of dinner— of a victory—getting farther away with each breath.

With one last push, the rabbit hopped over a rock and disappeared.

Ally cursed again when she skidded to a stop and saw the hole. Collapsing to her knees, she stuck her face in the opening, hoping she would come nose to nose with the vermin. But a small tunnel yawned open before her, showing nothing but dirt and darkness.

Jumping to her feet, she kicked at the hole and screamed at the sky, hurtling her rock as hard as she could. It bounced uselessly against the ground, and that made her scream in frustration again.

Stupid rabbit.

Stupid rabbit.

Her fit of rage passed eventually. Breathing heavily, she glanced around the wasteland before trudging back to her house. She never went back unless she absolutely had to, but she knew Jes would be looking for her today. And she'd show up empty handed, as always.

"Stupid rabbit," she growled under her breath as she walked. She should've smashed its skull the moment she saw it. She should've waited to chase it with the hope it would come back. She should've just kept digging. Now she had two extra sticks to bury tomorrow.

Ally's footsteps slowed until she stopped. Perking up, she turned around to glance behind her. A whisper of a smile tugged at the corner of her mouth.

Without another thought, she stomped back over to the hole and filled it with dirt.

"There," she said once she finished, brushing her hands on her dusty pants. "Now you're just like the rest of us."

And with that, she started the long walk back home.

* * * * * * *

Jesper really wasn't good for anything.

He winced as his tower of rocks wobbled, then toppled over, pounding against the broken table like a violent rain. He'd been at this for over an hour and he hadn't been able to get it right.

Heaving a silent sigh, he crouched down to recover the fallen rocks from the floor. Each was about the size of his palm, with a few smaller exceptions, and were the smoothest, prettiest, most interesting rocks he could find. He'd been collecting them for two weeks now, refining his selection process as he went, and had spent the morning scrubbing them all clean. These rocks had to be the best the Molds had to offer. He was halfway sure of it.

The house creaked and groaned as he went back to work. The humid air wafted in through the holes in the walls, making every breath stick in his lungs. It was never completely silent in the Molds—the sounds of lost, desperate, and warped souls never truly died off—but Monty had been gone the last few days, his time overtaken by work. And that meant brief peace. It meant Jesper could work on his creation in the kitchen without fear of being bothered instead of holing up in his tiny, shared room or just finding somewhere else to be, like Ally usually did.

These days, he saw his sister even less than his overworked father. He couldn't blame her for wanting to stay away from the house. He didn't try to stop her either. She just checked in with him every other day, sometimes two or three, before disappearing again. He knew she had nowhere to go—he'd gone with her often as she wandered looking for the perfect places to bury her collection of sticks. At first, her leaving made him worried, as nobody in the Molds was ever a friend, and stumbling upon anyone could mean trouble. Especially since they had never been taught how to defend themselves with magic, or anything else really. But Ally was smart and stayed in the abandoned part of the wasteland. She'd made that her life, considering her stick burials as important as breathing.

Today, though, she'd be coming back. And he had to be ready.

As if the stars had set up the joke, a knock sounded on the door: two quick ones, a slow one, then three fast ones. Jesper gasped and scrambled to push the rocks together on the table.

"It's safe," he called once the knock had finished. Despite his harried work, he still winced when the door banged open behind him.

"You wouldn't *believe* what happened to me today," Ally snapped as she strode in, her black cloak billowing around her ankles. She had a constant sarcastic growl to her voice, so you could never quite tell if she was insulting or threatening you. While he wished she would smile more—genuinely smile because she had reason to—he had come to find her no nonsense attitude endearing, if not a little frightening at times.

Officially out of time, Jesper gave a quiet sigh and stilled his hands, slowly turning to face his sister. She had her mouth open, but she closed it as her eyes narrowed on his creation. Jesper's gaze flicked to the table and he winced. It truly was pathetic.

But he opened his palm in presentation anyway and said, "Happy birthday Ally."

The right corner of her mouth pulled up in a sly smirk: Ally's version of a smile. She took a few steps forward, crossing the space with reverent ease.

"What is it?" she asked.

Jesper winced again. "It's…well it's supposed to be…a ca-ake." The word stuttered out of him. "Kind of."

Ally raised a sharp eyebrow. "A cake…out of rocks?"

"Yeah. I mean, we…we couldn't make a *real* cake—I mean, I wanted to, but obviously we can't, so I ma-ade one out of your favorite things instead."

Ally reached out and plucked a rock from the sad pile. Her thumb brushed along the edge of it. "These are good rocks," she said. Jesper couldn't tell if she was kidding or not.

"I pi-cked them out," he told her. "But if…if you don't like them…we can pick new…new ones. Or you can...you can. I know you're better at...at it."

The smirk grew ever so slightly. "Jes, you didn't have to do this."

Jesper released a breath. She liked it. "I just wanted your day to be special." Of course, they had no idea if it was really Ally's birthday—Monty would never care to say, so she had picked out the day when she was five, and Jesper made sure to celebrate it every year. It was the only reason he kept so careful track of the days as they went by, so he never missed it. An unreal birthday, but a birthday just the same.

Ally took a few minutes inspecting each rock, picking it up and testing the weight in her palm, studying the edges. Jesper allowed himself to relax slightly. She wouldn't spend time on it if she didn't like it, even to spare his feelings. Maybe he'd done something right after all.

Once she finished, Ally reached out and took his pinky, holding his one finger in her entire fist. The gesture didn't work as well as when they were younger, when his little finger was all baby Ally could hope to hang on to, but neither of them had been able to let it go.

She squeezed his finger tightly. "I wish she were here." Ally's voice always pricked with sharp spokes, but it was softest when she spoke of Her.

A jolt went through Jesper, one hard enough to make his bones ache. He pursed his lips and bit the inside of his cheek, willing his mind to stay clear, his eyes not to play tricks on him and materialize the woman who gave birth to them sitting on their torn couch. He'd do just about anything for his sister, but talking about Her was one of the few things he just couldn't give her. It was too much.

He forced himself to meet Ally's eyes and nod, at least acknowledging the loss in her expression, before turning back to his plain gift. That was the most he could do.

Ally opened her mouth to say something, but a crunching sound outside cut her off. She had time to let out a panicked breath while every muscle in Jesper's body seized up, then the door flew open, slamming hard against the dented wall.

Monty filled the entire door frame. He had to stoop slightly to get inside, and the already tiny room instantly became much too cramped. In a second, he was towering over them, his thick blacksmith build making Jesper shrink himself smaller. In comparison to his hulking father, Jesper was one of Ally's sticks.

The air went taut. Jesper and Ally ducked their heads slightly and looked at the ground, forcing themselves to be as still as possible. Maybe if they didn't move, they wouldn't be noticed. Maybe Monty would be too drunk to pick up on the presence.

It was too much to hope for. Monty scowled when he saw his children, as if unable to believe they were *still* here, that they were *still* alive in this hellhole he'd brought them to.

Monty ambled forward and peered at the pile of rocks on the table. A flicker of interest glimmered in his stormy gray eyes, probably hoping the table was somehow full of food, but it quickly snuffed out once he registered the rocks.

"Interesting," Monty muttered, his gruff voice as scratchy as the bushy gray beard that took up most of his square face. "Still not good for anything, are you Jes? A real man puts food on the table, not useless pebbles."

Jesper could feel Ally's internal wince at hearing her most prized possessions called useless. It made Jesper want to cry—those were all she had—but he knew better than to do that in front of Monty.

"So-sorry, um, sir," Jesper murmured, his eyes still trained on his father's boots stained with mud, soot, and blood. He tried not to imagine whose blood it could be. "I, um, I bro-ought them, brought them in. For, for Ally."

Monty's eyes narrowed, and Jesper did his best to keep from shuddering. "My boy sounds stupid. Stupid stutter."

Jesper swallowed hard and waited to see if a punishment would come for that, or worse, they'd both be forced to sit there until Jesper could speak a full sentence without a single stutter. Nothing rattled Ally more than having to sit still in the same room as their father, and Jesper hated himself when it was his fault she felt so trapped.

Thankfully, Monty just made a noncommittal grunt and stepped around the table. "What's done is done," he muttered as he started to search their cupboard. They all knew it was empty. Monty worked as a blacksmith for Pepperjack, Elaria's ruthless crime lord. Some said that Pepperjack was even richer than King Asher himself, but apparently none of that gold could be spared to feed employees and their families. Or, Jesper suspected, his father actually *did* get paid by his bloodthirsty employer—Monty was the best in his field, after all—but the money went to rent payment and the need for ale in his blood.

Regardless, it left his children with nothing.

"Why do you need them?" Monty grumbled at the rocks on the table. It had been years since either of them had heard him use Ally's name, much less acknowledged she existed. "Taking up space."

"The-they were, um, they were a present." Maybe if Jesper complied they could both get out of this interaction unscathed. "We, and uh we will mo-ove them."

Monty had his back to them as he reached above the cupboard for a bottle of ale. Jesper leaned forward to grab the rocks, slipping out of Ally's grip, and the tiniest gasp escaped her lips when their contact broke. Sixteen and nineteen years old now, and Monty could still make both of them feel like a tiny child with one breath. Sometimes Jesper wondered if he would be forever internally frozen, stuck back in the past while his body kept growing, oblivious.

Jesper winced at the gulping sound as his father downed a quarter of the bottle in one impressive swig.

"A present." Monty's repetition of the word was slurred. "What for?"

Jesper ensured his voice stayed utterly neutral, not a hint of stepping out of line, no trace of challenging why a father would forget the day his daughter was born. "Her, um, birthday, sir."

Something in the air changed. Crackled. Jesper glanced up from his hurried collecting just in time to get a vicious backhand across the face. He lurched and fell to his knees, the rocks in his arms clattering all over the floor.

"Her birthday?" Monty roared. He smashed his bottle of ale against the table, then upended the whole thing. Rocks flew everywhere. "Her *birthday*?"

Jesper's bones quaked inside him. His head rattled. He tasted blood. But he forced himself to scramble to his feet and stand, to plant himself in front of his sister just as their father swiped at her. He missed and they took the opening.

They scampered back into their room, slamming the door shut just as Monty's fists pounded on it. Ally and Jesper pushed their backs up against the door, straining all their muscles, using every ounce of willpower to stand against their father's brute strength. If his father really tried, they all knew he could get through with a snap of his finger.

"Birthday?" Monty raged from the other side of the door. "I wish you both were dead! I wish you both were *dead!* Dead like your blasted mother!"

Ally's breath caught. Jesper's heart pounded in his throat, pulse roaring in his ears. He could sense his body, but he didn't feel inside of it, didn't feel like anything at all.

Eternities passed before Monty gave up. They heard him grumbling as he stomped around, kicking a rock or crunching glass every couple steps. The house settled back into fragile calm.

Going slow, silent, Jesper reached into his pocket and pulled out the one rock he'd saved from the disastrous gift. Gingerly, he offered it to his sister.

"Happy birthday," Jesper whispered as loudly as he dared, ignoring his throbbing lip.

Taking the rock, Ally rested her head on his shoulder and squeezed his pinky tight.

* * * * * * *

A deep rumble in the earth jolted Jesper awake. His joints whined as he sat up, rubbing his crusty eyes. A lance of pain shot across his mouth coated in spots of dried blood, and he winced as he remembered the night before. The disastrous birthday party. Filtered sunlight poked through the boarded up window, the lines of light illuminating the two flat mattresses on the floor. Jesper had fallen asleep with his back against the door; Ally was gone.

For a moment, he couldn't remember what had woken him up. A rumble in the earth? Or had it just been Monty slamming the door?

Jesper got to his feet and put his head against the door, straining his ears. The place was silent, not a grumble or a snore to be heard, though Monty slept less and less the older he got.

A knot loosened in Jesper's chest. Monty was gone. He must've imagined it.

Stretching his arms, Jesper opened his door and started to step out into the mess of a kitchen when another deep tremor rippled through the earth, knocking him into the wall. Screams sounded in the distance, followed by another explosion and enraged shouting—loud enough to be heard even from their shack.

Jesper gulped. A lot of awful things happened in the Molds, but it never felt like the earth itself was going to crack open.

Stumbling through the mess of broken bottles, dirty rocks, and the overturned table, Jesper managed to make it to the front door and swing it open.

The smoke hit him first. His eyes stung as he coughed and stepped outside. Another tremor nearly threw him to the ground, and his gaze tracked the smoke in the sky to find the source.

Pepperjack's.

When Monty had first brought their family to the Molds and sold his soul to Elaria's monster, he had insisted on building their shack as far from his employer's estate as he could get while still being in the crime lord's range. Even as kids, even after their mother died, they knew never to get any closer. Always stay as far away as possible no matter what you saw or what you heard or who you wanted to help. Just stay away.

And everyone was so afraid of Monty, they stayed away from his kids too.

But with his father gone, his sister missing, and his world on fire, Jesper ignored his ingrained fears and forced himself to run for the flames.

He'd never been a fast runner, and with the horrible sounds grating against his bones, he found himself slower than ever, stumbling more.

He didn't see anyone until he got to the edge of Pepperjack's outer circle. The shacks were on fire, the weeds around them catching as well and burning up in a blink. Far behind he saw a cluster of people running away like their lives depended on it—running toward Racine, the scrappy village that connected the Molds with the rest of the kingdom of Elaria.

No employee of Pepperjack's was stupid enough to leave the Molds unless he ordered them to. He owned them, and even if they did manage to slide past the crime lord, King Asher's men would butcher them if caught. It was why he had never taken Ally and ran: because of their father, Pepperjack owned them too.

What was *happening?*

Coughing up the smoke in his lungs, Jesper stopped to lean against one of the few structures that wasn't burning and surveyed the chaos around him. People were running every which way like mad. There seemed to be some kind of fight closer to Pepperjack's estate—from here, he couldn't tell who was part of it.

An acidic pit opened up in his gut. Was Pepperjack killing his people? Was Monty dead? No, he couldn't be. Monty was one of his best. That was why they were still alive, largely untouched by the brutes that called this place home.

Jesper stepped forward—to do what, he wasn't sure yet— but a blood curdling scream froze him in place. A girl. A girl screaming as though her very essence was being shredded piece by piece. He'd heard a lot of screams in the Molds, but this…this tugged at the ends of Jesper's humanity.

His blood went cold. He tried to tell himself what he knew: Ally would never be stupid enough to wander over here, even if the flames made her curious. Ally wandered off all the time, careful to stay within the borders of this land but never coming this way. She was probably out digging with her new rocks and had no idea anything was happening.

Those were the facts Jesper knew. But the awful scream had his soul shaking inside of him. He couldn't move. Even when the scream kept going, then got cut off, then choked back to life again. There he stood, frozen in place, as destruction reigned around him.

Helplessness. It filled up his lungs, clogged up his throat, and kept his mouth constantly sealed shut.

Ally clutching his finger. Jesper backed in a corner. Their mother in the ground, their father standing over them.

Helpless.

The screaming stopped again. Jesper straightened, trying to get his bearings, to remember where he was. How had he gotten out here?

A crackle went through the smoky air, making the hair on Jesper's arms stand up. He recognized the presence of magic— a *lot* of it—and he stumbled forward, Ally's mumbled name on his lips.

A figure slammed into him. Bulky frame. Scruffy beard, The permanent smell of molten metal and cheap ale.

Monty.

Monty with fresh blood on his boots and red flecks in his beard.

Monty the Merciless, the blacksmith who forged indestructible cages and torture tools for the greatest monster the kingdom had ever seen. Whose creations kept men in chains and made girls scream.

What had he done?

"Get," Monty growled at him, voice strained. He shoved Jesper backward. "What do I tell you about coming out this way? Move."

"Bu-ut she—" Jesper winced when the girl screamed again. He should help her. He didn't know what he could possibly do, but he couldn't just leave her.

Monty shoved him harder, his voice black. "She made her own bed. Now move!"

Numbly, Jesper obeyed. He was surprised to find his father following him, his long steps quickly passing the smaller ones of his son despite his limp.

Jesper's eyebrows furrowed. *Limp?* Since when?

Monty noticed him looking and barked at him to be faster, then glanced behind his shoulder. As if checking for pursuers.

They were *running away.*

The chaos fell quiet once they reached their house. Monty pushed Jesper inside, then slammed the door shut and locked it. Then he sauntered over and sunk into a kitchen chair, sighing and stretching out his right leg.

Jesper's eyes widened. A deep gash ran from Monty's mid-thigh, over his kneecap, and across his shin. He couldn't remember the last time, if ever, his father had been coated in his own blood.

"What are you staring at?" Monty snapped. His voice had lost some of its power, his exhaustion showing through.

"You're hurt," Jesper murmured. He didn't make eye contact, but he felt Monty's eyes narrow all the same.

"A real man can take care of himself." The jab wasn't lost on Jesper.

Still, he couldn't shake the guilt that welled up from deep inside him. He'd long since accepted that's how he might die, drowning in the guilt that had plagued him for as long as he could remember. "But tha-at, but she, that gi-girl—"

"She's not our problem," Monty growled. "What's done is done. Now shut up and stay that way."

Jesper didn't understand the purpose, but he obeyed. He sat in a chair opposite his father, the kitchen table still knocked over between them, and stayed perfectly silent. Monty grumbled to himself as he tended to his wound. It was a crude attempt—his magic was suited for building and creating, never healing—but he got the wound closed and that seemed to satisfy him. Jesper couldn't remember the last time he'd seen his father do any kind of magic. He wondered about that a lot.

He didn't dare ask, though, as Monty muttered about Pepperjack, money, cover ups, and someone named Sterling. As more time passed, he grew more and more subdued, his eyes darting to the door.

Monty was waiting for something.

Jesper really didn't want to find out what, but the thought of retribution for moving without his father's permission kept him in place.

That something came about two hours later: a knock on the door.

Jesper stiffened and glanced at Monty. His father made a good show of pretending to be annoyed at the inconvenience, but Jesper could've sworn he saw Monty's face pale slightly under his beard. Grunting, he rose and answered it while Jesper stayed frozen in his chair.

"It's all over, Monty," a deep voice said as soon as his father opened the door. Jesper recognized it as Ralph, one of Pepperjack's other employees. Which meant he was probably with…

"It's a bloodbath," a scratchy voice piped up. Jesper scowled at Wendell's voice, Ralph's seedy partner. He had never liked the way Wendell looked at Ally. "We barely escaped ourselves."

Monty clearly couldn't care less about their survival. "Good for you." He started to shut the door, but Ralph's blurted statement stopped him in his tracks.

"Pepperjack's dead."

Despite still sitting in the rickety chair, Jesper felt the world fall out from under him.

Impossible.

Monty just barked a sharp laugh, a sound meant to make anyone feel about two feet tall. "The most powerful man in Elaria, killed during a little prison riot? I don't believe you."

"But we saw it!" Wendell screeched. "Stabbed in the chest with his own knife. A blast slaughtered nearly everyone: Towley, Bart, Nessa, Lizabeth, Dragon, and dozens more. All dead. Tons more injured, likely dead by tomorrow. People are staking claims, looting everything, taking cover. We sped outta there before Sterling could bring the royal army down on us. They've never come out here before, but he came for his daughter, is what I hear. I didn't see if he was the one that did Jack in, but I'd bet my left tooth on it."

Ralph's voice was sober and hollow. "It's true, Monty. Nobody would dare loot Jack's place if they weren't absolutely sure he wasn't around to skin them for it."

There were a few seconds of tense silence before Monty muttered, "Jack is dead?"

"We're lying low," Ralph went on. "Trying to see what factions rise up, which is strongest. Not sure how many of us survived the massacre. Anyone who doesn't hide fast will be arrested if Sterling decides to come back."

"And he'd just as soon chop off the heads of anyone who sets foot out of the Molds," Wendell added in disgust.

"But without Jack here…" Monty sighed. "No money flow. No food. We'll dry up."

Wendell snorted. "And no protection either, for you or your mangy kids. Might wanna start locking your doors at night and hide that daughter of yours."

"Are you threatening me?" Monty demanded, his temper flaring as the current in the air crackled. The doorframe shuddered and Wendell took a step back.

Ralph held up his hands. "We just came to pass the word on. Lines will be drawn soon. Without Jack, there's no doubt we'll all turn on each other. It's survival of the fittest now."

Shoulders sagging ever so slightly, Monty shook his head once. "It always has been." Then he straightened back up, the change so quick Jesper didn't think anyone besides him noticed. "Who are the frontrunners as of now?"

They continued talking about people Jesper had only heard of, discussing vague strategies without trusting the other with too many details, and cursing this Sterling guy again. Jesper steeled himself, took a deep breath to hold, then slowly got to his feet. None of the men noticed him slip silently into his room. He pulled the boards off his window, climbed through the opening, and ran.

* * * * * * *

When Ally woke up that morning, she left Jesper still asleep and climbed out their window, making sure to replace the boards. Not that they could really keep anyone out—it was a wonder their house stood at all, and just a flick of magic would pull them right off—but maybe the thought of extra work would make a possible intruder give up before they tried.

That was the idea, anyway.

With her new rock from Jesper tucked safely in her pocket, she set out into the wasteland to catch up on her work on her first day of being sixteen. Her first stop was to bury the two sticks she had missed yesterday. She did that quickly, glad to be back on track, then continued on her way.

She always made sure to wander away from the center of the Molds where total terror reigned. No, she was a girl that belonged on the fringe, on the edges.

Trucking through the lifeless yellow brush that spread out for miles around, Ally made her way back to where she had been the day before. It took some searching, but she finally found the tunnel she had caved in—the one the rabbit had used to escape. She pushed her foot against what once was the opening. Nothing gave. She had done a pretty good job.

Sinking to her knees, she started to dig.

The sun continued to rise as she undid all the work she'd done yesterday. Her broken nails scraped the dirt away as she went deeper and deeper, until the hole finally caved in and gave way to the tunnel.

Ally's mouth twitched into a smile as she considered her next objective for the day. She was going to find the rabbit.

Grabbing the stick she'd picked up on her way, she stuck it through the top of the tunnel, so it poked through the ceiling. Then she started to drag it and followed where it led her.

The tunnel weaved around in nonsensical patterns, going right then left, then looping around. Once it even went in a large circle, eventually bringing her back to where she started before launching in a different direction. Ally clenched her teeth but kept going. The sun climbed and her frustration mounted with every step, every pull of the stick, and no sign of dirty white fur.

After hours of trying to track it, Ally's boot caught on a rock and she tripped, collapsing into the dirt. Spewing profanities about the rabbit at the sky, she snapped her stick in half and threw it as hard as her throbbing shoulders would let her.

All she wanted was to win. To skin the stupid vermin and bring it to Jesper and finally get to eat something for once, to give something back to her brother, to break her long losing streak. But the rabbit had won. She'd lost to a *rabbit*.

Her father made her lose. Lose her safety. Lose her life. Lose her mother.

She just wanted to win. Just once.

Stupid rabbit.

"Ally!"

The sound startled Ally out of her stupor. She turned around to see Jesper staggering toward her, his dark shaggy hair slick with sweat. It must've taken him hours to find her, as far as she had gone. He collapsed when he reached her, doubling over and panting hard. Ally plopped on the ground and waited for him to catch his breath. Her brother was a useless runner.

"What's wrong?" Ally demanded once Jesper wasn't gasping anymore. Her eyes scanned him over and over, searching for an injury. She had so many nightmares stained with Jesper's blood. "What happened?"

What did he do? That was her real question. *What did our monster of a father do now?*

Jesper wheezed for a second longer before glancing up to meet her eyes. "Pepperjack is dead."

Ally blinked. Once. Twice. Three times. "What?"

"Pepperjack," Jesper repeated. "He's dead."

"But…" Early memories edged Ally's nightmares, of a milky man with colorful eyes who used his unlimited power to spill blood for fun. A man with so much magic, so much sway, that King Asher himself wouldn't challenge him. After that first initial meeting, her mother had kept Ally and Jesper far away from the man's claws—most other kids weren't so lucky.

"But how? Who could possibly kill him?"

Jesper shrugged. "Nobody really knows. But he's dead and so is almost everyone else."

Ally raised a hopeful eyebrow. "Monty?"

He shook his head. "He's okay."

Ally cursed in disappointment. Of all the bad luck. Jesper just looked at the ground, shifting uncomfortably and not agreeing, which made her scowl.

"He deserved to die too," she said.

A few beats of silence passed. "Well he didn't." He glanced back up. "And now there's no income. No protection. From what Ralph said, people are already picking sides with each other."

"And there's nowhere to go." Ally deflated, understanding what her brother meant. People in the Molds were cruel, but the two of them had largely been protected from the others because of Monty's high-ranking status. They hadn't been given much, had made their own way with what they found around them, but they'd managed to scrape by on his wages. Without either, they would die. They couldn't stay.

But the Molds, Pepperjack, had branded them. If they left, they'd be arrested and executed. Jailed for life if they were lucky. Even if they tried to explain they never had a choice, that they never did anything bad themselves, that they would do anything to keep from going back…nobody would listen to a child of the Molds.

Stay and die. Leave and die. Either way it was a loss.

Not to mention Monty. If all bets were off, then Ally would be safest in their house, and Monty wouldn't leave for work anymore. All day every day, trapped in that shack with him, the rampages becoming even more violent once the ale had dried up.

She'd rather die than be trapped like that.

The desperation swimming in Jesper's eyes washed over Ally in unrelenting waves.

"What are we going to do?" she whispered.

Jesper shook his head again. "I don't know."

The brush next to them rustled. Jesper went still. Ally leaned forward, peering over a mound of dirt to see the rabbit staring back at her.

The rabbit.

Back here.

Right in front of her.

Everything melted away into the background—Monty, Pepperjack, being trapped here—and she only saw those two black eyes. It was just her and this creature and the victory that loomed on the horizon.

This time, she was going to get it.

"Ally?" Jesper whispered. "What are you—"

The rabbit took off.

"No!" Ally lurched to her feet and ran, leaving Jesper behind. She couldn't waste the time explaining, and he would understand once she brought her prize back. He'd be so grateful. He'd congratulate her on her accomplishment, an amazing way to celebrate her birthday. They would eat, finally having at least one good thing, all because of her.

She could only imagine what her mother would say if she were still here to see.

Wonderful work, Ally. I'm so proud of you!

The little vermin was fast, but Ally knew that now. She knew how it would hop over obstacles and turn a random corner without warning. Despite its best efforts, the rabbit couldn't shake her.

Ally followed it farther than she'd ever gone before, until even the endless sea of brush ended and the ground got softer under her feet. Her lungs burned and her legs ached, but she relished in the feeling, in the chase, in the thought of having a goal greater than burying sticks and what it would feel like to accomplish it.

As she ran, the stench she'd grown used to changed. The air smelled smoggy and spongy, like the disgusting well they got their water from. She heard trickling and was surprised to come upon a stream she'd never seen before. The rabbit jumped over the stream with ease; she followed. Her boots started to squelch as she came upon a lake.

The lake was dirty close to shore, but it gave way to glittering green water, the sun bouncing off it in harsh rays. Ally stumbled in surprise—where *was* she?—and that gave the rabbit enough time to dive into the earth.

Ally cried out, but she was too late. She skidded to her knees at the opening just as the rabbit disappeared into a waiting hole and under the earth. As if it had led her there just so it could disappear again.

Panting, sweaty, and tired, she groaned through her teeth and pounded her fists on the ground, but she didn't move. The rabbit had to come back up *sometime*. She'd be waiting for it.

As her pulse slowly evened out, Ally surveyed the unfamiliar territory. Empty, dead land stretched on in every direction, interrupted only by the lake in front of her. She squinted but couldn't make out anything beyond the water. What was over there? Was it possible there could be a place other than Elaria? A place that had never heard of the Molds or Pepperjack or Monty the Merciless?

Minutes passed and she found herself edging toward the water. She hadn't cleaned up in ages; she smelled almost as bad as the stray animal carcasses. The water was stagnant but cool enough to be relaxing, and she just sat down in it, letting it come up to her shoulders. Then she closed her eyes and tipped her head back to feel the sun.

Maybe she should just stay here.

Forevers passed of course before Jesper finally caught up to her. By then she had gotten over the novelty of the water and now scoured the floor of the lake, marveling how different the soaked dirt felt in her palms.

Jesper collapsed behind her, just out of reach of the water. "What…what were you doing?"

"Chasing a rabbit." Ally didn't elaborate on the *loss* of the rabbit because the fight wasn't over yet.

"Why?"

"To eat it. Why else?"

And to prove I can.

"Where did it go?"

Ally gritted her teeth. This was supposed to be the victory she could share with him. "I'm looking for rocks now. The rabbit can wait." Then to prove her point, she started sifting through the dirt, looking for even the smallest of pebbles.

A shimmer under the water caught her eye. Splashing water everywhere, she scurried closer and gasped. Lodged in the bottom of the lake several feet from her was a blue-tinted rock. Oval shaped, just smaller than her hand, and covered in slight chips that looked almost purposeful.

"Do you see that, Jes?" she asked, mesmerized. Her fingers twitched in fists, suddenly aching to hold it, and she couldn't tear her eyes away. "I need it."

Ally didn't know how to swim, but she dived in anyways, her limbs flailing every which way as she tried to force her body down. The water was still at the surface, but down here the current ran in strange patterns, knocking her off path.

Coming up for air, Ally flipped her drenched hair in a huff. She'd get the rock. She had to. It glittered from the lake floor, taunting her.

"Ally," Jesper said, his voice laced with uncertainty. He never knew how to just *say* things. "I don't think—"

"I'm getting it." At least she could accomplish this today. "Help me get down there."

Jesper's eyebrows pulled down but he got in the water with her. They splashed around, trying to figure out how to push each other deeper into the water without drowning. Ever so slowly, they started making progress.

After several attempts, Ally finally got the hang of it. She kicked her legs wildly, and the closer she got to the rock, the easier it became. As if the water now pulled her to it. The new current swirled around her, seeming to cave in on itself, but Ally paid it no mind as she curled her hand around the rock. She felt a warm spark jolt through her.

Right then, she felt Jesper's hand wrap around her ankle. She tried to protest—she'd been doing just fine on her own— when her body jerked harshly. Her mouth opened in horror when she realized she was being sucked into the current where the water seemed to disappear instead of continuing on. As if hitting an invisible wall.

Ally screamed and struggled as Jesper tried to pull her back up, producing a stream of bubbles that floated to the surface easily, peacefully, unaffected by the violent way she flailed her body. She felt Jesper's grip tighten, but it was no use. It just sealed his fate with hers.

Water rushed into her mouth as both she and her brother tumbled into oblivion.

CHAPTER 2

DOWN THE RABBIT HOLE

The darkness never ended.

Jesper fell so far, so long, that eventually he ran out of breath to yell. The darkness sucked them in, pressed on all sides, swallowed absolutely everything, and he started to wonder if darkness is all he ever was. Had he ever been real? Or just a trick of the light?

Eternities passed before he crumpled on something solid. The ground, finally. Or was it? His eyebrows furrowed as his hands felt the unfamiliar surface, greasy and lumpy under his palms, no dirt or brush to be found. His teeth rattled around his mouth as he struggled to regain his breath. Only then he realized why it was so dark: his eyes were squeezed shut.

Jesper's body lay frozen in a heap on the strange earth. A sour scent invaded his nose and clung to his tongue, not even close to the earthy rotting smell he'd gotten used to. And the sound that buzzed in the air…no not sound. Nothing. No distant angry voices, no howling dogs, not even the sound of the weeds rustling in the wind. Was this what silence sounded like?

The ground, the smell, the silence—he didn't recognize anything and he had no desire to open his eyes whatsoever. A known hell was preferable to any unknown.

"Jes!" Ally hissed, slicing through the quiet. He jumped, then relaxed slightly at his sister's voice. Despite his constant worry over her, things were better when they could face them together. "Jes, wake up!"

He couldn't bring himself to look. "Where are we?" he whispered.

"I don't know." A brief breath of fear crept into her words, but she blew it away before it could take a real form. She shook his arm. "Open your eyes."

"I…I don't…"

"Come on. You're useless blind."

Steeling himself for the worst—though not even sure what that would be—Jesper hesitantly sat up and blinked his eyes open. He frowned. There wasn't much difference between his eyes open and closed.

"What…?" He waited to let his vision adjust to his murky surroundings. They were in a big…cave? It had to be. They'd fallen *down* after all, he thought, underneath the lake somehow, but…it didn't feel like there was anything above them. As if they'd fallen into a dead field. Everything was dark and shadowy, with no way to tell how far the land extended, or if there was anything above their heads besides a black sky.

"Well?" Ally stood over him with her arms crossed, as if mildly impatient, but her restless fingers gave her nerves away. "What do we do?"

"What do we do," Jesper repeated. "Um…I…how? How are we here?"

Ally shrugged, like it was obvious. "We fell."

"I remember that."

"Then why did you ask."

Jesper shakily got to his feet and took a breath of the thick, sour air. "Okay, um, I guess we…we should try to find a way out?"

She nodded in determination, as if counting sticks. "Good idea."

Is it? Jesper wondered. He was scared to move, scared to stay in one place, scared to breathe. Who knew what awaited them…anywhere.

But they couldn't stay. That *was* obvious.

He looked up to the non-sky or whatever it was, but he couldn't see anything besides darkness. No rip, no hole, nothing to climb out of. And nothing to climb with either. Just…nothing.

Forever.

"Do you think we're dead?" Ally asked. As always, Jesper couldn't tell if she was joking, though he could guess who she was thinking about. "Is this what happens to people?" She dug her toe into the questionable ground and scoffed to hide the waver in her voice. "What a waste."

"Maybe it's some kind of-of magic pit," Jesper offered, remembering the blasts that had rattled the earth earlier. Being from the Molds, you either already knew magic, learned by survival, or were a rake. Neither of their parents had taught them, so Jesper had no idea what magic could do outside of Monty's creations and Pepperjack's rumors. "With a-all the crazy things…Pepperjack did…maybe something happened."

Ally raised a skeptical eyebrow. "Have you ever heard of something like that?"

"No," he admitted. "But we…I mean, we wouldn't really be-be the ones to know, um, to know about it."

Ally huffed. That meant he was right. "This place feels like it's been here a lot longer than we've been alive."

That was true. The sour air held an ageless quality. How could you measure nothing in time anyway?

"Well," Jesper said as he looked around again. "Which way should, should w-we go?"

"Well, how am I to know."

"I don't know. You found the ho-ole." Or current. Whatever it had been.

Ally's eyes narrowed. "No, the *rabbit* found the hole. It brought me to it. It probably knew it was here and wanted revenge for chasing it or something."

The chances of that seemed low, but Jesper just shrugged it off. "Did you at least get the rock?"

She shook her head, pressing her mouth into a thin, angry line. "I must've dropped it when we fell." Then she straightened with confidence. "We need to find water. Water got us here. Water will get us out, I know it. It'll be easy."

It didn't look like there would be water anywhere in this place, and the situation seemed far from *easy*, but the greasy moisture of the ground had to come from somewhere, right? "Okay."

Ally surged forward, picking a direction at random, Jesper assumed, and he followed.

And they walked.

And walked.

And walked.

Nothing changed.

After what seemed like hours of walking nowhere, Ally let out a frustrated breath through her teeth and shoved her hands into her cloak pocket. Then she perked up and a sly smile cut across her face.

"I have an idea." She pulled a rock from her pocket and placed it on the ground. "Now we can make sure we're walking in a straight line." Her face beamed with a rageful kind of victory, and he knew she was thinking of Monty calling her rocks useless.

Jesper didn't see how that would really solve anything, but he nodded like it did for the sake of Ally's enthusiasm. More information couldn't hurt, anyway.

So with Ally periodically placing markers, they kept walking.

And walking.

And walking.

Jesper was about to plead for a rest for his feet, for a moment to close his eyes and get some kind of break from all the nothing. But then, something did change.

They came upon Ally's first rock.

A half scream escaped her. Jesper felt he'd been punched in the gut. He remembered Ally's words from earlier and got the sinking feeling maybe she was right. Maybe they'd drowned in the lake. Maybe they were dead.

"How is that possible?" Ally shrieked, and Jesper flinched at the explosive sound after hours of muted whispers and an eerie absence of background noise. "That doesn't make any sense!"

Her voice echoed through the empty space, again and again and again, until it sounded like her twin was shouting from miles away.

Something shifted in the stagnant air. The hair on the back of Jesper's neck rose and he shivered.

Ally started to shout again, but he held up a hand to quiet her. She snapped her mouth shut.

"Do you hear that?" Jesper whispered.

They both waited, listening. For a moment, Jesper thought he imagined it, but then the sound got louder. A hissing, growing into a rumble. Like…an animal. A very big animal.

Jesper pushed Ally's shoulder softly. "Run."

So they did.

They tried to run away from the noise, but it was hard to tell exactly where it was coming from. Several times they got too close—close enough for the rumbling hiss to verge on a screech—and Jesper's heart skipped a beat. But hours later, sweaty and spent, they'd finally found silence again. Jesper honestly didn't know which was worse.

Assuming it was nighttime and wanting to rest, they plopped on the ground to sleep. Though neither of them would probably sleep at all.

Seconds passed. Minutes. Could have been hours but it was hard to tell.

Maybe we are dead. Would it be the worst thing? Staying here forever would be a terrible kind of punishment, one he maybe deserved. But Ally? She couldn't stay here. The thought of getting her somewhere else, somewhere safe without fear of her getting hurt…that didn't make death sound so bad, even if it meant leaving Monty behind.

Instantly, sharp spokes of guilt stabbed Jesper in the chest, but Ally spoke softly and tore his attention away.

"Jes?" She didn't look at him. Just stared straight ahead into the darkness.

He followed her example. "Yeah?"

"I don't think I want to stay here forever. It might not be terrible, but I don't want to." She let out a frustrated sigh. "There has to be more than just here or there."

"I don't want to either," Jesper admitted.

A few beats of silence passed. "Are you afraid?"

"A little."

"Okay, well I'm not. If you were wondering."

"I know. I wasn't."

Ally nodded to herself, a harsh jerk of her head, as if making the declaration that she was truly not afraid. But Jesper knew her better. And she proved him right when minutes passed and she reached for his hand.

She didn't let go of his pinky once all night.

* * * * * * * *

Despite her exhaustion, Ally tried her best not to close her eyes. It wasn't too hard for her, at this point. Living with Monty the Merciless had given her years of learning how to steal rest without ever letting her guard down. To sleep for ten, fifteen minutes at a time and snap awake instantly, waiting for the next yell or slap or object thrown her way. Her body had adjusted and now she wondered if she ever managed to get away from this place and her father, a place where she knew she would be protected, if she would be able to sleep through the night.

40

Jesper may have dozed off for a bit here and there, but she sensed that he was mostly awake. That didn't surprise her. After all, he'd had to live with Monty longer than she had. She honestly didn't know how the puny kid had survived on his own those years before Ally had been born. Then again, maybe it wouldn't have been as bad. Less hits taken for his little sister.

Who chose families anyway? Why did she have to belong to a man that beat his wife to death and hated his kids? Sure, she had an amazing mother and a trustworthy brother, but one was gone forever and the other was the shattered reflection of their father's hatred. How did that make up for being chained to Monty the Merciless?

Seething, she reached into her pockets for her rocks, searching for a distraction. Sifting through what was left of her collection, her fingers paused when they reached an unfamiliar texture, and she pulled out the rock she'd found in the lake.

Ally couldn't explain to herself why she'd lied to Jesper about losing it. The moment she saw it, she just knew that she had to have it, that it was meant for her somehow. And after it had landed them here, she didn't want anything to happen to it.

Now that she could look at it out of the water, it was pale and drained of the blue tint she'd seen earlier. The strange, patterned chips in it made it seem like it would be lighter or crumble apart in her hand, but it felt firm in her palm. After years of finding the same kind of brown and black shards, this perfectly oval one looked purposefully made in comparison. Unique. Rare.

Maybe it was worth something. She imagined bringing it home to her mother, showing the proof of a hard day's work for Ally out in the Molds. Her mother's bright eyes would widen in surprise, her mouth breaking into a beautiful smile. She'd call for Jesper and the three of them would prepare their few belongings. They'd wait until the dead of night, after Monty had passed out with ale dripping from his beard, and walk out without a backward glance. Her mother would know exactly where to sell the rock at the highest price and they'd buy their freedom.

Some pressure in Ally's chest ebbed at the fantasy and her fingers started tingling as she gripped the rock. No longer a child of the Molds. Freedom with her mother and Jesper. They'd have enough to buy their freedom, buy protection, buy safety. They'd leave Monty to rot in that burning hell and never think of him again.

Thank you for getting us out of there, her mother would tell her. *It's all because of you and I'm so proud.*

The chipped patterns pressed into her palms as she squeezed the rock, the desperate need tearing through her. The longing. It might kill her. She glanced up before remembering that the sky wasn't there—she had fallen too far for the sun to reach her now.

Give me something better. If it weren't for the eerie silence, she would scream it at the non-sky. *Give me something better than this.*

To her shock, something answered: a flash of light from her palm pierced through the darkness, fading as quickly as it had come. Mouth agape, Ally glanced down at the rock in her hand.

"What was that?" Jesper mumbled as he snapped awake.

The air seemed to change, with a rising buzzing that she couldn't really hear, but sense. Something swelled and pushed softly against her, a gentle whisper scraping at the edges of her mind.

"I don't know," Ally answered him, hastily shoving the rock back in her pocket. "It came from over there."

A tiny yelp of surprise escaped her lips when something *did* appear in the direction she haphazardly pointed: a dot of light. Dim, but it seemed like a blazing star in comparison to the darkness they'd been trudging through.

Jesper straightened. "What is that?"

Such helpful questions. "I don't *know.* Probably a way out." She'd found it, after all. Maybe the sun had finally answered. "Let's follow it."

Her brother didn't look like he agreed, but he didn't argue either. Ally knew she would have to be the leader here. Jesper knew best at home—how to avoid Monty, how to survive him—but out here Ally could help. She was the better explorer. She could do this.

It was easier to keep going when there was something to walk towards, but Ally found her frustration mounting as, once again, they walked on and on and nothing changed.

Finally, Jesper spoke up. "Maybe it's just…"

He trailed off as the light flickered, then started to grow. As if moving closer.

Ally sensed Jesper open his mouth again, and she cut him off before he could speak. "If you're about to ask what it is again, don't."

He didn't.

Agitation built in Ally as the light grew bigger and bigger. It wasn't until the light was nearly upon them that she realized it wasn't alone. Glowing faintly, the ball of light sat in the palm of a woman's hand. She came with several others, shadowed men and women, on either side of her.

Ally gritted her teeth as the group of strangers formed a half circle around them. Surrounded. How had they managed to get surrounded in this wasteland?

She stuffed her hand in her pocket, gripping one of the sharpest rocks she had, and Jesper leaned forward to wrap his hand around her wrist. With a movement so smooth it looked like he'd just shifted on his feet, he slid slightly in front of her.

The woman appraised the two of them, the light flaring against her sharp cheekbones. There wasn't much that could be seen of her outside the light—much less anyone else—but Ally could easily identify the calculation in her eyes, the certainty.

Another moment of silent appraisal passed before the woman closed her hand and the light winked out, settling them into murky darkness once more.

"We a-are sorry for, um, for invading your, um…spa-ace," Jesper said in his softest way that only came out when something was wrong. "We didn't mean to, uh, we didn't mean to cause any, any trouble."

Ally gripped her rock harder and scowled despite Jesper's peaceable expression. She would never fault her brother's stutter like Monty did, but it *did* make Jesper seem weak. He may know how to dance around their father, survive in their house, but Ally knew that out here, they would need to take action instead of shielding their faces and hoping for the best.

As Ally predicted, the shadowed people didn't seem impressed.

"It's not wise to send out signals like that," the leading woman said, her voice rough in between words, in ways Ally had never heard before. "Attracts attention."

Jesper just blinked his wide eyes.

"It wasn't us," Ally lied, annoyed that she wanted to duck her head under the woman's gaze. She tried her best not to. "We felt it too."

Again, that appraising look. When had this woman taken charge of the situation? It seemed everyone was looking to her.

"Are you banished or a jumper?"

Banished? She'd heard the word before but didn't know what it meant. Not that it was a surprise—Monty the Merciless never put much into their education.

Jesper shook his head, just as confused. "I don't...um...we got lost."

Ally gritted her teeth and would've glared at Jesper if she wasn't watching the woman intently. Showing weakness was always a bad move.

"Lost?" The woman clicked her tongue. "This is a very unfortunate place to get lost in. What realm do you come from?"

Ally wanted to scream at the use of another word she didn't know. What did it matter anyway?

"The Molds." Unlike her brother, she kept her voice hard. As if daring one of them to mock them for the trash land they came from.

When the woman's eyebrows drew together, Jesper clarified quietly, "The Jacklands."

"Were you sent here?"

"No," Ally snarled. She straightened her shoulders and lifted her chin in defiance, trying to match the authority this woman thought she could just claim over everyone else. "And you have no business bothering us, so leave us alone."

Jesper pressed his thumb into her wrist in warning. She didn't care. If they didn't put up a strong front now, these strangers would eat them alive.

The shadowed people were quiet for a moment, silently consulting with the other. Ally checked her grip on the rock; Jesper shifted as if preparing to take a blow and stay standing.

The woman finally broke the quiet. "We can offer sanctuary until you can find your way. There are all sorts of creatures in this place you'd not want to meet."

Then she turned and started walking in the opposite direction, displaying the long sword strapped to her back. The others stepped to the side—Ally thought they were following at first and realized too late they had closed their circle behind Ally and Jesper and now herded them on as they followed. Once they were closer, she could see they all carried weapons of some kind, all sharp and deadly. The meaning was clear: move or be moved.

Ally imagined clubbing a few of them and making a run for it—there was no way the shadows could see that much better than them in this grimy darkness—but Jesper started walking with them. With a scowl, she let him pull her along.

"They could take us anywhere," Ally hissed at him. "They could do anything to us."

Jesper didn't deny it.

They walked forever, following the shadows that followed their leader blindly. Ally wondered how they possibly knew where to go in the never-ending nothingness—especially when nobody lit a ball of light this time—but once she had caught up to the leading woman, she noticed the rope. It was tied around her ankle and spooled on her belt. She wound it as they walked, the other end of the rope stretching past what Ally could see.

So they were following a rope. Interesting.

It took ages for them to finally reach the end. They came upon a cluster of assembled shelters surrounding a small pit in the ground. The rope was tied to a contraption made of a stick and a lump of what looked like metal that sat by the pit. As the shadows stopped walking, their leader bent down to untie her ankle and dropped the pile of rope on the ground.

The slight sounds of their approach brought a few more people from out of the shelters, including several children. Ally's stomach clenched. Jesper sidestepped closer to her.

They were truly surrounded.

Ally's eyes darted everywhere, trying to see everyone at once, trying to measure every possible threat. The people, in contrast, relaxed. As soon as their leader's rope fell onto the ground, they disbanded their loose circle around Ally and Jesper. Some started talking to the people around them, others went into shelters, and a few just dropped to the ground right then to stretch out their legs. Even weirder, it looked like they all had sticks tied to their boots—she hadn't noticed until now.

The four children ran up and embraced the leader, then she turned to face Ally and Jesper. From this close, Ally could see she was wearing a dark hood that concealed vivid white blonde hair and sharp silver eyes.

"I'm Astrid," she said. Ally couldn't tell if she was threatening them or baiting them. "This is our community. Here we have three rules: be quiet, do your part, and never travel alone. If you don't cause trouble you can stay as long as you want."

Jesper nodded rapidly, eager to show obedience.

Ally narrowed her eyes. "Who are you? Why are you here?"

Astrid didn't seem put off by the threat in Ally's voice. It made Ally hate her and envy her even more. "We are many people from many places, but that doesn't matter now. We are where we are and we make the best of it."

"We weren't *banished.*" Ally spat the term like it was dirty, despite still not being entirely sure what it meant. Again, she ignored Jesper's warning press on her wrist. "We need to get back…get back…"

A flash of Monty appeared in her head, pounding on her door. *I wish you were dead!*

"Home?" Astrid supplied when Ally fell quiet. "I'm sure you would. We all would. But we are banished and not allowed to return. If you're truly lost and want to return to the realm you came from, then you'll have to find the right portal, which is hard enough to do without swarms of vrykol trying to rip out your throats. Not to mention any other ancient, angry creature you may stumble upon." Astrid shrugged, unsympathetic. "Your choice."

"Vrykol?" Jesper squeaked. "What…what's that?"

"The creatures of the In Between. They are rather stupid and a prey to the darkness as well, but they're strong and fast and love the taste of flesh. If one finds you, you likely won't walk away with all your limbs intact, if at all."

Jesper swallowed hard. Ally refused to let her feelings show on her face. Instead she tried to mimic Astrid's firm stance on her feet, the no nonsense set to her mouth, and fierce gleam in her eyes. She refused to be taken prisoner like these people. They'd just given up.

"If it's so terrible here, why don't you just take another portal and go somewhere else?" Ally did her best not to trip over the unfamiliar word, to say it like she knew exactly what she spoke of.

Astrid's jaw clenched slightly, but otherwise didn't react. "Do you not know what banished means?" Ally's blood boiled at her tone, but Astrid went on before she could explode. "We are cursed, essentially. No portal will work for us. When we try, we are spit back out here."

Jesper gasped softly, as if not able to imagine the horror of it. Several of the people who had walked with them lowered their heads or clenched their fists at the reminder of their situation. The bald man who had walked next to Astrid and still sat not far from her just sighed loudly.

Ally raised an eyebrow. "What did you do to get stuck here?"

For the first time, a flicker of something flashed across Astrid's face—Ally couldn't pin what emotion it was before it disappeared. But she'd struck a nerve.

The bald man just snorted. "Now you're asking the interesting questions," he muttered. But none of them bothered to actually answer.

"Well *we* aren't staying here," Ally said, ignoring everyone else's heavy silence. "Either tell us where to go or get out of our way."

Astrid pursed her lips and stepped forward. Jesper teetered back, nearly falling onto Ally, but she held firm.

"You're brave," Astrid said. "Brave and stupid. It can get a girl into trouble, can't it?"

Ally scowled and opened her mouth, but the woman cut her off.

"I'll take you halfway to the largest group of known portals. The rest is up to you." Then she turned and stalked into one of the shelters.

Jesper released a breath, glancing around at the gathered people that were all minding their own business, eager to ignore the newcomers. For now.

"You really think we can trust her?" Jesper whispered to Ally.

"Of course not," Ally responded. "I'm not trusting her, I'm using her as a resource. There's a difference." She glanced around, hiding her unease. "I'm not staying here."

They sat on the edge of the settlement to rest their feet before their journey, careful to keep their eyes on everyone within sight. Rather than let Jesper's contagious worry come over her, Ally blocked out the sound of her doubts with thoughts of the sun and the lake in the Jacklands.

Her mind wandered as she glanced around the little community, as Astrid had called it. Small and right in the middle of a dangerous place, but everyone survived, deferred to her as their leader. Ally watched Astrid give advice, make commands, and even comfort the children. They looked to her for strength and guidance.

The idea took root in Ally. Here Astrid answered to no one. She didn't have to buy her way in, sell a rock or some other stupid thing to buy protection. No, her strength was her own, and this place was too. Surviving, despite the death and darkness around it.

Again, a fantasy wrapped around Ally, but rewritten: a cluster of small shacks full of a handful of people that had each other's back. And a fierce blonde girl leading the charge, strong enough to guard them from every monster that came their way.

Despite whatever she had done to get stuck in this place, Ally couldn't help but think Astrid's mother would be proud to see what she had built here.

Aren't you proud of me?

The fantasy in her mind popped like a bubble, and Ally snapped her teeth together so hard they almost cracked. She glowered at Astrid, perfectly at home in the middle of this hellish place.

How lucky was she.

* * * * * * *

Astrid rested for what Jesper guessed was about a day, maybe more. Maybe less. It was hard to tell, really.

He couldn't relax. He kept tabs on every person in the little camp, most of which began ignoring them after Ally had challenged Astrid. The exceptions being Astrid herself, and Duffer, a bald man with an inked design on the left side of his face. Jesper hadn't noticed it in the shadows while they walked, but when the man had sat down across from them, he couldn't help but be mesmerized.

"It's a symbol for balance," Duffer explained without provocation when he caught them staring, Jesper discreetly and Ally openly.

Astrid rolled her eyes as she sharpened her knife. "Here we go."

Duffer just grinned at her. "Oh, come on Triddy. You love it."

"Don't call me that." She stood and walked off, muttering something about food before they left. Duffer just smiled wider as he watched her.

"We got eternity in here," he said. "I still have time."

Jesper didn't know what Duffer would need the time for, but he didn't ask. He just waited in silence as the man went on about how he learned to tie knots to help them get around this In Between.

"It's a symbol too," Duffer finished, pointing to the spool of rope Astrid has used to lead them here. "As long as you're anchored to what matters, no matter how dark the journey may be, you'll always find your way back home."

Jesper nodded, like he understood what that meant, so Duffer wouldn't think he was stupid and stop talking to him. Ally just scoffed.

Astrid returned with a plate for the four of them. They ate this dark kind of meat that was tough to chew and managed to be both slimy and dry at the same time. Jesper didn't even want to know where it came from. His jaw ached but his stomach ached more, so he ate it anyway. At least it was food.

"When are we leaving?" Ally demanded for possibly the fourth time. Jesper nudged her foot with his toe, making her hiss, "What?" at him. He was used to her forceful attitude when it was just the two of them, but her new boldness in front of others made him nervous. The last thing he wanted to do was make anyone angry.

"*You* can leave whenever you want," Astrid said, licking her fingers. Jesper winced. "If you want me to lead you halfway, as I said before, then you'll have to wait until I'm ready."

"And when will that be?" When Astrid shot her a disapproving look, Ally scowled. "I don't want to be here anymore."

"Lucky that you *can* leave," Astrid said coldly. Duffer glanced sideways at her but she ignored him. "Lucky that you have the choice. Forgive me if I don't have any sympathy for your impatience. I'll leave when I'm ready, and if that's not soon enough for you, feel free to go get yourselves devoured by vrykol. See if I care."

"Fine!" Ally yelled, making everyone in the camp cringe and glare at her. Huffing, she lurched to her feet and stalked away.

"Bit harsh," Duffer muttered. Astrid scowled at him and took another bite.

Jesper mumbled an apology to them both, missing Astrid's response to Duffer, and jumped up to run after his sister.

"Ally, stop!" he called as loudly as he dared. "Wait!"

He finally caught up to her and stopped in front, barring her path. She scowled at him.

"You could be...just wait," he said. "We need their help."

"No we don't! We can do it on our own."

"They're trapped here, Ally. They—"

"I don't care! *I'm* trapped here!" Her voice cracked and that seemed to break her front. A glimmer of tears in her eyes shone through the dark as her knees started to shake, and Jesper caught her by the arms before she fell. He wasn't strong enough to hold her up, though, so he gently lowered the two of them down until they were kneeling.

Ally's fingernails dug into Jesper's arms. "I'm trapped. I'm trapped."

Jesper's chest constricted as his forceful sister unraveled before his eyes. "Ally. Ally look at me."

But her gaze was unfocused and far away. Her breath went ragged as she chanted again and again. "I'm trapped I'm trapped I'm trapped I'm trapped I'm trapped."

Jesper wondered where she was, what she saw. The first time Monty slapped her, when she was barely four? The first time Jesper bled and suffered broken bones in her place, when he was eight? The first time their father forced them to sit in chairs next to each other and threatened them until Jesper could say a perfect sentence?

Or, he feared, the day their mother closed her eyes forever and Ally's scream shattered the sky.

I'm trapped.

"Ally, listen," Jesper started softly. "Listen to my voice. I'm here. I'm here with you. Come back here. Listen to *my* voice."

It took a moment of coaxing, but eventually he felt her come out of it enough to hear what he was saying. Slowly she got in control of her breathing and relaxed, though she couldn't stop trembling.

"I'm scared," Ally told the ground. For a rare moment, the usual bite to her tone was gone, and she sounded like baby Ally again, the little angel that had both brightened and burdened Jesper's dark world. "I don't want to be here."

"I know," Jesper said quietly. While he loved his strong sister and hated her pain, these moments when her walls fell made him wistful. "We can start walking, if you want. We can just go. Maybe we can find it on our own."

Ally pursed her lips and nodded. She released her grip on his arms and took a breath, and Jesper felt her walls rising back up as she hardened into her usual self. He understood why she did it—why she had to—but it still made him sad.

Over Ally's shoulder, he saw Astrid walking toward them. He tensed and nudged Ally. She broke away completely from him, stood, and spun around, as strong as steel. Jesper got clumsily to his feet beside her and they watched Astrid approach with what looked like a roll of leathery parchment in hand. Ally had wiped all weakness from her face, as if she'd doused herself with a bucket of water and washed her fears away.

Jesper wished he could be as brave.

Ally opened her mouth, but Astrid beat her to it. "I'm leaving now," she said. Only then Jesper noticed the rope tied to her ankle. "Follow if you want." With that, she turned and started into the abyss, the rope dragging behind her.

Jesper wondered if there would ever be a place he would tie a rope to, making sure he could find it again. His stomach rolled a little at the thought maybe he already had—even from here, even after everything, he felt an itch under his skin, one he knew he couldn't scratch. One he knew would drive him insane until he got back home.

"It's about time," Ally muttered, breaking his uncomfortable train of thought as she stalked after Astrid. The darkness didn't look inviting, but he had no choice but to follow.

Duffer came along with them, which made Jesper feel slightly better. "Rule number three," he said by way of explanation. "Never travel alone."

"Yeah, well I don't *see* any monsters," Ally said.

"Vrykol aren't a laughing matter," Astrid snapped, as she referenced her parchment. Maybe a map then. "You take them as one and you'll be dead within the hour. We've found they are the only creatures that roam near the portals. So long as you don't go too far, they should be all you have to contend with."

"Where, um…where did the-ey come from?" Jesper asked. His feeble question sounded pathetic next to Duffer's confidence. "The vry, vrykol, I-I mean."

Astrid shrugged. "They were here before we were."

"Legend has it," Duffer supplied when Astrid didn't, "that the vrykol were actually human once."

Jesper winced. Ally wrinkled her nose in distaste, clearly not impressed. "Right."

"I don't make up the legends, little girl. They say vrykol are humans that spent too long wandering the darkness and went mad. The lack of sunlight changed their eyesight, their senses. They lost who they are in the nothing. And when they grew ravenous from hunger, they ate each other. The combination transformed them into what they are."

Jesper felt the color drain from his face, and he nearly vomited. Even Ally didn't have anything to say for a moment, though the moment passed.

"So if you can't leave," she said, "is that what will happen to you?"

Astrid stiffened and Jesper shot his sister a look, but Ally had her gaze trained on Astrid, as if marking every movement, every breath, and stowing it away somewhere.

"Not if I can help it," Astrid finally muttered.

Ally nodded once and straightened her shoulders, lifting her head and walking with long, steady steps—like Astrid, Jesper realized.

"That's why we must give ourselves an anchor," Duffer said, gesturing to the rope that trailed behind them. "So we don't get too lost."

Jesper almost asked what he meant, if he could help Jesper sort through his own messy and tangled ropes he followed himself. But then he thought of Duffer's calm face twisting into Monty's derisive scorn and bit his tongue.

As Jesper feared, they walked for ages. There was nothing to see in the shadows, nothing to hear besides Ally's loud footsteps as she tried to match Astrid without stumbling, and the occasional breath from someone in their group. The lack of distractions caused him to think, which he usually tried to never do.

He thought of what to do once they got back to the Molds—they had to go back. But Pepperjack was dead. Chaos would reign. A full war might even break out among the factions, with only Monty to protect them. What could he do to keep Ally safe?

He thought of Monty alone in their shack without work to keep him busy, money to keep him fed, and kids to keep him angry. Maybe he'd get involved in a faction war. Maybe he hadn't even noticed they were really gone yet. Would he care if he did? Or would it be a relief to finally be rid of them, of the reminder they provided?

He thought of his mom, broken and defeated on the couch. A shell of a human. The last words she'd said to him, the sound of Ally's scream when she realized—

Jesper jolted as if he'd been hit with a bolt of magic, and everything inside him throbbed. He hadn't meant to go down that hole in his head. He never allowed himself down there.

He thought of the rabbit that Ally had chased into the hole. How many of those holes existed in his mind, too deep and scary to risk getting even near them? What would happen if he fell down one and couldn't get himself back out?

Jesper shuddered. Suddenly the legends of the vrykol didn't seem that far-fetched at all.

Finally, after lifetimes of walking, Astrid stopped. Jesper looked around, but there wasn't anything different about their surroundings. Just the exact same nothingness.

For the first time in a long time, he found himself wanting to scream.

Astrid pointed straight ahead. Into nothing. "We came farther than halfway. The cluster of main portals is over there, about twelve hundred steps.

"How do you know?" Ally demanded. "There's nothing out there."

Astrid pocketed her map and traded it for a stick, offering it to Ally, who took it and tried to keep the pleasure from her face. "Use this to keep your steps straight," Astrid instructed. "Put it on the ground next to your feet if you need to and move it as you go." She gestured to the stick tied to her boots, and Jesper finally realized its purpose.

"I've used sticks for that before," Ally said proudly, almost glowing in the dark as she puffed out her chest. "I know how it works."

Jesper could've sworn something like an annoyed smile almost flashed across Astrid's face—or maybe he imagined it in the dark. She opened her mouth to respond, but suddenly Duffer slashed his muscled arm in the air, silencing them.

Ally gasped. Jesper held his breath.

The hissing was back.

Ally couldn't tell exactly where the sound came from—it was *everywhere*. Above her, below her, around her, in the space between each of them. Their silence seemed to feed it, make it grow louder and louder until it became a deep, screeching rumble that made her bones shudder. As if her body couldn't stand to hear the wrongness of such a sound. Her muscles locked up; her limbs froze. She couldn't remember how to breathe.

"What do we do?" Jesper whispered as he grasped Ally's wrist, the words barely more than a puff of air.

Astrid and Duffer had mirror expressions on their faces: tense and resolute. Ally tried to mimic the look on her own face. Lips pursed, jaw clenched, eyebrows furrowed.

"Keep going," Astrid answered. "There's no way to know—"

A hulking shadow appeared from nowhere and launched itself at Astrid. Duffer ducked in front of her and slashed his arm across the darkness. The shadow shrieked in a way that made Ally's ears ring and sagged to the ground, its stretched out claws twitching against the ground in a puddle of what she assumed was blood. It dripped from the wicked knife in Duffer's hand, so dark crimson it looked black.

Astrid opened her palm and an orb of light appeared, a knife ready in her other hand. Ally gritted her teeth at the feeble stick she held. Always left with the sticks.

"Keep moving," Duffer ordered, all fake friendliness scraped from his face.

"Moving?" Jesper squeaked. He hadn't taken his eyes off the mass of black limbs on the ground.

Astrid nodded. "It takes them time to locate their prey. If you keep moving they have a harder time catching on."

Another screech, so loud Ally slapped her hands over her ears, but then she froze. Three shadows surrounded them.

Roughly five to six feet tall—most taller than her—on two legs with black leathery skin, rows of mismatched sharpened teeth that jutted out of hanging jaws, and empty eye sockets that stared at nothing.

Ally's blood went cold and she choked on a scream.

In some corner of her mind, she hated herself for freezing, but neither she nor Jesper seemed able to move while Astrid and Duffer leapt into action. Wielding light and weapons like a king's warriors, they stood with their backs pressed together, eyes darting between each monster.

Astrid broke her concentration once to look at Ally. "On my mark," she said, "run."

A vrykol screeched. Duffer scowled, dagger raised in each hand. "Come here, kitty cat."

The monsters obeyed.

Two went for Astrid and Duffer. One went for Ally and Jesper. For a split second, Ally was insulted that the vrykol considered her the weaker prey. Then it slammed into her, knocking her flat on her back, and all air rushed out of her. Claws bit into her arms as the shadow screeched in her face. Its breath felt cold and rotten, enveloping her in a deep-rooted dread that told her death was near.

This was how she died.

She could not *believe* this was how she died.

Somewhere underneath her paralyzing terror, she found red hot rage boiling higher and higher. She'd survived the Molds. She'd survived her mother's death. She'd survived Monty the Merciless. She wasn't going to die like this, at the hands of a stupid monster who was too weak to fight against the world around it.

Ally screamed a war cry and started kicking and thrashing, feeling the monster's claws scrape at her skin. She managed to throw its balance enough that she could free her arm and reach inside her pocket. It snarled and lunged for her neck. She used all her strength to crack its skull with a rock.

Black blood oozed onto her shoulder. She tried to push the spasming dead weight off her but could only wiggle free when Jesper helped. He took one second to look over her, then they both jumped to their feet and took in the scene. Astrid slammed her sword into a vrykol's shoulder and it shrieked in agony, glaring at the orb of light in her other hand she wielded like a shield. Behind her, Duffer's inked face was puffy and bleeding as he slashed at the monster that managed to dodge his blade.

Ally yanked on Jesper. He didn't budge. "Remember what she said?" Ally shouted at him. "We have to go!"

Jesper pursed his lips, uncertain. "We should help them."

Ally huffed. His uncertainty was going to kill her someday. "They'll be fine. But we have to go. That was the whole point of this anyway, wasn't it?"

In the end, Astrid made the decision for them. With one glance at Ally, the reflection of flame dancing in her silver eyes, she jerked her chin forward. Ally knew the meaning of that look. Astrid closed her palm, then with a snarl through her teeth, flung her hand open again. Light burst from her palm, piercing the darkness with an edge as sharp as the sword she held, and vrykol shrieked as Ally had to cover her eyes.

That was the cue. She had to tug on Jesper again, but he obeyed her this time, and together they ran headfirst into the shadows. Even though he panted, she didn't let them stop until the sounds of struggle had faded and they were once again surrounded by nothing.

They stopped to catch their breath. "I hope they're okay," Jesper murmured after a minute. He actually sounded guilty about it.

"Of course they're okay," Ally scoffed. "She had a *sword*. Did you see how she used that thing with the light? She's obviously a professional."

"Where…where do you think she came from?"

Ally shrugged. "Don't know. Maybe a northern village we've never heard of." Truly, she didn't care. Astrid had done the job, had protected them, and she passed that mantle onto

Ally. Trying her best to channel the female warrior, Ally pointed with more confidence than she felt. "Let's keep moving this way. We'll find where we need to go."

"Ally...do you even know what...wha-at we're looking for?"

She shrugged again, remembering the strange way the water had flowed against itself in the lake before they fell. "I'm sure we'll know it when we see it."

"Okay." He didn't sound convinced. She would have to convince him.

And she would. She could be just as brave and strong as Astrid.

As they walked, the adrenaline slowly drained from her system and she found the maddening nothingness getting to her again. Maybe Duffer hadn't just been telling stupid stories to scare the newcomers. Maybe the monsters really had been human once.

Then they were the weak ones, Ally told herself. It made her feel better. After all, someone like her or Astrid would never fall to the level of the vrykol. Ally would search until she got her and Jesper out. They wouldn't be trapped here. He'd be so proud of her.

Time passed and her feet started aching. When she looked up from the black ground and saw a shimmering in the distance, she was sure her eyes were tricking her. She blinked once. Twice. Three times.

The shimmering remained.

"Jes," Ally murmured. Her tone rose with hope against her permission. "Jes, do you see that?"

Jes looked up from his feet, then went rigid. "What...?"

"It's our way out!"

Ignoring her cramping joints, Ally ran. The shimmering grew before her eyes, taking up much more ground than she previously thought, and hope exploded in her chest. This had to be it. They were going to get out.

The hope inside her stilled when she reached her destination. Before her, the ground gave way to a bunch of little ponds. The water inside was completely still and glassy, a frozen picture of deep gray fog.

"What is this?" Ally demanded. Then once Jesper caught up, she remembered how they got here in the first place. She turned to her brother and practically shouted, "The water will take us back!"

Jesper flinched and his face drained of color. "Ally, do you hear—"

An ear-splitting screech cut him off. Ally whipped around to see four vrykol across the second pond, nearly tripping over their own disgusting limbs as they raced toward them.

"Ally," Jes breathed, grabbing her wrist.

Not four of them. Six.

More.

More.

Ally turned to run only to see that another pack of vrykol had heard the noise and were running at the chance of dinner.

Surrounded.

Ally took a precious second to notice the revolting way the vrykol moved, limbs whipping like they didn't have bones, but even the blind monsters took care to go around the glassy ponds. To somehow avoid the water, even in their blindness.

The monsters were seconds away now. Ally made the decision. Grabbing hold of Jesper's hand, she jerked him forward and jumped into the nearest pond.

She never hit water. Instead she felt a rush of fresh air against her skin, so crisp and clean in comparison to the murky air they'd been breathing for however many days they'd been lost in this wasteland. A bright white light devoured the dark shadows and everything around them, including the screeching vrykol, fell away.

Ally didn't feel like she was falling again, or going upwards, or really anywhere. She could feel Jesper's hand still clutched in hers, but she couldn't see or hear him. As if she were suspended in never ending whiteness with nothing above or below her.

Then all at once, she hit.

Sludgy water slammed into her mouth, coating her tongue in grainy mud. Coughing, Ally pushed herself up on her elbows to keep her head out of the water and opened her stinging eyes.

They had washed up on the edge of a lake—a regular lake, not a glassy shadowed one. It was still dark around her, which gave Ally momentary panic, but the full moon shone through the clouds in the sky, illuminating the shadows of buildings in the distance.

They'd done it.

Ally whooped and jumped to her feet, splashing more water all over Jesper, who kneeled next to her and coughed so hard that he shook.

"I did it, Jes!" She spun in a circle on the shore, noting how vast the lake was: she couldn't see to the other side. Just water forever. The portal had probably spat them out on the other side of the lake they'd found in the Molds. "I brought us back!"

Jesper staggered to his feet, his face still pale and eyes red as he took in the unfamiliar buildings ahead. "But...where...where are we?"

"Does it matter? We're free!"

Apparently, her brother did not feel the same excitement. Relief flooded his eyes when he saw the moon, but he looked again at the buildings and frowned.

"Elaria?" he mumbled. Jesper would remember more of life outside the Molds than Ally, but he still didn't know anything about the kingdom's geography. Another education point Monty had missed—likely to keep them trapped in the Molds forever. "Maybe we should find King Asher. Explain our...our situation. If...maybe if we...if we explain that all then—"

"Then what?" Ally demanded. "He'll let us go? He'll give us a nice little palace of our own and we can pretend to be rich little orphans for the rest of our lives?" She scoffed. "That's not going to happen. And you know it."

"But if—"

"Hey!" They both jumped at the unfamiliar shout, the voice too commanding and much too close for Ally's taste.

She whipped around and saw two boys crossing a wooden bridge of sorts, heading toward them. One twice the size of Ally, the other as skinny as one of her sticks, but somehow looked exactly like the other. Maybe it was the red hair that did it. They were too close for Ally and Jesper to run now, and with the lake in the way, they didn't really have an exit anyway.

Jesper took a shaky breath and stepped in front of her. Ally slid her hand in her pocket and fisted a rock.

The skinny one reached them first. He wrinkled his freckled nose when he took them in and pulled something out of his shiny coat. For a second, Ally expected him to have a stash of rocks too, but his hand held something small and metal with a kind of handle. She didn't know what exactly it was, but the way the boy waved it around told her it was a weapon.

The taller guy whistled when he saw them sopping wet, his nose patterned with the exact same freckles as the other. Maybe they were brothers then. "What, did you just wash up outta the Pacific or something?"

"Never seen 'em before," the smaller one said, eyeing them in a way that made Ally straighten. "I say we just crack 'em now and leave 'em to the waves. Less clean up."

Ally's jaw clenched, but she sensed there was something more to the little metal thing in the kid's hand—something she should be wary of. She wasn't sure she could fight her way out, and Jesper certainly wouldn't be good for that. Red hot envy boiled in her veins that Astrid could defend herself and Ally could not.

Seconds passed and she couldn't find a way out, so she took her brother's idea and blurted, "We want to see the king."

She remembered a time long ago, when some betrayer had been dragged back into the Molds, brutes prepared to beat him to death. But he screamed that he wanted to see Pepperjack first, to explain himself, so the beating was postponed and he was taken to the crime lord's place.

Of course, he was still skinned alive that night, but Ally would come up with a plan before things got to that. She just needed time.

The big guy gave a disbelieving chuckle. "She serious?"

His brother narrowed his eyes. At least it made them both pause.

"King is dead." He did nothing to hide his suspicion. "Red is in charge now."

Ally blinked. That couldn't be right. King Asher's wife was Sara or Sydney or something like that, and everyone knew the prince's name was Roman. She'd remember a name like Red.

Maybe they really had been spat out on the far side of the lake, and they were in a different kingdom altogether. Maybe they would have never even heard of Pepperjack in the first place.

Now *that*, she could work with.

"Okay then," she said, jerking out her chin and squaring her shoulders like she'd seen Astrid do. "Take us to King Red."

The big guy let out another uncomfortable laugh and exchanged glances with his brother. Then the skinny one muttered something under his breath and started walking up the shore. The big guy gestured with his weapon for them to go first: Ally leveled a glare at him as a warning to behave while she had her back turned to him, and sauntered after his brother. Jesper swallowed hard and went with her.

As they walked, Ally imagined what she would say to this new king, the possibilities she had now that she wasn't tied to her father. This king wouldn't know about her family, where they'd come from. This would be her chance to start over. Be something more than Monty the Merciless' pathetic daughter, just another stick to be buried and walked all over.

This was her chance, and she wasn't going to let it go.

Once they got over the edge of the lake and made it to the road, the surroundings yanked Ally out of her thoughts.

She wasn't sure what the rest of the kingdom looked like, but she was pretty sure they weren't in Elaria anymore.

The roads were made of something hard and black instead of stacked stones or dirt, and the carriages that sped down them were unlike anything Ally had ever seen. They still had four wheels, but these were black and made out of something else, had four doors instead of two, and a big glass window and lights in the front. The black roads were lined with skinnier, white roads where it seemed the people outside of the carriages were supposed to walk. And beside those were the tallest buildings Ally had ever seen.

Hope and awe bubbled in her chest at once. What kingdom *was* this?

The royal guards led them deeper into the city and the few people around outside took one look at the guards and instantly parted for them to pass. Ally's mouth pulled up slightly. She could get used to that.

They finally turned a corner and went back into the space between two towering buildings. Most of the windows were dark or broken, but a few of them showed little rooms. As they got farther into the space, Ally noticed the people lurking on the edges along the walls. As if standing guard. Most of them, both male and female of all ages, wore shiny kinds of jackets and all carried little metal weapons.

Ally's fingers started twitching inside her pockets, dragging across her rocks. She stole a glance at Jesper's face to find it blank and pale, his eyes wide and taking in every single person they passed.

This is my chance, Ally kept telling herself, trying to keep her hope afloat and not drown in fear. Once again, she remembered the story of the man being skinned by Pepperjack. *This is different. This is my chance. I'm not letting it go.*

I will not let it go.

I will not let it go.

Ally waited to be taken into some kind of castle or at least a throne room to meet the king, but eventually they reached the end of the passageway. The wall facing them held a system of black rails that climbed up the building, a mix of platforms and ladders. One of the platforms had been torn apart, the sharp rails bent at weird angles to give the idea of a throne. And sitting on it was the fiercest woman Ally had ever seen.

Older than Ally but younger than Astrid, she gave off a scalding kind of power that made the hair rise up on the back of Ally's neck. Her long brown hair had been pulled up into a high ponytail on her head, the hair slicked back to showcase the severity of her cheekbones. Her eyes were big and cloudy and highlighted with black painted lines; her plump lips were painted a deep crimson. She wore thick black boots that tied up her calf, dark pants that clung tight to her legs, and a black jacket with a rose threaded on the sleeve. Scarlet thread dripped underneath it, as if the flower were bleeding.

No king after all.

The Red Queen.

"Well," she said as she looked down on them, the corner of her smirking mouth pointed like a dagger. "And what do we have here?"

CHAPTER 3

A RACE
WITHOUT RULES

The Red Queen's gaze left Jesper utterly paralyzed.

"And what do we have here?" she asked. Her voice rolled through the air, low and breathy, as if it had been locked up a long time and still wasn't used to freedom. Jesper had a feeling she was better left caged.

"Found 'em by the marina," said the smaller of the redhead boys that had brought them here. "Washed up outta nowhere with her cloak like some kinda old European guy."

Red arched an eyebrow. "That's new. You got names?"

The queen looked at them expectantly. Her dark eyes dragged Jesper's voice out of his throat.

"Jesper," he mumbled. "And my-my sis-sister, um my sister, Ally." He didn't dare give his last name—in case Red's territory wasn't friendly with the Jacklands, because, really, what territory was?—but an instinct inside him wanted to, to assert some kind of protection. Ally would never admit it to herself, but they only survived this long because of Monty Lewis's name.

And they were far from the shield of his reputation now.

"Ally and Jesper," Red repeated. She reached to her right and stroked a shadowed lump, something he hadn't yet noticed.

Jesper stiffened when he realized the lump was a massive black dog. The animal looked right at him and bared its teeth, as if sensing the recognition. "Huh. I've never seen either of you before. Did Dal send you?"

When Jesper shook his head, Red's gaze sharpened, those dark eyes yanking him into an abyss. "You know my price for trespassing?"

Ally seemed to have collected herself and opened her mouth, but Jesper spoke first. "We didn't mean to-to trespass, Your, Your Hi-highness. We, um, we got, got lost."

Red cocked her head. He felt like a skittering insect under her scrutiny. "Lost?"

"Yes, lost," Ally said, letting her voice out in a rush. "You can't really punish us for getting lost, can you?"

"Now that depends," Red mused. "What's the punishment for being someplace you shouldn't?"

Jesper's mouth went dry despite the moisture in the air.

Ally just shrugged, the picture of indifference. "Where we come from, the crown chops people's heads off." Jesper's stomach dropped. "I'm not sure what you do here."

The corner of Red's mouth twitched. "Ha, really? Now that would catch people's attention, wouldn't it. I'll have to spruce up my executions, then. Any other suggestions?"

"No, Your Highness," Jesper said quickly. "We...we don't mean to...to interrupt your night. If you could...if you could just give us direction ba-ack home, we-we will be on our way."

"Okay. This has been just *thrilling*." Red grasped two of the bars of her throne and pulled herself up, then stepped gracefully down the stairs. Though she wore those big black boots, her steps didn't make a sound, but the dog lifted its head and tracked each of her movements with its beady eyes. "I appreciate the entertainment, but I'm busy and this has gone on long enough. The game is over now."

The game? "We aren't...we weren't, we…" But Jesper trailed off as the queen strode right up to them. Thanks to the added height of those scary boots, he had to look up at her, and he felt as if his father stood over him now.

For the first time ever, he wished it was Monty instead. At least then, he would know what to expect.

"We don't play games." Ally's voice lacked its usual strength, like all the air had been let out of it.

Red didn't smile, exactly, but her mouth twisted up into a sly smirk. "Dal, McClain, Uma, they've all sent in little spies, and so many of them have played the dumb card, okay? I've seen it all and you can't get that past me. I'm out of your league. Besides, claiming to be lost?" She barked a laugh, a sharp lance across his chest. "Honestly, how stupid do you think I am?"

Jesper shook his head rapidly. "No-no, of course not."

"We don't think you're stupid," Ally added. She'd recovered a bit of her resolve, but her eyes were still wide as she watched Red. "You're a queen."

Red's smirk grew, clearly pleased with the recognition. "Well of course I am, Miss Ally, but sucking up won't save your head."

He could almost see the grisly scene dancing across her eyes: them getting executed right here, the massive blade cutting into their necks, blood flowing down the street. Bile rose up his throat when he realized that's exactly what the deep brown stains on the ground must be. Blood stains. Red Queen indeed.

The queen looked down on them, the amusement drying up in her expression, and Jesper wondered how many people had met their end here.

"Who sent you?" Red demanded. "One chance to answer."

"No one sent us," Ally answered, nearly insulted.

"N-no one, no one sent us," Jesper found himself repeating. When Red's expression started to teeter toward violence and she reached inside her bleeding jacket, he blurted, "We're from Elaria."

Ally cut Jesper a glare. Red opened her mouth, then closed it, then opened it again.

"Elaria?"

"Ye-es," Jesper breathed. The queen's expression demanded more, and he gave it. "There was a, a, a massa, a massacre. In the Ja-acklands. Where we're from...from the Ja-acklands. We escaped and-and fell. Astrid helped bring us he-ere."

Red pursed her crimson lips. "Astrid? From which gang?"

Jesper looked to Ally. Ally shrugged. "Um, a...a gang? I don't...I don't know—"

Ally jumped in, saving him from his ignorant stumbling. "We didn't align ourselves with anyone. We used Astrid to bring us here and disposed of her when it was necessary."

Jesper's eyebrows furrowed. It didn't happen like that. He started to clarify, but Ally pressed on, as if sensing he would.

"She led us through the darkness and we found our way ourselves after she became useless. Now we're here. On our own. Nobody sent us."

Red studied them, her eyes flicking between the two of them, as if taking the moment to catalog every detail. "What's the darkness?"

"A...a place...of, well..."

"They called it the In Between," Ally cut in. "It was like a dark cave under the lake. It stretched on forever with monsters everywhere. Astrid had been banished there, and we used her knowledge to bring us to the water, we fought the monsters off, and we ended up here. We've never been here before."

The one redhead eyed them like they were crazy. The other just snorted. "That's like Hawkins kind of crap. You sure you ain't just been binging too long?"

His brother laughed. "Next comes the demogorgon, right?"

"Cray-zay."

Red opened her crimson stained mouth and shrieked a laugh, the unhinged sound grating on the edges of Jesper's composure. It echoed in the space between buildings and scraped against the bricks. "You're seriously telling me you came from an upside down? That's the best you have?"

"We're not, we're not fro-om there," Jesper nearly whispered. "We-we're from Elaria. The Jacklands."

Again, Ally glared at him. "But we aren't aligned with any of the vermin there. We were held captive and escaped."

Why are you lying, Ally?

"Uh huh." Red's eyes swept over both of them as she ran her tongue over her teeth. Her hand disappeared into her jacket, and she twisted on her heel, beginning to turn away from them. Then faster than Jesper could blink, she snatched Jesper and dragged him with her, slamming him up against the ladder of her throne. He heard Ally shout, but all his senses narrowed in on the blade of a knife against his temple.

Red glared down at him, pressing him so the metal dug into his back. "Tell me the truth or lose an eye." She brushed the blade against his eyelashes for emphasis, and Jesper's knees buckled. He would've fallen if she hadn't braced him against the ladder.

"We aren't with them!" Ally screamed. Scuffling sounded, likely the redheads holding her back. "Pepperjack, Dal— whoever! We *escaped* the Jacklands—on our own—and we're not doing anything wrong!"

"Pepperjack," the redhead snickered over Jesper's pounding heart. "Apparently after the demogorgon comes the cheese."

The queen ignored them as she pressed the point of the blade right by the corner of his eye. He shivered, but couldn't find words inside himself. Her eyes held him captive as much as her knife did; he couldn't move, couldn't speak, couldn't think. For a moment he thought her eyes were as dark as the In Between, but then he realized they were opposite. The In Between had been empty, a cavern of nothing. But the darkness in Red's eyes was full to the brim, and he saw too many years, too many things, packed in them for being as young as she was. The thought echoed uselessly in his terrorized brain that she would've fit right into the Jacklands.

But it didn't matter: Monty wasn't here to protect them now. The only thing that mattered was keeping Red's knife from Ally.

So even though his knees shook and his eyes watered, Jesper just swallowed hard and whispered. "It's the truth." Then he clamped his eyes shut as a dribble of blood started to form from the knife.

"We will swear fealty to you!" Ally shrieked. "We have no allegiances to anyone else! We don't! We'll do anything you ask!"

Jesper waited to feel the knife dig into him, but after a few seconds, the blade lifted from his skin. He risked opening his eyes to find Red staring at him, her head cocked, her expression thoughtful.

"Interesting," was all she said. Mercifully, her knife went back into her jacket and she released him. Jesper sagged to his knees, breathing hard, and suddenly Ally was there, flinging her arms around his shoulders. When he glanced up, Red had seated herself back on her throne. He shuddered when their eyes met. She watched over them as if they were animals in the ring, ready to make them play a game.

He'd grown familiar with stories of the games Pepperjack would play with his indentured pets, but clearly they were someplace new. A whole new game.

Jesper didn't know the rules to this one.

"Well, Ally and Jesper, welcome to Ducat." Red's light tone didn't match her dark eyes. "I'll be watching you closely. Don't make trouble and I won't slit your throats." She smirked. "Or chop off your heads, if it makes you feel like home. If I think we can work something out, I'll be in touch."

The dismissal rang clear. The redheads waved their metal barrels at them and ushered them away from their queen, leaving Jesper and Ally alone in the dark on the unfamiliar streets.

* * * * * * *

Welcome to Ducat, the sign said. *A Land Full of Wonder.*

Ally rolled her eyes when she heard it. She and Jesper had made it to the edge of the territory, and he'd spent so long staring at the rusty sign trying to make out the words that some passing homeless—and very drunk—man read it out loud to them. Then he'd cackled at the sky and wandered off. Ally would've clubbed him with a rock if Jesper hadn't stopped her.

"Doo-cat," Jesper repeated, clumsily trying out the word. "I've never heard of it."

"Well you aren't exactly a world traveler."

Jesper frowned, and the movement pulled at the spot of dried blood next to his eye. Ally had been trying not to look at it.

"We need to leave," he said.

"Leave?" Ally blinked. "Why?"

"The queen obviously doesn't like us."

"She doesn't *not* like us. I convinced her to let us go," Ally pointed out, once again ignoring the close call etched into her brother's face. "That's much more than Pepperjack would've and you know it." Despite almost disfiguring her brother, Ally couldn't help but envy Red. All those big ugly men followed their queen without question, and she could clearly take care of herself. Plus she ran a whole *city*. Much bigger than Astrid's pathetic cluster of shacks.

Jesper didn't say it, but his doubt hung in the damp air around them. "Why did you lie about Astrid? About where we were from?"

Ignoring the questions, Ally looked up at the dark, cloudy sky, noting the sun was about to break over the horizon. It had been a long, strange night.

"I'm starving," she announced. "Let's find food and somewhere to sleep."

"We need to go *home*," Jesper replied.

"What? Back into the In Between?"

Jesper pursed his lips. She knew her brother didn't want to go back into that place any sooner than she did.

"We need to go home," he said after a minute. "We don't belong here."

Eyeing the spot of blood on his temple, Ally blew out a breath, then immediately took another one. The air was so nice and clean here. If she focused on it, she could almost forget that her brother nearly lost his eye.

"Can we at least find food first?" she finally asked. "It's pointless to go back starving and weak."

Jesper at least agreed to that, so they started walking back the way they'd come, heading deeper into Ducat. The strange vehicles rattled as they whizzed by on the road, some nearly clipping him. Most only carried one person at the front, but several had a whole group of people spread throughout the carriage. The wheels sped underneath them, and an unusual scent followed, some mix of smoke and metal and heat. Weirder, they seemed to be operated by humans rather than magic. When something wrong happened, a blaring noise came from the vehicle, and they all stopped and started based on a hanging light system Ally couldn't figure out.

The buildings were nearly as strange as the carriages. Sure, they were still made of brick or some kind of gray stone and had doors and windows—things she recognized—but most towered so high that she had to crane her neck to see the roof. Each had the metal ladders and platforms bolted to the walls, and they seemed to hold more than one household each. Like an inn, but on a much grander scale despite the permanent gloom to everything.

But despite the unfamiliar layout, buildings, and vehicles, Ally recognized the people they passed. Or rather, she knew the type. Hunched shoulders, shifty eyes, twitchy hands. People used to minding their own business and watching their backs. Their gazes raked over Ally and Jesper as they walked by, assessing threats, and Ally made sure to stare right back. Nobody bothered them.

Only one man said anything at all. They'd crossed a street through a racket of blaring vehicle noises to find him sitting in a rusty chair on the corner. He wore an oversized blue jacket with a lumpy hat pulled low over his head, and a cloud of smoke surrounded him. Both Ally and Jesper choked on it as they passed.

"You look lost," the man drawled, his voice husky.

Ally turned around to glare. "We aren't lost."

The man held a long stick between his teeth with some kind of cup at the end. Smoke billowed out of it in puffy clouds. "You don't. He does."

Jesper coughed again, but Ally forced herself not to, even though her throat burned and eyes watered.

"You kids wanna go somewhere else?" the man went on. "Somewhere the moon turns blue and the beasts are men?"

Jesper's face darkened. He took Ally's arm and kept walking, leaving the man behind in his smoke. She was so surprised by him that she didn't fight it.

"What was that?" she demanded. For all he'd lived through, her brother was soft, and the harsh lines of his clenched jaw looked strange on him.

"That man's on a drug." His tone clipped the words short. "He's not worth listening to."

Thunder rumbled overhead. The sky opened up and rain poured just as the first rays of sunlight started brightening the day. Ally reclaimed control and pulled Jesper into the nearest building full of people.

It was some kind of food place. A counter took up the left area with three droopy kids Ally's age standing behind little metal boxes. Lines formed in front of the counter and the seating to the right had nearly filled. People wearing the same purple shirts as the kids came out from behind the counter carrying plates or bags of food. They called out names between the chatter of people and clanking of metal, all of it melting together into a controlled chaos.

The new place leeched some of the harshness out of Jesper's face, replacing it with a fearful kind of curiosity. "What are you doing? We don't have any money."

Ally didn't answer. A slight smirk spread on her mouth as she watched the workers come out a door behind the counter carrying food, call out a name, and give it to whoever answered without asking for anything else. She waited until a red-faced boy came out carrying two bags.

"Mia?" the boy called, searching the crowd with heavy-lidded eyes. "Mia W?"

A few seconds passed. Either this Mia wasn't listening or she'd left without her meal. Her loss.

"Here!" Ally called. Jesper hissed in disbelief under his breath, but Ally broke from him to walk right up to the boy.

He didn't even look twice as he handed her the bags and muttered, "Have a great day" like he couldn't remember the last time a day had ever been bearable, let alone *great*.

Nobody paid them any attention, but Ally fisted both bags in one hand, grabbed Jesper with the other, and ducked out of the building. She protected their spoils from the rain in her cloak and ran, Jesper trailing behind her, until she thought they were far enough away. Then she ducked in between two buildings and found an empty spot that had stayed mostly dry thanks to an overhanging roof.

By the time Jesper caught up, Ally was practically drooling as she unwrapped each delicacy. A carton of golden circles that were crunchy on the outside and soft on the inside. Several stacks of bread with meat and egg smashed in the middle. Packages of freshly cooked meat slices on the side.

And it was all *hot*.

She stuffed three golden circles into her mouth and actually moaned. Flavor like she'd never known burst across her tongue. Salt, she recognized, remembering the taste fondly from her childhood back when their mother fed them, but everything else, the oily moist goodness, was a beautiful welcome. Her stomach grumbled the second she swallowed, demanding more.

Out of breath, Jesper started to protest, but she shoved one of the stacks at him. She could see the second the smell hit him: his eyes widened and the words died in his mouth.

"You have to," she mumbled in between another handful of delicious circles. "You just have to."

Need took over Jesper's conscience. He shoved a giant bite into his mouth and closed his eyes, half swallowing and taking more before he really even chewed it.

Whoever Mia was, she'd clearly been buying food for several people, but Ally and Jesper consumed it all within minutes. Soggy paper blew around them as they sat, panting, like they'd just run the most satisfying race there had ever been.

"Wow," Jesper murmured in a daze. "That was…"

"Amazing?" Ally licked her lips again, searching out every crumb and drop of flavor. "You're welcome." She smiled. She'd gotten them food herself, actually good food, and they didn't even get caught. For some strange reason, she wished Astrid had been there to see it—it was much better than the disgusting leather sticks she'd given them to eat in the In Between.

Her voice brought Jesper out of his food-induced stupor. He straightened and glanced around the wet passageway, the sky above them growing lighter with each passing second.

"Why'd you lie?"

Ally heaved a sigh. "Will you relax? I didn't *lie*. I just carefully selected my truths." When Jesper just stared at her, she shrugged. "The Jacklands *were* like a prison. Monty the Merciless basically kept us trapped there."

Jesper's shoulders scrunched in on themselves. "He…but he protected us. With-without him…we…we would've—"

"Left? Escaped?" Ally gritted her teeth. "Same difference."

"Yeah, but…I mean, not…it's…"

"I don't understand why you can't just call him what he is."

"I-I don't…it's more…it's hard."

Ally barked a sarcastic laugh and the words tumbled out of her before she had the chance to think. "Hard? What's hard is we lived with a monster. What's hard is without him hanging over us, our mother would be alive. *That's* hard."

Jesper looked away, focusing on his hands as he picked up the damp trash around them. Rage simmered under Ally's skin, and she struggled to keep it contained, to remember the victory of the moment before and the contentment of her full stomach. She and her brother never fought.

But Jesper never talked about their mother. Couldn't even sit around in a conversation about her. Ally had always tried to respect his right to grieve in his own way—after all, he had known her longer than Ally had—but sometimes it made her want to pull all her hair out.

The world acted as though their mother didn't exist, as if she wasn't ripped from her life and dumped in a grave, leaving a cavern in Ally's soul. Jesper was the only one left that could help Ally keep her memory alive, at least, and he stayed silent.

Look what I did for us, Ally wanted to say. *Don't you think she'd be proud of me?*

She'd be proud of me.

Wouldn't she?

Ally opened her mouth, but snapped it shut when a figure appeared at the entrance of the passageway. Jesper tensed. Ally stood.

A girl, about the same age as Ally and twice the size, blocked their path out. Her blonde hair faded into pale pink, her eyes were lined black and powdered pink, and her coat shone purple.

A slow smile spread on her round face, stretching her cheeks and showing blinding white teeth. "I found you."

* * * * * * *

The rain picked up, beginning to pelt Jesper's face as he stared at the newcomer. He stayed still, mentally trying to piece together an escape plan, cursing the fact he hadn't been paying more attention to where they were rather than the food.

But even without turning around, he knew this stranger blocked their only exit.

Ally stepped forward, hand in her cloak pocket, and Jesper winced at the threat in her voice. "What do you want?"

The girl's sly smirk rivaled even his sister's, though more colorful. "I saw what you did with the food at Gordy's."

Jesper's stomach dropped. Was this girl part of the queen's law enforcement? As good as the food was, it wasn't worth getting arrested. He shivered in the rain.

Or losing an eye.

Ally shrugged. "I don't know what you're talking about."

"Mia W. was in front of me in line." The girl's pale face wrinkled with her nose. "She had, like, a million kids all screaming everywhere and snot dripping down their noses. Believe me, she's one you notice. So are you, in that old school cloak of yours. I like the vibe."

"You can't prove anything."

"Ally," Jesper breathed. The remnants of trash blew around them. The girl looked at the wrapper pointedly, then narrowed her eyes.

"I've never seen you before."

"So?" Ally asked.

"I know everybody. Or, at least, I know *of* them."

"Congratulations."

"Ducat is a wasteland. Nobody in their right mind would *come* here, unless they're up to something."

"We're not—" Jesper started, but Ally cut him off.

"*You're* here."

"Because I'm stuck here. That's just how it works. You're born here, you die here. You're not born here, you never know this pathetic place even exists. It's like the land of socks the dryer ate."

Ally just shrugged. Jesper tried to gauge the distance between the girl and the wall. Could they hope to slip by and outrun her? She didn't really look like the running type, but, then again, Jesper wasn't so great either.

The girl ran a hand through her hair underneath her hood, as if she needed to fix it despite the rain pelting down. She gave a little bow; it seemed more mocking than respectful though. "The name's Cheyenne," she said, "but everyone calls me Kat."

Jesper raised an eyebrow. Ally barked a laugh.

"A cat?" Ally asked, her voice dripping with mockery. "You can't be serious."

She turned her nose up. "Middle name is Katherine and I couldn't stand my grandma Kathy when she was alive, but Kat works for me. It's memorable. It has personality, and in this digital age, you gotta be memorable. You got names?"

Ally laughed again. "Not animal names."

The girl rolled her eyes. "Look, rumors of newbies wandering around will spread really fast, especially if you aren't affiliated. People will be looking for you and won't mind some slicin' and dicin' if you know what I mean. Riley will move the earth itself to find you first—and you better hope he does— and if he can't part from his beloved WSU paper long enough then he'll enlist sweaty IT guys he works with and you don't want that. Plus, if they can't find you then he'll make me help and my newest vlog episode *has* to go up by Tuesday and honestly I just don't have the time to scour the streets looking for missing kittens, all right?"

Jesper blinked. He understood about half of what she had said.

Ally pursed her lips and thought for a moment. "You really call yourself a cat?"

The girl—Kat—threw her hands up and let out an exasperated sigh. "Why are you so stuck on that? Katherine is a perfectly normal *boring* name. Kim K freaking named her daughter *North* and nobody's crying over it. That girl's an icon!"

Jesper's eyebrows furrowed. He didn't know any Kim but he was afraid to let his ignorance show.

Apparently it did anyway because Kat's mouth dropped open. "Kim. Kim Kardashian? The only Kim that matters!" She dragged her hands over her face. "I can't even believe this."

Ally opened her mouth, but a sudden song slashing through the air cut her off. Jesper jumped at the sound, and the two of them glanced around wildly, looking for the source of the music. Only Kat wasn't bothered. She reached into her purple coat and pulled out a pink striped rectangle. She looked at it, sighed, then tapped the face and held it to her ear. Immediately, the song stopped.

"You know you can at least give me more than twenty minutes," she said flatly. Then she stopped talking.

"Um…" Jesper exchanged a glance with Ally, who, for once, couldn't mask the confusion leaking out onto her face. Were they supposed to respond?

"Yeah," Kat said out of nowhere, making them both jump. Was she communicating with someone else? "Two of them. I think they're siblings." A shorter pause. "I know because I'm looking at them." Another pause. "No, I don't think so. Don't got the vibe…yeah, yeah, I know. Jeez, Riley, you're such a buzzkill. Just take a chill pill. We're on our way." Then she tapped the box again and shoved it back into her pocket.

"What's that box thing?" Ally demanded, her arm still in her pocket. Likely holding onto a rock.

Kat put a hand against her chest as if hurt. "Hey, don't mock it, all right? I'm waiting for my next ad sponsorship to come in before I can get an upgrade."

"Is, is it ma-magic?" Jesper asked.

Kat snorted. "Sure, if you want to call AT&T magic."

Jesper pursed his lips. He'd never heard of that type of magic before.

"You used it to contact someone," Ally said, still on the offensive, "and told them about us. Why? Who is Riley?"

"Relax, kitten. Riley's the ultimate mother hen. The only thing you have to be afraid of is him coddling you to death. We all know he'll try." With a sweeping arm motion, she gestured out of the passageway. "Let's go." When neither of them moved, she rolled her eyes. "*Somebody* cut my breakfast at Gordy's short, and I'm starving. Let's go catch the end of Jenny's meal, shall we?"

Jesper saw Ally's lip curl as she took a menacing step forward toward Kat. He had no plans to go with the stranger, but it was much too early in the game to make enemies. Who knew what kind of allies Kat had, or how powerful Riley was?

"Okay," Jesper mumbled. Ally shot him a dark look, but he just stepped in front of her, as if to follow.

Kat nodded as she smiled, clearly proud of herself, and led the way out of the passageway. Stepping after her, Jesper wrapped his hand around Ally's wrist and squeezed lightly to silence her protest. He gave her a pointed look. She sighed when she realized his plan and rolled her eyes.

He was afraid she would attack anyway, but Ally followed his lead: the second they had gotten out of the passageway, they took off down the street in the opposite direction of where Kat had started to lead them.

We have to go home. The thought echoed over and over again, propelling him faster, even when Ally pulled ahead of him. *We have to go home we have to go home we have to go home.*

Eventually they had to slow down—Kat had been left far behind anyways. Jesper nearly doubled over trying to catch his breath, and Ally yanked him behind the nearest building. Running through the city probably hadn't been the best way to keep a low profile. The queen likely already knew about it. Surely one of her guards had seen them.

Doesn't matter, Jesper thought. *We are getting out of here.*

"Water," he gasped to Ally once he caught his breath a bit. "We have to go back to the water."

Ally jerked back in surprise. "What? Why would we do that?"

"We have to go back. We can't stay."

"Go back...you mean go back into the endless cave of monsters?" Her mouth fell open in shock when he nodded. "Again, *why* would we do that?"

"We have to go home." Just saying the words out loud caused his bones to shake. They should've never left in the first place.

"Home," Ally repeated blankly, as if the word tasted unfamiliar in her mouth.

"Yes. Home."

She just continued to stare at him, her eyes far away, and Jesper peeked out from around the building. He couldn't spot any immediate threats, so he took Ally's arm again and led her down the street. They made several wrong turns and had to backtrack a couple times, but eventually he found what Red's guards had called the marina. Land spilled into an endless expanse of water, thousands of rain drops creating a roaring mass of ripples. Despite everything, the magnitude of it took Jesper's breath away.

His sister stayed stiff and silent as he led her across the wooden beams and stopped at the edge. The rain had long ago soaked him to the skin, but the idea of just jumping right back into the waves suddenly didn't seem appealing.

Glancing around, he saw a wooden structure tied to the platform underneath their feet. It looked like a really long skinny bowl, and it floated on the water, gently knocking against the platform with each wave. Small, but still big enough to fit two people inside.

He'd heard of boats and ships before and wondered if this is what they looked like. In Elaria, getting on one was considered a death sentence, but, Jesper reasoned with himself, Red's guards wouldn't have come all the way down here to get them in the first place if there had been any danger of sirens.

"You want to steal it?" Ally asked, finally breaking her silence. He glanced over to find her staring at the boat too, her face unreadable.

Jesper's shoulders sagged. Of course he didn't want to steal it. But what other choice did they have? Maybe the waves would bring it back when they were done with it.

When he said as much to Ally, she just shrugged. She didn't offer any other comments as she climbed into the boat after him—it nearly tipped over, but they caught it in time. Jesper untied the knot holding it to the platform, and instantly the waves started carrying them out, away from the strange new land they accidentally found.

We are going home, Jesper repeated to himself again and again. A shiver that had nothing to do with his rain drenched clothes went through him.

They had to get home, even if Ally didn't understand it yet. Or maybe never would.

He hoped she would forgive him someday.

* * * * * * *

Ally pursed her lips as the waves rocked their boat farther and farther away from land. She had to squint in an effort to protect her eyes from the spray of water that splashed up on the side of the wood. Not that it really mattered—she'd been soaked a long time ago.

And isn't that a good thing? she wanted to ask her brother. *Doesn't the rain make you feel clean for once?*

Just the thought of going back made her want to scream, but for some reason she couldn't find her voice. Was it just the strangeness of her brother having such a conviction that made her feel hollow? Or was it knowing that she'd escaped— somehow, some way, she had managed to *escape* Monty and the Molds and her miserable life—and now that chance would be buried beneath these waves?

Jesper says we have to go back. Her brother rarely had a spine about anything, except when it came to protecting her from their father or refusing to talk about their mother. Or, she noted, when they passed that drugged up man on the corner. In all her life, those were the only times Jesper had ever had any kind of resolve.

Why now? she wanted to shriek at him. *Why start making decisions now?*

Why are you taking me back there?

She opened her mouth to ask, despite the fact they were too far away from land now to really do anything about it, when a wave slammed into the side of the boat. A squeak of surprise escaped her and she threw her arms out. The pathetic pile of wood nearly tipped over but stabilized at the last second.

Ally shot Jesper a look. "This was the worst idea—"

Another wave slammed into them, and Jesper cried out when the momentum tossed him like a clod of dirt into the water.

"Jes!" Ally snatched him by the shoulder before he could completely disappear, and she latched her other hand onto the side of the boat to keep herself from falling too. Water slashed at her violently as if demanding she let her brother go. Surrender. Be buried. Like a stick.

Gritting her teeth, Ally glanced up through her wet eyelashes to the sky, searching for the sun. But it couldn't be found behind the thick gray clouds.

"Give me something better than this!" she shrieked at the top of her lungs. She thought of the rabbit getting away from her, and the rage it brought gave her strength. Her arm screamed as she pulled her brother back into the boat. A momentary victory, as the next wave nearly tossed them both out.

Ally tipped her head back, the rain or waves or both splashing over her face in a rush, and screamed at the sky. Deep, rolling thunder roared right back.

She only had a moment to pause in wonder and listen to the thrill of the sound.

Then she tumbled into the water.

A brief glance of the overturned boat caught her eye next to a sinking mop of black hair, then she fell under the waves.

The storm was deceptively quiet underneath. For a second she wondered if this would be the better alternative than the boat, but the first whiplash proved her wrong. She thought her neck would snap as the water hurled her around, left and right and upside down and she didn't know which way was up. Each swing of the current felt like a brutal punch. She raged against her own powerlessness but there was nothing she could do. No matter how much she clawed and kicked, the water beat her down twice as hard. Just like everything else.

One blow. The Molds.

Another. Pepperjack.

Another. Their mother's death.

Another. Monty.

Another. The stupid rabbit.

Another. Monty. Again, Monty, again, if not a hit to her then one to her brother, again and again and again.

She survived Monty, but for what? She survived those monsters in the In Between just so she could grovel to someone new in an attempt to save her brother. Get beat up again just so she could fall right back into the water and drown for a place that had never really been her home.

A brief glimpse of air kissed her face, and her ragged lungs scraped what bit of it she could. Here she was fighting again. Powerless.

When the water dragged her down again, she crashed into something solid and fingers wrapped around her wrist. Jesper. Somehow, he'd found her again.

Fighting, again.

For nothing, again.

Her chest screamed for more air, her limbs exhausted, and she knew she didn't have much left inside her. Instinctually, she used her free hand to reach into her heavy cloak pockets, seeking the comfort of her rocks. She'd always been able to fight with them before, but now they were helping to drown her.

A zing danced across her fingertips when they brushed over an unfamiliar texture—no, not unfamiliar. Her rock, the new one that they'd fallen into the lake for. She clutched it in her hand, and she felt her desperation, her rage, course through her, making her hold on tighter to the piece of herself that she had collected. She knew her body was about to give out, but she wouldn't allow her mind to. She would not die here.

Her resolve grew like wildfire in her chest, snaking down her arm and into her fingertips as she held onto her precious rock. She kicked and thrashed her way to what she felt—and hoped—was land, dragging Jesper with her, and with each strike of the water, she made herself a promise.

She would never go back to the Jacklands.

She would never see her father.

And she would never, *ever* beg for herself or her brother ever again.

* * * * * * *

Once again, Jesper wondered if he had died.

He wasn't conscious exactly, but he knew he wasn't asleep—still aware, painfully, of the burning in his lungs and dead weight of his limbs. He couldn't find the surface of this darkness though, and for a moment he thought maybe they'd done it and were now in an even darker part of the In Between.

Then reality seemed to smash into him, and his eyes flew open just as he coughed up enough water to flood the entire Jacklands. It scorched his throat on the way back up, just as hot as the grainy sand in his eyes. When he could finally see clearly, he found himself staring up at the same cloudy sky he had been just as he'd slipped beneath the waves that had nearly killed him. The rain had already started to subside, just a light drizzle now.

It didn't work.

Disappointment crashed into him just as hard as the water had, and he pushed himself onto his knees in a desperate search. Thankfully, he didn't have to search far. Ally had ended up less than twenty feet from him. Her stringy blonde hair had tangled into a matted knot of dirt and debris, and it looked like she had already been through her own coughing fit based on the way she sat curled inward. Her eyebrows furrowed in skeptical wonder as she stared at something in her hand, but her cloak covered it from Jesper's view.

"Ally," Jesper rasped. His sister didn't break her stare. "Ally."

A screech sounded, making them both jump. Jesper's jaw dropped when he found the pink powdered girl from earlier—

Kat—rushing for them, someone unfamiliar close behind her. Ally's expression broke into a snarl and she shoved her hand back into her soaked cloak and jumped to her feet. The way Jesper's body felt, he couldn't believe she could just jump up like that.

"Are you *insane?*" Kat demanded once she got close enough to yell over the crash of the waves. "You could have drowned!"

"You don't say?" Ally muttered, her tone as dark as the clouds. She held a hand out and helped Jesper lurch painfully to his feet. Sandy water sloshed in the corners of his clothes, his shoes, his hair. Despite the itch, he forced himself to stay still as he examined the man with Kat: several years older than him wearing laced up shoes, skinny gray pants, a shiny black jacket, and a piece of gray fabric pulled tight over his head.

"Are you guys okay?" the stranger asked, dark eyes wide behind square frames. Why did his eyes need protection? Maybe from all the rain.

"Who's asking?" Ally shot back.

Kat, still bewildered, regained some of herself to start saying, "I told you—" but her friend cut her off.

"I'm Riley. Kat gave me a call when she saw you, uh, head into the water there."

"Which bears repeating," Kat added, glancing at both of them, "are you *actually insane?*"

Riley waved her off, which made Kat roll her eyes and Ally stiffen. "You guys are probably cold and tired—you can come crash at my place and then we can talk." His eyes darted around for a moment before resting back on Ally. "This isn't the side of town you want to be standing around in for very long. Trust me."

Ally scoffed. "Trust *you?* I don't even know you, okay? We're fine, just leave us alone. Come on, Jes."

She motioned for him to follow her, but he couldn't make his feet move. He could only think *it didn't work.*

It didn't work.

It didn't work.

What would they do now? How could they get back? Maybe the water only went one way. Maybe it could bring them here but nothing could leave. Was that what Astrid had meant by banished?

They had to get home. That knowledge bore deep into his bones, overriding everything else. If Monty knew they were gone…the thought made him shudder so hard that Ally turned back to glance at him.

"Jes?" she murmured uncertainly under her breath.

"Your brother looks like he could use some rest," Riley said, making Ally whip her head back around. "If you—"

"Back off *my* brother, okay?"

"We need to get home," Jesper said. His voice sounded as empty as he felt. "We need to get home."

That made Ally practically bare her teeth, and Kat raised her eyebrows and took a step back as if retreating from a rabid animal. Riley didn't so much as blink.

"Is Ducat home?" he asked.

Kat shook her head. "Can't be."

Ally hissed under her breath when Jesper managed to shake his head too. Why did his head feel so fuzzy?

"I can make arrangements for you then," Riley said, almost as if he were begging them. His eyes shifted around again. "You just look like…you don't look that great. Nearly drowning takes a toll. I can get you where you need to go."

"Save it, Riley," Kat muttered, but he ignored her.

"I don't know you and I don't need you." Ally glared at both of them. "Leave us alone."

Riley sighed. "Look, I'm just trying to help."

Jesper didn't recognize the look in Riley's eyes, the expression on his face—he didn't have a name for it, didn't know how to react to it, didn't trust it. But one need overruled them all.

"Yo-ou can help us ge-et…get home?" he asked.

"Yeah, sure." Riley shrugged as if it were easy. "Anything you need. We just need to get out of here. Kat can explain on the way."

Truthfully, he didn't think it through much. He didn't feel capable of much thinking at the moment. Jesper just gave a tired nod and motioned for them to lead the way. Ally shot him a disbelieving glance that only intensified when Jesper took a shaky step to follow Riley and Kat. He tried to give her a reassuring look. She just pursed her lips, something shifting in her eyes as if she'd just made a decision, and started walking with him.

So for the second time that day, Jesper and Ally trudged away from the endless water and into an unknown city.

Riley brought them to his own strange carriage. The color of it reminded Jesper of vomit, and the thought made him almost retch right there. Riley opened the back door for them before getting in the front seat behind a wheel, and Kat tapped her hand against the side of the car.

"Be grateful, kittens," she told them. "Riley rarely drags Billie out for anything." Then she slid into the other seat in the front.

Ally glanced at the open door before looking back at Jesper, as if to say *we are really doing this?* Jesper didn't have anything in him but a tired half shrug. What other choice did they have? Finding an empty street to try and sleep in with the hope Red's people wouldn't find them and try to take another eye?

His sister seemed to read his expression and nodded once, a sharp jerk of her head. Jesper couldn't help but breathe a sigh of relief. Together, they crawled into the back seat and shut the door. The carriage hummed to life with a violent shudder, and for a moment he wondered if this was just as dangerous as the small boat in the waves. But Riley pulled on a stick in between his and Kat's seat, shifted his feet, and they started to move. Jesper would've watched his movements with fascination—was he controlling the carriage somehow?—but nausea welled up inside him and he had to close his eyes.

Kat's bubbling voice filled the empty space that could've been tense or awkward, and Jesper found himself grateful to the strange, pink girl. She explained that Red was something called a gang leader—a really dangerous one—so she pretty much ran the city as she wished. Anyone who wanted to stay alive stayed away from her bad side.

"Since you're newbies with no discretion, it was only a matter of time before Red found you," she said, "so it's a good thing you decided to come with us."

Ally waved a dismissive hand. "We already talked to her. She said we were welcome here."

Jesper winced at how easily the lie rolled from her lips.

Kat turned in her seat and raised a painted eyebrow. Riley glanced at them in the mirror. "You saw Red?" he asked. "In her alley?"

"Yeah," Ally said, her demeaning tone rolling over everything. "I told you that."

"And she just let you go?"

"Yeah."

"So you're not one of Uma's spies?" Kat asked.

"No-no," Jesper said, finally finding his voice. That was the last thing he wanted anyone to think. "We are...aren't. Not."

Her eyes went over them again. "Huh. Interesting."

"Is it?" Ally bit back.

"Considering very few people walk out of that alley alive or at least bleeding," Riley answered, completely unperturbed by Ally's tone, "yes, it is."

Jesper saw Ally's gaze dart to his eye before she straightened her shoulders. "I convinced her that we aren't going to cause her any trouble. She was almost happy to have us. So this whole 'rescue mission' or whatever you want to call it is actually pointless."

Kat scoffed. "A few more minutes on the streets as an unaffiliated and you might've changed your tune, kitten."

Ally scowled. "Stop calling me that."

"Whatever." She went on to describe a guy named Davey—"beautiful hair, terrible kisser"—who was shot last week because he'd made Red angry. "He's in the hospital now, but I seriously doubt he will make it out, at least in one piece." That made Riley tense and grip the wheel a bit harder, but the reaction went away as quickly as it came.

Eventually Riley stopped the carriage at an old, white box of a building, the paint peeling like old fruit. "It's not much," Riley said as they got out, "but it's home." He said it with such certainty, as if 'home' were a real foundation, something stable—something Jesper just couldn't imagine.

They followed him up two sets of precarious staircases before he unlocked a door and let them through. Jesper watched him warily as he locked it again from the inside. He noticed Jesper watching and offered a soft smile. "Welcome to Bellevue One Forty-Five. Come on in and sit down."

Jesper's eyes roamed the new space. The stone floor matched the one outside, though in here there were three sporadic, mismatched rugs trying to hide it. Two worn couches and a short table crowded near the front door and a clunky black box. Behind the couches stood a square table with a counter running the wall on the opposite side. The left wall opened into a hallway.

Kat had taken a seat at the table next to a girl with a cloud of curly black hair, the story of her morning already spilling out of her in dramatic gusts as if she had nearly drowned in it too. A short lady stood at the counter, her back to them. With alarm, Jesper realized Ally had disappeared.

As if she sensed his building panic, Ally appeared again from the hallway. Her eyes were narrowed in skepticism as she took in the new space.

"It's not much better than ours," she muttered.

Riley crossed the room, either not picking up on Ally's attitude or choosing to ignore it. "You've already met Kat. This is H." He gestured to the girl next to Kat. She waved without looking up, staring intently at the little rectangle box in her hands. Then he pointed to the lady at the counter. "And this is my mom Jenny." Jenny offered a wave without turning around, clearly fully invested in whatever she was working on.

"H?" Ally scoffed. "Right."

The girl looked up at Ally, her cloud of black hair bopping with the movement. "What's it to you, newbie? Still waterlogged?"

Riley rapped his knuckles against the table, and H rolled her eyes. "What are your names?" he asked, looking from Ally in the hallway to Jesper still stationed by the front—locked— door. When neither of them answered, he gave a small smile and said, "Should I just call you One and Two?"

Was it a joke? Jesper couldn't tell. His head still was filled with fuzz and the room had started to tip sideways. His shoulders sagged with the weight of his limbs.

"Jesper," he murmured.

Riley's eyebrows furrowed. "Jester?"

"Jes*per*," Ally cut in sharply. "And I'm Ally. Now tell me why you forced us to come here."

We chose to come here, Ally, Jesper wanted to tell her. *We need to get home.*

"She's a winner," Kat muttered.

H gave a dramatic sigh. "Riley, if they're going to be this obnoxious then just set 'em loose."

Riley shook his head, ignoring the girls. "Just wanted to help, like I said. New people don't last long around here." A tense moment of silence passed before he sighed. "Look, why don't you two get cleaned up and rest—I have a spare room you can use. Then when you've recovered a bit from this morning we can talk about getting you home."

Again, Ally pursed her lips, a storm raging in her expression. Jesper sensed she wanted to argue. Since they'd arrived here it seemed like she unleashed every combative word that had built up over the years, meant for Monty. So he was surprised when she just gave a curt nod and motioned for him to come with her. Having already explored the place, she led him down the hallway and into the first room on the right.

They shut the door and pushed the small dresser in front of it for good measure, then Jesper couldn't hold himself up anymore. He collapsed onto the small mattress.

"Ally." His limbs were heavy, as if he would fall right through into the ground. He was no use to his sister like this—he needed rest—but he felt like he was drowning again, and what if the water buried him before he could explain? Could he explain?

We have to get home, Ally. We just have to.

Somewhere through the waves, she felt him grasp his pinky. Instantly he relaxed a fraction. "It's okay, Jes," she told him, her voice puffed up with importance. "I'll keep watch."

How did we get here? he wondered. How did they go from Jesper standing as a wall between Monty's ruthless rage and Ally's scared silence, to Ally picking a fight with everybody while Jesper sat uselessly to the side?

Despite how hard he fought against it, he couldn't help succumbing. He fell into sleep plagued with dreams of red rivers, snarling dogs, and gray smoke, so thick and dark that he couldn't find Ally anywhere. He pawed through the smog and screamed her name over and over again, but she was gone.

CHAPTER 4

JOIN US FOR TEA?

Of course, Ally broke herself out.

She planned on coming back for Jesper once she knew where to take him, how to find somewhere safe. The last time Ally had been brought to a new place against her will—when Monty had signed their souls away to Pepperjack without even asking—she had her mother to guide her. Her mother tended to their house, got them food, told them where to go and where to never set foot. Who to talk to. Who to avoid. And when she fell prey to a monster in the Molds, Jesper stepped up to take her place in the quest to keep Ally safe.

Now it was Ally's turn. They'd washed up somewhere new, and she'd already managed to save her brother from losing an eye. She knew she should take the responsibility of taking care of them here, a chance to give that back to her brother after all he'd done for her—to convince him they should stay here instead of going back.

This place gave new life to her. She could feel the clean air washing through her with every breath, strengthening her steps, giving her confidence. Ally could carve a place for them and everything would be exactly as she'd always hoped.

And she wasn't going to blow that chance by getting chained up by Riley five minutes into their adventure.

He'd left them alone—for now—in that bare and unremarkable bedroom: a single bed with ratty brown blankets, a small wooden chest with two drawers, and a square window on the far side. After helping Jesper to the bed where he promptly fell asleep, his mop of damp hair clinging to his head, she waited until she could hear soft voices pick up from the kitchen. Not loud enough to make out their words, the plans they were discussing for the new prey they'd found.

Ally hissed through her teeth. She would not be trapped here.

Her feet automatically gravitated toward the window, her fingers twitching with the itch for freedom. Several metal rods and pieces of wood had been shoved in between the wall and the pane to keep it shut, but yanking them out didn't actually do anything to help open it. Some kind of locking mechanism stuck on the side of the window stood in her way. She wasted precious time trying to get around it, and when she couldn't figure it out, she finally snapped it off and shoved the window aside. With a huff and last glance at her sleeping brother, she crawled through.

Ally took a deep breath and her body relaxed. The wet air was so *clean* here. It made her nose sigh and lungs sing. Standing on the metal platform stuck to the wall, she surveyed the area. Besides the puffy clouds, the brightening sky held no signs of the downpour earlier, and, more importantly, no yellow haze. She took another deep breath.

Yes, she was going to make this work for them.

The metal creaked softly under her boots as she descended the stairs. Ally peeked her head around the brick corner, noting the handful of people that littered the streets by the carriages that whizzed past. She waited until the coast was clear, then walked out, her hands stuffed in her pockets in case she needed a weapon fast.

Her eyes darted every which way, marking her surroundings as she walked so she could find her way back to Jesper again.

The white box of a building Riley tried to trap them in, stuck in a long row of similar chipping buildings like an afterthought; the square slab of street crammed with tall rectangles with attached hoses that people stuck into their carriages; the market stalls with flashing bright signs Ally couldn't even look at, let alone read. Most interesting, every few blocks she found a huge painting on the wall of a random building, stark color against the gray sky.

There wasn't a building in Ducat that wasn't crumbling in on itself with chipped, deadened paint, crime and poverty smeared across it all. And yet…she'd long since wished for something better, challenged the sun to give her more, but now she realized she had never wanted a perfect palace with marble floors and glittering jewels. Ducat wasn't yellowed and miserable like the Molds. It was broken, sharp, clawing for a place in the world, to survive.

A smile tugged on Ally's mouth at the thought.

Eventually, she made it back to the place she'd taken food from, the one cat girl had called Gordy's. Ally marked the place in her head too, the washed-out purple words painted on the gray brick. She'd need to learn to get around on her own, but also how to steadily get food for Jesper and her. The food they'd eaten had been the best Ally had ever had. She imagined how thrilled her brother would be when they ate like that all the time because of her.

The man in the strange hat still sat at his spot on the street corner, puffing a cloud of smoke around him. She had meant to keep going, but the sight of him from across the street stopped her in her tracks. He'd set up his chair in the center of it all—nearly the exact midpoint from Red's alley throne to Riley's white prison. Crowds of people came and went around him, ignoring him as if he were nothing but a rock in their path.

Ally stopped in an alley across the street and watched him for a few minutes. The things he must hear and see. The information he must have.

The Jacklands were full of rats, but a survivor knew how to pick the strongest ones out of the pack. And something told Ally this guy was one of them.

Once a lull had passed, the street now empty, a young man braved the cloud of smoke. With hands stuffed in his pockets, shoulders crunched, and eyes shifting around, he stalked up to the drugged man's chair tucked by the corner of the building. The young man spoke quickly. The drugged man blew his smoke. Ally squinted and leaned forward, noting an exchange that happened, though she couldn't tell with what. The young man shoved his share of it into his pocket and walked hastily away.

Ally waited until the young man was good and gone, then stuffed her hands in her pockets, curling her fists around a rock, just in case, and marched across the street. She had to hold her breath when she stopped in front of him. Stars, that smoke reeked.

The man still wore his blue hooded top from earlier. He leaned back in his chair as he surveyed her. "New girl. Lookin' for a high?"

For some reason, an image of Jes flashed in her mind: his sudden disgust—anger, even—with this man for his 'high.' She never wanted Jesper to look at her like that. Plus, living with Monty hadn't exactly made her soft toward alcohol. She shook her head resolutely. No, she would never, ever even resemble the shadow of her father.

The man looked her up and down. "You got anything for me, then?"

Ally scowled. "No."

"Then get lost. You're breathing my air." As if to prove the point, he blew a bunch of smoke in her face.

Ally couldn't help coughing once, but she cleared her throat through watering eyes and promised herself she wouldn't cough again.

The man gave a crooked grin, likely reading her resolve in her expression. "If new girl ain't lookin' for a high, what ya doin' talkin' to me, love?"

"You seem like a big player here," Ally said coolly, and the man raised an eyebrow in surprise. "I want to know what you know about Riley."

"Ah, I see." He sucked in another cloud of smoke. "Riley Hatton takin' you and your brother in, that right?"

It took everything in her not to roll her eyes. "No, he didn't take us at all. But he won't leave us alone and I want to know why."

"You don't trust easy, do ya chickadee? That's smart. Real smart. Especially if you're stickin' around here. But I don't know a lot about Riley Hatton. He don't like to talk to me much."

"But you've heard something," Ally pressed. "You've had to, working here, like this."

"I've heard a lot of things, about a lot of people."

"Like?"

"Like everyone knows he's obsessed with fresh chickadees like you. The ones he thinks he can 'save.'" He rolled his eyes. "Waste o' time if you ask me. Chickadees like you are going to find trouble no matter what."

"Saves them from what?"

"Red. Her people. The Black Cards. The rot of Ducat itself. When you have a horse as high as he does, it's easy to look down on everything else."

Ally furrowed her eyebrows. "And Red just lets him get away with that?" It didn't match the ruthless woman she'd met, the one that nearly took her brother's eye.

The man just held her gaze and puffed smoke out of the stick in his mouth, his lips quirking in a slight grin. "Interesting, isn't it?"

"Why doesn't she just get rid of him?"

"Dunno. Anyone who mentions it to her gets a bullet between the eyes. Just how it is. Riley keeps to his part. Red keeps to hers. As much as she does, anyway. Red tends to bleed out everywhere. Gets all over Riley's self-made white hat."

"His hat wasn't white."

"Figure o' speech, love."

Ally didn't understand what he meant, but she refused to show it. "What happened between them?"

"You seem smart. Why don't you figure it out?" When Ally glared at him, he pulled the stick from his mouth and leaned forward. "It takes a monster to hold off a monster, don't you think?"

A monster to hold off a monster. Ally glanced around the street, suddenly feeling like eyes were trained on her back, but nobody paid her any attention. Not just that, but avoiding—as if this street corner simply wasn't there. By ignoring it, they acknowledged its existence.

She turned back to the smoky man. "Do you work for Red?"

For a brief moment, his eyes darkened. He stuck the stick between his lips and leaned back in his chair. "No. I'm freelance. Gives me freedom."

"Who buys from you? Does Riley? Is that why Red hates him?"

He let out a breath that could've been a laugh if it weren't so scratchy. "Look at the fresh chickadee, finally asking questions that matter. Someone *has* taught you, haven't they?"

She ignored that, thinking of the desperate young man just minutes before her. "You don't do all of your transactions here. At least not the important ones."

"Now you're thinking."

"Who buys from you?"

"And what do you have for me?" He eyed her again, then laughed once when she scowled. It made her feel like a stupid little kid. "You think I'm just gonna offer that up? In Ducat there's no something for nothing. That's how this business works."

"I don't need the lesson," Ally snapped.

"I like you, love." The smoky man settled deeper into his chair and crossed his leg, a clear dismissal. "Consider your Riley question free of charge—a welcome to town type o' thing. But know in the future, if you come knocking on my door, you'll need something to trade. Something good."

Ally gritted her teeth, hating the fact she was still at the bottom of the food chain. Always being stepped on. "Fine." She turned on her heel and stalked away.

"You're welcome, chickadee!" the man called after her, singsong. He sounded utterly crazy, and Ally knew her brother had been right. She'd never try any kind of drug; she'd make her own way instead of taking that easy way out.

Chewing on the new information—what did white hat *mean?*—she wandered further toward the water, tasting the salt on her tongue. A sudden shout yanked her out of her memories of drowning. She turned to see a man running down the street two blocks from her, his eyes wide with determined panic, as another man chased him with bared teeth. After living in the Molds, she recognized a murderous rage when she saw it.

Ally's heart hammered as she slipped in between the next two buildings to let them pass and do what they would with each other. A horrible stench assaulted her nose, and she glared at the giant metal box that held what looked like a ton of garbage. She was about to pick a different hiding place when she heard the slap of steps against the ground getting closer, a faint shadow rounding the corner.

Swearing under her breath, Ally ducked behind the garbage bin and tried her best not to gag. Within seconds the first man turned into the alleyway, the other on his heels. A wheezing kind of groan came from the first as he realized what Ally had too late: it was a dead end.

She pressed herself between the wall and the metal bin as far back as she could go, willing herself invisible. Her breath caught as the second man entered the alley and pulled a knife from his shiny jacket.

Don't see me, she begged silently, hating that she instantly felt Monty standing over her. *Don't see me, don't see me, don't see me.*

The first man turned around, his face drawn and pale, a rabbit caught in a trap.

"Hey man," he said in a shaky voice. All three of them knew it was over for him. "Look, I didn't…I can explain."

The second man just growled under his breath as he lifted his knife higher. Ally barely caught a glimpse of some markings on either side of his mouth, inked on like Duffer's had been, though they resembled two elongated teeth. "They always think they can."

Ally held her breath as she watched the inked man pound the offender to the ground and proceed to slash him with his knife. A river of red ran down the street, seeping underneath the garbage bin and lapping at Ally's boots. She barely lifted her cloak in time before that got stained too.

It didn't take long. After a few minutes the inked man reached into his victim's pocket and pulled something out, too small for Ally to make out, then turned and left.

Ally waited until she was sure the inked man wasn't coming back, then she carefully stepped out from behind the garbage bin. His victim looked even worse up close, stained with blood and two vertical slashes down from his lips to his chin. Her stomach lurched when she realized the cuts matched the ink on the other man's face.

"Nasty business, isn't it?"

Ally jumped and spun around, yanking a rock from her pocket and holding it up above her head, ready to let it fly into someone's skull. She relaxed ever so slightly to find the inked man hadn't returned. Instead, a young man not much older than Jesper held his hands up in surrender, but the smirk on his face showed only amusement.

"A rock, huh?" he said. "Real cute. Good thing Governor already bit the knife. I shudder to think what your rock could do to him."

Her thoughts flitted to the other rock in her pocket—the strange one she'd picked up, the one she could've sworn guided her and Jesper out of the water when they almost drowned again this morning. A rock her instincts told her to keep to herself.

"What are you doing?" Ally demanded. Her eyes scanned him, doing a quick threat assessment. He held one of those barrel weapons in his right hand—clearly, he really wasn't afraid of her rock, and Ally decided she needed to find one of those barrels. He wore a slick black jacket big enough to possibly hide some strength underneath, and his hair had been shaved with swirled designs buzzed on the side of his head. His teeth were crooked, eyes dark, and a small black square with a symbol had been painted on his right wrist, peeking out from under his sleeve.

He was bigger than her. She didn't scare him, and she had no idea how to do anything other than hide behind her brother.

The boy dropped his hands along with the pretense she was actually a threat to him. "Could ask you the same thing. Newbie getting mixed up with the Walrus? Wouldn't recommend that for sure."

"A Walrus?" Her curiosity bubbled up without permission, and she internally cursed herself. She needed to stay focused. She needed to get out of here.

"*The* Walrus," the boy said, still sporting a devilish grin. "The guy who knifed Governor here. You can always tell who he got based on the marks he leaves."

Ally glanced at Governor's mangled and bloody mouth, and made a mental note to never cross the Walrus herself. "I see." She jerked her chin at the body. "So what do you want with him?"

"He actually has an appointment with Red." He smirked when Ally raised his eyebrows. "Yeah, *that* kind of meeting. Bill here has managed to piss off just about everyone." He rolled his eyes. "Red wanted to see him, and I knew he would run, so I just had to track him down."

She couldn't help but remember her brother pinned up against the metal bar with a knife at his eye, and shuddered slightly. "Too bad Walrus got him first. Looks like you're too late."

As if he'd heard her, Governor—or Bill? These people had the strangest names—moaned and turned his head. Not entirely dead then.

"Am I?" The boy just winked at her. "Name's AJ Knave, by the way. Didn't expect to see such a pretty thing out here. What's a Newbie like you doing wandering around?"

Ally straightened slightly, her grip still tight on her rock. "I was looking for someone. I'll be on my way now."

"Boyfriend?"

"Brother." Lately her lies had come so easily, she almost forgot they were lies. "I thought he might have gone back this way."

AJ looked her up and down. "Interesting."

"Is it?" Ally bit back.

"You got a name, Newbie?"

"Not one for you."

AJ laughed once, then reached down to grab Governor. The man wailed in pain as AJ easily threw him over his shoulder, like a bag of garbage to toss in the bin.

"Well, I can't be late for Red," AJ said, then leaned toward her. "Word of advice, Ally?" She went rigid at her name. "I wouldn't wander around these parts with only a rock in your pocket. Walrus will tear your face to shreds just 'cause it's pretty, and I like it too much for that. Go back to Jesper at Riley's apartment, right where you left him."

Ally's bones shivered, but she refused to let it show. Obviously AJ was trying to rattle her with his knowledge, and though her skin itched at the thought of being watched, she mostly felt grateful to escape the situation unscathed.

And that infuriated her.

Still, she took the chance. She ran out of the alley and down the street as fast as she could, eager to get away from AJ before he changed his mind or the Walrus came back.

Still just a stick, she thought bitterly as she ran. She couldn't help but envy how relaxed AJ had been, perfectly at ease despite the danger that had lurked just minutes before. The way he waltzed around like he owned the place, slow and sure, with

Red's influence and his own weapon to protect him. Ally needed that. She needed to do what he did, put herself on Red's good side, instead of the receiving end of her pointed blade. Or anyone else's for that matter.

Once she reached the blinding signs of the market stalls, Ally let herself stop running to catch her breath. She didn't want to keep running anyways. She wanted to *fight*. To defend herself. She was a rat of the Molds and had been raised in brutality. Really, was the Walrus that different from Pepperjack? Was Red's knife that different from King Asher's chopping block?

She had survived that place and she'd survive this one too. She had to.

I'm not going back. I'm never going back.

"Hey! Ally!"

Ally groaned as Riley ran up to her, the black frames on his face jostling, saved only by the skin-tight hat pulled down over his ears. A gray hat. Not white.

"What are you doing?" he demanded, though his voice felt more exasperated than angry.

She glared at him. "What's it to you?"

Why were you following me? They had met a few hours ago, and already Riley was tracking her down? *Why are you trying to trap me?*

Riley scanned the street with his eyes, as if looking for threats, and Ally almost snorted. Yeah he was older than her, but way too soft. Between the two of them, she would put her money on AJ any day.

"Do you have any idea how dangerous it is for you out here? A fresh face walking around? I can't even name all the sick psychos that would love to get their hands on you."

"Yeah, like the Walrus?" Ally shot back. She enjoyed the look of horrified shock on Riley's face. "That's old news to me now. I don't know what you're doing, but I'm not interested in becoming your new pet or prisoner or whatever cat girl is. Leave me alone."

He shook his head as if to clear it. "What about your brother? You would leave him?"

That pierced her, sharp as a dagger, low in her gut. She clenched her jaw. How dare he use her brother against her? "I was coming back for him. And I don't have to explain myself to you."

Deep down, though, she knew Riley had won with that line. She knew he wanted her to go back with him, and she would, just for Jesper.

Riley rubbed his face with his hand. "Look, maybe we got off on the wrong foot." The patronizing warmth to his voice grated on Ally's nerves. "I'm not asking for an explanation or expecting anything. All I ask is you hear me out. Let me help. Next to Red, the Walrus is the first in a long line of scary people you want to avoid—especially as someone that doesn't know the ropes around here."

Ally laughed once, the lashing of a snake, thinking of Pepperjack's laugh as he grabbed his knives, Monty's blood-soaked hands, her mother's lifeless eyes. "My father worked for a man who liked to skin people alive. If you want to scare me, you'll be very disappointed."

* * * * * * * *

Like most mornings, Jesper woke up alone.

Unlike every morning, he had no idea where he was.

Panic seized his chest as he glanced around, eyes bleary, until he saw the open window, the early afternoon sun filtering through. Then he remembered.

The bed squeaked loudly underneath him when he sat up, rubbing his eyes. He didn't realize the sound would be an announcement. Thirty seconds later, a knock sounded on the door.

Jesper froze. Ally was gone. She'd left the door barricaded with the chest of drawers, but he didn't know how helpful the old piece of wood would really be. Should he run? Duck out the open window and hope to track his sister down?

Another knock. Riley's warm voice came from the other side. "Hello? You guys okay?" When Jesper remained silent, he went on. "There's food out here if you guys want it."

Jesper glanced at the window, then back to the door. What did Riley want with them? The fact he didn't have an answer should've sent him crawling out the window, but the thought of running into Red again made him shiver and stay put. He hoped Ally hadn't gotten into any trouble, though he knew she had a knack for finding places she wouldn't be bothered.

In the end, he waited too long. The knob turned and Jesper heard Riley's grunt as he shoved his shoulder against the barred door. It only took two tries for the chest of drawers to scoot an inch, then topple over as the door flew open. Part of the wood cracked. Riley stared at it in surprise, and Jesper couldn't help himself.

"So-sorry," he muttered to Riley's tied shoes.

Riley glanced again from the cracked furniture to the open window before his eyes landed on Jesper. Jesper winced.

"Your sister?" Riley asked.

Jesper shrugged one shoulder. "She...she'll be ba...she'll be back."

The stirring of fear in Riley's voice caused Jesper's heart to start hammering. "Well where did she go?"

Jesper shrugged both shoulders now, as if that could prove his point.

"She left you here?"

That fact had never hurt him before, so Jesper didn't understand why it stung now, but he curled into himself and waited. For what, he didn't know. But he was ready to dive under the bed if Riley started throwing things.

You let your little sister take control? he could imagine Riley sneering. *How pathetic is that?*

Jesper watched Riley's foot take a step forward, and every muscle coiled so tight inside him that he thought he would shatter. A hand came down on his shoulder. He flinched and stumbled back, barely catching himself before he tripped backward over the bed.

The mattress creaked. Jesper winced. He took three breaths without incident before his eyes finally flicked up from the ground, anticipating the next move, the worst.

Riley just stood there, eyes wide, and somehow that was almost worse than him going on a rampage. A slight breeze came in through the window. Jesper wished it would blow him far away from here.

Then Riley surprised him: he took a step back. Air rushed into Jesper's lungs as Riley's expression settled back into its bright gentleness despite the extra lines around his dark eyes.

"How about this?" he asked. "You stay here and eat what you want, and I'll go find your sister."

Jesper's eyebrows furrowed. "Um, fine-find her?"

"Yeah." He glanced at the open window, and the lines around his eyes deepened. "Before she runs into any trouble. You can't go far without running into something, and it's never good. Will you please stay here while I go find her? I don't want to lose both of you."

Part of Jesper wanted to run the second Riley was gone, but he knew he wouldn't. So far nothing bad had happened to him here—what if he left and Red saw him and changed her mind? How long would he last?

No, just like the Molds, it was safer to stay put than to test the waters out there.

Jesper nodded, and Riley gave him a tight smile. He wasn't sure what to make of it. Then Riley gestured for him to follow down the hall.

They entered the kitchen to find nobody had moved from the last time Jesper had been here. He couldn't have been asleep for very long. Riley's mother stood at the counter, wiping it off over and over in a daze even though it already looked clean, and sung a song under her breath. Something about twinkling stars?

"Ally's gone," Riley announced. "I'm going to find her." Kat and her friend still sat at the table, bent over their magic boxes. None of them even looked up at Riley's statement.

"She-she does...does this...all...all the time," Jesper fumbled, trying to explain why nobody, least of all Riley, needed to go after his sister. "She's...she's strong. Strong."

"She's annoying," the dark-haired girl said without looking up.

Kat smirked at her box. "RBF anyone?"

She and her friend snickered. Riley gave them a disapproving look.

"Just let her go, Riley," the girl went on. "If the brat wants to get herself offed then let her."

Riley sighed. "Just try to pretend you both can be hospitable, all right? Be nice." Then he glanced at Jesper. "Feel free to help yourself to what you want. Kat and H will get you whatever you need. I'll be back soon."

Riley's mother—Jenny, he remembered—finally looked up from her cleaning rag like she'd woken up from a trance.

"Riley," she murmured. Her voice reminded Jesper of a frail weed shaking in the breeze. "You be careful."

Riley smiled and crossed the small space to wrap his arms around her, as if cradling a child, since he stood a head taller than her. "Of course, mama." He kissed her head softly once.

Acid rose in Jesper's stomach and he looked away at the wall. The floor. His shoe. Anywhere. Was the room spinning? He couldn't tell. He stumbled back against the wall, needing the feeling of something solid, and he heard Kat say, "Spaz" under her breath and her friend laughed.

"Be nice!" Riley called again before walking out. The sound of the door clicking shut shook Jesper out of his stupor. He glanced up, suddenly realizing he was entirely outnumbered without Riley pleading his case.

The girls kept tapping on their boxes. Riley's mom wrung out a rag in the sink before whirling around, as if suddenly remembering Jesper was still there.

She gestured to the empty chair across the table from the dark-haired girl—H, Riley had called her. Only now did he see the plate of round breads.

"Sit," Riley's mom told her, her quivering voice higher and more jarring than her son's, especially since it came out of such a small body. "Eat a muffin." Then she turned and kept wiping off the clean counter, singing about twinkling stars.

Jesper's knees wobbled, but he obeyed, if only because he still felt a little lightheaded and his stomach was growling for whatever a muffin could be. Sitting as lightly as possible, he perched on the edge of the chair and picked a muffin from the plate. He had nearly shoved it in his mouth when he noticed the paper holding the bottom. A quick glance around the table showed piles of discarded round papers with the muffins missing. Ducking his head, Jesper started working on pulling on the paper.

First, he tried softly. Part of the muffin crumbled, and in a panic, he yanked on the paper. A piece of it ripped off while the muffin tumbled headfirst onto the table. Only the softest of thuds sounded, but to Jesper, it was as deafening as a horn.

"You for real right now?"

He glanced up from his mess to find H watching him. Her skin was much darker than Riley's, and her eyes much wider, and she seemed to be a head taller than Kat, who looked paler and pinker in comparison. The girl's curly black hair stuck out in every direction, and it floated like a cloud when she moved. From here, he could see what looked like a metal circle hooked in her nose—for decoration? Or was it some kind of restraint?—and he guessed the shapes on her shirt were words, though he couldn't read them.

Her brown eyes flicked over him. The judgment was clear. He suddenly had the urge to impress her, gain her acceptance, or at least come off better than he was right now. Even in his own house, he'd never felt so out of place.

"I'm going to lay down," Riley's mom announced, more to herself, it seemed, than anyone else. She set her rag down on the counter and walked into the hallway as if her feet were floating above the ground.

Something passed between the girls, a moment he wasn't in tune enough to catch, and he used their distraction to pick up his muffin and rip off the rest of the paper. It only took two tries before it was free. Relieved, Jesper took a bite. Flavor burst across his tongue, grainy and sweet, and it was an effort to not shove the entire thing down in one bite.

H's eyes narrowed as he watched him chew. Jesper slowed the action until his jaw was still and the lump of half chewed muffin just sat on his tongue.

"What do you want?" she finally asked.

Mouth full, he held up the muffin in his hand to show he was more than taken care of.

"No," she said, "what do you *want*? Why are you here? Auditioning to be Riley's new project?"

Jesper swallowed. The muffin stuck to his throat. "I, um, I ne-ed to get...I need to...get home."

"All right." Kat dropped her magic box on the table with a flourish, making Jesper jump. "I've officially caught up on all my feeds. I'm ready to make travel plans for dirty, weird, emo boys."

H rolled her eyes. "Where's home? Seattle?"

Jesper shook his head. "Elaria."

Kat blinked. "Eh-whatta?"

"Um…" Jesper glanced down, his pulse thudding in his ears. "El-Elaria."

"Even if I could hear you, I'm confident I'd have no idea what you're talking about."

"You know where it is, right?" H asked him. "Like, where did you come from?"

"Across the…cross the…lake."

"Lake? You mean the *ocean*?"

Jesper's eyes widened. They'd crossed an *ocean*? Most people who tried that died, at least where he came from. Maybe he and Ally had managed to walk underneath it?

"Wow, okay," H said, using an airy kind of tone Jesper knew she reserved for people she thought were crazy. "That changes things. What else can you tell us? Any directions? Defining features?"

No. Jesper had never been taught. He knew his way around the Molds, knew he used to live somewhere *other* than the Molds when he was young, but that was it.

"The Jacklands. King Asher." He winced. Though the information may be helpful, Ally was probably right: contacting his king as a child of Pepperjack would likely get them arrested.

"A king?" Kat crowed. "Like a crown and palace and everything?" Jesper nodded and she sighed, batting her eyelashes. "What a dream."

A dream? Jesper thought. *More like a nightmare.*

H frowned. "If there's royalty then you're definitely not from here. America doesn't do kings unless, you know, it's like MJ or something."

"MJ?" What was with these people and their names?

"Michael Jackson? King of pop? Smooth criminal?" When Jesper didn't react, H's mouth dropped open. "What hole do you live in that you haven't heard of Michael Jackson?"

Kat turned her nose up. "He didn't even know *Kim Kardashian.*"

"Are you actually comparing a Kardashian to the king of pop?"

"It's not a comparison. Kim rules all, not just pop."

H rubbed her face. "You are past saving."

"I'm a goddess."

"You're a disgrace. I can't even associate with you. We can't be friends."

Jesper stiffened, suddenly afraid he was about to witness the destruction of this relationship. But the girls went on like nothing had happened.

"Okay, let's find a map," H said, picking up her magic box and tapping on it. The screen glowed and changed under her fingertips, and Jesper marveled at the sight. "It's probably in Europe somewhere, right?"

"Um…" Jesper had no idea.

The girls continued to ask him questions about places and things he'd never heard of, like Paris and coliseums and mopeds. Kat went on forever about something called a crepe, while H started commenting on historical sites, then stopped when Kat gave her a blank look and quickly switched to music instead. They talked so fast, finishing each other's thoughts and knowing what the other would say. Jesper hadn't gotten in a single word—not that he'd tried—when Riley came back through the door, an annoyed-looking Ally trailing behind him.

Her eyes scraped the place until she found him, and her shoulders relaxed ever so slightly. "Glad to see they haven't locked you in a cell and made you change your name to Dog."

Kat rolled her eyes. "Hurray, the wicked witch is back."

"Nah, that witch at least had style," H said.

Kat snorted. "You're right. I don't think she's even heard of shampoo."

"Maybe not," Ally sneered as she plopped down in the seat next to Jesper, "but I'm not stupid enough to roll around in pink glitter so I can pretend I'm pretty."

Kat's face turned red and Ally smirked. Jesper wanted to hide under the table. H opened her mouth, but Riley cut her off.

"Easy, girls." He knelt down between Ally and H and rested his elbows on the table, then nodded at H's glowing box. "What are you looking at?"

H sat back in her chair. "Trying to get Muffin Boy and his witch back home."

"I hope the house falls on her," Kat muttered. "That's what happens, right?"

Riley ignored her. "Where are we looking at?"

"I don't know." H shrugged. "Some European country I've never heard of."

"Europe, huh?" Riley glanced between Jesper and Ally skeptically, but Ally was too busy tearing apart a muffin to notice. "Interesting."

"He said they crossed the ocean," H added. "He's got a king named Ashes or something."

Kat's eyes widened. "Or he just hit his head *really* hard."

Then Jesper realized: they didn't believe him. They thought he was making it up.

Ally would say that was a good thing. She would say she didn't want anyone to know where they were headed, that it was better that way. Jesper would agree if he felt like they had any chance of getting home on their own. He wasn't sure what to make of the girls, but Riley seemed to know what he was talking about.

"Elaria," Jesper said, silencing the table. "We're from Elaria."

Ally licked her fingers clean, then placed her hands on the table. "And we'll be on our way now."

"Hold up." Riley's face was scrunched underneath his glasses as he tapped on H's box. "Elaria? I've never even heard of it."

"C'mon, Riley," Kat said. "Search that big brain of yours and find it."

"The *internet* can't even find it."

"I don't care if he can," Ally said. "We're leaving now."

"How do you plan on getting back?" Riley asked. It wasn't a challenge as far as Jesper could tell—his voice sounded just concerned and curious—but Ally pulled back as if insulted.

"None of your business."

"You don't have any money, do you?" Riley went on. "How are you going to get plane tickets?"

Jesper's eyebrows furrowed. That sounded important. "Plane ti-ickets?"

"Yeah. Isn't that how you got here? Or was it by boat?"

Jesper and Ally exchanged glances. After Red's reaction to their story of the In Between, they both decided it was best to keep it to themselves.

"I'm sure we'll figure it out," Ally said.

But Jesper's throat was burning as he remembered their disastrous attempt to get home themselves. He'd nearly drowned and, even worse, he'd nearly killed Ally too. They had no idea where the entrance to the In Between was, or if it could be reached from this side. If Riley knew a better, safer way to return home—one that didn't involve drowning or man-eating monsters—then Jesper wanted to find out more about it.

"How…how do we ge-et them?" he asked. "Plane tickets."

Kat laughed. H sighed. Ally grumbled. But Riley held his gaze without ridicule.

"Well, you buy them," he answered. "You can buy them online with money. Money you *earn*, not steal." He gave a pointed glance to Ally. Jesper could only imagine what their walk back here must've been like.

Ally's glare would've been enough to burn the building down, but Riley didn't so much as flinch.

"I'm serious," he continued. "There are a million ways to get in deep with the wrong people—it's easy and scary. It's best for you to get an honest job, stay away from people like the Walrus, and save up for your tickets out of here."

Ally laughed, the sound sharp enough to cut. "A job? Really? That's your great idea. Why don't we go into the family business, huh Jes?"

Jesper's stomach rolled. His muffin threatened to come back up. "Ally—"

"I'm sure this pink cat would love to sit and watch us cu—"

"Ally!" His voice wasn't loud, but it managed to pierce through everything, including Ally's bravado. She froze. Everyone's eyes slid to him, and he had to take a few breaths. "Stop."

Ally pursed her lips and looked away.

Taking another shaky breath, Jesper turned to Riley. "Jobs?"

"Uh, yeah." It took him a second to recover. "You ever had one?"

The shame clawed at Jesper's throat, his father's voice snarling in his mind, but he managed to shake his head. "No-not re...not really. No."

Riley pulled his own magic box out of his pocket—did *everyone* have one of them?—and tapped it a few times before setting it down on the table so both Ally and Jesper could see it. "Any of these look good?"

Ally's eyes skittered over the shapes, then instantly focused on the new muffin in her hand, pulling the paper off with much more care than she normally would have. Jesper's palms started to sweat as he took in the symbols: familiar but not understandable.

His mind raced, looking for something, anything, he could say to keep from this confession. While he drowned, Ally turned her nose up.

"They all look stupid to me," she lied evenly. She hadn't looked at the letters long enough to pretend, but Jesper hoped nobody would notice.

Riley did. He glanced from Jesper's surely panic-stricken face to Ally's forced calm one, and something clicked in his expression when he looked at her. "You guys can't read, can you?"

At that, Ally exploded.

"Read?" she seethed. "*Read?* Why are you so desperate to find something wrong with us? Do we have to be something to fix? Do we have to be something so sad and desperate so you can use us to make yourself look like the hero? Huh? I *won't* be your sad charity." She cursed, crumpled the muffin in her fist, then threw the bits in Riley's face. The girls erupted and all three of them started screaming at each other. When Ally had gotten in the last word, she headed for the door, only Jesper wouldn't follow. Having reached her limit, she stomped to the room he had slept in and slammed the door shut.

The second she was gone, Jesper dove to his knees, desperately trying to pick up the muffin crumbs Ally had thrown all over the floor. His bones rattled inside him. The yelling seemed to echo in his ears like in the vast cave of the In Between, and it made him feel just as empty.

From somewhere above him, Jesper heard Riley say, "Hey, you don't have to do that."

"Sorry," Jesper muttered to the floor. "I'm sorry."

A hand grasped his arm and helped him up, and Jesper stepped out of the contact the second he was on his feet. "Sorry. It won't...happen again."

Probably. It seemed this place brought out all the aggression that had built up in Ally for years. *At least, I hope not.*

The girls were still fuming, glaring at the hallway, but Riley already seemed to be over it. "No, don't worry about it. I've had worse, believe it or not."

Jesper didn't know what to say. Nobody had ever accepted one of his apologies before, let alone been so nice about it. The territory was new and he wasn't sure how to cross it.

When the silence stretched into uncomfortable lengths—and Jesper started to panic—Riley broke it with ease.

"You know," he started, his voice a little softer now. Cautious. "I could teach you. If you wanted."

"Teach...?"

"To read. Both of you. Just if you want—no pressure, or anything."

Jesper watched him for a moment, searching his expression, waiting for the scorn or disbelief or joke.

You can't read? Ha! A real man wouldn't be so pathetically stupid. A real man would take care of his family on his own, wouldn't he Jes, not get tripped up by something as simple as the alphabet.

No, I can't teach you. You think I have time for that? It's too late for you anyways. What's done is done. My kid is stupid as a rock, and always will be.

He waited for Riley's voice to echo his father's. It didn't. Unsure how to react, Jesper nodded once to hopefully appease everyone.

"Okay," Riley said, letting out a long breath. Jesper realized he'd waited too long to respond and had made Riley nervous.

"Stay here as long as you need to. I'll ask around about job openings, if you're interested in that."

Jesper nodded again, faster this time. This exchange was almost more tiring than being around Monty: the constant waiting, always pushed to the edge of your seat, unsure what would be the thing to set him off. At least with Monty, though, Jesper could anticipate reactions. These three strangers continued to surprise him, and that gave him a headache. In fact, he was exhausted.

Keeping his eyes on them, just in case, Jesper slowly retreated backward until he was in the hallway. He hastily opened the door to their borrowed room and ducked inside, but not before he heard Kat mutter, "Freakazoid."

The second he shut the door and turned, Ally glared at him. "We can't trust them."

Jesper sighed. "I'm not." He stepped around her and sat on the bed, wincing as it creaked under his weight. He tried to sit lighter. It creaked anyways.

"What do they want with us?" Ally asked as she paced in front of him, like a caged animal. "Why keep us here?"

"I don't know."

"It's suspicious."

"Isn't everything, to you?"

Ally opened her mouth in surprise, then clamped it shut. Jesper sighed again.

"I just mean…" he went on, "it wouldn't hurt to be…well, nicer? We don't have to…to trust them, but maybe…maybe they can still help."

"I don't want their help," Ally snapped.

"Well we need it." He knew that, didn't like it, but had to accept it. They were lost. "And right now…I think they're just afraid of you."

"I *want* them to be afraid of me."

"Why?"

Again, she opened her mouth, retort already on her tongue, but it must've been too close to something deep, because she snapped her lips shut before the words could come out. For a moment, though, just a second, Jesper saw the answer reflected behind her steely eyes.

Because then they can't hurt me.

The crackling energy she had moments before dried up. Ally collapsed down next to Jesper, keeping her face forward as she stared blankly at the wall. After a few long seconds, she reached out and took his pinky in her fist. Jesper gave her space to think. It took her several minutes to speak again.

"I don't like how they look at you," she said, her voice quiet and even. She almost sounded reasonable. "You're better than that. Than all of them. Than everyone."

The corner of Jesper's mouth tugged upward, his soul drinking in the words that from Ally—or anyone really—were so rare. She was all that mattered to him. In this big, scary world, they only had each other.

"We don't need them, Jes," she said, leaning forward. He'd never seen her so earnest about something. "I have a plan. We can do it on our own, and nobody would bother us. We'd be safe."

"But how? I don't know how we could find our way back on our own."

"Back." Ally licked her lips and took a deep breath. "To the Molds. To Monty."

"Yes." Jesper's eyebrows furrowed. "Isn't that what we were talking about? Your plan?"

She hesitated, and a pit opened up in Jesper's stomach. What if she refused to go back? What if he had to explain why they had to go back, why they both—but especially him—were more tied to their father than she thought? He wasn't ready for that conversation. Thought he'd never have to be.

But Ally nodded, such a sharp jerk of her head Jesper thought she'd crack her neck. "Yeah. The plan. I just mean, we don't need anyone. We can make our own way."

"What's the plan?"

"The plan?"

"Yeah. Your plan. For getting home. Didn't you just say you had one?"

Ally looked at him so long, he would wonder if she didn't hear him—but he could see the wheels turning in her eyes. After several minutes of thinking, she sighed.

"Fine, I'll do it," she said, slumping her shoulders slightly. "I'll learn to read. We'll get jobs and save up. But we only stick around here with them to get information and money. The second we can make it on our own, we leave and don't look back. Deal?"

Jesper thought of the yellow haze of the Molds and nodded once. "Deal."

* * * * * * * *

It was the first promise Ally made to Jesper that she knew she was going to break.

She didn't *lie* exactly. In fact, the words she'd said taken literally weren't lies at all. After racking her brain for every possible answer, Ally had finally accepted the fact that she couldn't convince her brother to leave Riley's place—at least not yet. If they left now and found more trouble, it would just fuel her brother's crazy desire to get back to the Molds. Ally figured it was better to stay trapped here than go back home.

So she'd submit herself to Riley's imprisonment if it bought her time. Time to learn Ducat. Time to gain resources. Time to make a real plan.

A plan to convince Jesper to stay here with her.

She didn't understand her brother's obsession with going back, but, if she really thought about it, it also didn't surprise her. Jesper would want to stick with what he knew. Going back would be all he knew how to do.

But look at Astrid, Ally wanted to tell him. *Look at Red. Look at what they made for themselves.* She could do it too, she knew. Get on Red's good side. Gain protection. Trade Monty's rotting kingdom for this rainy one. Jesper couldn't refuse once he saw what she was able to do for them. He'd be so proud. She could finally give him what he deserved, and *she* would be the one to do it. To pay him back for all the years he'd looked out for her.

She had learned from Pepperjack that the best way to gain the upper hand against someone was to exploit them first—and be scarier while you do it. So her first items of business were to get one of those barrel weapons and start building a collection of information.

Finding a weapon—called a gun, she discovered—proved to be more difficult than she thought. Not because she couldn't find someone that could get one for her but because it, and everything, demanded something she either didn't have or wasn't willing to give. Mostly money.

The smoky man had been right about one thing at least: no something for nothing around here. She resigned herself to taking the job Riley said he could find for her.

Finding information proved to be a bit easier. Time consuming and boring at times, but it gave purpose to her wandering away from Riley's apartment, even if she did have to watch her back more. And it gave her benefits she hadn't even considered.

One afternoon she spied a red-haired woman kissing a man in the alley behind Gordy's. Turned out, she really didn't want her boyfriend finding out she was kissing his drug supplier. She worked as a waitress at Gordy's and brought Ally a free meal every time she asked in exchange for her silence. Burgers, fries, chicken wings, milkshakes, onion rings, sandwiches, sodas—all because of a moment Ally was never supposed to see.

That tactic didn't work as well on Riley, though, a fact that infuriated her. He always seemed to be a step ahead. The only real piece of information she had came from a pile of envelopes she had leafed through. One held what Ally learned was a check, something you could trade for real money, for Riley. She remembered overhearing H tell Riley she'd dropped off a check from someone called Mama March. But when Ally asked Riley who that was, thinking she'd surprise him and trip him up, he barely even blinked.

"She's not really your concern," he'd said. He took the check from her and that was that.

Ally couldn't stop thinking about it. Was Riley trading for money too? Was he courting this Mama March woman? She didn't know, but she planned on finding out. Any dirt on Riley that could explain his interest in them or eventually convince Jesper away from him would be valuable.

These kinds of thoughts distracted her so much one evening as she made her way back to Riley's apartment, that she didn't notice someone following her until it was too late.

Barely a week in Ducat and Ally head learned about the different kinds of rain: the falling so light and smooth it felt more like a mist than drops, the pelting half frozen chunks that seemed to cut the skin, the unrelenting downpour like an endless pot tipped over and everything slushed out.

Tonight, the rain was deafening, huge drops hitting the pavement so hard that Ally couldn't hear anything outside of the water and her own breath. Her cloak and boots protected the majority of her, but she'd started to get used to the feeling of her hair plastered against her head.

Maybe getting used to it had made her careless. After a week in a new place with no incidents besides the ever-growing mystery of what Riley wanted with them, she had relaxed ever so slightly. She was nearly to Riley's when she noticed the man in step behind her.

Ally didn't know how long he'd been following her—she only noticed him now because he had become uncomfortably close, infiltrating her space, with no signs of passing her.

Her heart sped up, but she forced herself to keep her steps even. She was only a handful of blocks from Riley's, from Jesper. She would make it. She'd walk in dripping wet and shoot a nasty remark at either Kat or H, or maybe both, then give her signature I'm-watching-you glare to Riley before sitting next to her brother, listening to him quietly marvel over whatever he had eaten that day. She'd take his pinky in her hand, and everything would be okay.

She sensed it before it happened: the man surged forward and grabbed her shoulder. She reached into her pocket for a rock, but in the end, she was too late. His hand clamped over her mouth, the other holding her tight so she couldn't move her arms. In a smooth movement, he had twisted them around into an alley and shoved her against the wall. The old brick scraped against her scalp.

The man was at least a head taller than her with a weak mustache and metal hoops in his eyebrows. His pale face nearly glowed in the rain, the thrill of assured violence lighting up his blue eyes. Ally couldn't help but see her father in those eyes, and despite her best efforts, she felt herself starting to shrink under the weight of his shadow, her instinct to cry for Jesper. But he wasn't here.

Always beat on. Always nothing.

The man used his body to keep her pinned against the wall as he lifted the sleeve of her cloak slightly to check her wrist. A grin spread along his face. "Fresh new face, still fresh as can be. The Walrus requested a fresh, pretty face he can work on. It's your lucky day."

Ally shivered at the malice in his smile that told her being chosen by the Walrus was anything but lucky. She remembered Governor the thief, sliced to ribbons and left to bleed out in the street. This wasn't like her father. This wouldn't be something she could walk away from with a couple bruises and a wounded soul.

She tried to scream anyway, but between the hand against her mouth and the pounding rain, she barely heard it herself. The man laughed and brought his other hand to her neck, pressing her back harder against the wall.

"He never seems to mind when I take a little somethin' of my own first." He smirked at her as his hand brushed against her neck and started lowering to the collar of her shirt. "What do you say, sweetheart? Do you wanna have some fun?"

Scalding hate boiled up in her throat and she thrashed wildly. This couldn't happen. This *wouldn't* happen. But what could she do? Just a stick, always buried, always broken and left to fend for itself.

Ally managed to free a bit of movement in one arm, and the man was so busy trying to get a handle on her that he didn't notice her hand slip into her pocket. Her fingers closed around the first object she felt, and a shock jolted through her. All of the desperation and hate seemed to well up and surge through her fingertips—as if feeding the rock.

A light flashed from her pocket, and then the man was gone. Ally blinked, her eyes darting through the rain to see him crumpled in a heap on the ground, his head bleeding from hitting the opposite wall. He groaned and started to pick himself up. Ally didn't waste the chance. She sprung forward and drove her boot into his face, his stomach, his ribs, until he was speckled with blood and unresponsive.

Breathing hard, she willed her heart to slow down. She raked her free hand through her soggy hair and leaned against the wall until the fearful adrenaline coursing through her veins subsided slightly.

I'm okay. I'm safe. Not trapped. I'm okay.

When she had more of a handle on herself—and had kicked the man in the face one more time for good measure— she pulled the rock out of her pocket. In the dim light it had a purplish tint, but otherwise looked the same. This time though, she hadn't been disoriented in the In Between, or distracted trying to keep her and Jesper from drowning. She knew the rock had done something.

The sun had finally answered. The realization dawned on her as she stared at the miracle in her hands that would completely change the game.

It's magic.

A slow smile spread on Ally's face, and she put the rock back safely in her pocket. She'd made a promise to herself. And she would die before she broke it.

CHAPTER 5

THE GAME OF CROQUET

"Come on," Ally hissed under her breath, exercising every particle of patience in her body to keep from chucking the rock off the building. She'd spent the last few nights on top of the tallest apartment building in Ducat, using the darkness and height to give her cover. The last thing she needed was for somebody to find out that she carried a powerful miracle.

She glared at the rock in her hand. It *would* be powerful, anyway, if it would actually work for her. After three nights of braving the cold and trying to hold the rock a certain way or say certain words out loud, she hadn't been able to get it to do anything.

"But I know that you did!" She plopped onto the cement and placed the rock down in front of her. It glowed an even deeper blueish purple under the faint moonlight peeking through the clouds. "I'm not crazy. I know what I felt, what I saw. You *did* something."

The rock just glistened. Ally imagined it scoffing at her, and it made her want to break something.

"I know it. You can't convince me otherwise." She counted on her fingers. "First, you probably brought us here, didn't you? Or made the current that brought us here. Then there was that flash of light in the In Between. Then you helped me save Jesper from drowning. And just the other day you protected me from that sleazy pig." She shuddered at the thought. "I *know* it was you."

The rock just stared back at her, and Ally imagined the knowing smirk it was likely giving her.

Gritting her teeth, she cast her eyes up at the sky and willed herself not to scream. The last thing she needed was another one of Walrus's sleazebags finding her—especially when she couldn't get the rock to do a single thing.

"Okay," Ally said, rubbing her hands over her face and looking at the rock again. "What's the difference? Why did you work then and not now? What is different about tonight compared to those other times?"

She sighed and laid on her back, staring up at the clouds as she went over the scenarios in her mind. Each time there had been something new. She'd never left the Molds before, so going into the In Between could've triggered it. She'd never drowned before, let alone tried to swim, and obviously being attacked by someone other than her own father was new. But still…

Different answers sounded over and over again in her head, but in her heart she knew she was hiding from the truth. The common factor in every situation had been *her*. She'd been, well…she'd been scared. Terrified. Of being trapped in the dark new place and never escaping. Of her brother drowning because of his misguided attempts to get back to their father's prison. Of that monster taking something from her and then delivering her to a bloodthirsty man that wanted to use his knives on her.

She'd been scared. Desperate. Angry, even. Stars, so angry, angry at being buried forever, at losing her brother in such a senseless way, at the man who wanted to assault her for his own sick pleasure. The scared, desperate rage had coursed through her and given a sort of power to the rock. As if it fed on her emotion.

Strong emotion and intent. Was that the trick? That would explain why her mounting annoyance this evening wasn't enough to make it work. She needed to really mean it.

The sky rumbled overhead, and Ally sighed. She scooped up her precious rock and stowed it in her cloak pocket, then made her way down the side of the building. Now she was very careful to keep her hand on it at all times, just in case. Nobody would get the jump on her again.

I need more practice, she thought as she walked. *I need to know how to use it whenever I want.* If she had powerful magic at her fingertips, like her father or Pepperjack? She'd make a name for herself. Red would *have* to take her on at that point, and Ally could use her skills to buy protection for her and Jesper.

And get us away from Riley. Her jaw clenched. Her suspicion over Riley kept her up at night. Every time she left the apartment, he tried to stop her or give her some reasons why she should stay put. Every time she came back, he hounded her with questions about where she went, who she saw. It was relentless.

Ally didn't trust him—even less with her brother, who had surrendered to Riley in some kind of truce, duped into thinking Riley could actually help them. And clearly, Jesper wasn't the only one. Not just the insufferable H and Kat, but there were always people going in and out of the apartment, people who Riley had 'helped.' People under his spell. Ally had thought nothing could beat the chaos of the Molds, but living in Riley's shelter for lost puppies brought its own kind of controlled madness. And she wouldn't relax until she knew what he wanted with them, or got Jesper far away before they could find out.

As if on cue, Riley was on her the second she walked through the door. "Are you okay?" he asked, as if she would believe that the worry in his wide eyes was genuine. "What happened?"

Ally couldn't take it anymore. She bared her teeth. "I actually ran into Red. She said she'd pay me to slit your throat."

The worried light in Riley's eyes sputtered out into something dark and sharp. Behind him on the couch, Kat, H, and another lost cat looked up in shock. H scoffed in disgust. "That's messed up."

Ally just glared at Riley, refusing to back down. Riley licked his lips and swallowed hard. Within a second, the dark glint in his eyes had winked out. How frustrating that nobody else noticed except her. Could anyone else see that he was plainly hiding something?

"Well I gotta go." The stranger—Cass or something, Ally couldn't remember anything but her shaved head—stood and walked out the door. The sound of it slamming behind her broke the spell. Riley shook his head slightly and backed into the kitchen. Kat and H muttered to each other under their breaths, accusing eyes on Ally.

She didn't care if they hated her. In fact, she hoped they did. The more they hated her, the more they would leave her alone, and the easier it would be to get Jesper out of here.

"I gotta go too, Ry," H called, standing up and slinging her backpack over her shoulder. "Mama's here to pick me up."

Riley poked his head around the cabinet to wave at her. "Good luck on your test tomorrow. I know you'll ace it."

"Yeah, yeah." H made sure to slam her shoulder against Ally's as she left. If there hadn't been a door between them now, Ally would've grabbed a fistful of her hair and punched her in the face.

Breathing through her teeth, Ally sauntered over to the kitchen table to grab a muffin from the basket. When Jenny, Riley's mom, wasn't in bed, she was making muffins and singing weird songs to herself. Something was definitely wrong with her, but Ally hadn't figured out what yet. At least she made good muffins.

Riley stood at the sink, washing dishes. He glanced over at her like the tension between them had evaporated. "Your brother's asleep by the way." He said it like he knew Jesper was more likely hiding than sleeping, and that bugged Ally. A week here and already Riley acted like he knew Jesper better than a manipulative stranger would. "Probably resting up for the big day tomorrow."

Oh, right, she'd forgotten about the job. H had thrown such a fit about it, which, Ally admitted, had been enjoyable. Riley had asked H to see if there were any positions open at the place she worked at: something called a coffee shop. She knew her boss would take Ally and Jesper on "under the table" and she was not happy about it. Even though Ally hated accepting anything from her, she got so much satisfaction from intruding on H's space. Jesper started tomorrow, and Ally the next day. The reminder made her insides flutter with nerves.

Ally wanted to strike back somehow, get under Riley's skin just like he always got under hers. Maybe if she could make that dark glint in his eyes come back, she could prove to Kat how messed up her owner really was.

It takes a monster to hold off a monster, don't you think?

"So," Ally slid into the kitchen chair closest to Riley and stuffed the muffin into her mouth, "how did Red become queen anyways?"

Did she beat you out for it? Is that why there is this strange truce between the two of you?

Riley startled slightly at Red's name, then breathed a laugh as he reached for the towel to dry the plate. "A queen? I guess that would make more sense to you. She's not a queen, in the royal or political sense of the word. She's just a gang leader. *The* gang leader, actually. She's run all the other prospects out of town."

"Or slaughtered them."

Ally jumped at the voice right behind her, and turned to see Kat sitting at the table, gobbling up a muffin. Ally hadn't even heard her move. When Kat looked at her, she gave her a huge grin. "Now this is a good story. You gotta make sure you tell it right, Riley."

Riley rolled his eyes. Ally caught the thread eagerly. "He lies about it?"

"No—" he started, but Kat cut him off.

"He doesn't *lie*, he just likes to leave out all the dramatic, gory details, which, really, is why we all care."

Riley blew out a long breath and sank into the chair on Kat's other side. "Whatever, Kat."

She took that as permission to tell the story herself, and Ally couldn't deny she was curious about what the cat had to say.

"Once upon a time," Kat started, the purple powder on her face highlighting her wide, green eyes, "Ducat was overrun with bloodthirsty gangs. As in multiple of them. They all hated each other, and they spent their days fighting over recruits and territory, duking it out over and over. Tons of people were hurt or killed, and no gang could get the upper hand. So really, Ducat was just terrible to live in. Like arguably even *more* terrible than it is now.

"Slowly but surely, though, there was a young recruit that rose through the ranks of the Black Cards gang. He started out as a nobody, but it wasn't long before his bloody reputation got around. He was a brawny guy, all muscle—gorgeous, by the way, in that scarred, dangerous kind of way." Kat batted her eyelashes; Riley groaned and shook his head. "By the time he was…what? Sixteen?"

She paused and glanced at Riley. He shrugged. "Eighteen? Something like that."

"By the time he was seventeen, he had taken control of the Black Cards and nearly squashed all other resistance. He called himself King and he pretty much was one too. Everyone paid for protection or he would send his band of crazies on you until you gave in. It was nuts. Literally everyone bowed down to this kid."

"So where does Red come in?" Ally asked.

Kat held up a pink-nailed finger. "Patience, kitten. So King built up his empire for, like, eight years or something, right? He's untouchable. Everyone knows him and everyone is shiz-your-pants terrified of him. And he forces all these kids to join the Black Cards, right, because that's what gang leaders do, and one of these high school kids he drafts is Red.

"Now, what's *really* interesting is nobody really remembers much of her before she became 'Red,' you know? Her past is super murky. Nobody has ever heard of her, and all of a sudden she's high up in King's ranks, doing all this dirty work for him, right? She must've been good at it too, because within a few months she's King's girl."

Ally's eyebrows shot up and her mouth twisted with distaste. "Really?"

"Yeah, hard to believe now, right? But she was always with him during their power meetings, basically sitting in his lap and wearing sleazy dresses and whispering in his ear, and if you weren't so scared of them, you'd just throw up because they're so nauseating, right?"

"You talk like you were there," Riley muttered, a dark edge to his voice that surprised and excited Ally. "You were a kid."

Kat turned her nose up. "I hear things, kitten. My gossip is as good as gold."

"You're exaggerating."

"You're no fun." Kat turned back to Ally, as captivated by the story as she was. "So King's got his queen, right? You think that's the end, and they ride off into the blood-soaked sunset. No. One night, Rockwell, one of King's bodyguards, calls 911. You get that? A gang leader's bodyguard calls the *police*. Of course, he called the officer King had in his pocket, but still. Only get this: the police never show up. Right before he called, Rockwell had made calls to some of the other gang members, and word had gotten around that something had gone down. They try to call him back, but get no answer. They track his phone and find him dead. So they rush to King's apartment and out walks Red. With a butcher knife. Like, ten times bigger than the one Jenny uses to cut up a rotisserie. The most powerful man in the city, stabbed to death in his own bed by his girlfriend."

Ally's mouth fell open. Riley's gaze fell to the floor.

Kat just bounced in her seat, eager to have such an audience. "Yeah, this stuff's crazy, kitten. Turns out, she'd been planning this for *months*. She'd gone under King's nose and worked with some of his boys that liked her better, like AJ and the twins, and she'd been undermining him. She walked out of his place in this frilly little nightgown he'd bought her, drenched in his blood, and proclaimed herself the new leader of the Black Cards. Anyone who challenged her would meet the same fate. Only two or three idiots were stupid enough to go against the girl who had murdered King, the most dangerous man they'd ever known, and she mowed them down easily." Kat sat back and blew out a breath, her show now over. "So she's been running the place in her fabulous boots ever since."

"Wow." Ally couldn't help some of the awe that crept into her voice.

Riley glanced up at her tone, his expression focused yet far away at the same time. Ally wondered where he went. "She's really bad news, okay? Getting mixed up with her is a death sentence no matter what way you spin it. Stay away, all right?"

Ally narrowed her eyes. "Why do you care so much? Why does Red—the most powerful and scary person in this city—leave you alone?"

His face stayed blank, but she could see the measured calculation in his eyes of an animal trapped in a corner. And he was trying to find himself a way out.

To Ally's annoyance, Kat answered for him. "Because he's the last of the good ones left in this forsaken city." She grabbed another muffin and headed for the TV again, bored already.

"You have homework," Riley told her, picking up his laptop and heading for his room. "These grades aren't going to raise themselves from the dead." A muffled moan from the couch sounded in response. Kat had already managed to bury herself under a mountain of blankets. "I tell you, Kat, once you graduate high school I'll leave you to sleep away your days in peace."

"No rest for the wicked," she groaned back.

Ally glared at Riley's back as he walked down the hallway, as if she could mark it with a target.

No rest for the wicked indeed.

Jesper knew this was a bad idea the moment he tripped over his own feet. He fell into H, who jerked herself around to catch herself before she hit the edge of the counter, and her elbow knocked a cup to the ground. It cracked. He winced.

"Sorry," he mumbled. Maybe he'd get kicked out already based on that entrance alone.

H leaned down to pick up the striped cup and put it back on the counter. "Sure." She turned on all the lights, then gestured to the space. "This is Miguel's."

Jesper didn't know what coffee shops were supposed to look like, but this one seemed okay. The bitter smell hit strong, the lights flickered every few minutes, and the floors looked like they hadn't really been clean in a long time. Maybe twice the size of Riley's apartment, the space was filled with a couple of tables and chairs shoved into the corners and the long dark counter H stood behind.

"You clock in over here," she said, pointing to a square stand on the counter. It looked just like H's magic box, only bigger, and it too changed as she tapped it. "This will keep track of your hours so Miguel knows what to pay you. Just type in your code and hit 'in.' Then when you want to leave, you do the same and hit 'out.' Not rocket science."

Jesper wasn't sure about rocket science, but he had to have H tell him which button said in and which said out. His second failure of the day so far.

"We have an hour before the place opens," she told him. "So we turn everything on, make sure it's working, count the tills, and all that." Jesper knew she didn't want to work with him and Ally—and why would she, really?—and it showed in the dull tone of her voice. He did his best to be quiet (which he succeeded in) and out of the way (he wasn't as good at that) and helpful (which he failed at). It became clear very quickly that he was only going to slow H down despite his best efforts to memorize everything she said.

When it came time to open, H brought a stool out from the back and set it behind the counter, away from everything important. "Just sit here for now." Jesper's shoulders sagged in defeat, but he knew she was right. So he sat.

The rush came quickly and with vengeance. Within minutes of opening, the line went to the door, and the small space barely had enough air for everyone to breathe. A few people sat at the tables, slow and relaxed, but most customers were bouncing to get in and out as fast as they could. They all talked over each other—many of them on magic boxes—and the clamor mixed with the roar of the machines created a monster of sound that had Jesper sitting on edge.

H, to her credit, didn't stumble once. She wasn't very cheerful, but she always knew what to do, and she handled the people, taking money, and making the orders with a balanced control that he began to envy. In contrast, he just sat there watching with his mouth half open, his body aching from every muscle tensed. How she handled it all, he didn't know. But he was starting to think this whole job thing had been a huge mistake.

It got even worse when a lady started yelling over the noise. Jesper's stomach dropped when he glanced over and realized she was yelling at *him*.

"Excuse me! *Excuse me!* Don't you work here?"

Jesper froze at the murder in the lady's blue eyes. H was busy at the counter and hadn't noticed the disturbance yet, but the woman's blazing expression demanded attention. Against his better judgment of wanting to be helpful, Jesper got shakily to his feet and leaned forward.

The woman held up her cup of coffee and the printed paper H had given her after she'd paid. "I was overcharged." She shoved the paper in his face as if it were an execution order. Probably his execution, from the way she was glaring at him. He had to grip the counter to keep from falling over as his eyes flicked over the endless lines of letters and numbers. It all jumbled into a mess; he was going to be sick.

"Hello?" the woman said, shaking the paper in his face. "Did you hear me? I was overcharged."

Jesper nodded and swallowed hard. His throat was closing in. He couldn't find any words, didn't even know what words he should look for.

"Are you stupid or something?" she demanded. He flinched and drew back, prepared to just take the beating and wait for the yelling to stop, when a beautiful cloud of black hair broke through the storm.

"Take a chill pill, lady," H said, taking the paper from the customer. "I can take care of that for you. We'll get you your dollar back." Then she muttered so low only Jesper heard. "Since you can't afford decency."

The woman scowled but followed H back to the magic screen to fix the problem, and Jesper watched in awe at how collected H stayed throughout it all. When the woman finally left, H turned to Jesper and said, "Maybe you should go sit in the back."

The dismissal crushed what was left of Jesper's spirits, yet he still felt a wave of relief when he stepped into the quiet of the back room. He could hear the whirring of the machines and the chime of the bell on the front door, but it was much better to manage. He collapsed into a chair and focused on breathing. Surrounded by old machines, bags of dark beans, and mountains of cups, home seemed farther away than ever.

A good hour passed before H came into the back and plopped into a chair. "Mornings are the worst," she groaned, rubbing her leg with one hand as she produced her magic box with the other and began tapping on it.

They sat in silence for a few minutes until the bell dinged again. Jesper winced. H sighed, then broke her glazed gaze from her box to glance up at him.

"You wanna go back out there yet?"

"Um…" Jesper swallowed. "Sure."

So they both got up and went back out front. Two young girls stood in line, the only ones in the place, both of them tapping on a magic box. Jesper had to wonder why everyone was so attached to them.

He started for his stool, but H waved him over to the screen. "You're gonna help this time, Muffin Boy."

Jesper's palms started sweating as the girls said what they wanted—words that sounded like complete nonsense to him—and H turned to him. "All right, we're gonna put that in."

He didn't recognize the words, but numbers were more familiar thanks to a week of lessons with Riley, and he mostly kept up with H's guiding instructions. The girls paid with credit cards. Jesper got to swipe them while H asked for a name on the order. When the payment finished, she pulled Jesper to the machines and told him what to do. Actually making the orders came easier—as long as he knew what ingredients to add, he could remember the order to put them in, and what buttons to push. But it worked. Within a few minutes, he had successfully produced their orders.

A warm bubble formed in Jesper's chest when he handed the girls their drinks. They thanked him and walked out just as a young man in a shiny jacket came in.

He'd never felt so accomplished in his life. Turning to H, he asked, "Can...will you...can we do...show me that again? Pl-please."

H just shrugged. "If you want."

Jesper nodded, and they did it again. He still relied on H for the ordering part, but the preparation got easier, and he found he loved learning how to make the different kinds of drinks. The order to it helped him focus. Now that he actually worked, the time went by fast, and it wasn't long before another girl came in, her skin covered in art, and took over.

"It's not always a picnic," H told him as they walked out the door. "But it's fine."

Jesper glanced at her. "I li-ike it. Thank you."

"You're weird, Jesper, I gotta say, but I'd rather hang with you than your wicked witch any day."

The rest of the week went okay: he averaged less mistakes. H had 'release time' from school, meaning she had permission to work during school hours. Until he and Ally were both fully trained, she had to be with them during their shifts, so Jesper went with her on the days she worked mornings, and Ally the days she worked after school. Ally didn't seem to like it much, but Jesper didn't mind. It gave him purpose. And the thought of getting money from that purpose—money that could take them home—was more than anything he could've hoped for.

On his fifth shift, he met Miguel, the owner of the coffee shop and Jesper's new boss. He was younger than Jesper expected, with a short build and eyebrows so bushy they almost looked like one connected line.

Miguel was only there for a few minutes to restock some supplies. He shook Jesper's hand and told him as long as he didn't steal anything, he'd be fine. Then he winked at H on his way out.

H wrinkled her nose. "He's, like, eighteen years older than me. It's weird."

They sat in the back, taking a much needed break after the morning rush. Jesper still relied on H, but could be trusted to make most of the common drinks by himself, and he'd slowly become more comfortable with asking the occasional question.

After tapping on her magic box for a bit, she dropped it in her lap and sighed. "I'm making a frap for myself. I deserve it. You want anything?"

"Um...no." Jesper shook his head. "I don't think so."

She eyed him skeptically. "What's your poison?"

"What?"

"What coffee do you like? What would you order?"

"I don't...I don't know."

She raised a sharp eyebrow. "You've never had coffee before?"

Jesper shook his head.

"You've worked here for a whole week and you haven't snitched any?"

"No." Was he supposed to? He thought Miguel had said no.

"Your sister is already addicted. Pretty sure she won't even have a paycheck left by the end of the period." She stood and went to a machine. "I'm making you a basic. Gotta start somewhere."

H insisted on doing it herself, so Jesper sat back and watched her work. In no time, she handed him a steaming cup and sat down with one of her own.

"Careful," she warned. "Don't burn yourself."

"Thank you."

"Yeah, yeah."

Jesper waited a second, letting the steam blow up into his face. He glanced up to see H watching him with those steady dark eyes. It startled him to realize she was actually interested in what he thought. Funny, since she never seemed to be interested in anything other than her magic box and Kat.

She dropped her gaze to her own cup, pretending to wipe a spot on the side, but somehow he knew she was really paying attention to him.

He took a sip. The hot liquid seared his mouth, nearly frying his tongue just as the awful bitter taste invaded. Without thinking, he spat it right back out, and coffee spewed onto the floor.

His mouth dropped open in surprise when H burst out laughing. Her face completely changed, the musical sound lighting up her entire expression. "What did you think?" she asked between laughter.

"It's gross," Jesper blurted. "People pay for this?"

That just made her laugh harder. A smile started to spread on Jesper's face until he saw the puddle of coffee on the floor.

The warm feeling brought on by H's laugh froze over, and he ducked his head. Why didn't he just swallow it? Stupid.

"Sorry," he mumbled.

"No, no, no," H said, her voice brighter with leftover laughter. "That was so worth it. You should've seen your face!

Man, I should've been filming. Can you imagine the boomerang we could've made?"

A laugh bubbled out from his chest now, pulled by hers, though his was more relief that she wasn't angry. H still chuckled to herself as Jesper cleaned up his mess.

"Gold," she said. "Pure gold."

The bell rang. H put her own cup on the counter and gestured for him to follow. "Break's over. Tomorrow we'll try something else. There's gotta be *something* here you won't spit out." She smirked at him and Jesper found himself giving a small, embarrassed grin back. He couldn't remember the last time he had looked forward to another day.

* * * * * * *

The alphabet was absolutely impossible.

Impossible. The word kept drilling into Jesper's brain as he sat slumped at the kitchen table with Riley. Twenty-six letters, all with two different looks and a million different sounds. How did anyone keep track? Maybe making words required a kind of magic—one that Jesper just didn't have.

When he got another letter wrong, he ducked his head and apologized. Again. 'Sorry' was the only thing he'd said to Riley all day.

Pathetic. Stupid, stupid, pathetic.

"You don't have to apologize," Riley told him, which somehow made Jesper feel even worse despite the patient tone. "Though it doesn't go unappreciated. Earlier your sister threw a cup at my head when she got a letter wrong." He laughed as he said it, but Jesper sunk deeper into his chair. They were hopeless.

The sink dripped in the moment of silence, echoing throughout the stale air. Jenny had burned a casserole earlier, and the place still smelled like it. Jesper had still eaten his share

145

within minutes. He still hadn't gotten used to the general supply of food, or Riley's willingness to give it.

Riley must've decided to take a break because he leaned back in his chair and stretched his legs out. "You know, it's interesting you speak English. Are there other languages in your country?" They hadn't found Elaria on a map yet, but that didn't stop Riley from pretending like he believed it was real.

Jesper shook his head. He didn't realize there could be more than one—everyone he'd met had talked more or less the same.

"Really? No outside cultures or anything like that?" When Jesper gave him a blank look, he gestured to himself. "Anyone that looks like me? Or H? Different ethnicities than you?"

He didn't know what ethnicities meant, but he thought he understood. "Yes."

"Interesting." He tapped his pen against his mouth, lost in thought. "Yeah, this one is a puzzle."

"Do you...have mo-more?"

"More? More languages? Yeah we have quite a few. English is the most common, obviously, but you can find lots of others depending on where you go or who you meet. I can read Mandarin, but I can't speak it fluently yet."

"Mandarin?"

"Yeah. It's a language from a country called China. My ancestors are from there. Have you ever heard of it? It's pretty big."

Jesper shook his head. The more he heard about the world, the more he wondered if he was actually supposed to fit in it.

"Did it...did it take you long? Long time, I mean. To...to learn it?" He was too ashamed to admit he didn't think he could learn his own language. Though Riley had probably guessed that by now with how badly he'd been doing.

"Yeah, it's been a few years, actually. It's easier when I have another language to fall back to. Learning from scratch must be daunting. It usually takes kids years to learn to read once they start."

Jesper stared at his hands and didn't respond.

Riley shifted in his chair, leaning his elbows on the table and pushing his glasses up. "You know, I notice you stutter a bit."

A stab of panic went through Jesper's gut. Stutter. He knew that word.

Your boy stutters, Monty. Is he stupid or something?

He felt the color drain from his face, and if his knees weren't so shaky, he would just run.

"Oh, no." Riley held up his hands, and it relaxed Jesper slightly to see them, to be able to track them. "Sorry, I didn't mean to offend you. It's okay." When Jesper took a shuddering—and embarrassing—breath, Riley nodded at him. "It has to be frustrating for you, to not get to say what you want."

Frustrating. Humiliating. Suffocating.

Even when he spoke, Jesper was helpless.

But the usual panic over this subject ebbed a bit when he realized Monty would have never said it like that. No, Monty would've demanded he stayed seated until he could speak clearly, smacking him if he moved an inch. *They'll eat you alive if you talk like you're stupid,* he'd say. *Talk to me like a man.* Never would he have sat calmly at the table and asked what it was like for him. *My kid is stupid. What's done is done.*

The sharp contrast between the two encounters made Jesper do something utterly crazy: he nodded. "Frustrating."

Riley leaned forward on his elbows again, his eyes focused as if this conversation were the most important thing in the world. It made Jesper sit up straighter. "I'm sure. Are there ever times when you can speak without it? Or is it pretty much constant?"

Jesper stopped to think. Nobody had ever asked him that before, and he didn't really keep track of it himself. "Not always. Only sometimes when...when it's just me and Ally it goes...it goes away. Or when…well it's there when I'm sc-scared but not when...when it's…" He thought of all the times he'd spoken clearly to Monty, whether to save Ally or himself.

Something inside him just clicked. A survival instinct. "When I have to. I don't choose...though. It just...it just happens."

Riley nodded. "I've heard you a few times. I'm no professional, of course, but it sounds to me like it's more of a nervous tic than a speech impediment. Who knows? That might make it easier to get rid of someday."

"Really?" It seemed too much to hope.

"Yeah, sure. I imagine getting more familiar with vocabulary might help. Practicing that and reading will probably make you feel more comfortable with words in general, and that might help when you talk. I mean, it can't hurt."

Jesper nodded eagerly, looking back down at the printed page of the alphabet. There had to be a way, right? If Riley believed he could...

He glanced from his simple alphabet sheet to the notebook Riley had open next to his laptop. Ink marked up the pages, lines upon lines of complicated words he didn't understand.

"Do you, um, go to academy?"

Riley brightened behind his glasses. "I do, actually. I take online classes from WSU. It's a university. This stuff is for one of my IT jobs though."

Jesper's eyes widened. A university? "You're smart, then?" Not that it came as a surprise. Clearly Riley was on a different education level than anyone Jesper had ever met.

"Well, I don't know about that," he said with a smile. "But I like learning. Keeps me busy and my brain working."

"And you...you know lots of words. And you think...think that I can do...do this?" He pointed to the alphabet page.

The smile didn't leave his face, but a seriousness passed over his expression like the spreading of a blanket. "Absolutely I do."

Jesper took a breath. "Okay. Let's keep going."

"I was hoping you would say that."

They spent the next hour going over the letters called vowels that seemed to be more magic than the regular ones, then the others. Jesper stopped on H, recognition dawning.

"H," he said. "Like H."

Riley grinned. "Yeah, it's short for Harriet. It's also her grandma's name, so she likes to go by the initial instead."

"What's mine?"

"This one." Riley pointed. "J."

Jesper traced the hook with his finger. This shape was the beginning of his name, the beginning of him. Picking up his pen, he circled it and wrote a shaky number one next to it. "What's next?"

"E. That one."

They kept going until he had circled all his letters in order. Then, at the bottom of the page, he carefully scrawled out his name.

J-E-S-P-E-R

He looked over the imperfect letters, his shoulders straightening with pride.

Jesper. That's me. I'm here. I exist. There is proof.

"There you go!" Riley exclaimed, holding up his hand. Jesper was so caught up in the victory that he didn't think twice about returning the high five.

"I think…I think I would recognize it now," he told Riley. "My name. Now that I've seen it…written it…if I see it again, I-I would know it." He reached into his pocket and pulled out a folded piece of paper, his shoulders sinking with nerves. Gingerly, he offered it to Riley.

Riley took it and opened it up, his eyes scanning the list of uneven words. "These are from Miguel's?"

Jesper nodded. "I've been tracing them when H is bu-busy." They were words on ingredient containers, the menu, the tablet screen. "Can you…um, can you tell me…what they mean? I want…I want to be able to help her more. Be better."

"Uh, yeah. For sure." He set the paper down on the table between the two of them. "That's actually really smart. Good job."

A grin tugged on Jesper's mouth.

Suddenly, the door flew open and a cloud of black hair stormed inside. Jesper snatched his list and shoved it in his pocket just as H slammed her hands down on the table, making him flinch.

"Your sister is the *worst* person to *ever* walk the face of this planet."

Jesper shrunk away from the angry heat in her eyes, a pit forming in his stomach.

"Cool it, H." Riley held a hand out toward Jesper, as if calming a spooked horse. "Take a walk."

"Oh I plan on it, a freaking long walk off a freaking cliff because I would rather drown than spend another second with her." When Riley started to speak, her scathing glare cut him off. "She's impossible!"

"I know," he said. "She chucked a teacup at my head this morning. Shattered all over the floor." He shrugged. "We survive."

"No," H seethed, "no we don't. You don't have to spend all day with her trying to force her to be decent. She breaks things, yells at customers, drinks a crazy amount of coffee—and all that caffeine does *not* help, let me tell you—and she throws everything on me. She freaking broke one of our machines and then told Miguel it was me!" She threw her hands up in the air. "I'm done playing your stupid superhero game. You find her somewhere else to work." Then she stomped out and slammed the door behind her.

The tension H left behind clung to the air, pressing down hard on Jesper's shoulders. Underneath the strain in his chest, though, he sensed a burning flame of...shame? Was he ashamed of Ally? He'd never been before; he'd never had reason to before.

Riley cleared his throat. The sound grated against the tense air. "Should I go find her?"

"No," he murmured. Ally hadn't exactly made it a secret that she didn't like Riley. Plus, she could take care of herself.

Just not anything else. He flinched. The thought came unbidden, and the flame of shame inside him exploded into inferno.

"Do you want to keep going or break for the night?" Riley asked.

Jesper sighed, trying to blow out the fire burning him. It didn't work. "Keep going." One of them had to, after all, if they were ever going to get home.

* * * * * * * *

Ally *hated* H.

What kind of name was 'H' anyway? Just a letter? It was completely stupid, just like her.

Fuming, Ally had taken off early from her shift, abandoning H to the pit of Miguel's and hoping she'd be buried alive in it. H had yelled that she'd be fired, but Ally didn't care—the coffee shop had been a waste of her skills, anyway. She could find something better. She *would* find something better.

The chilly night air helped cool Ally off, and she breathed it in as she walked down the street, her cloak billowing around her as she cleansed herself from the inside out. Riley had given them some old, ratty clothes they could live in, but she refused to part with her cloak. No, Riley couldn't take that from her.

The rocks in her pockets beat against her legs with every step, and she found comfort in that rhythm. For the first time, a beat of homesickness hit her, but the wind blew it right away. Instead, she thought of the special rock in her pocket, what she'd been able to do with it.

She needed to find something else, another job. Something to get her money. Influence. Without it, she wouldn't be able to build up her own life, convince Jesper to stay with her, to leave Riley. They'd only been there a few weeks and already she could see that Riley had started to sink his claws into her brother. She needed to act faster. But where to start?

The city had started to become more familiar to her with the time she had spent wandering it. She recognized certain people now, people who had patterns: who worked certain places, ate certain places, had their fix at certain places. Knowing people's patterns was valuable—then you can find weaknesses and capitalize on it. Pepperjack had built his empire on that. So, it seemed, had Red. Ally just needed to find the right opportunity.

The wind whipped through her hair as she came closer to the edge of the city, where the water met the earth. She found herself coming here often. She wasn't sure why. The water felt large and powerful. A reminder of where she'd been, where she could go, and the promise she had made to herself.

You're making patterns, she scolded herself, curling her fingers around her special rock in her pocket. If someone had noticed it, they could ambush her here. The Walrus, AJ, even Riley. She knew bodies were buried in the water at night, and she wasn't going to be one of them.

As if on cue, a shout shattered through the air, followed by a chorus of other voices. Ally didn't even turn to see who it could be. She just ducked her head and darted across the shore, her boots kicking up sand. Using the few abandoned cars in the parking lot as coverage, just in case, she turned at the old bait shop and scaled the locked gate in the alley. Within four minutes she had put a parking lot and a building in between her and whoever had crashed her party.

The stench of old fish had her gagging. Holding her breath, Ally walked behind the string of moldy buildings until she could breathe clean air again. She hadn't quite memorized this part of the city yet. If she kept going, she would risk getting lost, and she just wasn't in the mood for that tonight.

Ally turned the next corner to make her way back to the street, then stopped short. The sun had gone down fast, and in the night she could make out shadows already in the alleyway.

Two bodies, crumpled on the ground, their heads blown open and their blood staining the cement. And a girl, almost a head taller than Ally, with long brown hair cascading in waves over her bare shoulders. No makeup on. Black jacket in a heap on the ground despite the chill, next to a bag of painting supplies and a giant black dog.

Ally swallowed hard. Red.

Red's piercing eyes glanced over Ally, her pale lips pursed. Her dark shirt didn't have sleeves, and she had to be freezing. But she didn't shiver once as Ally's gaze roved over her lean figure, looking for where she could have stowed a killing weapon.

"Jabber didn't sound the alarm," Red finally said. Her low, razor-sharp voice didn't match her free flowing hair and face stained with paint. "That's strange, as you can imagine, given his name."

Steadying her feet, Ally cleared her throat and forced the words to come out smoothly, refusing to choke on the stench of brain and blood. "Maybe he just likes me."

Red stared at her another minute. She and Jabber the dog seemed to somehow have the same expression, and yet, Ally thought out of the two of them, Red would be the one to eat her alive. "Maybe."

Ally tried to keep her stance relaxed, but she didn't know what to do. Would Red dismiss her and let her go? Or had she wandered into the very wrong alley tonight? She wrapped her hand around the rock in her pocket and poured her desperation into it.

I don't want to hurt her, but I need to stay alive. I need to survive and I need to win her protection.

I need her to give me a chance.

Glancing at the white wall, Ally realized she recognized the beginning of the painting: it matched the other nonsensical murals that were sprinkled around the city like sugar on Kat's breakfast toast. Her stomach rolled when she tracked a stream of blood from the bodies to the wall. Not entirely paint, then.

Her eyebrows furrowed. "*You* paint these? Why?" She tried to hide her disdain, but couldn't deny the bad taste in her mouth. Red was a queen, not some little painter. Maybe the paintings were some kind of secret code to her gang members. Now *that* would be interesting.

Red glanced back at the smear of blood on the wall and sighed. "My city can be such an ugly place."

Ally loved the sound of that. *My city.* Untouchable.

"Did you really murder your boyfriend to rule this place?"

Red's lips quirked to the side in an almost smile. "You think it's such a horrible story, don't you? Everybody else does."

Ally just shrugged. "I've heard worse."

Red raised a thin eyebrow, looking over Ally again. "Really? Have you ever heard the story of Little Red Riding Hood?"

No. She glanced at the dog, Jabber, and tried not to wince when its dark eyes were trained on her. The need for Red's approval burned bright in her veins. "A long time ago. I forget the details."

Red smirked, and Ally wondered if she saw right through the lie. She stroked her brush along the wall as she spoke. "Once upon a time, there was a little girl who lived in a village by the forest. She always wore a red cloak—kind of like yours, actually—so the people called her Little Red Riding Hood. One day her mom bakes a cake or something and tells her to take it to her grandmother. So she grabs her basket and heads through the woods to good old granny's house.

"Along the way, she runs into a wolf. The wolf wants to eat her, of course, but Red Riding Hood doesn't know that. He asks where she's going and like an idiot she tells him she's off to her grandmother's house. She doesn't realize that the wolf heads her off and beats her there. He eats the grandmother, then dresses up like her and stays in her house. When Red Riding Hood gets there, she thinks the wolf is her grandmother."

That sounded crazy to Ally. They told this story to kids? "Well what happened?"

"Depends on which version your mom read to you at night. In mine, the wolf eats the girl and she's never heard from again."

Keeping an eye on the dog, Ally took a step forward to get a better look at the painting, trying to see the bigger words in the story.

Red leaned down to dip her paintbrush in the puddle. Crimson smeared over the white bricks, almost in the shape of a rose. A red cloak. A puddle of blood.

"Are you Little Red?" Maybe Kat had gotten the story wrong. Maybe the story had become so legendary that it had become based on myth more than fact.

Red jerked so hard Ally thought her neck might've snapped. The night air seemed to tense as Red turned her gaze on Ally, and Ally took a sharp breath at the fury she saw there. She forced herself not to move—retreat—like every instinct in her body screamed, even as Red stepped toward her. Another step. Then another. Ally's heart pounded in her chest and she felt the rock warm in her palm.

I don't want to hurt her, I need her, but don't let her hurt me.
I need her.

Ally sucked in a small breath when Red took her free hand and slashed her palm with a tiny knife Ally hadn't seen until then. Not reacting to the pain was easy; Monty had taught her that.

Red stared at Ally's palm as the blood welled to the surface, and she squeezed the hand so it would really start to flow. Ally didn't even wince at the searing sting. The knife was gone as quickly as it had appeared, and Ally watched as Red pressed three of her fingers into the small puddle of blood in her hand. Then she brought those fingers to her mouth and licked the blood off of them. Ally's mouth went bone dry.

Red let out a laugh, a jarring stab through the tension, and dropped her brush. She stared as it rolled away from her, still laughing. Then she pressed her fingers against the scarlet color on the wall, painting roses with Ally's blood now.

"Little Red Riding Hood," she scorned, painting with her fingers. "They thought so. They thought I was just a little girl, and I was, at first. But I got lost in the woods. So very lost. You know what you find when you're lost in the woods?" She laughed again, the darkness in it rivaling the In Between. "Right. *That.* So I put on the hood and I played the part they wanted me to."

"The part?" Ally tried to make her voice stay even, but it still squeaked slightly.

Red's hand movements became jerky, violent even, streaking the wall in blood. "I had a barbarian of a father that touched me in all the wrong places, and never softly. He loved me like that. He forced me into the hood, and when I wandered lost in the woods, I ran into King. Just like him, but with ambition. So I let myself become his instead, and King loved me too, because he thought I was so small, so broken. Little Red Riding Hood.

"I didn't question him. I had no self-respect. I did what he said, *everything* he said. I tortured people, I killed people, I let him bash my face in, use me however he wanted. I did it so three hundred and sixty-eight days later I would be completely alone with him, so I could stab him to death in his own bed. They remember that part of the story. They always remember that. It's funny. They didn't find me at King's place. They found me blocks away on the fire escape of a no name building with my knife. Nobody asked what I was doing in that apartment. Nobody realized that I was up to my elbows in my father's blood."

A slash of a smile cut across her face as she stopped painting and turned to look at Ally again. "I rid the world of two monsters that day, and I've butchered more since. Does anyone talk about that? What I've done, what I've given the people here? I freed them. The paintings appeared. I gave order and beauty. But everyone only sees the blood on my hands. They only talk about how I cut down the roses in their life and painted them red.

"Is that the story you wanted to hear, little Ally? So you can run home to your new pathetic friends and tell everyone they were right about me? Or were you hoping for a happily ever after?"

A happily ever after. Everything clicked into place as Ally looked over the frenzied girl in front of her, the one who had crowned herself queen. The one who had survived her father and made something for herself, a place she could be safe. That *was* the happily ever after.

Ally swallowed and her words came out shaky and barbed. "I would kill my father too," she said quietly. "If I had the chance."

Red cocked her head and stepped forward, closing the gap between them. Jabber let out a low warning growl. Ally stiffened.

With predatory grace, Red took Ally's chin in her hand, smearing blood and paint along her face.

"I sense it in you too, Ally. The fire. The rage. You wear the hood too." She smoothed her thumb along Ally's jaw, painfully close to her throat. "My advice? Use it."

"Use it?"

"Let them underestimate you. Let them label you and think they know what you are and where to put you. Let them think they have power over you."

"Why?" Ally breathed. That went against everything she knew. You always showed yourself to be the strongest in the room. Never let anyone see a weakness, even a misplaced one.

"Because the day someone finally thought to take off my hood, they didn't find a scared, lost little girl. They found a wolf." She grinned, and the slash of paint on her face in the shadow looked like her mouth gushed blood. "And I ripped them all to pieces."

Ally shivered. Red leaned in closer, and for a terrifying second she thought the girl would actually rip out Ally's throat with her teeth, but instead she pressed her lips to Ally's ear.

"You tell anyone about any of this tonight," she whispered," and not only will I deny it, I'll shoot every person you tell and yank off all your fingernails to feed to your stuttering brother before I gut him. Understand?"

Ally gave a shaky nod. Red waited another weighted second before finally releasing her. The air rushed back into Ally's lungs, and she hated herself for staggering back a step. Only then did she notice that the rock in her palm had gone cold. Only then did she realize that Red was letting her go.

"I like you Ally." Red retrieved her paintbrush and shook her hair out. "If you prove yourself to be more than a crappy barista, I'd like you on my side. I mean, you can dance around with Hatton and his strays all you want, but they won't get you anywhere." She gave her a knowing, blood-soaked smirk. "Come find me when you're ready to join the wolves."

* * * * * * * *

Jesper couldn't help but think the last time he had been this lonely was when their mother died. But he never allowed himself to remember that time, so he skipped around it in his mind, narrowly missing the rabbit hole of bad memories.

What were you thinking, Ally?

He'd gone to Miguel's—for what, he still didn't know—and found the place had been razed in his sister's wake. Miguel had actually been there trying to put out fires (and Jesper was overwhelmed with gratitude to find that 'putting out fires' was just an expression, not an actual fire).

Damage had been done, though. Miguel said that to make up for equipment she had broken plus all the coffee she'd taken, Ally wouldn't get a cent of her paycheck. Jesper apologized again and again. He told Miguel he would work the rest of that shift Ally had walked out on and wouldn't expect to be paid for it.

Thankfully, the night didn't wind up being very busy. Jesper's bones felt hollow as he filled the few orders and cleaned every possible surface and dish, some of them twice. But he forced his shoulders not to slump and focused on not making a single mistake. Miguel didn't trust Jesper to work on his own apparently, because the man sat at a table and pretended to be on his phone, but Jesper could feel eyes on his back.

Once again, Jesper wondered if he was ashamed of Ally. Maybe he just couldn't understand what she had done here. They had a chance to make something for themselves, and these people were nice enough to let them. Why did she have to throw it away like it didn't mean anything? It meant something to *him*. Couldn't she at least see that?

She's just scared, Jesper reasoned with himself, shaking his head hard to get rid of the thoughts against his sister. Stars knew the Molds had made them both feel they were constantly backed in a corner—literally in most cases. That left a scar on people, one that stayed with them. He knew she was doing her best. He shouldn't hold that against her.

Once closing time came, Jesper helped Miguel clean and lock up. The owner eyed Jesper doubtfully when he gave another stuttered apology, but Miguel nodded and gave Jesper the money he'd made in the last two weeks. The thin stack of green bills felt like blocks of gold.

At the awe in Jesper's face, Miguel's mouth quirked into a slight grin. "Don't spend it all in one place, all right?"

Jesper smiled back and nodded rapidly. "Yes, yes tha-nk you, sir."

"Sir? Now a guy could get used to that." Then he nodded in farewell. "'Night Jesper."

"Good—goodni-ght, sir."

Jesper counted the bills three times after Miguel had left—darkness had settled too heavily for him to see what numbers were on them, but he had twenty-six in all. Twenty-six! Twenty-six bills he had worked for himself, had earned. He couldn't wait to show Ally and H. Maybe Riley would even be a little proud, and Kat would smile at him and make one of her nonsensical jokes he didn't understand. It would be a great night after all.

Kneeling on the damp cement, he folded a few bills and tucked them in each shoe, just as he'd seen people do in the

Jacklands. He couldn't fit all of them, though, without his feet feeling too weird, so he put the rest in his jacket pocket and set off for home.

While he walked, he found his thoughts wandering back to Monty. What would he say if he could see what his son had done?

I'm not as useless as you think, Jesper thought. *I made my own money—real, honest money, not blood money. When was the last time you could say the same?*

A jolt of guilt struck him, the taste like bitter fruit in his mouth. The strength of it knocked him off balance, made him dizzy—why would he think such a thing?—and he stumbled, crashing into someone.

Immediately, Jesper jumped back, his forehead creasing in confusion when he saw the guy he'd slammed into: long blonde hair, crooked eyebrows, and a giant splat of ink on his neck Kat had called a tattoo. Jesper had seen him out of the corner of his eye, leaning up against the brick wall in the alley. How had he suddenly appeared in the center of the sidewalk?

"Sorry about that," the guy said, though his smirk looked anything but sorry.

Jesper dropped his gaze to the guys' dirty red shoes and muttered an incoherent apology back before continuing on his way.

The guy just pushed Jesper back. "What was that? Don't I get an apology too?"

A laugh slashed through the air, making Jesper's heart leap into his throat. He glanced down the alley to see four other people gathered, all different heights and clothes, but all with the same dangerous smirk on their faces.

Jesper swallowed hard as sweat beaded on the back of his neck despite the cool air. No, this was not good.

"Hey guys," the guy called to the group. "This guy crashes into me and doesn't even apologize for it."

The shorter girl laughed again and the dark-haired boy standing next to her gave a thumbs down. "Boo!"

That movement in the alley caught Jesper's attention, and he made the mistake of turning his head toward it. The guy used his momentary distraction to shove Jesper again, this time into the alley, closer to his group of friends. Jesper stumbled and barely caught himself before falling. A short-lived victory. He knew what was coming next.

He'd never hit someone before, even in self-defense, and even if he knew how, he didn't think he ever would. Instead, he just accepted his fate.

It all happened fast, and yet time seemed to stand still right there in that alley. He managed to dodge the first hit, but others quickly followed, each harder and more violent than the last. Jesper tried to stay standing as long as he could, but in the end they got him on the ground. The kicks hurt worse than the punches and new pain exploded every second for what felt like hours.

Jesper had been hit a lot of times in his life. But somewhere in this new kind of ocean of pain, a realization surfaced. One that he had always unconsciously thought about deep in the back corners of his mind, one that was dug up with each strike from his attackers. These people took pride and pleasure—sick, grotesque pleasure he could never understand—in hurting him, exerting power over him.

Monty didn't. The only things ever in Monty's eyes were rage and regret.

Finally, it stopped. Jesper couldn't help moaning in pain when hands sifted through his pockets. Far away, he thought he heard someone laughing, voices joking about a pay day. He knew they were robbing him; he knew he couldn't do anything about it. His precious, hard-earned bills, gone.

Jesper stayed very still as the far away voices slowly retreated, leaving him in a buzzing, painful kind of darkness. He could've been in an alley in Ducat or back in the In Between for all he knew. He just lay there, painting the ground red and wondering if all money ended up being blood money eventually.

CHAPTER 6

A RAVEN AND A WRITING DESK

Come find me when you're ready to join with the wolves.

Red's voice echoed over and over again in Ally's mind as she made her way back to Riley's place. The conversation had shaken her up more than she cared to admit, but she still couldn't stop replaying it. Red's bloody truth. Her absolute power. The way she'd clawed her way up the ranks and then made herself a spot at the top—beating King, her father, and anyone else who was out to get her. Just thinking about it made Ally's stomach flutter.

Apparently, cat girl hadn't been exaggerating at all when she told Ally the story.

So why would Riley say that? Why would he imply that Kat's version of the truth wasn't right, even when Red herself said it was?

Despite Riley's warnings, Ally knew Red's kingdom was something she just had to be a part of. After all, Riley couldn't really offer them protection. He obviously had some kind of deal with Red, and Ally planned on figuring it out, and exploiting it if she could. But she knew from the beginning Riley wasn't the answer to the life she wanted here. She didn't need stray cats to pretend to protect her. No, she needed wolves. And she needed to become one herself.

Red had obviously extended an invitation. A conditional one, of course, but all worthwhile ones were. Ally had to make herself valuable. An asset. Once she did, Red would welcome her into the ranks, give her a sure foundation to build something on. And when Jesper saw how safe they were, how powerful and protected, he wouldn't hesitate to stay with her instead of going back to the Molds. He would understand that *this* is what their mother would want for them.

Are you proud of me now?

The first step was to continue to expand her skillset and make a name for herself. Where to start though? She needed the right platform, one to help her make connections and one that Red would not just notice but be impressed by. Nothing Riley or H or the stupid coffee shop could ever hope to give her.

She also had to keep her eye on Riley and his crew. Kat was annoying and talked way too much, but that didn't make her an actual threat except maybe to Ally's patience—any girl with pink hair wouldn't be. H, though, could definitely be someone to watch out for. Riley treated her like his favorite, and she spent too much time with Jesper. She could easily get to her brother when Ally wasn't looking, before she had even noticed. On the other hand, Riley's mom wasn't an issue and never would be. The woman spent her days either cooking in a trance or sleeping, hardly ever in the main room and had never been able to hold a whole conversation. Pathetic.

That left Riley. Ally hadn't trusted him since the moment she saw him.

He was forcing the hero act. She knew it, had suspected it since day one when he was so adamant about keeping them, but she still couldn't figure out why or push him far enough to break the charade. And there was something with him and Red. Ally knew it. None of Riley's strays had the mark of the Black Cards and didn't seem affiliated with the gang or Red at all.

Why would a girl like Red give Riley any kind of space? Especially when King before her made everyone join or die?

It takes a monster to hold off a monster.

Riley was hiding his monstrous claws somewhere, and Ally would find them before they managed to sink too deep into Jesper and bleed him dry.

Ally opened the door to Riley's building and made the climb to the third floor, relieved to escape the frigid night air. Her racing thoughts screeched to a halt when she saw Riley's apartment door ajar, light spilling out of the crack into the hallway.

Something sharp pressed into Ally's chest as she forced herself forward. When she pushed the door open, she found the kitchen full, voices talking over each other. Kat stood with her phone in hand, waving her arms as she yammered on about something. Riley's mom was at the sink, wringing out a red cloth, while H and Riley huddled around a bloody figure slumped in a chair by the table. Nobody even noticed her walk in.

Ally's first instinct was to check behind her shoulder, heart hammering in her chest, mind racing and tripping, because Monty had to be here but Monty couldn't be here because Monty had never been here. Had he? Her brother only looked like that when their father was around. She thought she saw a glimpse of his gray beard in the corner, but she blinked and it disappeared.

Ally's fear snapped into rage. She stomped forward, slamming the door behind her, and H turned at the sound as Ally shoved her hard.

"What did you do?" Ally demanded, shoving her again.

Kat shouted, "Hey!" as H fell into the table, and Riley turned just in time for her to punch him in the face. Her knuckles screamed, but she didn't care, barely even felt it. Jesper was bleeding. Nothing else mattered.

H swore at her, picking herself up as Riley held his jaw, both of them turning on her. H was closest, so Ally launched herself at her, prepared to rip her apart, but a hand wrapped around her arm and pulled her back.

"Ally!" Jesper yelled. "Stop!"

Ally only half heard him, trying to wiggle out of his grasp so she could yank H's hair out bit by bit, but Jesper pulled on her arm again. He used the leverage to pull himself to his feet and swing her around, so her back now pressed against the table and he stood in her way. Her eyes found his automatically, and somehow they always made her take a breath.

"Ally," he said again, softer this time in between hard panting. "Stop. I'm okay."

She glanced over him and assessed the damage: several bruises on the left side of his face, bloody lip, gashes on his upper left arm and both palms, and some kind of rib injury, she guessed, based on the way he stood curled slightly to one side.

Memories hurled themselves at her, of Jes stained purple and red, voice soft as he desperately tried to calm her down, keep her quiet, so the monster wouldn't come back.

See, Ally, I'm okay. You see? It's just a scratch. I'll be okay.

She remembered once, right after their mother died, Ally had gone hysterical at the sight of her injured brother. He had to hold her tightly in his lap and restrain her until she finally broke down into sobs.

Is he going to take you away from me too? she had asked between tears. *Are you going to leave me like mommy did?*

Jesper's eyes had clouded over. *No, I'll never leave you, Ally, okay? Never.*

But despite his promise, that fear had haunted the back of her mind and she'd never been able to get rid of it.

Another glimpse of gray hair, and Ally gasped, jerking her head around to find nothing. She thought she heard the sound of her father's low growl in the tense silence, but she couldn't register anything except for Jesper's raspy breathing.

I thought we were safe. I thought we were finally safe from him.
But we aren't.
He's everywhere.

Ally stepped forward again, needing a target, her narrowed gaze landing on Riley. "But what did they—"

Jesper pushed her back, soft yet firm. "Nothing. They helped me. It's okay."

"What happened?"

"I, uh...I tripped and fell."

"You tripped and fell," Ally repeated, the words dripping with the skepticism pecking at her bones. How many times had he made that excuse? How many times had baby Ally accepted the explanation because she was too full of fear and guilt to face the truth? Somewhere, Monty laughed under his breath, the chuckle low and derisive.

"Yeah...after, um, someone pushed me," he admitted. "I left Miguel's and was walking home and ran into some...people."

Ally clenched her jaw and fists. "Who were they?"

"Nobody. I don't know. They were gone before I could really see most of them. H found me trying to walk back." He gave a lopsided shrug. "Wrong place, wrong time."

Ally could feel H's heated glare burning into her, and she fought the urge to hit her anyway. H had no right coming in here, taking over Jesper when Ally would've done a much better job helping him. Who did she think she was?

Her fists loosened in defeat when the full situation hit her, the reason H was especially judgmental: Jesper shouldn't have been at Miguel's. He should've been here. It was Ally's shift, one that she had ducked out early on in a rage. H must've told Jesper, and he went to check on either Ally or the place, to apologize. He shouldn't have been there at all.

Wrong place, wrong time.

Ally could see in his face that Jesper had made the connection too, but she also knew he would never voice it. Just like the other hundred times he had taken a hit for her without complaint.

I wish you were both dead! Monty had screamed. *I wish you were both dead like your blasted mother!*

Jesper must've registered the fire draining out of her, because he slumped back into his chair, barely hiding a wince. His composure seemed to crack with it. He glanced between H and Riley. "So-sorry. You can, um, go back to your ni—or um, your things. I can…I can take ca-are of…this."

Riley blinked and took a breath, his face red where Ally had hit him. "No, of course not. This is just how it goes around here, sadly. I never should've let you go alone but…" He sighed and his shoulders caved in, making him look smaller than he ever had. Ally was too rattled to enjoy it. "Oh well. What's done is done now." She stiffened. "We'll get you taken care of."

Jesper ducked his head and nodded. The gesture gushed disbelieving gratitude, and Ally's chest burned at the thought that nobody had ever offered to help Jesper tend to his own injuries in…years, at least. Probably since their mom died.

Ally turned her glower on Riley, eyes narrowing. He recoiled slightly in surprise at the murder in her gaze. Her hands balled into fists, and she was ready to scream accusations of manipulation at him, to rip him limb from limb. But a shadow in the kitchen caught her eye: Monty reaching for the ale.

No. Jenny holding a glass of water.

Jesper pulled softly on Ally's arm, telling her to sit. Instead of taking the chair next to him, she sat on the floor right next to his chair, acting as guard dog while H and Riley continued their pathetic attempts at helping. Every few seconds, her eyes would check each corner of the room, searching for the gray beard flecked with blood.

Jes flinched when Riley touched his skin, which Riley must've noticed because he was careful to only touch cloth and bandages after that, even if it meant bending his fingers at an awkward angle. H, on the other hand, didn't do anything useful. She just passed supplies from the counter to Riley, holding a bandage in place even when she didn't really need to. Ally could have done it herself, and done it much better.

Kat started talking again toward the end—the girl couldn't be quiet for more than five minutes—going on and on about this Kim lady she never shut up about. Her voice grated on Ally's nerves, but one glance from Jesper kept her from speaking up.

When Riley said he'd done as much as he could do, he walked with Jesper to the couch, encouraging him to spread out and relax when he tried to scrunch himself into the corner. Ally sat on the floor. Riley's mom went to bed—Ally had been shocked the lady was still up at all—and H and Kat got their stuff together.

"Text me when you both get home," Riley told them. "Please be safe. I heard the Walrus is out looking for the Carpenters. Just be careful."

Ally snorted. What a stupid thing to say. Telling someone to be safe didn't actually keep them safe. It just taunted the skies.

"Kat's stayin' at my place tonight," H said, slinging her backpack over her shoulder and adjusting her shoe. She stopped when she saw Riley's expression. "We'll be fine, Ry, okay?"

"I can video chat you the whole way." Kat fluffed her pink-tipped hair. "I *am* an internet personality after all. Actually, maybe that would make a great segment for the vlog." She tapped something into her phone.

H rolled her eyes. "That won't be necessary."

"You sure I can't take you home?" Riley asked.

H glanced at Jesper, then promptly ignored Ally's returning glare. "Yeah, we're good."

Kat walked to the door with her eyes still on her phone, then looked up at Jesper as she went out. "Feel better, kitten. I'll bring you marshmallows and Meryl Streep movies tomorrow."

"Thanks Ka-at," Jes replied, his voice strained and weak despite his bright tone.

"Take care of yourself, Muffin Boy," H called. Ally rolled her eyes.

"Okay. Thanks for...for finding-ing me."

Ally gritted her teeth.

"Yeah, yeah." H waved her hand, then she and Kat were gone.

Riley locked the door behind them, then walked over and picked up what they called a remote to turn the TV on so they could watch the moving pictures. It had been over two weeks living at Riley's—too long, in Ally's opinion—but the TV still amazed her.

Turning the noise down low, Riley set the remote down on the couch next to Jesper. "You can watch whatever you want— or whatever you can find, really. We only have limited cable, but you can stream anything too." Neither Ally nor Jesper asked what any of that meant. "How are you doing, Jesper?"

Jesper blinked in surprise, as if the question were the most unexpected thing Riley could have asked. "Um…I'm ok-okay. Thank you."

"If you get worse over the next couple days we'll consider finding someone to help." He frowned, his forehead creasing. "I don't trust the hospital here, but we'll figure something out." He pointed over his shoulder, down the hallway. "I'll be up doing homework for a while, so let me know if you need anything, all right?"

"We'll be fine," Ally snapped.

Riley really looked at her for the first time since she barged in. She couldn't read his expression, and it infuriated her. His gaze stopped on her hand. She twisted her arm to hide the bloodstained strip of cloth wrapped around her slashed palm, and his eyebrows furrowed. Her scowl dared him to ask.

He just sighed. "Okay." He turned out the lights, which made the TV seem to glow brighter. "Goodnight." Then he disappeared into the shadows of the hallway.

Jesper started dozing within minutes of Riley leaving, but he couldn't stay still, tossing and turning constantly. Even when he wasn't moving, his body twitched, as if it just couldn't relax.

Ally watched the TV. A bunch of people were standing behind screens, spinning a giant wheel of numbers and pointing to a board of letters. Sometimes the people looked happy and sometimes sad. Maybe if Ally could actually hear it, she'd know what was going on.

It wasn't enough to distract her, and her mind kept playing tricks. Was that the crunch of boots in the gravel? The stench of metal and blood in the air? The silhouette of the man who was supposed to take care of them, but had only ruined them?

Breath catching in building fear she just couldn't shake, she reached into her pocket for her special rock. If Monty *was* here, it wouldn't be like before. It couldn't.

I wouldn't let him hurt you. Her shoulders slumped and a lump got caught in her throat as she glanced over her brother's restless form. *I could've protected you. For the first time in our lives, you wouldn't have had to take the hit for me. I could've kept it from both of us. And I missed it.*

She looked down at the rock in her hand, faintly blue in the TV light. "I need to protect him," she whispered softly. "I thought…I thought we were safe now. I thought he couldn't…I thought he couldn't find me here." Her fingers clenched around the stone. "I need you to help me. I don't want to be the lost little girl that has to hide anymore. I don't want to hurt anymore. I need to get away from him, once and for all. I need to protect us."

A sudden creaking sounded in the hallway. Ally straightened up and hid her hand under her cloak, hiding the rock from view. Her heart pounded in her chest as she recognized a hulking shadow in the hallway, coming for them.

Monty. Here.

Just as she was about to scream for Jesper to wake up, the shadow shifted and Riley stepped lightly into the kitchen. She struggled to fix her composure as he opened a cupboard, then walked over to them.

He jumped when he got close enough to see her eyes, as if he hadn't realized she was awake. He looked younger in the glow of the TV screen: his dark hair a mess without its beanie, his rumpled plaid pants clearly for sleeping, and his glasses pushed up his nose like an afterthought. He carried a glass of water in one hand and two white circles in the other.

"Hey," Riley whispered. "I just came to give more medicine to your brother. He'll be pretty sore in the morning without it."

Medicine. Just right there, so easy to get inside a cupboard.

If Riley hadn't whispered, Ally would've forgotten to. "I can give it to him," she snapped. "He doesn't need you."

Riley kneeled down in front of her, setting the glasses on the ground and the medicine in her palm. Then he hesitated. Why was he hesitating? Couldn't he see that nobody wanted him here? Surely the know-it-all could figure that out.

"You know," he started, his voice smaller than before, "he could've died tonight. He's lucky he didn't."

The words struck something soft and vulnerable deep inside Ally. Her eyes stung with...tears? When was the last time she cried? She couldn't remember. But hearing someone else say it out loud, having someone validate her absolute worst nightmare when Monty could be right around the corner waiting to make it happen, was more than she could handle.

She scowled. "Luck had nothing to do with it. You pretend like you know him, but you don't. Jesper is the…he's…" She faltered. She didn't know the words, couldn't find them, but she didn't want to give them to Riley anyway. "He's more. Than everyone."

Riley nodded—like he *agreed* with her—and Ally felt her blood start to boil underneath her skin. She narrowed her eyes into dangerous little slits and leaned forward, her voice sharp enough to kill.

"So if any of you hurt him or even look at him wrong, I will personally carve you into pieces to feed to your stray Kat and burn this place to the ground with everyone inside. Do you understand?"

Her hand tightened its grip on the rock still hidden by her cloak, and she felt the tiny electric zing of it waking up.

I could hurt you. I could make you regret you ever took us captive here. I could make sure you never, ever dare to speak to my brother again.

Riley leaned back a little, as if sensing the murder in her heart, his expression still blank and unreadable. Ally hated that. She wanted to see the fear take root in his eyes. She wanted to know that here in a dark room with a stranger and her injured brother, she had the upper hand still. She could protect them. She could win.

He could be anywhere. He could be right around the corner.

Riley watched her for a long, silent moment. Then he just said, "It's nice to see you caring about something besides yourself, Ally." He nodded at the medicine clenched in her fist. "Make sure he takes those." Then he stood and disappeared into the hallway.

Ally sat for a minute, fuming. Riley Hatton. Who in the skies did he think he was?

Jesper stirred, and the sound snapped Ally out of her rage. Remembering the medicine in her hand, she turned on her knees and gently shook her brother's shoulder.

"Jes. Wake up."

His eyelids fluttered open, and he winced, trapping a groan behind his teeth. "Ally? Are you okay?"

"I have medicine for you," she said, offering the circles and water. "I knew you'd want it."

Jesper's eyes widened and the TV light reflected off of them in little colored shapes. He didn't say what she knew they were both thinking: how could someone just have medicine in their cabinet, free to take whenever they were hurting? "Thanks, Ally." A wince fractured his face when he sat up, but he did it anyway and swallowed the medicine with one drink before collapsing back onto the couch.

Ally didn't know what she was supposed to do next, so she just turned back and resumed her position. Except now she couldn't focus on the TV. Now she remembered why she'd been so good at watching it tonight, instead of looking at her brother's beaten face and bandaged hands.

Silent minutes passed. She wasn't sure he was still awake, wouldn't turn around to check, when she whispered, "Were you scared?"

Jesper took a shuddering breath. Awake, then. It took a whole spin of the TV wheel for him to answer.

"Terrified."

Her eyes closed, and she tried not to imagine it: her brother up against a group of dangerous people, all twice his size, twice as tall, laughing as they made him bleed.

Too late.

"Ally?"

"Yeah?"

"I, um...when they...I lost some of the money. From working. They robb-robbed me. Not...not all of it, but...but some. So it'll...probably take us longer. To get...to get home. I'm so-sorry."

Shame scalded her. She had worked just as long as her brother, but that stupid Miguel had kept all the money she'd rightfully earned. H probably had something to do with it, as a form of revenge.

"It's okay," she said, impulsively wanting to please him. "I'm getting a job too."

"You are?"

Ally perked up the excitement in Jesper's voice, bordering on pride. "Yeah. It's at one of those gas places, you know, where people take their cars. I would be putting supplies on their shelves inside the building." She'd passed by the other day and seen someone doing it, and it was the first thing that popped into her mind. "This job would be much better for me. They said they'll think about it, but I should pretty much expect to get it."

"That's great Ally! That really is." He sighed in contentment, and Ally reveled in the sound, that she had brought it. "Now we'll be even closer to getting home."

The words felt like a bucket of ice water had been dumped over her, smothering the catching flame of Ally's victory. She let out a long breath and leaned her head back against the couch, right next to Jesper's elbow. He moved his arm so it dangled over the side of the couch, and her hand automatically found his pinky.

Just as his breathing started to deepen, Ally thought she heard a sound by the front door. She whipped her head around, breath catching violently in her chest, before she heard it again, coming from the TV.

The waiting was agony. The waiting would kill her. Waiting for him to barge in and scream at her and beat her brother senseless. She could feel him out there, watching her. A wolf waiting for his Little Red Riding Hood to wander back to his corner of the woods, so he could finally eat her up and bury her for good.

* * * * * * *

Ally couldn't remember the last time she stayed in one place for an entire day, but she made it a point not to leave Jesper's side. She hoped it proved to *everyone*—especially H and Riley—that she was the first and only person in her brother's life, despite the fact that not moving built up a hot kind of static in her bones. Like a hive of bees had nested under her skin, buzzing loudly and restlessly. It made her itch.

Every few minutes she reached into her pocket and turned her rock over in her hand, and imagined setting something on fire. The rock would send little tingles through her fingers, and she knew she could do it with barely a thought. The knowledge calmed her. More than once, she could've sworn she saw Monty's shadow in the corner, but it always disappeared. If she ever blinked and found the shadow was still there, she thought, she would burn the place down, and that would be that.

Nothing to worry about.

Jesper stayed quieter than usual the entire day, and that left a solemn void in the air. He didn't move from the couch except to go to the bathroom, and even that only happened twice.

Riley and his mom took turns bringing him food periodically. Jesper would give a faint smile and thank them, then push it around the plate for a minute before setting it on the floor. He did the same with water, and only really drank it with the medicine she'd learned were called pills. Ally had started eating and drinking the leftovers for him, just so Riley would stop bugging him about it.

See? she wanted to scream at every single person. *I am the best caretaker for him. He doesn't need any of you.*

The only light in Jesper's eyes lit when Kat and H walked in that afternoon with stuff for him. Ally's fingers tapped against her leg in agitation, begging her to expose their manipulative plot. Jesper faked excitement for their benefit—she was sure— sitting up a little to eat a handful of Kat's promised marshmallows and drink from the Miguel's cup H had brought for him. They laughed about something that had happened at work; Ally's jaw clenched so tight it nearly shattered.

I could burn this place down, she thought as her thumb stroked her rock. *I could make sure you never touched him again.*

When Jesper thanked them for the twelfth time, Kat actually snorted. "You're acting like we're bringing you solid gold, kitten. It's just processed crap." She popped at least six in her mouth and tried to talk around them. "Nofin' to get exthited abut." It was the most reasonable thing Ally had ever heard her say.

Jesper slept slightly better the second night, still on the couch, and by the next morning Ally felt like a caged, rabid dog scourged with bee stings. She needed space. She needed air. And she needed a plan.

The sun had just broken over the horizon when Ally left her brother sleeping and hit the streets. She had two places to go, a job to get, money to make, and a plan to create. After all, based on what she'd witnessed the last two days, she knew she was running out of time. If she didn't act fast, H and Riley would have Jesper trapped in the palm of their hands. And that was if somebody else didn't get the chance to hurt Jesper before that.

The first stop she made was quick, easy, and fulfilling. It took her all of fifteen minutes, and then she went on her way again, her shoulders looser, her steps a bit lighter. When she heard sirens in the distance, she smiled.

The second stop would take more of her wits. Ally had spent the last two nights thinking of how to approach this moment, what speech she should prepare. In the end, she decided simplicity was better. It suited him anyway.

She found the Smoky Man still in his chair, smoking away. How was he here all the time? She didn't hesitate, walking right up to him with squared shoulders.

"I want a job."

"Hey, there, it's the chickadee." He wore the same clothes Ally had seen him in weeks ago, the first time she'd met him. He probably hadn't showered, though it was hard to tell behind the stench of the smoke. Maybe that was the secret to a dirty life. "You wanna go someplace where a cave in the ocean sings a silent song of death?"

Ally gritted her teeth. "I want a job. I want to work for you."

"Ha!" He broke into a grin, highlighting rows of surprisingly white teeth. "Remember what I told you, love? No something for nothing. Why do you wanna work for me anyhow?"

"You see everything that goes on here and everyone talks about you like you're some kind of ghost. From what I understand, you run your own ring without any kind of outside influence or support, unlike anyone else—and for that reason, you're the biggest supplier in Ducat, even better than Red's people."

He narrowed his eyes at her observation, nodding thoughtfully. "Well flattery ain't gonna take you the whole way. I know you're cookin' up something. What's in it for you?"

Ally saw no reason to lie to him. He'd probably be able to tell anyway, as strange as he was. "A paycheck, of course. A reputation. And I get to learn how this place works—insurance

for me and my brother. Then eventually, maybe a promotion."
It would check off all of Ally's boxes. They'd see what Riley
had to say when she discovered all his dirty secrets, and once
she had proven herself through this job, she knew Red would
come knocking on her door.

Smoky Man raised an uneven eyebrow. "Information is key,
you know that, love?"

"Yes," she said, "that's why I want it. It's both the armor
and the weapon." Pepperjack had said that once. Ally never
thought she'd be quoting him of all people, but apparently
there was a first time for everything.

Ally could tell the line impressed Smoky Man. He sat back
in his chair and slowly looked her up and down, sizing her up.
The minute seemed to last years.

"When you say reputation—and don't get me wrong, love,
I think the right reputation is the greatest shield a person can
have—how do you mean to use that?"

She shrugged coolly. "Stop the people preying on my
brother. Make the right friends."

"You mean Red?"

Ally kept her expression smooth, and shrugged again. "I'm
not really looking to tie myself down to anyone. Just need a
job."

"Ah ha." He took a puff of smoke. "You know, she runs it
different now. Not just anyone can join. Gotta prove
themselves first." She thought a flicker of annoyance passed in
his eyes, but she blinked and only found him to be
contemplative. "I run my business the same way, matter o'
fact."

Ally just stared at him, unwilling to show the nerves
bubbling in her stomach. She wouldn't allow herself to be
rejected. This was her chance. For her. For Jesper.

Finally, he blew out a smoky breath and said, "McKennis is
a buyer of mine. Not the newest, not the oldest, and not the
biggest. But he's gone off the radar. I got word he's selling me
out to someone. I dunno who." He pulled his stick from his
mouth and gestured to her. "You're right about one thing: my

stuff, vac, is the best there is. Call it an old family recipe from my homeland—very exclusive—and I don't want it leakin'. You find McKennis and get him to talk, bring me back the information, and you and I will have a talk. Understand, love?"

Swallowing her excitement, Ally nodded seriously. "Yes."

"You have a week, chickadee, and then you blow your chance and I move on. Don't waste it."

Ally turned on her heel with a sly, victorious smile, plans already forming in her mind. "I won't."

* * * * * * * *

Someone set Miguel's Coffee Shop on fire.

The fire professionals, firefighters, couldn't tell how it had started. The flames had just seemed to appear and catch onto the building with a vengeance, and concentrated there. Despite the other small buildings crammed on either side, only the coffee shop burned. Thankfully they managed to put it out before the entire building went down, but it scorched the back area, damaged one machine beyond fixing, and ruined nearly all the stored ingredients.

H gave Jesper this update, since he was still out and injured the day it had happened. She said Miguel had gone crazy over the incident, and refused to leave the place during the day, as if his presence could ward off any other disasters. Against the firefighters' advice, he opened the place back up after just four days.

Jesper's body still felt like it had been ground up and strewn all over, but he picked himself up and went to work anyway. Based on H's updates, Miguel probably needed all the help he could get. And if Jesper let every ache, inconvenience, or difficulty stop him, they would never get home.

He'd stayed on the couch for five days—something he had never once done before—and everyone had looked after him. Even Ally. She stayed with him for an entire day, and knowing how much that must have taxed her meant the whole world to him. Not to mention Kat's marshmallow visits, and H's gentle gaze, and the way Riley handled everything and Jesper could just relax for the first time in his life. He had to admit, part of him had sunken into the feeling of being taken care of, but now the guilt gnawed at him from the inside.

A real man would get up after he'd been hit, Monty would say. *A real man wouldn't take it lying down.*

And Jesper had done just that. The experience had shaken him up mentally more than anything, and thinking about it made his palms sweat and heart hammer. But he'd never been given the opportunity to just put something like that in the past and move on. Instead, he usually *lived* in the warzone, existing in a space that perpetually picked at all his scars so they could bleed again, never healing. Now he wanted to take the chance to move past what had happened, no matter how uncomfortable it was to do so.

Riley blinked in shock when he saw Jesper up and dressed that morning. Jesper had planned on being out before Riley woke up, but changing his shirt had proved to be a more painful and difficult task than he thought.

"You're going out?" Riley asked, eyebrows raised as he looked over Jesper's pathetic form.

"Just to work." He carefully shrugged on a gifted brown jacket two sizes too big, trying to avoid angering his ribs. "I'll be back later." It filled him with both comfort and dread to say the words. A place to come back to. Somebody waiting for him. Was that what a real home felt like?

"Um, do you...okay." Riley seemed to change his mind halfway through speaking. "H will be there today, right?"

"I think so."

That made him relax slightly. "Good. How are you feeling?"

"I'm okay. Did you see Ally this morning?" Glimpses of his sister had been scarce the last couple days.

Riley walked to the counter and poured milk in a mug. Almost four weeks of living here and Jesper still marveled at how accessible food was. "No, I didn't. Do I need to check on her?"

Jesper shook his head. "No. I'm sure she's okay." She certainly wouldn't have taken almost a week to recover had their positions been switched. Again, his chest warmed at the thought of her sitting on the floor by the couch all night. His sister wasn't meant to stay in one place.

Filled mug in hand, Riley turned to look at him, one corner of his mouth pulled up. Jesper froze. What had he done? He'd been on his feet for two minutes and already he was tripping up.

"Hey," Riley said, "did you notice that?"

If he meant all six hundred of Jesper's inadequacies, then the answer was yes. "Notice what?"

"We just had a whole conversation and you didn't stutter once."

Jesper paused and thought back, realizing it was true. A small grin spread on his face and he ducked his head. "You're right."

"Progress."

Jesper beamed and straightened his shoulders, the one word setting a light inside him that seemed to make everything shine a little brighter. "Thanks Riley. I'll see you later." He smiled again knowing it was true.

Maybe getting lost in this place wasn't the worst thing, he thought as he walked out the door. Then he heard Monty's voice in his head, as broken as Jesper's body had been when those people had mugged him, and the light from Riley instantly went out. Jesper ducked his head and trudged the rest of the way to work, the back of his neck prickling uncomfortably.

He'd barely walked through the doors of the coffee shop when Miguel jumped in his face, teeth bared and eyebrows popping off his forehead.

"You!" he spluttered, making Jesper flinch back. "Did you set my place on fire?"

"Uh...um, I…" The accusation floored Jesper. His neck felt hot and scratchy, and the gashes on his bandaged palms started to ache. "No-no."

H walked in from the back, then did a double take when she saw them. "What are you doing here?"

Miguel stabbed his stubby finger in Jesper's chest like a dagger. "He set my place on fire! I knew he was shifty, what with the shaggy black hair and sullen silence. Like a vampire."

H rolled her eyes. Jesper expected her to move on—she rarely cared about anything besides her breaks and phone when at work, let alone anyone else's business—so she shocked him by scoffing and walking to his side.

"Please," she said. "Jesper an arsonist? Even you know that's bull."

Miguel panted like he'd just sprinted here, eyeing her. He'd always paid too much attention to H. "You think?"

"Trust me, boss man, this ain't your guy."

"You're right." He backed off, and Jesper breathed again. "It's probably Lory. He's always been out to get me, since eighty-nine when I beat him at the track meet. Some people can't let go." And with that, he walked into the back, muttering to himself the whole way.

"Tha-thank you," Jesper breathed.

H waved her hand at him. "Yeah, yeah. What are you doing here? Shouldn't you still be slumming it on the couch scarfing down marshmallows?"

Jesper shrugged as well as he could.

"You're actually here to work?"

"Is that...I mean, is that ok-okay?"

H shook her head in exasperation. "Whatever, I guess. It hasn't really been the same without you—Alex isn't nearly as good of a listener and she just dumps stuff in. Doesn't even measure."

"What?" He found it easy to settle into their coffee shop work routine. He didn't realize they had one until now, but it felt nice to rely on something.

"I know, right? Barbarian."

He slipped behind the counter and their day began. The morning rush couldn't even be called a 'rush.' H said everyone assumed the place was closed this soon after a fire because "that's what a normal person would do." He found she watched him a lot, hovering a little, and it made Jesper even more self-conscious than usual. He tripped over his few words and struggled to think through his building headache.

Their shift was nearly over when he caught H staring at him again, her dark eyes narrowed. He couldn't tell if she was thinking or angry. Or maybe both.

"Wha-what?" Jesper finally asked. Had he done something wrong? Probably. His ribs were killing him.

"Don't think I haven't noticed."

"Um...noticed?"

"You're obviously still hurt. You look like microwaved shiz. If I were you I'd be on the couch milkin' Riley for everything he's worth."

Jesper didn't know what she was getting at, so he just shrugged again.

"But you're not. You're here. I haven't even heard you complain once. Or even mention it."

"I don't...um, I don't...it's over."

"Yeah, but I'm sure you still feel it. Kat stubs her toe and goes for the oscar nomination. I can't get her to shut up. You don't even make a sound."

Jesper didn't understand. Was she criticizing him? Wanting him to behave more like Kat? Even he had realized Kat was a once in a lifetime kind of person. Besides, why would complaining help? The pain was there whether he talked about it or not. No reason to drag others down with him.

When Jesper didn't answer, H shrugged and looked at her phone, moving on. "Speaking of, she should've been here, like, fifteen minutes ago. I swear, that girl's flakier than Tony the tiger."

Alex showed up, marking the end of their shift. H was still grumbling about Kat being late as Jesper hung up his apron and clocked out.

Then, like magic, the door flew open and Kat strutted in. She'd pulled her hair up on the top of her head, highlighting the pink powder around her wide eyes, bright with excitement. Jesper found himself a little excited too. The more he was around her, the more he soaked up whatever energy she put out.

"What is up everybody?" she sang. "Your favorite Kat is in the house!"

Alex sighed and cursed under her breath. Kat ignored that.

"Jesper!" She smiled at him, exposing all her teeth, and he couldn't help grinning back. "The magic mallows worked, I see." She put her hands on the counter and leaned forward. "Look, we don't got a lot of time—"

"Because someone was late," H cut in.

"If we were in a musical, this would be the reprise, and you got about sixty to ninety seconds to either join our adventure or not. Then the show must go on."

"Adventure?" Jesper asked.

"So here's the skivvy." She held up a black circle with a metal stick jutting out of it. "I begged and groveled and sold my beautiful soul to Riley so we could use his car, Billie. That's a big deal, kitten, in case you haven't noticed. Gas is ridiculous here and Riley is overprotective. *Anyways,* H and I are heading down to our favorite spot. There'll be a view, snacks, gossip, and general merriment. You wanna come?"

"Oh, um, I..." Shock took his words, leaving the all-important question. "Why?"

Kat blinked. "Why? For fun, kitten. Jeez, I'm starting to think that King Ashes of yours ran an Elaria prison."

Jesper choked on a laugh, making both girls stare at him. They had no idea. "No, um...I mean, why me?"

"This might be shocking for you and your self-imposed emo-ness to believe, but I like you. You're fun." She held up her phone. "Besides, I've been super bored ever since I showed you the workings of my phone and I want to find something else to freak you out."

"You're her new ball of yarn, is what she's saying," H threw in. He couldn't tell if she wanted him to come or not, though he had a feeling the girls had talked about it already. Probably on their phones.

Kat leaned forward and winked at him. "Don't listen to her, kitten. You're my number one." When Jesper hesitated, she went on. "Look, you don't have to, of course, especially since you still look like someone ran you over, but think of it this way: you've been through a trauma. You've been on the couch all week—not that I don't aim for that on the daily, but still. Your sister is MIA with her new job, which is a big fat bummer, and Riley would either smother you with worry or alphabet worksheets. As fun as *that* sounds, coming with us would be way funner."

Jesper's mind went blank. He didn't know what to say. They actually wanted him to come with them? For fun? He didn't want to offend them, but, despite Kat's claim, he wasn't sure they really wanted him along.

Understanding these girls would be a magic he wasn't sure *any* kingdom had, phones or not.

"Tick, tock, kitten. Reprise is almost over. Show must go on."

"Um...okay?"

Kat beamed. "We'll work on your delivery, but good enough. Welcome to the crew."

* * * * * * *

Ally wasted no time getting started on her new assignment.

First, she stopped by the police department after hours. If McKennis had been buying drugs for a long time, there was a good chance he'd been arrested for it at least once. There had

187

to be a record somewhere of what he looked like and where he lived.

The crumbling building looked just as pathetic as Riley's apartment building, but a shade of forgotten brown with flickering lights that Ally found both unflattering and lacking any intimidation. This was the home of the law enforcement? No wonder Red had full reign of the town. Ally had never seen the place where King Asher's royal guards trained, but now she imagined something like this since Pepperjack stood so powerful.

He did, she corrected herself. Somehow the reminder of the crime lord's death made her shift uncomfortably. She didn't like to think of what was going on in the Molds now. It wasn't her concern anymore and never would be again.

She heard the crunch of heavy boots behind her and whipped around, only to find the street empty.

Pushing her hair out of her face, she made herself focus. The front door was locked, but she tried it just in case someone had forgotten. Her plan involved breaking a window and climbing in—she cursed when she found every window reinforced with steel bars. On the back side of the building, a rusty ladder led the way up to the roof, but that proved useless as well. Only a cellar-type door showed any kind of promise of entry, but it had been chained and padlocked and rusted over, so Ally knew she wasn't getting through it.

She hissed through her teeth as she climbed back down the ladder. Now what? She could only imagine Smoky Man laughing at her getting tripped up on her first assignment by a locked door. And Red? No, this was not how it should go.

Frustration rising, she shoved her hands in her cloak pocket, seeking the comfort of her rocks. Then she stiffened. Of course. Her special rock had helped her this far. Why would it stop now?

Ally made her way back to the front door and clutched her rock in her palm. Instantly, the electric surety coursed through her, as if becoming more in tune with her needs and desires. She hardly had to concentrate at all when she'd started the coffee shop on fire; she'd just focused on her rage, not actual thought, and the flames had appeared out of nothing. Snapping the lock on the door was even easier. She barely had to look at it before she heard a click and it opened right up for her. She waltzed into the police department with a smile on her face.

The plan nearly fell apart again when she realized the records weren't kept on paper. She sat at the front desk computer and just stared at it for a minute, wondering how in the skies anyone knew how to work it. Her fingers tapped some of the letter boxes like she'd seen Riley do on his. The screen lit up and hope ignited in her. But after a few minutes of pressing every box, her excitement dimmed with the screen. There was no way she'd figure out how to get in, let alone work it. She couldn't even read the words for star's sake.

Somewhere, Monty laughed at her. She raked her hands through her hair, accidentally pulling a few strands out. The sound sank into her bones, drilling into her again and again, until she thought she'd come apart.

"I'm more than this," she whispered to him under her breath. "I'm more than you. And I'll prove it." She pushed herself up from the desk and scampered out of the room, unwilling to admit she was *still* running away from her father.

Turning the corner, Ally saw the dim lamp light spilling from behind an office door. The momentary distraction was welcome in her frenzied mind. She crept forward and listened to the sound of people shuffling inside. It only took a moment to realize what they were up to.

Ally rolled her eyes. How pathetic.

Sensing Monty still behind her, she barged into the room and nearly burst into laughter at the scene: two half-dressed people sprawled on the desk, a look of shock on the man's face and one of absolute horror on the woman's, as if one of her nightmares had just come to life.

Noting the expression and ring on the woman, the corner of Ally's mouth pulled up. "So," she said with casual confidence, "I'm guessing your husband doesn't know about this?"

The words broke the spell that hung over the room. With a small squeak, the woman shot to her feet and started pulling her skirt straight and fixing her shirt, while the man just sat up and stared at Ally, his hair tousled and lips red.

"I've never seen you before," he said, and Ally could practically see his brain working overtime to try and place her. "Who are you?"

Ally shrugged. "I'm new in town and looking for an honest officer to help me out with something." She smirked. "Sorry to interrupt."

"What do you want?"

"I need some information and can't quite seem to get into your computers here."

At that, the man's eyes narrowed and he started buttoning up his shirt, like she wasn't worth his time or concern. "Yeah, sure. I'll just arrest you now for breaking in. Whoever you're working for will have you replaced by morning."

Monty grunted a chuckle, and Ally jumped. His shadow lurked in the corner of her eye and she jerked her head. *You're nothing,* he said, *and always will be.*

The man stared at her. "What are you look—"

"Nothing!" Ally shouted back, gripping her rock tight in her pocket. Energy surged from it in a small, concentrated wave, holding the man and his lover captive against the wall. She screamed, and Ally silenced her—and Monty—with another flick of her wrist. She still held her mouth open in a shriek, but no sound came out. When Ally turned her head again, Monty's shadow was gone.

The man, to his credit, kept fairly calm for someone pinned by an invisible force. His eyes were so wide she thought they would burst from their sockets, but he kept his mouth in a firm, even line, as if fighting for control over his emotions.

Ally breathed hard, then straightened her shoulders. She liked this. Nobody could put a finger on her.

I'm in control. Not him. Me.

She painted a smirk on her face and sauntered up to the man, her voice dripping with sickly sweetness. "I need some help, officer, and you need mine. You think you wouldn't mind giving me a few minutes of your time?"

He scoffed. "And why would I need help from a rat like you?"

Ally cocked her head. "To keep the pictures secret, of course."

The woman kicked her heels against the wall in an effort to free herself, still screaming silently. Her eyes darted from Ally back to her lover in a desperate plea.

"How is this possible?" the man asked, more to himself, as he looked down at his bare chest. Then he looked at her. "Who are you?"

"Your worst nightmare," Ally said with a grin, "if you don't do what I say. Trust me, I don't need much."

He scowled, but it only took some voiceless pleading from the woman for him to cave. Within fifteen minutes, Ally had a copy of the file on McKennis, including a picture, and had tricked the officer into reading the address listed out loud to her.

Tucking the papers into her cloak pocket, Ally let her captives go. They both fell to the ground in a heap, the woman hitting her head on the desk as she went. Her lover cradled her against him as his scalding glare found Ally ducking out the door.

"I know everyone here," he said, "but I don't know you."

Ally just smiled. "You will."

* * * * * * * *

Their adventure started with a stop.

Kat had left something at H's apartment—something called a charger as well as some kind of phone picture stick—and she claimed they couldn't go without it. H lived just a few blocks

down from Miguel's, so they decided to walk instead of drive
the car since, according to H, "parking was a joke." Jesper
didn't know why parking would be funny, but he just went
along with it.

H's apartment building was half the height of Riley's and
painted a sour green. On the wall by the door, though, a spread
of different colors in bursts of design caught Jesper's eye. They
didn't have anything like art in the Molds, but he thought this
choice of sharp shapes and an array of colors created a nice
picture to look at, even if he couldn't tell exactly what it was
supposed to be. A field of flowers, maybe?

"The murals just show up," H said when she noticed him
looking at it. "Some kind of mystery painter. They're all over
the city."

Kat shifted her eyes dramatically. "I still think it's a secret
cult. I'm gonna do a vlog episode on it."

They walked up to the second floor and stopped at number
215, which, Jesper was proud to note, he could read. H shifted
on her feet for a moment, her hand hovering over the
doorknob. Then she turned to look at him.

"Wait out here, all right? We'll be right back." She barely
gave him a second to register the words before she cracked
open the door and slipped inside.

Kat glanced sympathetically at Jesper's bewildered
expression. "Don't take it personally, kitten, she doesn't let
anyone in. BRB." Then she went in too.

Jesper didn't mind, the more he thought about it. If they all
somehow returned with him to the Molds, he wouldn't want to
bring H or Kat inside his house either.

He could hear muffled voices from the other side of the
door, but he didn't try to make out the words—they weren't
for him, after all. He just leaned up against the wall for support
and wondered what he'd gotten himself into.

After a minute, the door flew back open. Jesper glanced up,
expecting H, and was shocked to find a different version of her
in the doorway. She stood shorter and thicker, with carefully
cut gray hair, wrinkles on her face, and no ring in her nose. But

they had the same eyes, nose, and mouth pursed into an unimpressed expression.

"You actually left him out here?" the woman called without turning.

"Leave it alone, old woman!" H shouted from inside. "Why are you like this?"

Her dark eyes roamed over Jesper. "Hmph. Well you better come on in here."

For a second, Jesper didn't know if she was talking to him, but then she gave him a pointed glance and gestured inside. "I don't have all day, boy."

Jesper ducked his head and stepped lightly inside. The place was smaller than Riley's: the kitchen and living area were both shoved into the same box of a space, and the narrow hallway showed two doors opposite each other with a cramped bathroom at the end. Green drapes hung over the two small windows, both of which had bars on the inside. That combined with the low lighting and distinct smell of tea and smoke made Jesper think of a prison cell, but the space gave off a cozier, if not more unique, feeling.

"I'll have you know," the old woman said, "I taught my granddaughter to leave trouble at the doorstep, but that's no way to treat a friend."

H gave an exasperated sigh and stomped into one of the rooms, while Kat grinned her huge grin and gestured to the woman. "I present to you the OG Queen of All, the one, the only, Harriet March."

The corner of Harriet's plum lips turned up. "Hush now, Kat, I already put on my blush today." Jesper automatically straightened when she looked at him again. "Now what new kitty have you found to play with?"

Kat stood on her tiptoes and slung her arm around Jesper's shoulder. He tried to hide both his wince and surprise. "This is Jesper Lewis. Newbie, quiet, insightful, and makes above average coffee. Might be one of the last of the endangered species 'Nice Guy' but my sources are still confirming."

Jesper stood still and tense as Harriet inspected him. H had always given off an uninterested yet magnetic feeling that made him desperate to impress her while knowing she couldn't care less about giving any attention. Under Harriet's gaze, though, the need to be something more burned so painfully inside him that he worried his face had turned red.

"Newbie, huh? Strange. Tell me, boy, why would you come to a diseased landfill like Ducat?"

Jesper's throat dried up, too intimidated to find words. Thankfully, Kat's words were never in short supply.

"My current theory is he's ex-CIA on the run," she said, "but Jes here is a tough nut to crack. Truly, we may never know."

Harriet's eyes widened. "I knew one of them once. Drove a truck as big as Texas and did his belt two notches too tight. Claimed he was runnin' from a big wig out to get him."

None of that made sense to Jesper, but Kat gasped. "Really? What happened?"

Harriet smirked, an echo of her granddaughter. "Now, Kat, you know I got all that southern hospitality for any gentleman lookin' as fine as he did."

Kat laughed and clapped her hands. "Oh, Mama March you are a *queen*!"

The woman didn't look like much of a queen in her drab apartment and scuffed shoes, but, Jesper reasoned, she did hold herself like one. Proud shoulders, raised chin, elegant hands. Maybe the title meant something different here to be used so commonly.

"H said ya'll are going' down to your spot," Harriet went on. "Let Mama March pack you a bag, all right?"

"Half the reason I'm here, Mama," Kat said.

While Harriet went to her cupboards and H could still be heard digging around her room, Kat took it upon herself to give Jesper a tour, which lasted less than a minute since they didn't even go down the hallway.

Mama March didn't make Jesper feel like he was invading, but he couldn't shake H's expression when she told him to wait outside. She clearly didn't want him in here. So he tried to make himself as small as possible in the corner. Several frames hung on the wall, and he occupied himself with studying the photos.

There were twelve in all. Most were of H and Harriet together throughout the years, each of them posed in the same crushing hug at the same angle, as though H held the camera. Two photos captured a younger Harriet sitting with a man in a hat, both of them laughing and staring at each other with so much admiration that Jesper could hardly look at them. The last one was of a family: a mom, dad, and two kids. Jesper recognized H, about eight or so, curly hair as wild and free as her smile as she clung to a baby boy.

H had never talked much about her family except for quick, hasty remarks about her grandma. Not that Jesper really did either.

Kat noticed him looking at the photo and slid up to him. "Her dad's dead," she whispered. "Shooting at the gas station a few years ago. Bad news. And don't bring up her mom or Leo either. She left and H never forgave her."

She left and H never forgave her.

The room started to spin. Jesper put his hand out against the wall to steady himself, gasping a low, choked breath.

She left and I never forgave her.

"Whoa, hey," Kat said, holding her hands up. "Not a big deal, all right? Just don't bring it up. Easy peasy."

H walked into the room carrying a white box with a tube sticking out of it and a long black stick with a box on the end. "Found it," she muttered, shooting an annoyed look at Kat while completely ignoring Jesper. "Thanks for the help."

Kat plucked the items from H's hands and kissed her cheek. "Thanks kitten. Let's roll."

Harriet turned with her arms full of three giant brown bags. "Don't forget your cornbread cakes. Life ain't worth nothin' without cornbread cakes."

"Truer words have not been spoken." Kat took a bag, then bowed. "'Til next time, Mama."

"You be careful out there, all right? I don't wanna get a call tonight sayin' I gotta come clean you out of the gutter."

"We'll be fine," H retorted.

Harriet's glare was so heated, Jesper took a step back. He wasn't sure how H survived it without shuddering. "Same thing your daddy told me, ain't it? Didn't stop him from getting mowed down in the Chevron."

H sighed and looked up at the ceiling in frustration. "You know I'll be careful, Mama."

"You better. You're my favorite granddaughter."

A glimpse of a smile appeared on H's face and she relaxed slightly. "I'm your *only* granddaughter, Mama."

"Same difference."

H scooped up both bags—one of which was marked with a 'V' and Jesper felt a flicker of pride at his recognition—then turned her back on him and walked out. "Come on, Jesper."

Jesper lurched for the door, pausing only to bow to Harriet like Kat did. She was a queen, after all, in some way. "Ni-nice to, um...nice to meet...meet you."

Harriet gave him a half smile. "Likewise, Jesper."

He had to rush to catch up with H, and Kat had surged even farther ahead. Jesper glanced at H, then ducked his head, his heart pounding. He hadn't been imagining her reaction. She was angry with him.

"Sorry," he murmured. As if that word had ever helped him before.

"She shouldn't have done that," H bit back. "You shouldn't have been in there."

Instincts told him to freeze and shrink, but he forced himself to keep walking. It felt important to him that she knew. "No-no. I under...I understand. You want to-to protect her."

She stared at him a long minute, lips pursed, as if deciding if he were joking or not. Apparently she realized he wasn't and relaxed a fraction. "It's not that I don't like you. It's just...she's special. That's all. I don't like anyone knowing her that shouldn't. Especially in a place like this." She snorted. "Not that Mama can't take care of herself."

"Seems like...you tw-wo are close?"

"Close, yes. She's my everything."

She's my everything. Jesper nodded, thinking of Ally. Yes, he understood.

"I'd say she's the only family I got left, but..." She shrugged. "Riley says it isn't just blood. Family is also who you find along the way. He's big on stuff like that."

"You think?"

"It's gag-yourself-cheesy and totally cliche." She shrugged again. "But I guess cliches are cliches for a reason."

By the time they made it back to Riley's car, Kat was already in the passenger seat talking at her phone.

"My travel buddies have *finally* arrived," she exclaimed, watching herself on the screen. "Of course, I never travel without my new Mitzi Berry lip gloss, which you can get twenty percent off of using my code, or Mama March's cornbread cakes, which, believe it or not, is not a sponsorship. I'm telling you because I cannot live without them." H sighed loudly and Kat glanced at her. "Well, the H of my heart is calling. Talk to you later, kittens!" Then she clicked a button and dropped her phone in her lap.

H rolled her eyes and started the car. "Whenever you're ready, Your Highness."

Kat beamed and hit the roof of the car, making Jesper wince. "Let's go!"

✳ ✳ ✳ ✳ ✳ ✳ ✳

All in all, Ally considered the evening highly productive.

With some (but not much, she reasoned) difficulty, she managed to find where McKennis lived. More of a mass of mismatched bricks than a building, stacked precariously and ready to collapse at any moment. She didn't really want to risk her life by going inside it.

197

After an hour of staking out the perimeter, she had a bit of luck: McKennis himself strode out the front door, his hands balled into fists and his hair a wild brown mane. Ally smiled and followed him.

First he stopped at a convenience store and purchased a few black and red packages. Not wanting to miss a speck of her research, Ally grabbed two of the same packages and purchased them with tip money she'd stolen from Gordy's.

"Lots of jerky fans this evening," the old man said as he scanned her items. "Curious."

Ally didn't have the time or patience for small talk, so she took her jerky and ran out the door, not wanting to lose her mark. Once she had McKennis back in her sights, she ripped open a package and popped a piece of jerky in her mouth. Tough and chewy and so flavorful, Ally nearly melted right there. It reminded her of the leathery meat Astrid had given them in the In Between, but so much better.

She straightened at the thought. If only Astrid could see her now.

McKennis went to the other end of town Ally hadn't seen before, and the pavement turned to clumped dirt under her boots. She thought he was heading for the trailer park, but he took a right and they ended up at a giant…building? Instead of wood or brick, the walls were a kind of slick and heavy fabric. A spire reached up to the sky and the fabric spilled out in a circle around it. Faded white and red stripes went down each side.

He didn't hesitate. He walked right up to a slit in the wall and ducked inside. Ally gripped her rock in her pocket, stowing her jerky away in the other, and followed.

The smell hit her first as if she'd walked straight into a brick wall. Sickly sweet and sour, it burned her eyes and left a tickle in the back of her mouth, and underneath that, the stench of too many bodies that hadn't been washed.

Barely holding in a cough, Ally glanced around the space. A dim light illuminated dozens of groups of people clumped sporadically, most of them slouched or just laying down on the ground. Some wore thick coats, others wrapped in slick cocoon-like blankets, all in varying degrees of falling apart. Everyone had a glazed over look in their eyes.

"First time?"

Ally turned to see a mass of wrinkles next to her bundled in an oversized gray coat. Something in Ally's expression must've confirmed it, because the old lady nodded.

"Name's Pat," she said, her voice like rubble. "Welcome to Crims." She held up three small bags, each holding fine white powder, tiny leaves, or pills. "First hit's free. After that you gotta bring your own or pay up."

Drugs. That's what he was here for.

A flash of Jesper's face appeared in her mind again, and she shook her head fast. She'd never surrender her strength anyway just for a hit of some drug. That would be the ultimate disappointment to her, Jesper, and her mother, she was sure. "No, I'm not here for that. Just looking for someone."

Pat shrugged. "Don't get high off the fumes or I'll charge ya." Then she settled back into her corner and puffed on a tiny stick.

Ally kept to the outskirts, her eyes darting over the shapes and looking for her target. She finally spotted him on the opposite side. For a moment, she worried Pat would kick her out eventually if she had to wait for McKennis to take his hit. He could be here for hours; it sure seemed like everybody else had been.

She watched as McKennis stopped at a mound of a person and kneeled down. He gave the person something, though she couldn't see what it was. After a few moments of talking, the person handed over something small and metal, she thought. Then McKennis straightened and headed for the exit.

Relieved, Ally followed. She didn't like this place and didn't want to stay here any longer than she had to. It stank like failure and regret. Two things that would never apply to her. But as she trailed behind McKennis, she thought she saw a wisp of a blood-flecked beard in the corner, dripping with ale.

She clenched her jaw and scurried a little faster to the fresh air.

I'll never be you.

Her nerves rattled, but she did her best not to lose focus. She had a job to do and she would do it well so she could escape Monty for good.

Thoughts of her father bounced around in her mind, and she kept having to check over her shoulder as McKennis unwittingly led her across town again. She snapped to attention when she realized where he was headed: the docks.

Ally's excitement started to bubble in her chest. He'd set a time up with that person at Crims, some kind of deal, and now she would catch him right in the act. Only one day on probation and she was already so good at this!

She breathed in the salty air and chewed on more jerky, wanting to keep her energy up for her big break. McKennis walked through the parking lot and made it to the stretch of mud that led to the dock. Ally was expecting him to divert to a corner and make a deal, but he walked right out to the edge of the dock and just…stood there.

Taking position around the corner of the bait shop, she watched him. And watched. Seconds turned to minutes, and after a half hour she was aggravated to find that he hadn't moved. He just stood there and stared at the ocean as if lost in thought or searching for something.

Ally sighed in annoyance. Maybe he was already high and she'd been following him for nothing. Maybe she should just push him into the ocean and tell Smoky Man the problem had been solved.

The back of her neck prickled just as a voice drawled from behind her. "What's up, Newbie?"

She jumped and whipped around to see AJ leaning against the wall, staring at her with a smirk, and gritted her teeth.

What do you want?" She blew a piece of hair out of her face and glanced back over her shoulder to check on her target. McKennis was still standing there with his back to them, staring out into the ocean.

"Staking out, are we?" He tracked her gaze to the ghostly figure. "Interesting."

"You ask a lot of questions."

"That's my job. Informant for Red, ya know." He jerked his chin out in pride. "I'm her top dog."

Ally leaned back against the wall and regarded him with a cool expression. "Doesn't she already have one of those? Big ears, sharp teeth, not as ugly as you?"

AJ laughed and stuffed his hands into the pockets of his black leather jacket. "Something like that. I'm her eyes, ears, *and* teeth. But I haven't met a girl that doesn't like my bite." He winked. Ally wrinkled her nose in disgust and he laughed again.

"Why do you shave designs in your hair?" she asked, jerking her chin toward his buzzed head. She wanted to change the subject, be cool about it, and insult him in one go.

He brushed his palm against the side of his head, as if striking a pose. "It's dope, classy, and intimidating."

"It's boyish, ugly, and pathetic."

"Well," he said, touching his hand against his chest with a small smile, "I'm hurt but not surprised. If you're going to just stand around insulting my hair instead of enjoying my company, I guess I will leave you to it."

"That's the idea," Ally muttered. She turned to peek around at McKennis again. Still just standing there staring. "What's his problem?"

AJ stepped forward to stand right behind her. Ally stiffened but forced herself not to move away. This was *her* job.

"Allan McKennis?"

"Yeah. Know anything about him?" When AJ didn't immediately answer, she cut him a sideways glance. "What, I thought you were Red's eyes and ears and knew everything. You really can't tell me anything?"

In the dim streetlight, she saw his mouth pull up into a mocking grin. "Ah, but no something for nothing. Tell me why you want to know."

"I'm doing a job." Even as she said it, her shoulders straightened and chin lifted. She had a job. She was *doing* something. "Somebody is paying me to find out more about him."

"Who he's selling to, you mean?"

Ally's sharp gaze darted back to him. "How do you know that?"

"I'm trying to figure out the same thing. Whoever the new seller is, they aren't on Red's radar."

"They aren't on my boss's either," Ally conceded.

AJ nodded his head toward McKennis. "His parents worked for King. The wife messed up a job and got hacked to pieces—that was kind of King's thing, the way he dealt with people. They forced her husband to watch. He went crazy and took the other kids on this tiny boat out in the middle of the ocean, like he could actually run away. McKennis thought he was insane and wouldn't get on the boat. I guess he didn't think his dad would actually do it. But the big guy did, and McKennis watched the rest of his family drown in the waves from the shore. He's been a hard user ever since."

Ally shivered, and she blamed it on the chilly night air though her cloak shielded her well enough. "Where does he stand with Red?"

"He was a Black Card, of course—everyone was, back in King's day. He supported Red for taking King out, but he's not affiliated anymore. And he's so strung out on vac all the time that he's not worth trying to recruit. The only people who care are the ones that sell to him since he's such a consistent customer."

So that's why Smoky Man wants to know what's going on. "So he went crazy like his dad and now just stares at the ocean all night?" Even just saying the words out loud made Ally's bones ache and her stomach tie itself in knots. She ignored it.

AJ shrugged. "Does he look sane to you? One thing you learn in this line of work is everyone's got a tragedy. Some of them more stupid than others, but nothing motivates people more than pain." Out of the corner of her eye, she saw him say it with a sadistic smile that Ally both wanted to appreciate and lean away from. "What's yours?"

"My what?"

"Tragedy."

"Tragedy is only a word used by pathetic people," she answered with a scoff.

"Deflecting type then. Interesting. Combined with the emo-slash-medieval cloak and constant glare, I'm guessing daddy issues?"

Ally scowled. "Is this really how you do your job?"

He shrugged. "You'd be surprised how much the direct approach works in the right circumstances."

"Fine then. What's yours?"

"I'm irresistible to women."

She rolled her eyes. "You're pathetic."

"Is pathetic your favorite word?"

That made Ally stop and think for a second. Did she have a favorite word? Did she know enough words to have a favorite? Then she realized she sounded like Riley and shrugged. "It describes most things and most people."

"Fair enough. If you're staking out McKennis too, maybe we could help each other. You could learn at the master's feet."

Ally rolled her eyes. "Not interested. I'm only one day on the job and I already discovered something." She straightened her shoulders with importance. "McKennis made a stop at a place called Crims."

AJ laughed. "The Crims tent is common knowledge for everyone, so I'm sure your boss knows about it too. Won't get you far—used to be a circus tent back in the day for the Crimson Troupe. Now Pat's runnin' the place, but her stuff is crap, so people mostly just use the space. Everyone knows Ricky has the best stuff if you can afford it."

Ally just stared at him in annoyance, filing away that information. So she hadn't made a big break like she thought. She still knew more than the average newbie in this town.

At her expression, AJ held his hand out. "Come on, Als, clearly you need the help."

"I don't *need* your help," she growled back.

"I don't *need* your help either. But I know how to take advantage of the right opportunity. And it's an opportunity for you too, isn't it? Everything I see gets back to Red. From what I hear, you'd like to make an impression."

At that, she turned around to face him completely, watching his expression. "So basically you're asking me to do your job for you and you'll talk me up to Red."

AJ flashed her a wolf smile. "Something like that."

Ally wanted to be one of Red's wolves so badly. When was the last time AJ had been scared of anything? From what she could tell, he just walked around the place like he owned it. Because he'd bought himself protection, earned it, and now had a place here, in Red's ranks. If she had his resources, her skills, and the rock? She'd be unstoppable. Red would have no choice but to take her on as one of her own.

I want a place. She wanted it more than anything. *I want a place and I want to be able to give one to Jesper too.*

I want to escape Monty, just like she always hoped I would.

I could do it too. And she'd be so proud of me.

Wouldn't she be proud of me?

"So?" AJ asked, snapping her back to the sound of the ocean waves in the night and the stench of McKennis's family tragedy. "What do you say?"

Ally turned to face him completely, ignoring his teasing grin and she puffed herself up proudly. Let him underestimate her too. She couldn't wait to prove him wrong.

"Show me the way."

* * * * * * *

Jesper had no idea what to expect from their 'adventure.' Something similar in the Molds would've been breaking into a house, starting something on fire, or getting into a fight. He didn't *think* Kat and H had anything like that in mind, but, really how was he to know how things worked?

Within the first hour, though, Jesper realized the only sparring going on was with words. The girls talked about everything, offering up bits of information and then rolling onto the next thing at frightening speed, like the car racers that tore down Heartland Avenue for money. He could barely follow along, but even still, he learned so many things he didn't know.

Like that Riley's mom had a disease called Depression, which explained why she almost always stayed in bed and lived as if in a daze. Jesper had just thought that's what all moms were like.

Or that H was vegan, which explained why Mama March had marked a 'V' on one of the food bags. H's eyes lit up with so much animation, he couldn't help but be enraptured, even if he didn't quite understand why not eating certain things helped combat what she called "humanity's mass murder of beautiful animals." He admired her passionate dedication.

Or that Kat often spent time on a dating app and had kissed either sixty-two or seventy-five guys in her life (H said the first; Kat said the second). Jesper's face had gone bright red, and Kat laughed.

"Aw look at him! What about you, Jesper, did you leave behind any broken hearts in your kingdom?"

Jesper blushed deeper and shook his head.

"Not even one?"

H snorted. "Not all of us make it a goal to get around town twice, Kat."

Kat just smirked back. "Jealous much?" she sang. Then she picked up her phone and scrolled through dozens of pictures of men, all ranging in looks and ages, telling Jesper about each one.

"You...you are with...all of them?" he asked, incredulous. He didn't remember much about courtship, but he was pretty sure the whole point was to end up with just one person.

H burst out laughing, smacking the wheel with her palm.

A grin spread on Kat's face. "They don't really know about each other. Keep my secret, okay kitten?"

"Yeah," H laughed, "'cause it's *such* a secret."

Jesper smiled at H's laugh—it was so rare to not admire. He glanced at her in the mirror above her head. "Do you have a...the dat-ing app?"

"I wish!" Kat exclaimed.

"No." H firmly shook her head. "Not for me, you know?"

"It's because she's still hung up on Nez. They broke up last year and despite being such a fine catch, your girl still hasn't moved on."

H rolled her eyes. "Past is past, Kat. I'm over it."

"Then move on!"

"Keep singin' that same tune, Kat. Nobody's listening."

Kat just turned and winked at him, like they shared a joke, and Jesper beamed. Despite everybody else's complaints, he liked listening to Kat ramble on. After years of being trapped in the void of the Molds, her constant over the top bubbliness was a welcome relief that he'd come to rely on.

As they drove, they left the dirty city of Ducat behind. The high and broken buildings disappeared and the sky opened up into a wide new world, empty of crumbling walls and grimy gutters. Jesper watched out the window in fascination. He didn't know how a place could remind him of the vastness of the Molds and yet be so completely different.

"Why do you stay?" he asked during one of the few breaks in the girls talking. "In Du...in Ducat."

Kat shrugged, the question not interesting enough for her.

"I don't know," H said. "We just do. Ducat leaves a stain on you. Even though you *can* leave, technically, you can't, you know?"

Jesper nodded. Just like the Molds.

"But that doesn't mean nobody ever does," Kat said. "Riley could be out of here if he wanted to."

That perked Jesper up. Sure, he didn't plan on staying in Ducat forever—he had to get home—but the thought of Riley leaving sent a clean slice of pain in his chest. "Why?"

"He's one of the few around here with a brain."

H nodded. "Ry's different. He actually had scholarships to a lot of different colleges. They wanted him, even though he was from this wasteland."

"He was stupid not to take them," Kat muttered.

"And where would we all be if he had?" H snapped back. Then she glanced in the rearview mirror, as if she sensed Jesper stiffen at her tone, and sighed. "He *was* stupid not to take them. Sometimes I wish he would've."

While it had been nice to sit back during the drive, the jostling of the car didn't help Jesper's injuries much, and he breathed a sigh of relief when Kat announced they had arrived.

Going slowly, he eased himself out of the backseat and looked around, then sucked in a sharp breath. They were in the middle of nowhere: the road they'd come from looked like it stretched on into nothing. Ahead, the hard surface turned into sand, and the sand into water. A little bubble of ocean seeped in, spreading out forever in every direction. The air smelled salty and clean, no fumes or mold or blood anywhere, and it seemed to cleanse his lungs as he breathed it in.

He imagined what it would have been like if he and Ally lived here instead: still a big expanse of nothing, but accidental and pure in the way the Molds were intentional and rotten. If he breathed enough of this air, would it cleanse him completely? Could it possibly be enough to wash away where he'd come from, what he'd been, the stain that his father left on him? He could be someone else. Some*thing* else than just Monty's pathetic son that would grow up to be just as awful.

Was that his biggest fear? Even more than losing Ally? He'd try to bury that terror as deep and dark as possible, but sometimes at night he dreamed they ended up just like their parents. He knew the history. It would be just too easy.

It's too late for you, he could hear his father saying. *What's done is done.*

He nearly doubled over at the punch of guilt to his gut, and he felt sick as he looked around at the perfect serenity.

No, Monty's voice didn't belong here. It would taint the beautiful place, this little piece of the world Jesper had found and wanted to take for himself. Using all his mental strength, he shut Monty's voice from out of his head. His palms actually broke out in sweat from the effort, but Jesper was determined.

Not here. Please, not here. Just give me one place of peace.

When Kat came back, they all sat on the blanket and opened up their sacks from Harriet. At first, Jesper wouldn't take one, sure that it hadn't been meant for him even though there were three. He protested until Kat dropped one in his lap.

"It's for you, kitten, I promise. Now eat it before I do." That made Jesper gape and try to hand it back over, but Kat pushed it away. "I'm kidding! Come on, Jes, just take it and say thank you."

"Thank you."

"Besides," she went on as she bit into a yellow bar of bread, "you would be stupid to turn one of these babies down. Mama March came straight outta New Orleans and can cook with the best of them." Then she turned to her giant purple bag and dug around in it until she found a jar. Thanks to his job and Riley's never-ending patience, he recognized the words on the label: peanut butter.

"That's disgusting," H said as Kat dipped her yellow bread into the jar.

"You say that every time, and I will never be offended." She offered the jar to Jesper. "You wanna try, kitten? It's called cornbread cakes Arlo Style."

H wrinkled her nose and shook her head at him. Kat broke into her wide smile and cocked her head, like a little kitten, and Jesper shrugged. The air here empowered him. When he nodded, Kat whooped in victory and helped him scoop some peanut butter onto his little cake. When he took a bite, his eyes widened. How could something taste like so many different things at once? He felt overwhelmed by all the contrasting flavors, but he couldn't stop himself. It was magic.

Kat cackled with glee when Jesper reached for more, and H rolled her eyes, trying to use her food to hide the small smile playing on her lips. Jesper thought if he could stay here with a jar of peanut butter for the rest of his life, it would be the happiest he ever thought he could be.

"What's Arlo?" he asked in between licking his fingers. When had he ever licked his fingers for pure pleasure instead of desperation?

Crumbs fell from Kat's mouth as she answered, "Not a what. Who."

"Riley's grandad," H said with a soft smile. "One of the greats."

Kat's eyes widened, realizing Jesper had never heard this great story, and so he sat back and ate while the girls told him all about Arlo McFry.

Arlo's parents came to America from China before he was born. His investor father had a lot of money, an eye for successful business, and no room for anything outside the traditions he'd been raised in. He believed that had brought him to prosperity, and he struggled with his son Arlo, who constantly tried to push the boundaries. When Arlo was eight years old, he heard jazz music for the first time and fell in love instantly.

"Arlo McFry wasn't even his real name," H said. "He changed it because two of his favorite sax players were Arlo Jackson and Marvin McFry."

Kat shook her head as she licked peanut butter off her own fingers too. "Goals, honestly."

At fifteen, Arlo got kicked out of his house, so he played sax on the streets and earned just enough money to make it to his dreamland: New Orleans. He was young, but talented, and he found a jazz band willing to take him on. During a performance, someone in the audience got so into the music that he threw his bowler hat onto the stage. Arlo picked it up, put it on, and never took it off.

"He *lived* for that hat," Kat said. "He worshiped it. He became known for it. Even if you didn't know who Arlo was by his name—which, let's be real here, made you a loser— you'd recognize the Chinese sax player in the bowler hat that performed actual musical miracles with his saxophone."

H smiled. "He actually wanted to name his first son, Riley's uncle, Bowler Hat. That didn't fly, of course, but he got the last name Hatton to stick. Marla was a saint."

After a few years of making his name, Arlo met a girl and they fell deeply in love. Her dad didn't like him very much since he didn't have a steady job, so they were going to run off and get married. When her dad's job changed, he made her move to Washington with the family. Within a year, her dad sent Arlo her wedding invitation. Arlo was crushed.

But he kept playing and eventually met a woman named Marla. They got married and had two boys together. When the boys were young, Marla's aunt got sick, and since nobody else could take care of her, Marla volunteered. But the traveling wore on her, and after a while she decided she wanted to move the family up to Washington. Arlo was angry and refused to leave his home, but eventually he agreed just for his sons.

Jesper got stuck on that last part. Kat snapped her fingers at him when she realized she'd lost him, and he was grateful she pulled him out before he fell down that hole.

"So." Kat wagged her eyebrows. "They live in Washington for a few years, then guess who he bumps into one day?"

"The one he loved?" Jesper guessed.

"Ding ding! Correct. They are both married, but they pick it back up right where they left off. They don't even try to hide the affair that well. It was *that* crazy. Eventually their spouses found out and they were both so angry, they got divorced and married each other. Like, what?" Her pink-rimmed eyes widened dramatically. "But it gets. Even. Crazier. Can you guess?"

Jesper shook his head, mesmerized.

"Guess who the woman was?"

"I don't know."

She sighed. "Guess, Jes."

"Um...you?"

H snickered and Kat threw them both a dark look, but she also grinned, so Jesper didn't think she was actually mad.

"I would be *lucky* to do as well as Arlo McFry. No, the sweeping heroine of this romance saga is none other than the OG Queen of All, Harriet March!"

Jesper gaped. No, he couldn't have guessed that.

"Can you believe that?" Kat crowed. "So Arlo marries Harriet, Chris and Marla get married, and the kids have the weirdest mixed family thing going on. It's messy for a while, hearts are broken and everyone leaves to start anew, but Arlo's sons stick around because even though he hurt their mom, Arlo is just impossible not to love. Impossible. Not long after, Riley is born and the world becomes a substantially duller but better place."

"Arlo gave him his first beanie," H added. "When he was, like, six or something. He totally passed on the hat obsession. He was always telling us to show our soul to the world." She tapped her nose. "I got my nose ring without telling anyone, and when I came home, Daddy and Mama March started to chew me out, but Arlo blew on his sax until they shut up and told me he loved it." She lowered her voice in an impression. "'Ain't nothin' wrong with a girl expressin' herself, Mama. She's just showin' us her soul. A beautiful one too.'"

Kat nodded. "A legend."

Silence settled, drying the paint of the image they had drawn in Jesper's mind. He had never wanted to meet anyone before, especially since all the grown men in his life were ones to run away from. But something in his bones yearned to meet Arlo, to see it for himself, to ask him questions.

How did you do it? How did you become what you did? The girls weren't even his, really, but they were talking about him as if they were part of the bloodline.

Family is also who you find along the way.

"Where is he?" Jesper asked, breaking the soft silence.

The lighthearted mood plummeted into the cold ocean. "Cancer." Kat kicked at the dirt and H dropped her head. "Played his sax 'til the very end though. We buried him in his hat."

"Rest in peace," H murmured.

They stayed still for a minute, out of some kind of respect Jesper wasn't sure he had the right to give, but he wanted to. The thought of a man, a good man, and man who made mistakes but a man who still did right, who left a good mark on his family, who was brave enough to take a different path than his father, whose sons grew up to be as good as Riley and whose daughters would ask for rest for his soul rather than spit on his grave...that was something worth Jesper's reverence.

Maybe, just maybe, it could be possible for Jesper too.

After a minute, Kat reached for her phone and turned on music. It wasn't anything like the slow strum in the coffee house or the heavy beats that often poured out of H's headphones—no kind of music Jesper had heard before. The sounds slid into each other like spreading butter, rolling and weaving and melting into something smooth and soulful. They didn't say it, but somehow he knew it was Arlo's music.

The song flooded the air and wrapped around Jesper as he sat with two people that had never hurt him and called him Jes, watching the sun dip into the vast ocean. And for the first time since his mother died and left them all alone, Jesper could finally breathe.

* * * * * * *

Ally's week was up.

The sun thrust the last of its rays into the cloudy sky as she made her way down Heartland. Night was settling on her seventh day of probation, and there was still so much left to do.

Despite the fact that she had approached Smoky Man from behind, he started talking to her the moment she turned the corner.

"Hey there chickadee," he called, puffing away. "Wanna go someplace dragons roam and tell stories from the skies?"

Ally rolled her eyes as she came face to face with him. Nothing had changed about him—still high and crazy. He had different clothes, though, since they'd last talked, so apparently he had a place somewhere, but he still wore a hat she now recognized was like Riley's. She frowned. Maybe everyone who wore those stupid beanie hats were insane.

"McKennis is a pawn," Ally said. "He's strung out and thinks he needs a higher dose, and someone else offered him that in exchange for being his runner. He's definitely betraying you, and selling out your other customers too, but I don't think it's a regular. Somebody new."

Smoky Man bit on his stick and watched her with narrowed eyes, then blew a cloud of smoke into her face. "Interesting, chickadee. But how do I know you ain't lyin'?"

"McKennis will tell you himself." She handed over a folded slip of paper with an address written. Ally had to lie through her teeth to get AJ to write it for her without admitting she couldn't. "Right now he's tied up in the basement of a tattoo place. It took me about twenty-eight minutes to make him talk, but I think he'll be quicker the next time around."

He laughed in a way that made Ally's hands ball into fists. "That's cute, love, but this isn't schoolyard politics. What makes you think he'll tell me who his buyer is?"

"He won't have to. That basement is his meeting spot with the buyer. They're under the impression a deal is going down between them and McKennis in forty-five minutes." She nodded at the paper in his hand. "You get there in time, you'll get them both."

Now he sat silent, mouth halfway open and smoke stick dangling out. Ally's pulse raced with exhilaration.

Look at what I'm doing for us, she wanted to tell Jes. *Wouldn't she be proud of me?*

She'd be proud.

Wouldn't she?

"Name's Ricky." Smoky Man held out his hand. "And you've got yourself a gig, love."

Ally grinned and shook his hand.

CHAPTER 7

VANISHING ACT

Time hadn't meant much in the Molds. With its perpetual yellow haze that stuck to the air even in the dark, and absence of any kind of structure—academy or work or anything besides sitting home and trying not to die—time had melted into one blob that rolled over Jesper as one day morphed into the next. And the next. Again and again. Survival was no respecter of time, and time waited for nobody.

Here in Ducat, though, Jesper had things he needed to pay attention to. Like what time his shifts at Miguel's started, or when the unspoken curfew hit and for safety he needed to get inside. Some were even more subtle. Like when Kat's favorite show was on or when Riley had an important homework deadline. And now that he tried to keep track of time, it amazed him how fast it went.

Almost three months had passed since Jesper and Ally had washed up in Ducat and stumbled into Riley's apartment. That sounded like a lot to Jesper, but, then again, he wasn't really used to what months usually felt like. He found himself thinking more of Ducat and less of the Molds. Did he even remember what it looked like? Their house, their room, their father...sometimes the images became murky in his mind. Did people normally start to forget after they'd been away from home for three months? Or was he doing it on purpose by accident?

Jesper couldn't allow himself to fall down that rabbit hole. The guilt would suffocate him.

So he didn't. He focused on his routine. He took on more shifts at Miguel's. He'd come home and do some reading exercises with Riley until everyone—usually Kat and H, but sometimes others he met like Torsen and Cath who used to stay with Riley—showed up for dinner. Even though Jesper found new people to be scary, it wasn't *as* scary to meet them with Riley, H, or Kat around. Turned out, some people could be pretty nice with some interesting stories. Not *everyone* was out to hurt someone.

Torsen liked cars and this game where he helped animals cross the street. Or something like that. He loved to find things and take them apart and then build them back bigger or better. He'd been working for Red, fixing up anything and everything she needed. But something happened (Torsen didn't go into details and Jesper didn't ask for them) and he decided he wanted out. So he came to Riley, full of shame because Torsen used to hate him. But Riley buried the past and helped Torsen get out. He had stayed here during the process just like Jesper did—and many others before, he found out.

Cath had a similar story, but she wasn't afraid of sharing all the details. She'd been an enforcer for King, then Red after, and had supported Red in her overthrow of King. Cath had done a lot of things. A lot of things that made Jesper's stomach turn. But after a gruesome murder of a girl the same age that her daughter would've been, something inside her broke. She didn't want to keep it up. Like Torsen, she'd been cast out on the dangerous streets with a target on her back, and found a home at Riley's. He helped her change her ways, and she got a permanent inking, called a tattoo, during that period.

"It's so I don't forget," she said, pointing to the crimson tear tattooed on her cheek, just below her right eye. "So every time that I look in the mirror, I remember what I was. And what I will never be again. If you forget, you get careless. So I made sure I won't."

Jesper had seen quite a few tattoos on Pepperjack's thugs, but Cath's tear was his favorite by far. The second time she came over, he dredged up some bravery and asked her how she got the tattoo. Everyone—Riley, H, Kat, Torsen, Cath— glanced at him in surprise. He had practiced talking more around the apartment, and H even more at Miguel's, but still, especially compared to Kat, he stayed pretty silent.

Cath, thankfully, didn't miss a beat. "There's a place on Heartland down from the gas station. If you go anywhere, go there. Elanore will take care of you."

The thought hit him that maybe if Monty had gotten a tattoo to remind him, things would've turned out differently. The rebellion caused his stomach to lurch so violently, that he had to excuse himself to vomit up his food in the bathroom. As he flushed it all away, he hung his head. What a waste of food. But when he glanced up in the mirror and saw his face, he imagined having a tattoo.

Maybe he would get one someday. So he didn't forget. Like Monty had.

If you forget, you get careless.

He splashed water over his face, as if he could just wash off the sins of his father. Scrubbing at his cheeks, like he could wash away any residue Monty left on him. But when he looked back at himself in the mirror, despite the water dripping down his chin, he could still see the reflection of Monty's haunted eyes in his own. Would that harden into hatred one day? Would there be a time when Jesper would only recognize his own reflection because it mirrored his father's?

"No," he whispered to his reflection, still tasting the residue of vomit in his mouth. He thought of Arlo playing his sax in his beloved hat. "I won't forget. I can be something else." His voice wobbled, but the words held strong.

It wasn't just Riley's friends that taught Jesper these new things with their old stories. The more H and Jesper became...well he wasn't sure they were *friends*—what qualifications did you have to have to call it a friendship? Did you need a certificate or something? He hadn't found the right way to ask yet—but they were friendly with each other. H had taken an interest in Jesper that he couldn't understand, but he found himself constantly grateful for it. She even put down her phone to talk to him more than she did with Kat.

As time wore on, she talked to him more about misadventures with Kat, or growing up with Riley, or her thoughts on the world. He learned that someone close to her and Riley (Jesper didn't know who and didn't ask) had been cut to pieces in a brutal execution by King. Shortly after, she'd accidentally wandered into a butcher shop and saw a cow being sliced up. She went home and didn't eat for almost a week— her grandma became worried she would starve herself to death—and after that she became vegan.

"I talk about the politics of it because that's what Kat would understand," H told him one time when they were cleaning coffee machines. "Plus I wouldn't want to hurt Ry by talkin' like that. But it's really because I just can't stand it. Just the sight of raw meat will keep me up for days."

The conversations they had in the coffee shop were the deepest, most real talks Jesper had ever had. If it weren't for the fact that H couldn't stand Alex, Jesper would wonder if 'co-worker' actually stood for a different, stronger meaning of 'friend.'

Their relationship also brought Jesper closer to the infamous Mama March herself. Somehow, Jesper had proven himself worthy to H, and she brought him around her grandma's apartment a couple times a week. Sometimes they just stopped in to grab a change of clothes for H or a few bags of cornbread cakes.

The third time they stopped by, Mama March shocked Jesper into immovability by giving him a giant hug the second he walked in the door. His skin prickled at her warmth, nearly scalding him. He got so dizzy that H had to steady him.

But despite Jesper's admittedly rude response, Mama March just grinned at him. "Welcome home Jesper." When he furrowed his eyebrows in bewildered confusion, she turned her gaze to H. "Now what do I always say?"

H sighed and rolled her eyes. "Any friend of Mama March has a home with Mama March."

"That's right, that's right." She turned back to Jesper, the wrinkles in her face folding over as she smiled at him again. "You remind Mama so much of Riley. He's like my other son, that kid. Couldn't be prouder of him."

Jesper's eyes widened and he shook his head in disbelief. "Oh I...I don't kn-know. I mean that's...like Riley isn't...I am..."

I am bad. I come from bad. I could never be like Riley.

But Mama March just fussed over him, fixing his hair. "Now, Jesper, Mama has seen a lotta bad folks in my time. Lotta good ones too. But golden ones, now they're the rare ones. Riley's a golden one. My granddaughter is too. Mama's got an eye for gold, and I can see that's you."

Jesper ducked his head as he felt his face flush. But he couldn't stop smiling. Even when Mama March ran her fingers through his shaggy hair and declared she would give him a haircut.

And the next week, she did just that. She cut off all the hair that had grown scraggly and curled over his ears. H complained she'd done it way too short despite Mama's insistence that it was dashing, but when Jesper looked in the mirror, he found he loved the way his hair now spiked up toward the sky. He no longer looked like an overgrown weed in the Molds that had been forgotten and left to die.

"Thank you," he told Mama March again and again. It blew him away how changing his hair felt like a new start. "Thank you very much."

Jesper would never admit it to anyone, but he went to the bathroom more just so he could look at his hair in the mirror. And afterwards when Mama March opened her stout arms for one of her giant hugs, Jesper bent himself over to return it wholeheartedly.

"Such a respectful boy," Mama March said, patting his back. "Arlo would've loved you." Jesper beamed. Then she rushed to take her fresh batch of cornbread cakes out of the oven, having already left a jar of peanut butter on the counter he could take to share with Kat for their Meryl Streep movie night. The next one on their list was about a devil that liked to wear fancy shoes. Or something. Jesper hoped it wasn't too scary. The one they'd watched the other night had lots of singing on a pretty island. He would love to watch it again. Everybody had seemed so carelessly joyful, and they all danced to every song even if they were bad at it. Jesper would love to visit that island.

The only thing that would've made the night better was if Ally had stayed to watch the movie too. Her new job at the gas station kept her pretty busy; he hardly ever saw her any more for longer than an evening, and even that only happened every few days. Jesper missed her, but at the same time, that's what their relationship had been like for years. Except now, she didn't leave him alone anymore. He had other people now too. And when she did stay for dinner, she talked about how great her job was going, how much she had learned, how much she loved it in Ducat. It made Jesper happy.

Happiness. It had always seemed like a faraway ideal that could never be reached, at least not by Jesper. And now here he was, with new hair and a mother that didn't hate to mother him and friendly people who waited for him to come home safely.

Nobody had brought up Elaria in a long time. A day didn't go by when he didn't think of it, but he didn't want to ruin the peace he had found. Was that so bad? Wasn't it okay for him to appreciate what he had while he had it?

Truthfully, each day he didn't try to go back added a new weight of guilt on his shoulders. It made him sick at night. But he told himself he was still going home. He had things to do, but he still would go. Eventually.

Sometimes the guilt would wake him up in the middle of the night. He'd go into the bathroom in case he threw up. He'd stand at the sink and scrub at his face. But when he'd look back in the mirror, he'd still see Monty's eyes staring back at him.

* * * * * * *

When Jesper got to work that day, he found H wiping off counters with her earbuds in. She took them out once she saw him, and he caught a glimpse of what she had been listening to on her phone—too fast for him to try and read, but he recognized the picture. It was a talking show called a podcast. Kat had seen it on H's phone a few days earlier and had made fun of how boring they were. H had snatched her phone back and said Riley had made her download it.

H caught him looking at her phone and raised an eyebrow. "What, snoop?"

"I thought…I thought Riley made you. Made you listen to tho-those."

H shrugged, her eyes on her earbuds as she carefully wound them up. Strange. She usually just shoved them in her bag. "Okay, maybe Riley's not *making* me. But Kat doesn't need to know that, all right? I'd never hear the end of it." Jesper gave a faint grin and nodded. H glanced down at her phone. "Speaking of, she won't text me back. Stupid vlog takes up all her time."

For the twelfth time that morning, Jesper patted his pocket and straightened with pride when he felt his own phone still safely secured. Ally had given it to him over the weekend, having bought each of them one with the money she earned. It wasn't the fancy touch kind like everyone else had—she'd called it a 'burner flip phone'—but Jesper couldn't be prouder. That night he had spent an hour carefully typing everyone's name and number into his contacts.

223

Now he understood why Kat and H practically kept their phones stuck to their hands at all times. He could just *talk* to someone, whenever he wanted. If something bad happened. If something good happened. If he wanted to tell Kat that they should watch his favorite Meryl Streep movie again that night, he could just text her, and he would get a bunch of exclamation points and pictures of pink cats smiling.

Magic, right at his fingertips. If he didn't love it so much, he'd be almost angry that he'd been deprived of it his whole life.

The day was slow, so after cleaning all the machines twice, Jesper took out his phone and spent fifteen minutes typing out a message to Ally:

HI HAVE GR8 DAY JESPER

Then he sent a similar one to Kat before putting his phone away to clean the tables.

H had been right: the vlog did take up all of Kat's time. She didn't show up for dinner that night, which wasn't the strangest thing since she always had something going on, but when Jesper and H got to work the next day, she still hadn't texted either of them back.

Sure, Kat wasn't known for being reliable—even Jesper knew that—but she *always* had her phone.

"Nobody else is even concerned," H complained, watching Jesper put an espresso shake together. "I mean, yeah, sure, Kat is the flakiest flake I've ever met, but it's been *four days*. She would've texted me back."

Jesper reached for his phone. "Should I try...try to call her?"

"Yeah, tried that already."

That night at dinner—just H, Riley, and Jesper—she brought it up again.

"I hear you," Riley said, "but I'm sure she's fine. Remember when Beyonce's album dropped? Or when the last season of Kardashians released? She didn't come out for a week."

H grumbled, "I know. It's just…"

"You're annoyed she won't text you back."

"Am not," she snapped.

"Look, the last time I went looking for Kat when she didn't want to be found, she filled all my shoes with mud and tried to flush one of my beanies down the toilet." Riley laughed softly. "We need to give our Kat license to wander or she'll never come home."

"I know." H sighed and slumped back in her chair, the harsh annoyance draining from her expression. She stared at her plate. "I'm just…with Mary Ann. I'm worried."

Jesper's eyebrows furrowed as he shoved another bite of spaghetti in his mouth. He *loved* spaghetti. The delicious sauce had little bits of tomato, and the lump of long noodles always captivated him. He found comfort in the fact they could be all tangled and confused and still tasted so good.

Mary Ann…he'd heard the name before, mentioned by Kat in passing once or twice. A tense stillness settled over the table as Riley took the name in. Jesper stopped eating. His limbs stiffened as his eyes flicked back and forth between the two of them.

Riley pursed his lips. "You really think—"

"I don't know what to think, Ry, that's the point," H exclaimed in exasperation. "I'm probably wrong. I hope I'm wrong. If Kat knew I was even thinkin' it, she'd be pissed. But I just can't shake it."

He gave a curt nod and glanced at the clock. "It's not too late. I'll head down to West End and see if I can find her."

"No, I'll go."

"Absolutely no—"

"You have a deadline," H reminded him, gesturing to the textbook and notebooks that littered around his plate like soggy leaves. "Besides, it'll be better comin' from us. Can't risk another one of your beanies gettin' flushed."

Riley's eyebrow arched to the line of his blue beanie. "Us?"

"Yeah." H sat up straight and folded her arms. "Me and Jes."

Jesper's eyes widened. She wanted him to go with her? He'd never really been picked for anything before.

Riley glanced at him in question, and Jesper didn't hesitate before nodding. "I'll go."

"Like you said," H went on, "it's probably nothin'. We'll just make sure and then come straight back. An hour tops."

With a sigh, Riley sat back and rubbed his hands over his face. Both Jesper and H perched on the edge of their seats in anticipation.

When he finally spoke, his voice sounded as tired as he looked. "Listen to me, Harriet Maybelle March, you will *drive* straight there, you will keep your phone on you at all times, you will knock on Mary Ann's door, you will be the perfect picture of polite, and then you will come straight back. You will call me if *anything* even smells wrong. Do you understand me?"

The stern edge to his tone surprised Jesper and set his nerves on edge, and he half expected H to fight back—her usual style. But she surprised him too.

"I will," she said, her hair bopping up and down as she nodded fast. "I swear. We'll be fine."

Riley's hands dropped from his face and he looked at Jesper. "You sure you're up for this, Jes? West End isn't the nicest place."

Fear curled tight in Jesper's stomach. Or maybe it was spaghetti noodles. Either way, he felt a little bit sick, but a certainty coursed through him as he glanced at H's hopeful face. A surge of protectiveness overcame him when he looked at her, or thought of Kat waltzing in to bring him marshmallows after he'd been mugged.

Jesper nodded. "Anything for Kat."

* * * * * * *

The last few months had been some of the best of Ally's life. Not that she really had much competition in her short, sad life since her mother died, but still.

She'd thought having a job and reporting to somebody would be the worst thing in the world—turned out, that was only the case when working at stupid coffee shops with stupid H. Everything about that situation had held Ally back. Probably purposefully so. But working with Ricky taught her so many things and opened possibilities for her future right up.

Possibilities. The freedom to even have possibilities had seemed so foreign. But now here she was, making her own life.

This life also gave her independence, namely from Riley. She went back to his place less and less, choosing to stay in one of AJ's empty places if she needed to crash. The time on her own had helped her learn more than Riley ever had, arming her with knowledge that mattered: knowledge she could use against people, knowledge she could protect herself with.

Of course, Jes had stayed with Riley. She hadn't created enough stability for the two of them yet, so she hadn't presented her plan. But she did have a plan. Once it was ready, she knew she'd be able to convince Jesper to stay with her in Ducat, and she could finally give back to her brother what he had given her all these years.

She did go back to Riley's every now and then, just to make sure they hadn't done anything to her brother. Riley himself looked busier than ever and she didn't talk to him much. But Kat and H had picked up the annoying habit of acting like Jesper's best friends. They cut off all his hair and convinced him to dip everything in peanut butter. They forced him to watch despicable movies in the name of fun, surely trying to indoctrinate and confuse him so his guard would constantly be down and they could control him. She'd seen part of one of the movies: everyone had sat around singing instead of doing anything productive, and the moral of the story was that everyone could just get along.

Absolute garbage.

Ally couldn't wait to pry him out of their clutches.

"Why haven't you stolen him back already?" AJ asked her once while they were running surveillance. Ally hadn't ever talked about Jesper, but she ranted constantly about Riley, and AJ must've connected the dots. "If you want him back so bad."

"Don't talk about my brother," Ally snapped back. She rested her head back against the passenger seat. AJ's car was surprisingly clean.

"Just sayin'." He glanced in the mirror as he smoothed his ridiculous hair with his hands. "You seem like the kinda girl that takes what she wants."

A small smile curved the corner of Ally's mouth. "I am. I want to make sure when I take him back, I leave nothing left."

"Ruthless. I like it." AJ popped another fruit snack in his mouth. He had an unhealthy obsession with them. Ally much preferred jerky. The idea you could just have a giant package of dried meat on you at all times made sense to her. Every time she did a supply run, she always grabbed at least three bags—any or all flavors.

"Does Ricky know we hang out so much?"

Ally shrugged, her eyes glancing up and down the street. Still hadn't seen their target yet. "I'm sure he does. I don't really care. I still get my job done so he can't complain."

And he didn't. Ricky didn't hide the fact that he viewed Ally as his best investment. Because of her, his sales were up twenty percent, and customer loyalty had been perfected. Nobody dared cross Ally. Whoever did learned the hard way.

"I've got plans for you chickadee," Ricky had started saying. "You and me, we're gonna go far."

Ally didn't bother to correct him. They both knew she would take an offer from Red the second it came. But for now, being Ricky's right hand worked well for her.

"Where does he go?" AJ asked nonchalantly. He always tried to weasel information about Ricky's operation from Ally, which surprised her. AJ seemed to know everything that went on in Ducat. Truthfully she didn't know much about the inner workings of Ricky's craziness—he said she didn't need to know and she didn't care to. She only cared about her own name, and her reputation had slowly started to spread.

Plus, even if she knew anything, she would never tell AJ. If Red wanted to know, she could ask Ally herself. This question, though, she could answer.

"You must suck at your job then," Ally replied, digging for the last piece of jerky left in her bag. "He's always sitting on his corner. I've never met him anywhere else."

"He's never there."

"He's *always* there."

AJ shook his head. "I never see him there. Maybe a handful of times in my entire memory and only when he's running a job himself."

"Again," Ally said, ripping off a bite of jerky with her teeth, "you must suck at your job. He's right on Heartland. Everyone can see him."

"At least come up with a more interesting lie than that."

Ally started to protest. That *was* the truth. How stupid was he to miss it? But then the gate around the apartment complex across the street finally opened, stealing both their attention.

"Aha," AJ murmured, leaning forward against the steering wheel to get a better look at the girl darting out from the gate. "The rabbit finally pokes its head out of its hole."

A flash of memory hit Ally: chasing the rabbit through the Molds. She gritted her teeth and shook it from her head. "Let's go hunting then."

They waited until the girl had gone down a couple blocks before AJ started his car and they began stalking their rabbit.

She called herself Duchess, which told Ally everything she needed to know about how stupid this girl was. Twenty-four years old, long curly blonde hair, a gap between her two front teeth. She'd kept King's men cozy and satisfied during her time as a Black Card, and now Red mostly left her to her own devices. But someone had caught wind that McClain, a rival gang leader from the next town over, had infiltrated Red's ranks somehow. AJ had spent months trying to piece it together, and the trail led to little Duchess.

Ricky had wanted Ally to get more information too, in case someone making a power play tried to take his business. Inevitably, the course had put her on AJ's path, so here they were again, running a job together.

It started to rain as AJ wound the car down the road, being sure to keep a reasonable, normal speed. No need to tip Duchess off. She kept a brisk pace down Hazelwood Lane, and they almost lost her when she dodged through some apartment buildings. But through the rain, Ally saw her duck underneath a bridge and climb into a car.

"License plate," AJ reminded her lazily, but Ally didn't need it. She had already picked up her phone to take a picture of the plate. When she glared at him, he chuckled. "Just seein' if all that jerky is putting you to sleep on the job."

Whenever they rode in the car, AJ liked to sing along to the radio. "I need background music," he would say. And as the car cut through the rain puddles on the street, he sang with the guy on the radio. She thought AJ was better than the guy—who names themselves after a candy anyways? That's not scary—but she would never ever admit it.

"Here we go!" AJ gasped, turning up the music. "Queen Rihanna, let's get it!"

Ally rolled her eyes as a woman's voice blared through the speakers. "Can we focus?"

"Come on, Als, it ain't a party without Queen Rihanna. We gotta get some disturbia going on after this."

"Don't call me that."

"Why not? Aren't we friends?"

"Ha." Ally made a point to lean forward and turn the music down, her eyes never leaving the car in front of them. "I don't have friends."

"I don't either. Bad for business."

"The business of spying and murdering?"

"Yep." He popped the 'p' at an unnecessary volume. "All my friends end up dead."

He didn't sound very sorry about that. "Really? Who was your last friend that died?"

"King."

A chill shivered down Ally's spine. She glanced sideways to see a vicious, victorious smile on his face. "You say it like that was a good thing." Evidently, the death of the last gang leader didn't put him out of a job. "Why?"

"His whole act wore itself out. I got bored. Once Red made her intentions known, I knew she was the better bet." AJ smirked. "Got me a promotion, anyway."

"So you helped Red. You were one of the double agents that took King down." She did her best to not sound impressed.

"That's right. My best friend is power. Don't really care who it's coming from." He turned to give her a knowing glance. "I'm pretty good at knowing it when I see it."

Ally turned her eyes back to the car they were following, refusing to let her smile rise to her face. AJ was right about at least one thing.

"Speaking of, somebody became Ricky's favorite girl fast. I've never seen somebody rise his ranks so quickly. What's your secret, Als?"

"I'm just that good."

She thought he would argue, but instead he whistled. "I know you are. Three months you've been here and already people know your name."

Ally couldn't help but smile a bit at that, though she tried her best to sound a bit bored. "Really."

"Yeah. Ever since you took out one of the Walrus guys, you've put yourself on the map. New girl comin' in and shakin' things up…doesn't happen often. How'd you do it?"

Now that's what I like to hear. Wouldn't she be proud of me?

"Just my charm."

The song changed as the car in front of them drove past the city line, leaving the sparse city lighting and plunging them into the dark. AJ's shoulders stayed relaxed, his head lolled back against the seat. Driving in the dark didn't seem to bother him. Ally tried her best to take notes on his skill—not that she could get a car anytime soon, but it would be nice to know how to drive one, in case of emergencies.

AJ noticed her looking at him, and flashed her a devilish smile. She wasn't stupid. She trusted AJ enough to learn from him, but even that trust didn't extend far. She never dropped her guard around him. Her hand always hovered over the pocket with her rock, just in case.

"Hey, eyes on the road," Ally snapped. "The car is turning." She watched as the headlights ahead of them turned onto a side road. It had been invisible in the dark until the light spilled out over it. Where was she going?

When AJ kept driving straight, Ally whipped her head around. "What are you doing? We're going to lose her!"

"Hang tight, Als," AJ said, talking down as if to a child. "If we turned right in after her, she'd know we were following. I'm not down for a shootout tonight."

"So then what? We just go home?"

"Patience. Learn from the master."

Ally scowled and folded her arms across her chest. Sometimes she wondered if AJ was really worth the sanity.

A few minutes later, AJ turned the car too. For a moment Ally thought he would drive them straight into a bunch of trees, but once the headlights turned, she saw the tiny gravel road. Then the lights went dead.

Sensing her alarm, AJ chuckled softly. "Don't worry, I know where I'm going. Memorized these back roads a long time ago. Just don't want the lights to alert anyone we're spying."

Ally made a mental note to learn the roads too. She'd already memorized the ins and outs of Ducat. If Ricky didn't have anything else to add to her load tomorrow, she'd come back down here and start mapping it out.

The car crawled its way forward, snaking through the pitch-black night. Ally forced herself to stay calm. AJ couldn't sense her nerves. Besides, this wasn't the In Between at all. She was above ground. She wasn't lost. She was still in control.

AJ flipped the music off, then crawled forward a little more before cracking the windows open and turning the car off. A deep, final silence settled. Too thick. Ally took a breath. She'd gotten used to the constant buzzing of sound in the city. She found comfort in it. But this absolute silence suffocated her. Was that the dash of a vrykol claw?

I'm above ground. I'm in control. I will never be buried again. I'm in control. I can protect myself.

"You good, Als?" AJ whispered.

Ally shot him a scalding glare. "If you're thinking of ditching me out here, I'd think again."

He chuckled again. "Wouldn't dream of it. Listen."

Ally sat there fuming for a moment before reigning herself in. She sharpened her senses and strained her ears as she stared out into endless black. Eventually, she heard the distant sound of car tires against the gravel.

"Shortcut," AJ whispered. "Admit it. I'm a genius."

"Shh!"

Two car doors opened, then one shut. Ally pressed her ear through the open crack of the window as distant voices spoke up.

"Hey, baby," a deep voice gruffed. "You got something for me?"

Ally saw the barest shadow of AJ's head nodding. Confirmation of McClain's voice.

"You bet I do," Duchess responded. "Hope you have something for me too."

"Always." A moment of silence passed before a car door shut. More silence.

"They're in his car," AJ whispered. "We'll have to wait it out so they don't hear our car leave. Then we can take this confirmation back."

Ally had to admit, Duchess had found a brilliant place to meet, shielded by the relentless night. Any speck of light from someone following would be seen so easily and give them enough warning to get out fast. Of course, Ally could wield that power too. Spying with the same shield.

"If you want to do anything to help pass the time," AJ said, and she could hear the smirk in his words, "I wouldn't say no."

Ally scoffed. He managed to work that in at least once every time they saw each other. "In your dreams."

"Oh, I do dream about it. Frequently."

"You're pathetic."

"Just making an offer."

"And it hasn't worked out so far, so I wouldn't hold your breath."

Time dragged on. Ally could not sit still. How could anyone stand this? Confined in a tiny, uncomfortable car, no room to move, trapped and caged and just waiting? When AJ offered her fruit snacks, she took them, just to have something to do with her mouth. An entire hive of bees buzzed violently underneath her skin, screaming to be set free. They pricked her skin again and again and again. She could go crazy like this. She *would* if McClain and his little Duchess didn't hurry it up.

She felt the breath on the back of her neck first, then heard a low, grating chuckle from the backseat. The stench of ale and metal smothered AJ's citrus car freshener.

Every muscle in her body froze over.

No, not here. He couldn't find her here. She was trapped here. Trapped and lost and buried, never to see the light again. She could feel a hand from behind her, reaching out to grab her neck, and she opened her mouth to scream.

In the distance, a car door opened, making Ally jump. She could see a faint light, then heard tires roll against gravel again, retreating to silence.

"McClain will go first," AJ said, oblivious to the monster Ally was sure sat in the back of the car. "Typically she'll have to wait at least five minutes before leaving. Once she's gone, we can go."

Ally blinked. It took her a moment to understand what he said. "Just go? She's right there. Why don't we go question her?"

"I'm not on enforcement, Als. Intelligence, remember? We gathered our intel, now we go give it back to Red—or I will, and you to Ricky—then it's over. Gets handed to someone else to take care of."

Ally gritted her teeth. She had waited around in the dark like a caged prey just to go home?

In the darkness, Monty laughed, the sound sharp enough to draw blood.

Typical, she could hear him say. *Always weak.*

"That's your job," she ground out, not sure which of the men she was talking to, "not mine." She opened her door as quietly as possible, ignoring AJ's hissing protest, and left it hanging there instead of slamming it shut like she wanted. For a moment, the ground lurched under her feet. Darkness swirled around her. Was that the cry of a monster in the distance?

No. No, I'm not there. I'm not trapped. I'm in control.

Reaching in her pocket, she closed her palm around her rock. Surety coursed through her. She could breathe again. Pouring her desire into her palm, she followed the slight influence that pulled her forward until she broke through the trees and found the waiting car.

Ally crept up behind it, noting the two shadows inside—a driver in the front and Duchess in the back. Nothing she couldn't handle. The rock could knock out the driver, and with a flick of her wrist, she did exactly that. By the time AJ had found her, she had dragged Duchess out from the back seat by her hair and pinned her to the ground.

"What did you tell McClain?" Ally demanded.

Duchess struggled underneath Ally's knees. "Screw you!"

A derisive chuckle from behind her shoulder. Ally gasped and whipped her head around, catching a glimpse of a bloodstained beard.

You don't have what it takes to survive, Monty spat at her. *You never have. You're better off dead. Both of you.*

Ally swallowed hard, unable to stop the image of Jesper's corpse from assaulting her mind.

Duchess whined, reminding Ally she was there. "What are you looking at? What's out there?"

Baring her teeth, Ally turned back to glare at her. She was in control. No matter what he said, she'd never be the one cowering on the ground ever again.

I'll make a place for us, Jes. I promise.

With the first spark of the rock, Ally relaxed. When she glanced behind her shoulder again, Monty was gone.

She smiled.

Despite the dark, she had to admit the location did end up working in her favor. Nobody was around to hear Duchess scream.

* * * * * * * *

Jesper had never been to West End, and he quickly found that he never wanted to come back.

At first, he marveled at the unfamiliar set up: dozens of shiny metal boxes—trailers, H reminded him—all arranged on a big square of empty land. Night had fallen, but people were still out, sitting around little campfires, eating together, sharing smoking sticks. You obviously had to belong to be a part of the group, but it seemed like a nice group to be a part of.

It had rained earlier, and eventually H said they needed to park the car and keep going on foot. She didn't want to get stuck in the mud. As they got out and started walking, Jesper found his opinion of the trailer park changed drastically. The trailers became smaller and dirtier. Rats ran around, including huge ones with striped tails and angry eyes. The air smelled of smoke, vomit, and waste, and what few people he saw had sunken eyes and hard mouths.

It reminded him of the Molds. He'd never been closer to home since arriving in Ducat, and he hadn't felt this lost since their first day here.

"Over here," H said quietly, pointing to another cluster of trailers up ahead. She walked with her shoulders straight, eyes ahead, doing her best to hide the tension that radiated off of her tense muscles.

"Why here?" Jesper whispered back. Kat's bright pink personality didn't belong in such a colorless place.

"Kat's from here. She hates it. Usually stays with me or Ry or her newest boy, and she hardly ever comes back. She says it's bad enough she's from Ducat: she doesn't want her vlog watchers to know she's trailer trash too. Between you and me, I think that's where, like, all of her insecurities come from."

Jesper nodded. He could understand that. "But if...if she's never here...then why are we?"

"Mary Ann's her mama. Nice lady, I guess, but she's hard on vac."

"What's a vac?"

"It's like a drug—Ricky's brand. Super addictive. Wrecks you."

A shudder went through Jesper, and he picked up his pace. They had to find her in time.

"Kat's seen what it's done to her mama, and she knows she's got the same obsessive personality, so she stays far away. I worry...I worry that one of these times Kat will stop by and Mary Ann will convince her to try it." Her face hardened. "There wouldn't be much hope after that. Kat would nosedive into everything, and she knows it too. Even if she drinks, she's real careful. Growin' up by Crims does that to you. You go one way or the other."

"Crims?"

H pointed behind her shoulder. "Back that way. Used to be a big circus tent—the town was built by performers way back in the day. Anyways, it went to ruin and now Pat runs it. People just take drugs and waste away somewhere the police are paid off not to look. It's pretty terrible."

The blood drained from Jesper's face. "What if…what if she…what if she's there?"

"If someone you know ends up there, you won't see them again. Not the person you know anyways." H shivered and hunched her shoulders. "So she won't be."

After winding through what seemed like endless trailers all shoved together, H finally stopped at a rusting brown one. Jesper stayed right on her heels as she marched up to the door and banged her fist on it. Now that he had stopped moving, Jesper wondered if he would throw up his spaghetti.

"Mary Ann?" H barked. Her voice shot through the stagnant air, making Jesper wince. "You up?"

A long, painful minute passed before the door opened and a woman stepped out. Her stringy blonde hair tangled at her neck, and it seemed extra skin hung off her short frame, as if she'd once been fairly plump but had lost too much weight and her body didn't know what to do.

Her eyes narrowed, then she broke into a grin once she recognized the girl on her doorstep. Even in the dark, her teeth were yellow. "Harriet! What a pleasant surprise!"

H gritted her teeth, and Jesper could feel her straining to hold herself back. Apparently she was taking Riley's instruction to be polite to heart and it cost her. Jesper admired her fierce protection of her friends. "Kat here?"

Mary Ann's light eyebrows pulled together, crinkling her whole face. He couldn't force himself to look her in the eye. "Cheyenne? Why the devil would she be here? Haven't seen that girl in months."

"Uh huh." H took a step forward and forced herself inside. "I'll see about that."

Jesper's pulse thudded in his ears as he peeked inside the doorframe. The place was a disaster. Mounds of garbage lined the floor, the counter, the bed. A nasty stench came from the pile of rotting dishes in the small sink, and the light that shone from the ceiling had shattered, leaving an exposed bulb. Mary

Anne followed H as she blew through the trailer, calling Kat's name and looking in every corner. Jesper stood watch at the entrance. He couldn't bring himself to step inside; there wasn't much room for a third person anyway.

The search took all of two minutes—Kat wasn't here. Mary Ann hurled question after question, but H just ignored her and left, sighing in relief.

"Don't tell her we came here, all right?" H told him as they made their way through West End back to the car. "It'll just piss her off."

Jesper nodded. "I won't." The words came out like a wheeze.

H glanced at him, then did a double take. "Hey. You okay?"

He closed his eyes and nodded again, faster, though he felt lightheaded.

"Don't play with me, Jesper."

What game could they possibly be playing? He cleared his throat and opened his eyes. The ground lurched under his feet, but if he concentrated, he was fine. "I'm okay."

H raised an eyebrow, but kept walking. "Whatever. The good news is Kat isn't slummin' it with Mary Ann. She's probably just shacking up with a new sugar daddy."

Jesper flinched at the mention of Mary Ann. H stepped closer to him and slowed her pace so he could keep up. "Let's just get home."

He nodded. Yes. Home. Away. Away from here. Away from the rabbit hole in his mind before he tumbled into it. Anywhere else.

When the muddy gravel under his feet gave way to pavement, his shoulders relaxed a fraction. Until H swore, and he glanced up to see a couple people had surrounded their car.

Four guys. One of them was bigger than Jesper and H combined. Jesper immediately thought of the mugging in the alley, and his first instinct was to grab H and run. But he couldn't run very fast. Could H? Maybe he would tell her to run, then offer up the money in the beginning, and they would leave him alone.

They'd heard H, though, and as soon as Jesper skidded to a stop, the guy closest to them looked over. A grin spread across his face as he took a swig from the can in his hand, then he tossed it on the ground and elbowed his buddy next to him.

"See, Nez?" he cackled. "Told ya I recognized the car."

His friend turned to look too, and H sucked in a sharp breath, nearly tripping over her own feet. She would've if Jesper hadn't lurched forward to grab her arm.

"Are you kidding me?" she demanded, balling up her fists. "You idiots scared the shiz outta me! What are you doing?"

"What am *I* doing?" the guy—Nez—repeated. His words slurred a bit. Jesper couldn't tell if he had been mocking them or angry. "What are *you* doing this way? Not like you."

Jesper had heard that name before. He sifted through every conversation until he remembered Kat's voice talking about H's ex-boyfriend.

Oh. *Oh.* Jesper did not know what to do in this situation.

H stuck her chin out. "None of your business, Nez."

"'Bout time it should be again, don't you think?"

"Get out of the way. I'm going home."

Nez just sneered and gestured at Jesper. "What, goin' home with this beanpole? Lowered your standards, baby." His friends burst into laughter. Jesper felt stupid, but he didn't really understand how he'd been insulted.

The jeering didn't rattle H, though. She just glared at him even though she barely reached his shoulder. "You're drunk."

"Who cares?" He reached for her hand and she yanked it away, nearly smacking Jesper. "Come on now, baby, let me remind you what a real man feels like."

H gritted her teeth and her eyes narrowed into tiny, angry slits. "You're drunk," she said again. "You're drunk and you're stupid and I refuse to talk to you when you're wasted."

"I'm stupid?" he repeated, which made him sound pretty stupid. "Six months I haven't seen you, ain't even heard from you, and I get I'm *stupid?*"

"Yeah. Now get out of my way."

Jesper saw it in slow motion: H shouldered her way past Nez, reaching for the car door, his friends started laughing at him, and Nez's face darkened in a way Jesper understood.

Instinct took over his body. He lurched forward just as Nez grabbed H's shoulder, spinning her halfway back around and slapping her across the face. She staggered back and fell into the side of the car. Nez struck out again, rage bleeding from his expression, but this time Jesper was there. Nez stopped himself before his hand touched Jesper. He blinked, as if waking up from a dream, and his eyes widened in horror when he registered H bent in half clutching her cheek.

"Whoa, no, baby, no. I'm sorry, I didn't—" He reached out, H cringed away, and Jesper took a step forward.

"Don't touch her," he said quietly. "Just go."

Nez hesitated, but then he pursed his lips and stumbled back. His friends glanced at each other, either confused or shaken, but they followed his lead.

A few feet back, he tried again. "H, I—"

She just shook her head. Nez sighed in defeat and walked away.

Once he was sure they were gone, Jesper turned back to H. She'd hunched her shoulders so her head hung down and her cloud of hair covered most of her face. Through the cloud, though, he could see her hand still on her cheek and her eyes filled with tears. He'd never seen her so small; his heart ached. Without saying anything, she got back in the car and started it.

"Do you want to go home?" Jesper murmured.

She shook her head, speeding down the road. "Mama's at bingo night." He could barely hear her soft, shaky words, but he understood. She didn't want to be alone.

The drive back lasted only seconds. They walked up the stairs. Jesper opened the door for H, and they walked in to see Riley bent over his books on the table where they'd left him, exhaustion etched into his face.

"How'd it go?" he asked.

H stayed hidden in her hair as she mumbled something, then nearly ran for the hallway.

"She's tired," Jesper told him. "Kat wasn't there."

Riley nodded. "Thanks for going with her." Then he dived back into his work, and Jesper knew he wouldn't be coming out any time soon.

Steps heavy, he walked to the room he and Ally shared. Ally wasn't there, of course, but H had curled up on the bed, her back pressed into the corner.

Jesper softly shut the door, then sat across from her on the bed and leaned his head back against the wall. What a night. He felt buzzed and gutted at the same time.

When H's voice finally came through, it was rough and grasping for control. "You tell Ry?" she whispered.

"No."

Another few minutes of silence passed before she unearthed herself from her hair. Her dark eyes shone wet and fierce, and her lip trembled despite its best efforts.

"He wasn't like that," she snapped, like Jesper had accused her of something. "When we were together. He wasn't like that."

"Okay."

Her eyes narrowed. "You don't believe me."

"No...I mean, yes...yes, I-I do, I..."

"You don't believe me."

"I do." He held up his hand, asking for time, and took a breath. She huffed but gave him a second to find the right words. "I just...I don't under-understand why you feel like you have...have to tell me tha-at."

"I don't want you to think I'd pick someone like that. I'm not Kat."

"Okay," Jesper said.

She huffed again. "Sorry. That was mean. I don't really think Kat..." Her breath caught and she bit her lip, then rubbed her face with her hands. "Ugh, I feel so stupid."

Stupid. Humiliated. Alone.

Helpless.

Jesper remembered.

How strange it felt to be on the other side. Relieving in an uncomfortable kind of way, like an itch on a phantom limb.

Watching her struggle with something he was too familiar with sent a new jolt of pain through him. The words came out before he knew what he was saying.

"I know how you feel."

H tried to be discreet as she wiped her eyes, covering up the action with sarcasm. "Yeah? Your ex-girl ever go wack on you?"

"No," Jesper admitted, staring at his hands. "But my-my dad, he...well, um…" The words dried up. Guilt prickled his stomach. What was he doing? "Um, nevermind."

A heavy silence settled on their shoulders. After a second, Jesper risked a glance up, hoping she had been so preoccupied with herself that she hadn't heard him. But H had come out of her hair, the tears in her eyes forgotten, as she stared at him with her mouth halfway open.

Jesper dropped his eyes. The guilt started climbing up his throat.

"He hit you?" H whispered.

He flinched. "Once."

"Once?"

"Um…" He blew out a breath, the words going with it. "More than once." She didn't seem to know what to say, which was good because he needed a minute to sort through the thoughts in his mind and pick out the best words. "I feel your...confusion. Humiliation. Helplessness. When you get...get that pain from someone...someone who shouldn't give it to you. It-it changes how you...how you see. Everything. The world. Yourself. All of a sudden...you are very...very sma-all. And hurt."

"And alone," H added, her voice empty.

Jesper shook his head. "Not alone. Not me. I had Ally."

Just the mention of her name made H scowl. "She's a real piece of work."

"She doesn't mean to-to be."

Her face softened again, and another tear snuck out of the corner of her eye and trickled down her cheek. "You've done a lot for her," she murmured. "Haven't you?"

He shrugged. "I tried. I'm an easier target. Better than her. He...he worked for...an awful man. Did awful things. I was always...always afraid of wha-at he would do. To her."

Silence again. Too much. Too heavy. Stars, he wished it would just crush him already. He deserved that, didn't he?

"Wow," H breathed. "No wonder you two are crazy. Your dad's a monster."

Your dad's a monster.

A monster.

Monster.

Guilt clawed up his throat, scalding his mouth. It was all he could taste, see, smell, pounding in his head in time with his heart. He'd never once said the words before—it had been ages since he even thought them—but he threw them out now in a desperate attempt to soothe the burning on his tongue.

"He wasn't always like that."

He wasn't always like that.

Monty the Merciless.

Monty the Monster.

"What do you mean?" H asked.

Too much. Too much, too much, too much, he said too much, he thought too much, he tiptoed too close to the edge and now he was falling down the rabbit hole. Endless black, dark forever.

"Nothing," he muttered. Movements stiff, he jerked himself off the bed and stumbled into the bathroom. He spent a few minutes scrubbing his face until it shone angry red. Not enough. Still not enough. Not ever enough. He could scrub himself to the bone, and he could never wash away his father's stain.

Riley didn't even look up when Jesper walked into the kitchen and made an ice pack. He took it back to the room and handed it to H without meeting her eyes.

The bed creaked when he sat back down. His hands fidgeted in his lap as she brought the towel to the side of her face. Her eyes stayed trained on him, though, as if she could see right through him. He couldn't take it. Right when he was ready to stand up and walk back out the door—for good this time— she broke the silence.

"Around here, bad things happen. They happen and it makes people harden right up. Sometimes they turn into jaded, messed up monsters. Sometimes they hurt other people too. Just because."

He waited. She didn't go on. "So?"

"So. You're made of different stuff."

He winced. "That's bad."

"No, just…" Her eyes glistened again, and she dropped her gaze. "Just don't let it harden you too."

* * * * * * *

"That was amazing!" AJ crowed over the stereo as he and Ally sped down Heartland. He hadn't stopped talking since they'd left Duchess to fend for herself. "I had no idea McClain had infiltrated through Crims. Like, no idea. And now we know his plan, his contacts…" He whooped and hit the top of the car with his fist, and it sent a thrill of proud exhilaration through Ally. "You're amazing. How did you do it?"

Ally smirked. Thankfully, it had been too dark for him to see she had just been holding her rock. He probably assumed she had a knife on her or something. "I'm the best."

"You're the best student I've ever had."

"Pft," she scoffed. "I did this myself. If it were up to you we'd would've left an hour ago with nothing."

AJ laughed. "Got me there, Als." Then he gave her a sideways glance. "Wanna come with me to tell the boss the good news?"

"You mean…go tell Red?"

He nodded and Ally's eyes widened. The chance to show Red what *she* did, all on her own. That was exactly what she'd been working so hard for. "Yes. Yes, let's go."

"Thought you might say that."

As the night blurred past her window, Ally's mind raced over the possibilities on how to present herself and the information she'd gleaned from Duchess, the best way to really show to Red how impressive she'd become.

Her hand curled around her phone, and the overwhelming urge to call Jesper came over her. She hadn't seen him in almost a week, and while she never felt tied down to him, she did miss him. He wouldn't even believe what she'd accomplished tonight, basically stopping a rival gang leader in another city from taking over before he could really start. Not just a pathetic little stick any longer.

I'm doing this to protect us, she itched to tell him. *Protect us like she did.*

I'm doing this for you. Aren't you proud of me?

Wouldn't she be proud of me?

AJ parked on the curb under the streetlight with little care and Ally got out of the car, shaking her head to focus and smoothing out her cloak. She couldn't mess this up.

"Ready?" AJ gestured to the alleyway with a smirk.

Not just any alley. Red's.

Taking a breath and squaring her shoulders, Ally nodded. Time to prove herself.

The redheaded twins nodded at them as they rounded the corner. They each leaned against an opposite wall, near perfect mirrors of each other.

"B," AJ said, nodding back at each of them in turn. "C."

These people and their weird names, Ally thought. She couldn't help remembering the first time she'd come here, how the two brothers had ridiculed her and called her crazy. Now they just regarded her with cool, if not somewhat respectful expressions. It made her smile.

Just you wait.

Per usual, a giant bloodstain smeared along the cement leading up to Red's throne, though the source must've already been dealt with, because the alley was empty. AJ strode right up to the fire escape like he owned the place, and Ally tried to match his ease. From her seat above them, Red smirked, her hair pulled back tight and lips painted crimson. Jabber sat next to her, and she had her arm around his massive neck, highlighting the bleeding rose on the sleeve of her jacket.

"Look at that," she said as she watched the two of them approach. "Dynamic duo at it again. Nice to see you around Ally."

Ally raised an eyebrow at that. She figured AJ was keeping Red in the loop about how much time they'd spent together—she *hoped* he talked about her a lot—but hearing it from Red still sent a jolt of anticipation through her.

"You'll never believe what we dug up tonight," AJ said, his eyes bright even in the dim light. "Duchess broke the whole thing open. Actually—" His gaze cut to Ally. "Als here broke it open herself."

Now it was Red's turn to raise an eyebrow. She glanced between the two of them, curiosity bleeding out from her expression. "Let's hear it."

Ally didn't let AJ take this moment from her—she plowed ahead before he could. "McClain is trying to infiltrate through Crims. He's slowly dropping drugged up people there to keep their ears to the ground and gather information about operations here."

"Hm." Red's expression was contemplative, the most sane she'd ever looked. "I guess nobody would question another body coming out of Crims. How have we not been able to ID them though? We know McClain's people."

"He's not using his people. He's put a stop on his dealer's drug supply and hoarded it all. Users can only get their fix if they go undercover for him."

"Ah ha." She nodded appreciatively. "Clever."

"So you have a dozen extra bodies in there with Pat desperate to find information. A lot of it is false or made up because they are so desperate, but enough truth about your operation leaked through over the last year. He was planning to infiltrate within the next six months."

"How? We'd notice somebody building an army, even in Crims or West End."

At that, Ally lost her nerve momentarily, and a gust of frigid wind blew her hair over her face. She struggled to tuck it back while AJ smirked and picked up the trail for her.

"Ricky," he answered. "McClain is hoping he's bitter and will strike a deal with him."

Red tipped her head back and let out a cackling laugh, and Jabber's ears perked up. "Ricky, huh? That's his master plan? More likely trying to get his hands on vac."

"I didn't know," Ally said, finally finding her voice again. "I don't think McClain's approached him yet." Not that Ricky would share with Ally if McClain *had,* but she was desperate to keep herself in Red's good graces.

Red laughed again. "I know, Ally. I don't think you're stupid enough to wander into my line of sight if you were a part of this."

Silently, Ally breathed a sigh of relief. She could still salvage it.

"Where did dear Duchess end up anyways?"

"Bleeding out on a side road just outside of town," Ally answered. She couldn't help the pride that came over her, the strength in her limbs. "It'll be a while before she recovers."

Red's lips pulled into a sharp smile. "Based on the stories I'm starting to hear about you Ally, I have no doubts about that. If she does dare to make her way into town again, we'll make sure she's taken care of." She scratched behind Jabber's ears. "Hm hm hm. So many things to do. First thing's first. Ally? I have a job for you."

Ally didn't think she could stand any straighter but she tried, her veins pulsing with excitement. This is what she'd been waiting for, what she'd dreamed of all those days staring at the sun.

She tried to keep herself from sounding too eager when she nodded. "Yes."

Red grinned, as if seeing right through her nonchalance. "You're Ricky's new golden girl, right? Lasted much longer than any of his other misguided protégés, even after the Walrus tried to take a stab at you. Here's the deal: you convince Ricky not to align with McClain. No strings on my end—he's smart enough to know it'll be bad for business to have things change around here. If you can pull that off, then I want you as one of mine."

Each word filled Ally up and up until she could've sworn she was glowing. She couldn't keep the triumphant grin from her face. Everything she'd survived, everything she'd worked for, coming down to this.

Strength. Safety. A place to call her own with her brother at her side. Never looking over their shoulders again.

Aren't you so proud of me?

With a smile that matched Red's, Ally nodded. "I'll get it done."

* * * * * * *

When Jesper opened his eyes again, he found himself back home.

His breaths came unevenly as he glanced around the familiar living room, a sharp stone settling in his gut.

He didn't just know this place. Somehow, he knew this day. The Day.

His focus zeroed in on Ally first, as she had always been his priority. The harsh lines that would become her defining feature only just barely showed on her six-year-old face. She sat on the floor next to the couch, playing with her new collection of rocks and sticks Jesper had helped her find. Already she'd whined for food five times today. Jesper stood in the kitchen, desperation long since gone as he sifted through their empty cupboards numbly, trying to make something out of nothing. He didn't even glance at the figure sulking on the couch. It had been a long time since he'd looked his mother in the eyes.

"Mommy, look," Ally said, reaching up to tap the leg drooped over the broken arm of the couch. "Look."

Ally continued to whine, her voice getting louder, and Jesper ignored it. She was always trying to get their mother's attention. It rarely, if ever, worked. He just had to get her to quiet down before Monty got home.

The real issue: what were they going to eat?

He closed his eyes and tried to think through his sister's shouting, wondering if he should just go admire Ally's things to satisfy her. Heaving a sigh, he braced himself to turn around just as Ally went silent.

Something cold and sinister shivered up Jesper's spine. As if he'd just been dunked into a pool of freezing water.

Even before he turned to look, he knew.

Ally had climbed into their mother's lap, eyes wide, gasps shaking her little shoulders. "Mommy?" Her voice broke and a wheezing breath shook her. "Mommy, wake up."

He looked from her to the figure on the couch, always unresponsive but now as still as death.

Still as death.

Dead.

Their mother was dead.

Ally opened her mouth and her scream shattered the sky.

The pieces of the sky rained down around him, the entire world caving in on Jesper's small and frail shoulders.

He wasn't strong enough to carry it.

He snapped clean in half.

"Mommy!" he screamed, the name unfamiliar on his tongue. "Mommy, wake up! Wake up. Don't leave us here with him! *Don't leave us here!*"

Jesper collapsed to his knees, then scrambled back, because *he* was there, standing over the couch, his boots, his hands, his beard all covered in blood, his face contorted with a kind of rage that could shake the earth.

When Monty's scalding gaze jumped from his dead wife to his screaming daughter, Jesper's sense slammed back into him. He dove forward and pried Ally off the body, snatching her away before Monty could turn on her next.

He barricaded them in their room as he held sobbing baby Ally in his lap, knowing it wouldn't be enough if Monty truly wanted to get inside.

Monty the Merciless.

Monty the Monster.

The ground started shaking violently, the earth splitting wide open. Their screams echoed back at him.

Don't leave us here with him.

Please.

Mommy come back.

She left them and he never forgave her.

He wasn't always like that.

Jesper scrambled away from the edge, but he wasn't fast enough. Both he and Ally tumbled into the hole of endless darkness, lost forever.

"Wake up," Jesper rasped as his eyes flew open. Sweat dripped down his back, plastering him to the thin mattress. His throat ached. He'd been screaming. His breaths came harsh and choppy, and his lungs wheezed like all the air had been squeezed out of them. "Wake up. It was her fault. It was your fault. Wake up."

"Hey now," someone said softly. Riley. "You're awake. Take a deep breath. You woke up."

Jesper pushed himself up, wild eyes scanning the room, looking for Monty, or even Ally. Instead he found a rumpled Riley standing over the bed. H sat on Jesper's other side, her hair matted and face stained with tears. One glance at her and Jesper remembered what had happened. What he'd said. The safe inside him that he'd unwittingly broken open.

"I don't talk about it." The words jumped from his mouth so fast it was hard to tell what they were. "I do-don't talk about it, I don't, I don't ev-ever talk about it. Ever. I'm the only, I-I am the only one. That knows. Remembers now. And I-I don't ever ta-talk about it."

Riley raised his hands and Jesper jerked away so fast his head smacked against the wall. H put a hand on his shoulder, but dropped it when he flinched. She glanced at Riley, tense fear splayed on her face, then followed his example and raised her hands in the air so Jesper could see them.

Somewhere in his brain, Jesper registered the sign of peace. His heart still thumped violently, his breaths ragged, but he slowly started to see clearly and pull the nightmare away from reality—or, really, the past from present.

He'd sat on the bed with H until she rested her head in his lap and fell asleep. He had been happy she stayed close to him and drifted off himself. He'd dreamed of that day, the day he never let himself think about, but it was a dream and nothing more.

"We aren't going to hurt you, all right?" Riley went on. "You remember us, don't you? Riley and H."

Jesper jerked his head in a nod. He remembered them, but he'd once trusted his mother, his father. Look at where that had gotten him. Just because he had vague memories of reading and coffee and spaghetti didn't mean they wouldn't hurt him now.

"It's just us, Jes," H whispered. She sounded rattled. He'd never heard her sound so scared, so unsure. When he looked at her, with her usually immaculate hair snarled and emotions smeared on her face rather than hidden behind a mask of indifference, something shifted inside him. He'd never seen her that way either. Not until tonight. She'd lowered her walls too. His had come tumbling down. Maybe they were both vulnerable. She needed protecting just as much as he did.

That thought, the shift in focus, helped him breathe a little easier, think a little clearer. When Riley asked if he wanted water, Jesper nodded. His eyes tracked every movement as Riley left the room.

H watched him with tears in her eyes, as if his wounds made her bleed too. He wondered what possible stake she could have in his pain. Was that the mark of friendship? When you had no choice but to bleed along with someone?

She opened her mouth, then hesitated, probably afraid of setting him off again, but she didn't stop. "Earlier...earlier you said it was her fault. Did...did she…" Her voice broke. "Did your mama leave you too?"

Ally's scream echoed in Jesper's head. "Yes," he gasped, then winced.

"She left you with him?"

Monty the Merciless.

Monty the Monster.

Don't leave me with him. Don't leave me with the monster you made.

"Yes." Jesper sucked a breath through his teeth. "Yes, she did."

"Where did...do you know where she went? What she left you for?"

She left us and I never forgave her.

"Drugs," Jesper spat. The truth burned on its way out, but it was such a relief to let it go take up space somewhere else. He'd carried it alone for years. It had eaten him away. "She left us for nothing."

Understanding broke on H's face. Her shoulders sagged as she opened her mouth, then closed it, then opened it again. "She overdosed?"

"Over-dosed?" The new word came out clunky.

"Yeah, you know, you take too much and it kills you."

"Oh. Yeah." He swallowed, both relieved and devastated there was a simple word for what had happened to his mother. "Overdose."

"How old were you?"

"Eight." Three years living as the only child. One year of happiness with Ally and their parents in a village he couldn't remember. Two years of things rolling steadily downhill.

Another two years of nightmares before their mother left them to burn in hell on their own.

That was the truth, the truth that only he and Monty carried. The truth that bound them together, despite everything. The truth that tied Jesper to the rotting Molds, the chain tight and thick enough that he knew he would never break free from it.

A new panic seized Jesper's chest. He leaned forward so fast that H pulled back. "Don't tell anyone. Please." Ally's memories had built themselves into images she could handle, and Jesper never had it in him to correct them. It wouldn't matter anyway. She thought Monty had beat their angel mother to death, and Jesper knew she wouldn't believe anything else. "Please. Anyone."

H nodded rapidly. "Okay. I won't."

Jesper nodded back, then let out a breath that lasted years. Exhaustion rattled his bones as he sat back against the wall. Everything hurt, but on the inside, like he'd been mugged again but they'd beat his heart instead. He'd take the physical beating over remembering any day. He *had* taken Monty's beatings over it, letting himself get hit again and again so long as he could still dance around the hundreds of rabbit holes in his head.

As the minutes passed, his breaths evened out and his muscles slowly started to relax. H slid closer, little bits at a time, until she felt safe enough to lay down next to his legs.

"I was ten," she whispered out of nowhere, like the conversation hadn't ended. "I was ten when my mama left me. Took my little brother with her too. Went off to go live with his real daddy: some mouth-breather named Don."

Jesper shuddered in spite of himself. What if his mother had taken Ally with her? He wouldn't have made it. He'd only survived this long for his little sister.

"Leo was my whole world." Her voice shook with a sob. "I loved that little boy so much. But she didn't care. She just took him. Broke my daddy's heart too, but she said Leo was more hers and Don's than ours. The affair hurt my daddy, of course, but he let her keep cheatin' if it meant she wouldn't leave. It worked for a few years. Then it didn't." She took a breath. "Gone. Just like that."

"Just like that," Jesper echoed softly.

They heard Riley puttering around the kitchen, Jenny's door opening at the end of the hall, and his soft voice, too quiet to make out words.

"Will she ever get better?" Jesper whispered, thinking of the deep crevices that lined Riley's face when he tried to coax his mother to do anything.

H shook her head. "I don't think so. She loves him a lot though. Can't fault her for that." She sighed, and the sheer emptiness of the sound resonated with the hole in Jesper that had been left in his mother's wake. How could you possibly fill something like that?

Seconds passed, then H reached for her phone laying on the bed. She stopped halfway, let her hand hang suspended in the air for a second, then continued on to grab it.

"Can I...can I show you something?"

Jesper nodded. H turned her head so she could look at him, and the tracks of the tears on her cheeks reflected in the light of her phone. She showed him the screen.

"This was us." The screen displayed a photo similar to the one Jesper had seen hanging on Mama March's wall. This one was just the two of them though, brother and sister, H's smile carefree, her eyes bright and unguarded. A little boy in her lap with the same bright eyes and mouth open in laughter. "He was, um...he loved bubbles. Like so much. My daddy had one of those bubble guns and was spewing them in Mama's face. It made Leo laugh so hard every time."

The image pierced Jesper's heart, and his thoughts jumped to Ally. How could H have lived with such a loss? He could see in the way her arms wrapped around the little boy, so tight and protective, so loving, that she too had been shaped by the one that came after her. Their younger siblings had molded their hearts—take them away and what could possibly be left?

"How did…" Jesper swallowed. "How did you…survive…that?"

She shrugged. "How do we survive anything?"

Her phone buzzed, a notification banner spreading over Leo's face. She clicked it automatically and the corner of her mouth twitched into something almost like a smile.

"Kat?" Jesper asked hopefully.

Her face fell. "Nah, I wish. Just a new video." Her eyes darted to Jesper's face, then back to her screen, as if nervous.

"You can watch it if you want to." Stars knew Jesper could use a distraction.

"Well, I…" She shifted slightly. "It's kinda stupid."

"I like most things."

"Okay well…" She started tapping her phone to bring it up, and her other hand twisted in her matted hair. "My hair is…well, it's hard to do. Like know how to do. My, um, my mom used to help me but then…"

Then she left. The words hung between them in the air.

Jesper cut them down. "I love your hair."

H snorted, her eyebrows furrowing. "Nobody likes my hair." The words sounded vacant, like they'd first come from somebody else and she'd learned to repeat it. The thought made Jesper unbearably sad.

Your boy stutters, Monty. Is he stupid or something?

"I do. It's like a cloud. The clouds here are amazing. Reminds me of that."

She stared at him so long that Jesper's face turned red and he wondered if he had done something wrong.

"You mean that," she stated.

"Um…yes? I mean…I mean what, what I-I say."

H blinked as if taking that in, then glanced back at her phone. "Thanks," she murmured so softly he wondered if he heard right. "Josh made fun of my hair once in sixth grade and Kat punched him so hard she broke his nose." A faint smile pulled at her mouth before it disappeared. "I really *really* hope she's okay."

"Me too."

"Anyways." She showed him the young woman on her phone with skin darker than H's and her hair just as curly. "So this girl has a channel with a bunch of tips for hair. Well, not like tips, but tutorials. Breaks it down step by step so I can follow along."

She turned up the volume slightly, and the woman on the phone started welcoming everyone back. She sat at a chair in her bathroom, and behind her you could see her bed with seafoam blankets and a small dog curled on top. It looked very homey. Jesper liked it immediately.

"Sometimes," H started, her voice so small. "Sometimes I just turn it on, like in bed, tryin' to sleep. Just to listen. And pretend that maybe somewhere, in a different life, she stayed. To show me how to…do my hair."

Her voice broke on the last word and silence settled between them like a blanket. Jesper liked listening to H breathe. It reminded him to breathe too. Maybe that marked friendship: something as simple as helping each other breathe.

They watched video after video long into the night, each holding onto a ghost.

* * * * * * * *

The next morning, Ally found Ricky on the corner of Heartland, as always, smoking his pipe from his camp chair.

"Wowee!" he exclaimed when he saw her, cloak billowing behind her. "Look at this here. Chickadee's skippin' like somebody gave her a big ol' lollipop. What's got you lookin' so happy, love?"

Ally couldn't hide the excitement radiating through her bones, and she didn't even care. "Just a good day."

"I'll say. We got a clear sky and good opportunities today. I like the jingle in the air."

She rolled her eyes, but even his standard nonsense couldn't bring her down. It would be better for him to be in a good mood after all. "Sure. What's going on today?"

"Couple o' meetings. In fact, chickadee I was hoping you'd be around for them. It's about time you start running more things around here."

Ally's heart soared. He couldn't have been more right. "Who are they?" she asked, practicing her professional tone so everyone would take her seriously.

"First up we got a Miss Lori Gordon stopping by. Think you can handle her?"

She snorted. "Not even a question. Who is she?"

"Just a regular lookin' for her vac. Hasn't paid on time in ages so I've been holdin' out on her. Ten to one she's comin' to beg. Can you hold your ground, love?"

"Hold on the ground?" Her forehead creased, and she felt the frustration rising in her that there was *still* something she didn't understand. She was supposed to belong here; she had run herself ragged making sure that to anybody looking, she *did* belong here. "You mean like hold her down? I can do that."

Ricky's bushy eyebrows rose so high they looked like they would fall off his forehead. His usually distant and drugged eyes sharpened, and she didn't like how his gaze seemed to take more from her than she was willing to give.

She just glared back at him and after a long moment, he blew out a cloud of smoke. It had been a long time since it had made her cough, but she still felt the urge in her throat.

"Where are your parents, kid?"

The question surprised Ally and threatened to entirely ruin her good mood. "What?"

"Your parents. Where are they?"

"They're dead," she answered flatly. He'd never asked about her personal life before. "Anything else?"

"Just you and your brother then, huh?"

"Why do you care?"

"Curious." He chewed on his pipe. "I never see him with ya much. Word is he hangs around Riley Hatton."

Ally gritted her teeth. "And?"

"Riley just doesn't seem like your scene, love, that's all."

"Riley is nothing but a manipulative, stars-forsaken leech."

If Ricky had opinions on the venom in her voice, he didn't share them. "Interesting stuff, interesting stuff."

"Is it?" she bit back. "Are we going to do our job or what?"

He chuckled. "Always business. I like that about you chickadee."

She didn't have time to retort before a woman nearly ran up to them. Her frizzy, blonde hair was towered precariously on her head, almost falling over several times with her quick movement, and her hazel eyes stayed trained on Ricky.

"Lori," Ricky greeted with the tip of his head, as if he'd run into an old friend by surprise. "How ya been?"

"Been fine, Ricky," Lori answered, a bit too fast and harsh against his slow ease. Ally didn't care for the way she completely ignored her presence. "Been a while since I've seen you here."

Ally frowned. That was the second person that had said that, but Ally saw him here every time she passed by. When she glanced at him, Ricky winked.

"Well I've been busy, love, been real busy. Hopin' to get some sun here soon. Tryin' to grow orchids this year."

"Uh huh, sure." That seemed to be the end of Lori's patience. She narrowed her eyes and hissed. "Come on, you know why I'm here."

Ricky sighed and took his pipe out of his mouth. "Tragic thing around here. Nobody has time for friendly conversation." If Ally didn't know better, she'd think he sounded truly sad about it. "Fact o' the matter is, love, I haven't gotten payment for your last two deliveries."

"I told you I'm good for it!" Lori practically yelled, her hands balling into fists and her hair nearly toppling over. Ally slipped her hand into her pocket to find her rock, just in case this lady decided to actually fight. "You know that I am. You *know* that I am."

"Do I?" Ricky asked, the barest edge to his voice for the first time. "'Cause lately I ain't seein' that."

"Charge me double. Interest. I don't care. I'm good for it and I'll get you the money."

"Ha. Appreciate the dedication there, truly. But it's not my call to make." Then he sat back and sucked on his pipe, as if settling in for a show.

Lori laughed, but it sounded more like a scream. "What? Not your *call*? You make sure everyone here knows vac is yours and only yours, Ricky. You're giving it up now?"

"Course not, chickadee. Just have a bit of help today." He gestured with his pipe. "You haven't the pleasure of meeting my new enforcer, Ally, have you?"

For the first time, Lori looked at Ally, then blinked, as if just realizing she was there.

Ally smirked. "Hi."

Slowly, the color started to drain out of Lori's face. "You're…you're her. But then…"

With those words, Ally's souring mood went high as the sky. "Heard of me, have you?"

Lori swallowed hard, connecting the dots of what it must mean for Ricky to have his enforcer there for their meeting. "Ricky…Ricky, look, I didn't mean any disrespect. Just business, you know?"

Ricky took a puff from his pipe. "I hear ya, Lori, I hear ya. I consider my clients the closest kinda twisted friends I can find in this place. So I'm gonna leave it up to Ally, here." He winked at Lori. "Just business, ya know?"

She spluttered for a minute before realizing Ricky wasn't going to budge, then she turned to Ally. "Look…Ally was it? I just need a little bit to tie me over. That's all. I can pay whatever you want."

Ally snorted. Based on the holes in her faded pants and the broken clasps on her overworn shoes, this lady had nothing else to offer. "I'm sure. How long have you been using vac?"

"How long?" Lori furrowed her eyebrows. "Why does that matter?"

"Just curious."

"Um, eight years. Almost nine."

Ally didn't try to hide her disgust. How could somebody just surrender themselves like that for so long? "Interesting."

"I'm willing to pay—"

"I'm not interested in money," Ally cut in. "The money is for Ricky." She didn't know how far Ricky wanted her to go—up to this point he'd given such specific instructions for her interactions—but it seemed like he didn't care. It was Ally's show now, and she was more than happy to try out the new part of being in charge.

It took Lori a moment to get over her surprise. "Okay. If you don't want money, then what?"

A sharp smile spread on Ally's face as the idea came over her. "I want you to beg."

"To beg?" Lori's voice rose with anger again. "Come on, Ricky, this is ridiculous."

Ally shrugged. "If you say so." Then she turned as if to walk away.

"Ricky!"

"Not my show, chickadee," Ricky said indifferently. "Far as I can tell, you're about to let your chance walk away."

"Wait! Please wait!"

Slowly, Ally turned back around, pleased to see Lori's wide eyes trained on her. "Change your mind?"

Lori could hate her—stars knew how much Ally loathed her father when she begged for mercy, to spare her brother, only to have those pleas fall on deaf ears. Monty hadn't so much as looked at her in years. But in that moment, Lori only displayed a hateful kind of desperation, knowing that she had Ally's full attention.

"Please," she said. "Please just give me a little more, just to hold me over."

Ally clicked her tongue. Truly, she just wanted to see how far she could take it. "On your knees."

"But…" Lori blinked and glanced at Ricky, but he just sat back in his camp chair, watching Ally with a clear gaze. He wouldn't be any help to her.

"Well?"

To Ally's amazement, Lori closed her eyes, then slowly got down on the ground, one knee at a time. When she opened them again, they held the whisper of tears.

"Please, Ally. Please give me more vac. I'll do anything for it. Anything you say."

And Ally knew she meant it. She would throw herself in front of a car if Ally asked her to.

Ally had never felt so invincible in her life. For the very first time, nothing could truly touch her, and the exhilaration of that knowledge brought so much relief she was almost dizzy.

She'd never be the one on the ground again.

"Okay," Ally said with a smirk, and Lori sucked in a sharp breath of hope. "I'll give you half your usual dose for triple the cost. You have a week to pay that off along with the other two you missed."

"A week?" she breathed. "But that's…I can't do that."

"That's my offer. Take it or leave it. Either way, if there's no money by next week I'll be at your door, and the only reason you'll be on your knees is to clean up the blood."

Lori swallowed again, the tears in her eyes on the verge of leaking over. Ally expected her to fight back at least a little more, but she just deflated in defeat. In the most pathetic display Ally had ever seen, Lori turned to Ricky like a dog looking for a bone, and when Ricky tossed a small bag at her, she snatched it like a vulture.

Seeing the handful of tiny leaves in the bag made Ally wrinkle her nose. Why would anyone trade their pride, their strength, for that? It was beneath her.

She let herself feel the sun on her face as she watched the sniveling Lori slink away.

"Well what do ya know!" Ricky exclaimed once she was gone. "The chickadee's got some steel in her, doesn't she?"

The admiration in his tone, however slight, made her beam. "I'm the best for a reason." Then she remembered the real reason why she'd come to talk to him today. "Speaking of that, I tracked down Duchess for AJ. We had a nice talk."

"Yeah? Learn anything good?"

"McClain wants Red's territory, and he's trying to infiltrate through Crims. He thinks he can strike a deal with you to get all the way in."

She didn't know how he would respond to that, but he just chuckled. "Course he does. Somehow I get the feelin' I'm not the first you told, huh love?"

Alarm threaded through her, and she did her best to keep an impassive face. How did he guess that she'd already talked to Red? "I don't know. Word can get around fast."

Ricky scoffed, puffing some smoke. "Sure, kid. It ain't my first time around the block. What did Red want?"

"She doesn't want you to take the deal, but with no strings attached on her end."

Something dark flashed in his eyes, almost too quick to catch, and he muttered a curse under his breath. "Well somebody sure thinks they own everything, don't they? Lemme guess: she would give you something if you got me to agree to her terms, right?"

He seemed to know, so she didn't bother lying. "Yeah, she did." Did her voice still sound as confident as she hoped? She couldn't tell. She wanted to get Lori back here on her knees again so Ally could go back to being in control.

"I don't blame you, love. Newbie wants to get in with the biggest fish in the sea. I've seen that before; I can respect it. Makes the most sense for someone wanting to rise in the ranks.

"Now here's your second lesson of the day: Red will give you protection through others' fear. That's helpful to have, to be sure, to be sure. But with me, love, you get power through others' desperation." He clapped his hands together. "Combine the two and you're unstoppable."

Unstoppable. This whole time Ally had considered Ricky just a means to an end, a way to get Red's attention and build her skills. But clearly Ricky had a kind of influence that Red couldn't touch by being the sole supplier of vac, the far superior drug that everyone wanted their hands on.

With the two of them backing her, she really would be unstoppable. She and Jesper would want for nothing.

The corner of Ricky's mouth pulled up around his pipe as he watched the idea take root in her. "I won't hear McClain, you have my word on that. Don't trust him. The guy's as slippery as an oiled fishie. So you can share the good news." He nodded at her. "Do what you gotta do to get into Red's crew. But once you're there, love, you bring me with you. Deal?"

Ally considered it for a moment. Red had never talked about Ricky with anything other than disdain, but maybe Ally could change her mind. She could prove how useful it would be to align with Ricky. Between the three of them, they would have everyone in this city on their knees, bowing to them.

Except for Riley. The irritating thought buzzed in her ear, and Ally wanted to swat it away. If she had her way—and based on the way things were going, she knew she would—Riley wouldn't be a problem for her for much longer. She'd yank Jesper away from him, and after he saw what she could give him now, her brother would never look back.

Look what I did, Jesper. Look what I made for us. For you.

This is payback for all the hits you took for me. This is revenge for our father trying to bury us as nothing. This is a legacy for our mother sacrificing herself to save us.

I did this for her. For us.

Wouldn't she be so proud of me?

When Ricky reached out his hand, Ally shook it. "Deal."

CHAPTER 8

SENTENCE FIRST, VERDICT AFTER

High on her victories, Ally made her way to Riley's apartment. It had been almost a week since she'd been there, and she hoped there hadn't been too much damage done while she was gone. It was already going to be hard enough to convince Jesper to break free of their cage, but she was confident she could do it. Once she showed him what she had done for him, he'd be so grateful. He'd be tripping over himself to follow her, to thank her, to praise her. And her life will finally have been worth it.

Today, though, she'd have to do some damage control and make a plan. If she caught Jesper there alone, then today would be the day. Without their influence confusing him, she'd take him with her and they'd never look back. If Riley, H, or Kat were there, she'd need to be patient and create the right opportunity.

Ally used the rock to unlock the front door of the building. After the night with Duchess, she noticed it had turned a darker color, spots of purple so dark they were almost black. For a moment, she had been afraid whatever power it was gifted with had been lost, but it worked just as well as before.

Even better now that she had learned how to use it. Her perfect secret.

She pushed her way into the apartment to find only one person inside. Ally wrinkled her nose at the familiar blob of black hair.

"Surprised to see you here," H said as a greeting while she shoved things into her backpack. It could've been Ally's imagination, but the girl's voice wasn't as sharp toward her. Shame. "Jes is at work."

The words stung Ally more than she wanted to admit. Not only did H know Jesper's life better than his *sister*, apparently she felt like she could call him Jes now. Only Ally called him that.

He's mine, not yours.

Jealousy coursed through her with a vengeance. "What's wrong? Did Riley finally decide he likes the stray cat more than you?"

H froze in her tracks and scowled. "My best friend is missing," she bit back. "But maybe you'd know that if you ever gave your brother the time of day."

Rage boiled under Ally's skin—how *dare* H use Jesper against her?—but she forced herself to smirk. "Wow, people are *that* desperate to get away from you, huh?"

Something in H's eyes snapped and broke open. She raised her arm, as if to punch Ally, but suddenly stopped herself. Ally deflated in disappointment. She'd love nothing more than to rip that girl's hair out.

"I really don't know why he loves you so much," H said. Somehow the soft words hit Ally harder than a punch would've. "I don't. You're a witch. And don't give me some sob story shiz just because your dad's a monster and your mom OD'd. Those things happened to Jesper too and he's ten times the person you could ever hope to be." And with that, she turned and stalked out the door.

Ally stayed stuck in place for a few moments. A few minutes. An hour? Time had stopped, time didn't matter anymore. Dozens of thoughts clamored over each other in her mind, each screaming louder than the last. Her heart thumped wildly in her chest, as if it would shatter her ribs and break through, leaving her to bleed out on the ground.

Finally, she forced her legs to stumble forward, down the stairs, outside. The fresh air that had seemed freeing earlier today now threatened to suffocate her. She ducked into the alley and pressed her back against the brick wall, breathing hard. Her hands shook as she pulled out her phone and made a call.

Jesper answered halfway through the second ring. She could hear the coffee machines whirring in the background. "Hey, Ally!" She'd relied on the steadiness in his voice her whole life. "How are you? I've been trying to get a hold of you—"

"What's an OD?" Ally cut in, her voice hoarse.

Three beats of silence passed, just the sound of those stupid machines that should've burned. "What?"

"An OD," she repeated. "What is it?"

Six beats of silence. The machines grew quieter as Jesper's breaths grew shaky. "I, um…Ally, I…I don't…"

"I know you know," Ally bit back. She wanted to be fierce and demanding, but it came out desperate, as pathetic as Lori had been. "Tell me. Now."

It took her brother a painfully long time to pull himself together before the words rushed out of him like she'd broken through the dam in his heart.

Alice Bonham was the youngest of four kids, and while she had been raised in a loving home, she often went unheard in the racket of her older siblings' lives. This made her into a loud and daring child that grew into a reckless teenager. She had an ease with magic, but her parents couldn't afford to send her to academy after they'd paid for her siblings, and she said she didn't care. She'd rather have fun. And she did.

At only fifteen years old, she'd become a heavy drinker, had tried every drug she and her friends could get their hands on, and been with her fair share of boys. She always got into trouble, but she managed to keep most of the dirtiest details hidden from her parents.

When she turned eighteen, she met Monty Lewis, a young blacksmith apprentice. Though he led a respectable and boring life—completely different from Alice's crazy world—she fell madly in love with him. She decided to give up her party life and clean herself up so she could be the kind of girl the gentle giant would want to marry. Both Monty and his brother were extremely talented blacksmiths, and they both received opportunities to train in Synan with the best of the best. But Monty knew Alice didn't want a life that could lead to a career for the crown, and he had fallen in love with her too, so he let his brother go and stayed to marry her.

And they were happy. So amazingly, painfully happy.

And then Alice got pregnant.

Becoming a mother had never been on Alice's list for life. She hadn't thought about it much, but she found she enjoyed the attention of being pregnant and slowly got more and more excited about her coming child.

The family celebrated the birth of Jesper, and Alice loved watching how much Monty adored his son. But eventually the party ended, everyone went home, and real motherhood started.

It wasn't as glamorous as she'd hoped.

Alice didn't like it. She liked Jesper well enough, but she resented the responsibility of his life and the changes birth had made to her body. She became distant, sad, and tired, and couldn't shake herself out of the cloud.

As time went on, she didn't know what to do. She loved Monty with her whole heart and the only bright spot in her life was seeing him so happy. She didn't want to disappoint him, so she kept up the cheerful wife and mother charade. Until one day, she couldn't take it anymore. She reached out to one of her old friends and asked for a dose. Just something light, something to get her through the day. And it worked for a few years.

Until Alice got pregnant again.

She thought sharing a name with her first daughter would inspire some kind of mothering fire inside of her, but Alice fell even deeper and darker than she had before. She and Monty started arguing about little things—about everything—and she'd get him so riled up that he would actually raise his voice. Hearing his father yell always scared Jesper and made baby Ally cry. The yelling didn't match the gentle father they knew.

Monty would always come to Jesper's room and apologize after the fight had ended. He stayed with Jesper until he fell asleep with his little sister cradled in his arms. He didn't know what was wrong with Mommy, Monty would say, but he would help her. There wasn't any reason to be scared.

And despite watching his mother sink further away every day while Monty was at work, Jesper believed him. Until the day it all came crashing down.

Alice had spent all their money getting doses. Her parents and in-laws had finally cut her off, as she'd borrowed so much, and soon all their friends did too. She had started asking Monty's boss for advancements on his pay.

The day Monty discovered his wife was an addict was also the day he found out they had no money left and he lost his job.

They'd screamed at each other for hours that night. Jesper cradled baby Ally against his chest on his bed, doing his best to keep her from getting scared. The shouting finally gave way to sobbing. Alice told Monty the entire story. Her crazy past. The struggles of pregnancy and motherhood. The way the skeptical doctors laughed and said she wasn't trying hard enough. How much she couldn't stand what her life had become. How she missed the days when it was just the two of them.

After Monty had comforted his wife, he came into Jesper's room to hold his children, not realizing that Jesper had heard the whole thing. Monty promised that he would take care of it all. Jesper wanted to believe his father, who was strong and could handle anything, but even that young he had started to learn that some things were outside of his father's control.

Monty's name had been discredited; nobody would hire him. Alice had turned their families against them. They lost their house. Within months, they had to move to the edge of Racine, the grimiest village in the kingdom, worlds away from everything they knew.

Alice still got drugs. Monty didn't know how, couldn't find a way to stop her, but at the same time his children were homeless and starving. He promised he would take care of them. He'd give his soul to save them, he loved them so much.

So he did exactly that.

He walked into the Jacklands, right up to Pepperjack himself, and made a deal: money, shelter, and full protection for his family in exchange for his services. Above all, nobody could touch his children. Anyone else might have been turned away by the crime lord for asking so much, but Monty had a reputation as the best in his trade. By that night they had moved into the Molds and became ensnared in Pepperjack's web.

In the end, it was Monty's attempts to save them that killed them all.

As the months wore on, their father began to change. Instead of coming home with a bright smile as he told Jesper about what he'd made that day, he came home defeated and stained with blood, unwilling to look anyone in the eye. Pepperjack made him build despicable things. Prisons and chains and torture devices. With each passing day, Monty grew hardened and gruff.

Alice was heartbroken over the change in her soft and loving husband. Could she not stand the guilt of where she had brought her family? Or did she truly believe none of it had been her fault? The only thing they knew for sure was that she blamed her kids. After all, she'd been perfectly happy with Monty until they'd come along and ruined her life. She punished them for the simplest mistakes and screamed at them constantly, often reminding Jesper that none of this would've happened if it weren't for him. He almost found relief when she started using hard again and grew distant, even though that left six-year-old Jesper in charge of his baby sister.

The longer Monty worked for Pepperjack, the more valuable he became, and the more hours Pepperjack demanded from him to ensure protection for his kids. Sometimes he wouldn't come home for days at a time. When he did, he'd find his wife high and his children starving. He stopped smiling, stopped laughing, stopped joking, stopped coming into his children's room at night to hug them. Once he came home and four-year-old Ally wouldn't stop crying because she hadn't eaten in so long. Jesper desperately tried to get her to quiet down, and when he couldn't, Monty slapped her. Jesper's eyes had gone huge. Monty broke down into tears and apologized, but Jesper never looked at him the same after that. He knew.

He had already lost his mom and he was losing his dad too.

Monty became numb. He drank to keep the horrors of his job at bay, and would stumble home just to black out next to his wife. She hated him for what he had become; he hated her for doing this to them. They only remembered their kids when they were angry.

As Jesper spoke in broken sentences over the phone, Ally slowly slid to the ground, memories unfurling in her mind, the once sharp edges now becoming fuzzy. She'd always remembered her mother doting on Ally, cooking for her, holding her, playing with her, calming her, protecting her, loving her. A bright light in a happy world that Monty the Merciless had destroyed.

A headache came on as those treasured memories blurred and shifted. Yes, someone doted on her, cooked what they had for her, held her, played with her, calmed her, protected her, and loved her. But it hadn't been the beaming angel with golden hair. Instead, she remembered the scrawny kid with big eyes and a dark mop on his head.

The one true memory Ally did have was twisted: yes, Monty had beaten their mother that day, but only after he'd come home to find her dead. He'd beaten the corpse. He had been angry at her too.

Their mother had left them all in hell.

Ally remembered the rest.

When Jesper finally finished, he wheezed into the phone, as if he'd just run across town and back.

"You're lying," Ally whispered, but the words sounded false even to her own ears. It felt so wrong, so undeniably, completely, and totally wrong, but somehow she knew it was true too. How could something be both wrong and true? That didn't make any sense. That was madness.

"Ally." Jesper choked on her name. He might have been crying. He hadn't cried for their mother in years. Maybe never. Hardly even talked about her. Ally had always hated him a little for that. And now...what was it worth now? "Ally, I...I'm sorry. I...I'll come fi-ind you. We can...we can...we can talk more—"

Ally's voice came in strong now, but still hollow. "No. Don't."

"Ally—"

"I don't want to see you. Don't look for me." Then she hung up the phone.

She sat in the alley for a long time, staring at the wall, as if she could watch her memories play out one more time, the good ones, where her mother had loved her. Where she had been enough. Happy. Had she ever been happy?

From down the alleyway, she heard her father chuckle.

The endless thoughts rose up in her like a brutal ocean wave. She could feel the water thrashing down her throat.

Finally, Ally forced herself to her feet and started walking. If she stayed still she would drown. She just walked. Walked away. The waves followed her. She started to run, but she could still hear the water crashing behind her. She would drown. She needed to drown. Maybe then it would stop.

It didn't. Instead it started to rain. The sky opened up and dumped torrents of water on her, the wind whipping her hair in a frenzy. Blind, she skittered to a halt and tried to pull her sopping hair away from her eyes.

Panic rose inside her. Drowning. Drowning again, in between worlds, in between lives, at the mercy of the waves. Always the weak one. Always useless. Always overpowered. Always the one that didn't matter.

Why did you bring me into this world at all?

"Ally," someone whispered, their eerie voice somehow piercing through the deafening rain. "Ally."

Ally gasped and spun around, her nails scratching her face as she clawed her hair away only to find the sidewalk beside her empty.

But her mother had just said her name.

Did you bring me into this world just so it could kill me?

"Ally!"

This time she screamed as she spun around again, only to find AJ staring at her from inside his car. He'd pulled over to her and rolled down his window, watching her with a bewildered expression.

"What are you doing?" he asked. "Do you need a ride or something?"

"What?" She glanced behind her shoulder again but there was nothing there. Something in her chest cracked open. She'd never felt so much pain in her life.

Without thinking it through, she yanked open the passenger door and threw herself into the car.

"Just get me away," she snapped before he could ask. "Anywhere but here."

AJ looked her over with a raised eyebrow. She trembled so violently she almost bit her tongue, and somehow she knew he figured it wasn't from the cold. "Jeez Als, you look like crap. What happened?"

"Nothing!" she yelled back. "Are you going to drive or not?"

He raised his hands in surrender. "Whatever." Then he finally started driving. Ally craned her neck to watch the empty

spot of sidewalk until she couldn't see it anymore. She kept
fidgeting, reaching into her pocket for her rock, then releasing
it, then fisting her hands in her lap, and then back into her
pocket again. A pained, labored breathing was the only sound
besides the rain slapping against the windows, and it took her a
few minutes to realize it was hers.

Did you ever even love me?

AJ stopped the car, and Ally looked up to find they'd made
it across town already, parked in West End. To the left, trailer
homes. To the right, the Crims tent. She shivered.

"This far enough for you?" he asked, then reached toward
her. Some kind of snarl came through her teeth, and she
would've bit off his hand if he'd come further, but he retracted
quickly. He gave her a look of disbelief then gestured toward
the glove box. She deflated and turned to look out the window,
still tensing when she sensed him reach over and pull
something out of the glove box.

"You need to relax, Als." She heard something slosh and he
swallowed. "Take some."

Ally glanced over to see him offering her a silver flask
printed with the design of a playing card. Two of spades.

"Why not the king?" she asked, snagging onto the
distraction. "Why the two?"

AJ glanced at the pattern and a flash of darkness passed in
his eyes. Then he took another swig and it disappeared. "It was
a joke. From a friend." The word had the slightest air of
bitterness to it, though Ally could've imagined that. "He was
big into cartomancy stuff."

She wrinkled her nose. "I thought you don't have friends."

"I don't. Not anymore." Then he shoved the flask at her, as
if suddenly annoyed. "Just drink it before you drive me crazy.
You need to calm down."

Ally had to take the flask before it fell from AJ's grasp, and
she glanced at it warily. Despite Monty—or maybe *in* spite of
him—she had never tried alcohol. She'd always looked down
on it, thinking that needing it was a sign of ultimate weakness.

Now, though, she just wanted something to drown out the pain before it drowned her. Anything.

AJ scoffed. "Don't tell me you've never had a drink. What, your mommy teach you to just say no?"

She couldn't help it; she flinched. The lance of agony that went through her made her lift the flask to her lips. It burned. It burned like fire, but Ally forced herself to swallow, to let the flames lick at her and scorch her throat and keep her from drowning. The flames settled into her stomach, emanating a kind of haze that barely dulled her senses.

That's what she wanted. She took another drink.

And another.

And another.

Too soon she'd drained the flask, but somehow AJ had produced more. He gave her his wolf smile as they both drank and the haze seemed to settle over the car. Her thoughts slowed down, so sluggish that it took her minutes to remember why her chest ached from the inside out. When the memory caught up to her, she washed it down.

By the time the drink really ran out, Ally couldn't see straight. She fumbled for the car handle, not sure where she could go, but she just knew she needed *more*. And she needed to find it fast before the stars-forsaken memories surfaced again.

Before she could figure out how to get out, AJ took her arm and pulled her into him. She didn't even fight, didn't stop him when he crushed his mouth against hers, hot and heavy and all teeth. No pleasure came from the sensation but she relished in the distraction at least. Somewhere in her brain she knew she should panic, but she didn't care. Nothing mattered anymore.

AJ was all over her for what seemed like ages, until he finally passed out. She shoved him away so hard that his head hit the car door, then she ducked outside, grateful for the fresh air. Her legs wobbled and her feet faltered. She fell in the mud several times, and the last time she felt her stomach heave and she threw up. As she stared at the pile of sick underneath her, all the bones in her body seemed to hollow out. She wanted her mother to hold her; she wanted to scream for Jesper.

For the first time in years, she was truly alone—without her strength, her brother, or even the memory of her mother to save her. And Ally started to cry.

Did you bring me into this world just so it could kill me?

Did you ever love me at all?

Somehow, she got to her feet, stumbling through the mud, tears streaming down her face. The rain pelted against her skin. She couldn't see in front of her. Darkness everywhere. Was this the In Between? Would the monsters finally take her now?

By the time she reached shelter, every part of her was caked in mud and vomit. From the tent entrance, Pat watched Ally with a raised eyebrow.

"Please," Ally choked out. Even to her own ears, she sounded pathetic. Broken. Like baby Ally screaming for her mother to come back. "I just want to forget. I need to forget."

Unmoved by her pitiful display, Pat held out her hand expectantly. Ally stared at it for a minute before finally realizing what Pat wanted. She reached into her cloak and pulled out a wad of cash, not bothering to count it before handing it over. Any price was worth getting rid of this agony.

The eyebrows on Pat's forehead just climbed higher. Without a word, she handed Ally a small baggy filled with tiny circles. Pills. Then she pushed Ally inside the tent.

Ally swallowed hard, staring at the dozens of pills she'd just purchased. She thought of her mother, who she'd thought always guarded and protected her. Instead, she had succumbed to something like this. And Ally had wanted to be just like her.

She didn't realize she'd consciously made the decision before she popped all the pills in her mouth, having to swallow several times before they all went down. It wasn't long before the darkness rose from the corners and wrapped its talons around her, pulling her down far past where she'd been meant to go.

Ally had fallen into a deep, dark hole.

And this time she wasn't climbing back out.

Are you proud of me now?

* * * * * * *

"You all right there, Jesper?"

The question shook Jesper out of his thoughts, and he was grateful. After his dream the night before and the rough conversation with Ally this morning, the holes in his mind had been blown open by landmines. Everywhere he looked, he saw destruction. His insides felt like they'd been scrubbed raw. Every second spent not actively engaged in a distraction left his mind wandering dangerously, falling again and again into dark caverns of past memory he'd tried so hard to bury.

He blinked and focused his eyes. Mama March stood over him, her soft, expert hands making quick work of his latest haircut. H sat in the chair next to him, knees pulled up and arms curled around them. After spilling their guts to each other, they hadn't been able to be more than a few feet apart, as if they were each the hasty bandage covering the other's bleeding wounds.

Jesper glanced at Mama March and gave the most encouraging nod he could muster. The look in her dark, knowing eyes told him she didn't buy it. He shrugged apologetically. She sighed and kept working on his hair. The snipping of scissors filled the silence. Out of the corner of his eye, Jesper saw little bits of his hair raining down on the ground like blackened ash.

"You know," Mama March started, as if they had been mid conversation, "my granddaughter only pulls a face like that when she's been talkin' about Leo."

H curled in on herself slightly. Jesper felt the pang of her pain in his chest as he thought of Ally.

I don't want to see you. Don't look for me.

Mama March's voice pitched a bit softer. "We all got people we've lost. Don't get any easier, either. You got a Leo, Jesper?"

Throat thick, Jesper swallowed, then nodded again. He hadn't been able to find his voice since the call with his sister.

She clicked her tongue as she inspected his hair. "My love passed rather unexpectedly. Cancer came on fast, of course, but it wasn't just that. He was so *alive*, that man, in a way I'd never seen. I thought for sure I'd be dead long before Arlo." She sighed again, and the heaviness to it, the weight, nearly drowned Jesper right there. "Riley's dad, Leo, my son. It all piles up. Makes an old woman want to lock herself in her apartment and never come out again."

Jesper had certainly done that. He'd locked himself up in their house in the Molds, refusing to come out. A known prison is safer than unknown freedom.

"But, we can't do that, now can we? We gotta keep our hearts open. The pain of loving is always worth the pain of losing. Even if the loss is worse than we ever could have imagined."

The words settled somewhere in Jesper's mind, but he couldn't bring himself to focus on them. He just nodded his thanks to Mama March as she set her scissors down on the counter.

"Remember that, Jesper." She turned back to pull him to his feet and give him a hug. The gesture felt so foreign that it nearly scalded him. "After all, I keep these doors locked and people like you can't walk through. And that'd be my loss, wouldn't it?"

Jesper just stood there, too aware of his own skin, as H and Mama March said their goodbyes, Mama handing over several paper bags filled with cornbread cakes.

"You heard from our Kat yet?" Mama March asked before they walked out the door.

H's shoulders sunk even farther. She just shook her head. "Not yet."

The lines around her eyes creased with worry. "She'll come back to us. She always does."

Neither of them said anything on their way back. They'd both settled into a pained kind of comfortable silence, and Jesper wasn't inclined to break it. Instead he watched out for every person they passed, hoping and dreading to spot a head of messy blonde hair.

I don't want to see you. Don't look for me.

When they walked into the apartment, they found Riley pacing around the kitchen in a frenzy. Jesper skidded to a hasty stop when Riley practically yelled into his phone.

"Why? *Why* would you take her there?"

The surprising hostility emanating from Riley made Jesper's heart stop, but he forced himself to stay. If this was news about Kat, he had to hear it.

H had the same idea. Her eyes widened with the most animation in days, and she bounced on her feet as she watched Riley with eager anticipation.

Riley turned in his pacing and froze in his tracks, his gaze stuck on Jesper. All the angry fire in him went out like the flip of a light switch. The faint sound of another man's voice came through his phone, but after a moment Riley just hung up without a goodbye, his expression somber.

"What is it, Ry?" H asked. The desperation in her tone gave way to impatience. "Who was that?"

He let out a long breath and dropped his head, the most defeated Jesper had ever seen him. He ran a hand over his beanie before glancing up at Jesper again. His eyes glistened with possible tears.

"It's Ally," he said quietly, like the words pained him to say. "She's at the hospital. She, um, she overdosed."

And with that, the world seemed to stop.

The dead body on the couch, still as death.

The scream in the distance that shattered the sky.

The pieces of the sky rained down around him, the entire world caving in on Jesper's frail shoulders.

He wasn't strong enough to carry it. Truly, he never had been.

He snapped clean in half.

The next thing he knew somebody was calling his name in the dark. The voice came from far away, echoing through a cavern. Was this death? Was this what happened to people when they die?

What a waste.

"Jesper!" A new voice pierced through the haze and found him. "Jesper, wake up!"

For a moment, he thought it was Ally, and he struggled to find air. To get to her. To save her. When at last he broke through the surface and opened his eyes, he found a girl kneeling over him, her hair like a cloud and face stained with tears.

He flinched away from her. He didn't recognize her, didn't recognize this place, and even though there was a sense of familiarity lodged somewhere in his brain, his bleeding heart told him to run.

"Ally's in the hospital."

Jesper turned to see a young man kneeling next to the girl, holding his hands out and loose. They stared at each other in the silence.

"Ho-ow…" Jesper had to clear his throat, and even then his voice came through low and scratchy. "How do, how do yo-you know her? Ally. M-my sister."

The girl glanced at the young man with a fearful expression. The lines in his forehead deepened. "I know her because I've met her. You've stayed here for the past few months, and she comes to visit sometimes. Do you remember that?"

Jesper recoiled at the word. Remember. Of course he remembered. He remembered everything, always, the one cursed to never forget. All his remembering would ruin him. It had already. What he would pay to just be able to forget.

Ally might just give her life to forget.

The thought shook him out of his stupor. Despite everything, he knew he *had* to remember. The remembering was all he had. And the one thing he remembered more than anything else is he had to protect his sister, no matter what.

He recognized that feeling at least, and it brought a bit more clarity. Riley and H. Ducat. He knew them now, logically, even if he couldn't reach any of the emotional attachment he might have once had with them. How strange to stare at strangers that he still remembered as friends.

Riley relaxed slightly when he saw the recognition in Jesper's eyes. "She's alive, Jesper, and she should be okay. I need to go get her. She can't…she can't stay there. Did you want to come with me?"

H gasped, and she started crying again. "No, Ry, you can't. I'll go, I will take him—"

"No," Riley cut in sharply, making Jesper flinch back. He sighed and scraped his face with his hands, as if he would pull himself apart. "I doubt you're old enough. They won't release her to you. And I don't want you setting foot anywhere near there ever. You understand?"

"You're letting Jesper go."

"It's his sister, H. I figured he would have to be there." Riley glanced at Jesper. "Am I right? You don't really have to come, but I'm going."

Jesper just nodded. Of course he would have to go.

H opened her mouth to protest, but Riley just closed his eyes, as if he might break apart. "Please just stay. Get the bed ready for her. It won't take us long."

Seeing Riley so upset made H back down. Jesper didn't understand the reason, but he didn't ask, feeling too detached from the situation. He didn't say another word as he followed Riley out the door.

Neither of them spoke on the drive to the hospital. Riley seemed to be preoccupied, and Jesper couldn't muster any concern amid his panic. He kept getting flashes every time he blinked. One second he was looking at the road in front of him, the next a stretch of dead weeds in the Molds. One second he could smell the rusty heater and old car freshener, the next old ale and molten metal. If he didn't have Ally to hang onto, he would just succumb to the madness of it all.

Riley parked the car, every muscle tight and tense as he got out of the car. He didn't seem particularly excited to go into the brown building, so it surprised Jesper when he actually ran toward the entrance, not bothering to check and see if Jesper was following.

By the time Jesper caught up, Riley stood at the circular desk in the center of the room, rapping his knuckles against the counter impatiently. Chaos abounded around him: people in uniform running around and calling names, two young guys covered in blood getting wheeled away, phones ringing constantly. The place seemed too small for how many people were crammed inside. Jesper had to step around several people to get to the desk. Riley kept checking over his shoulder as if afraid somebody would attack him any moment.

Overall, it was not Jesper's favorite place.

"Her name is Ally Lewis," Riley was saying to the harried looking lady at the front desk. He'd never sounded so unfriendly before. "She's about seventeen, blonde hair, always wearing a black cloak. She overdosed."

That word again. It made Jesper flinch so hard that he caught the lady's attention.

"Who are you?" she asked.

"Her brother," Riley answered. "Have you seen her or not?"

The lady scoffed. "Right, like I don't have fifteen overdose patients in here right now. I don't have the time or the authority to dis—"

She stopped talking when Riley slid something to her. Jesper's eyes widened at the thick pile of cash. He didn't know whether he was relieved or disgusted when the lady didn't even hesitate—she just snatched the money and stuffed it in her pocket.

"Room 1865," she said, already looking back at her notes with disinterest. "She's been here a while and already been pumped so you'll have about a twenty-minute window before the nurses make their rounds again."

Riley left before she was done talking, already speeding toward a set of double doors on the opposite wall. Nobody stopped him as he went through, and Jesper struggled to keep up with his pace. Here in the hallway it was a little quieter. The people they passed paid them no attention. He started to get dizzy as he went by door after door after door, wondering which held his sister.

He'd barely caught up when Riley suddenly stopped and pushed his way inside a room. It took everything Jesper had left inside to follow him.

The sight nearly made him black out. His head pounded violently as he tried to merge the two images in his mind: Ally's pale and ragged form unconscious on the bed, nearly swallowed up by her black cloak covered in crusty mud. He blinked. Alice's pale and ragged form unconscious on the couch, her chest going up and down one last time.

How could this be happening?

"They didn't even bother to clean her up," Riley muttered darkly to himself, softly wiping away a smudge of mud on Ally's hand. She was covered in it, as if she'd been dragged from a hole in the ground.

All the cords connected to her overwhelmed Jesper, but Riley wasted no time pulling them off of her, somehow knowing where they all were. Within five minutes he had scooped her up into his arms and gestured for Jesper to get the door. His stomach rolled when Ally's head tipped back over Riley's arm.

Mommy!

Don't leave me here!

Don't leave me here with him!

"Jesper!" Riley's exasperated tone snapped Jesper back to the room. "Look at me. Your sister is alive, okay? She's alive and she's going to be okay. But we need to get out of here." He took an unsteady breath. "Now."

Jesper nodded and lurched into action, holding the door open so Riley could take Ally through. He was afraid somebody would see them with her and stop them, but nobody cared. They made it back to the car with no problem.

The second they were out of the building, Riley seemed to relax a little. He took extra care in gently setting Ally down in the backseat, twisting her leg back one way, fixing her neck, folding her arms nicely, as if making her comfortable. Jesper would've cried if he didn't feel so dried up inside.

Once again, the drive was silent, but this time Jesper stayed turned around in his seat, watching over Ally like a vigil. Had she always looked so pale or sick, or just now? Had she always taken drugs, or just today? Had she tried them by accident, or had it been Jesper's fault?

He would've thrown up if he had eaten anything in the last two days.

Riley parked the car at the apartment building. He turned the key slowly, as if all the energy had suddenly been sucked out of him. He sighed and the breath weighed thousands.

"It wasn't your fault," he said quietly. His voice wasn't as soft as usual, but the softest it had been in the last hour. "I don't know what happened, but I know that. I hope someday you can believe it."

Somewhere in Jesper's brain, the thought echoed that Riley sounded like it was *his* fault, but Jesper didn't have the time or care to figure that out. He just watched Riley carry his sister up the stairs and back into the apartment.

H opened the door for them, her eyes puffy and wide as she watched Riley take Ally into the bedroom. She started to say something to Jesper but he skittered past her like a frightened animal, his gaze trained on the floor. He didn't look up until he saw Riley's shoes standing next to the bed in their room. Jesper still thought of it as theirs, even if she hadn't been there in weeks.

It hurt Jesper to look at her, but he did anyway. She was so *still*. Frozen, lifeless, except for the rise and fall of her chest. If he squinted his eyes—and he tried not to—the blonde hair and sharp cheekbones matched his mother's perfectly. He hadn't thought of her face, the real details of it in so long, but now it was laid before him in violent clarity, just in a form twenty years younger. He hated it and longed for it at the same time.

Don't leave me here!

Jesper blinked. Ally on the bed. Blinked. Alice on the couch. Blinked. His sister. Blinked. His mother.

Are we just destined to become you? If Ally was their mother, would that make Jesper his father someday? Being here had messed with Jesper's head, made him think that maybe there could be a chance for them to have another life than what had been laid out for them, to take a different path than their parents had. But now Jesper saw that it was foolish, childish thinking.

There really was no hope for them at all.

✳ ✳ ✳ ✳ ✳ ✳ ✳

When Ally woke up, she found her mother standing over her.

She'd always remembered her mother as soft and warm, her full lips turned up in a slight smile, with a halo of golden hair as she reached to embrace her daughter.

Now her bones stuck out and her skin had a twinge of blue to it. Her hair fell snarled and lifeless at her shoulders. Rotting, empty black sockets stared back at Ally, and her mother smirked just as she raised a knife and plunged it into her daughter's heart.

Ally startled awake with a gasp. Pain crackled everywhere: her chest, her stomach, her limbs, her head. Her body was so heavy she could barely manage to lift her head and see the figure standing over her now.

Not her mother. Riley.

Riley was going to kill her. She could see the knife glinting in his hand, recognized the wicked smile on his face as he finally got rid of her, now free to keep Jesper trapped forever.

"Ally?"

The voice silenced the violence around her. Something inside her cracked open at the sound of her brother's voice, at Jes gasping her name as if taking his last breath. He knelt on the ground next to the bed she laid on. She didn't have time to ready herself before her traitorous gaze jumped to his eyes.

Haunted. Tired. A lifetime of sadness.

Why did you keep it from me?
Was she really like that?
Why didn't you tell me?
Was that how it really happened?
Did she ever love me at all?

Standing beside him was Riley with a cell phone in his hand.

He'd just had a knife, hadn't he?

"Ally." Her brother's voice again, quiet and raspy but somehow still steady. He reached for her hand. "Can you…can you hear me?"

She recoiled away from his touch, and Jesper's expression shattered. The devastation in his eyes was so absolute that she wanted to reach back to him, if only to make it better, but before she could he retracted his hand.

"What happened?" she whispered, the words grating against her sore throat. She glanced around the room with a sour expression. "How did I get back here?"

This is the last place I want to be.

"Riley brought you back from the hospital," Jesper answered. Her eyes flashed to Riley with distrust. Where did he hide that knife? Why else would he want her back here if not to finish her off?

As if to prove her point, Riley leaned in with a severe expression on his face. "Where did you get it?"

Even feeling like she'd been run over multiple times, his tone made her bristle, and she glared at him. "Excuse me?"

"Ally—" Jesper murmured.

"Where did you get it?" Riley demanded. "Who gave it to you?"

"Like I would tell you," she spat. "I hate you, remember?"

Jesper pulled back like Ally's fury was aimed at him, which just made her angrier, but Riley didn't even flinch. "This isn't about me, this is about you. Did you get it from Ricky?"

Ally blinked, stunned for the first time. Had Riley been watching her?

Riley cursed under his breath. "Ally tell me that you didn't take vac."

"Why does it matter to you?"

"Ally," Jesper whispered. "Yo-you have to. You have to te-el us."

"I don't *have* to do anything." Ally's voice rose as she pushed herself up on her elbows. "You're coming to play the big brother now? Where were you? Where were you to stop us from falling?"

The agony that spasmed over Jesper's face nearly killed her right then. Maybe she deserved that. Because they both knew exactly where Jesper had been: he'd been right there. Right with her. Slashing himself on the broken shards of their lives, bleeding out on the ground to try and save everyone else.

Despite the pain in her body that the pills had brought, she wanted the emptiness back. This was too much. "I needed it." She didn't mean to say it out loud, but the words cascaded out of her like a waterfall. "I needed it, to forget. The pills were the only way I had."

"How long?" Riley asked her. "How long have you been doing this?"

Not long enough. "It doesn't matter."

"Where did you get the pills from? Pat, AJ, Walrus?"

"It doesn't matter!" Ally shouted at him.

Jesper grabbed her by the shoulders and shook her roughly, wild desperation in his glassy, too-wide eyes. "Mom!" he screamed with the desperation of a young boy that had seen too much. "Mom, you have to stop!"

The world stilled. Ally froze. She felt her heart hammering, but everything else had stopped. Her arms throbbed under his tight hold; she couldn't bring herself to move. She just watched as the dazed look slowly drained out of her brother's eyes. He blinked again. His eyes started to focus. She could see the moment when he realized where he actually was, who he actually spoke to.

Ally knew she probably looked like her enough. She'd always prided herself on sharing her mother's traits, part of her name. For the first time in her life, she hated the resemblance. She wanted to scrub any part of her mother from her skin, even if she bled.

Jesper's mouth dropped open in horror. He let her go and leaned back, glancing at his own hands like traitors. "I'm sorry," he choked out. "I...I'm so-sorry. I never...I...I would ne-nev-never..."

"You would never hurt me," Ally said quietly. The truest thing she knew. Everything her brother had done, even lying to her, had been to protect her. She could see that now. "You're the only person in the whole world I know for sure would never hurt me."

Riley let out a long breath and pulled on his stupid hat. "I'll give you guys a minute." Then he ducked out of the room, keeping the door open. Likely so he could still spy on her.

Exhausted, she dropped her head back on the pillow and stared at the ceiling. Too many feelings swirled inside her. Too much. She itched for another pill, cursing the fact she had already gone through the supply she'd hastily bought from Pat.

After a long minute of heavy silence, she saw Jesper rub his face with his hand out of the corner of her eye.

"Was it..." he started, then stopped. Took a breath. "On purpose?"

Yes. No. Maybe. Ally had just wanted to escape her feelings, and she'd done that for a while, hadn't she?

"I don't know," she answered.

"First time?"

"Yes."

"Because of…because I told…because of her?"

Ally squeezed her eyes shut. She saw her mother standing over her with the knife again. With a small gasp, she opened them again.

"I'm sorry, Ally." His voice caught and broke. "I'm so sorry."

It took every bit of her strength to reach toward him. She didn't even have to look at him to find his pinky.

"Everything you ever did was for me," Ally said. Even if the truth hurt, she still knew it was true. "I'm not angry at you."

Jesper sagged in relief and rested his forehead against the edge of the bed. They didn't say another word for a few minutes. Maybe an hour. It was hard to tell. At one point Riley came to check on them—Jesper didn't budge so Ally assumed he was asleep and pretended to be asleep too. She lay tensed and ready in case Riley took the opportunity to take her out while she was vulnerable, but he just left. Probably wanted to wait until he could get her alone without risking Jesper seeing.

Jesper. Her older brother. Her true protector. Ally had wasted so much time trying to be her mother, to make her proud, and now she *had* in a twisted way. Her mother deserved none of it.

Now more than ever, she wanted to prove her father wrong, and her mother too. She wanted to give Jesper something better, to make up for what he had done for her. He was all she had left.

How long had she been unconscious at Crims before somebody had dumped her in the hospital? Days? Weeks? Had she missed her chance?

Maybe she could still salvage it. Merge Ricky and Red, if they hadn't replaced or lost interest in her already. If she could be the bridge for that alliance she could demand something from the two of them. Surely between Red and Ricky they could obliterate Riley and give her Jesper back. She'd do anything for his freedom. She owed it to him.

Trapping a groan behind her teeth, Ally slowly sat up and fought off the dizziness that came. She frowned. Every part of her, including her clothes and hair, were caked in mud. She'd need to find a way to wash out her cloak at some point, preferably before she talked to Red. She could probably bully AJ into letting her crash at his place until she was presentable enough.

I'm going to be something better than you, she thought, hating that she'd wanted to prove herself to a dead woman for so long. *I'm going to do what you should've done.*

It took a frustrating amount of time to crawl out of the bed without jostling Jesper awake or doubling over from pain or dizziness or near vomiting. She was a bit unsteady on her feet, but she leaned against the wall and made it to the door. Then she poked her head into the hallway.

Per usual, Jenny's door was closed. The room to Riley's door was open with the light on, and Ally could hear him typing on his computer in there. She tiptoed the opposite direction into the living room. H, thank the stars, was asleep on the couch. Ally slipped right out the door without waking her up.

The trip down the stairs was a bit precarious given how unsteady she felt on her feet. Strange winds whistled through the tight space, and in them she could've sworn she heard whispers.

"Ally."

She almost tripped on the last step, and her foot came down hard on the pavement. Squinting her eyes against the setting sun, she glanced down the sidewalk. Nobody was there.

"Ally!"

"What?" she snarled, whipping around to where the voice came from behind. Her stomach bottomed out. Leaning against the wall of the apartment building with dirty boots and a bloodstained beard, was Monty. He stared at her with violence in his gray eyes.

I wish you were dead!

Ally stumbled back, fumbling for the rock in her pocket, but a frigid breeze blew into her ear and froze her.

"You really think magic can help you?" her mother whispered. Ally gasped and turned to see her leaning against the opposite wall, black sockets wide and unforgiving. "It didn't save me."

Ally ran.

Several cars honked at her as she darted across the street, but she didn't care. When she hit the sidewalk again, she checked behind her shoulder to find the stairs to Riley's apartment empty.

Breathing hard, she wiped her eyes. If these strange visions or whatever were a side effect of the pills, then maybe the pills weren't worth it.

She turned towards Heartland and started walking. When she made it half a block, she found her parents watching her from the next alleyway.

Ally flinched and picked up her pace. The next time she passed an apartment building, her mother was there again, running toward her with a knife.

Heart plummeting, Ally dashed up to the next street. A taxi was parked on the sidewalk, left running with the driver's door open. The driver was helping their passenger put something in the trunk.

Ally didn't hesitate. She jumped into the driver's seat and slammed the door. The driver and passenger both yelled at her; she paid them no mind. Her foot jammed against the pedals on the floor and she pulled on everything she could get her hands on, trying to make the thing *go*. All these months she had never driven herself, but she'd studied AJ doing it for hours.

After a harrowing second, the car lurched forward and she sped down the street. Her eyes darted around wildly as she tried to maintain control, knuckles white around the wheel.

Once Ally turned onto Heartland, she relaxed slightly. Her father could follow her, her mother could run, but they couldn't catch her in a car. It was one of the many things Ducat had that Elaria didn't—it would win.

Something brushed against her throat, soft and cold. Ally shivered and glanced in the small mirror above her head. Her mother's black gaze stared back at her from the backseat.

"You really think you can outrun me?" she asked, her hold on Ally's throat tightening until she choked. "I *am* you. And you are me."

Ally screamed and jerked the wheel, barreling down a different street and onto the sidewalk. She had just a moment to see the car hit something—someone?—then her head smacked against the wheel and the world went black.

* * * * * * *

When Jesper woke up, he wasn't alone.

Through his muddled brain, the thought arose that not waking up alone was strange. Ally had usually left by morning, gone to wander the Molds and find the treasures that brought meaning to her life.

"Jesper!" a man's voice called, shaking him. "Wake up!"

Before he was all the way conscious, Jesper flinched back. The only man in this house was not one he wanted to cross.

"Jesper! She's gone."

Jesper blinked slowly, his chest aching at the words. Who was gone? His mother who had thrown them in this prison or his sister who spent her days pretending like she could escape it?

The scene settled around him, and Jesper's eyebrows furrowed. A room he wasn't familiar with. A young man in front of him. Did he know him?

"Jesper," the young man said again, his face stricken with panic. "Ally's gone."

Ally's gone.

Jesper glanced at the bed next to him—stars, his knees were sore—and found it empty. All at once, the memories rushed back at him.

Ally's gone.

Jesper jerked to his feet, ignoring the protest of his aching knees, and patted down the bed with his hands, as if his sister were just invisible and still lay there sleeping. The sheet puffed up and fell back down. Nothing.

"I tried calling her a couple times," Riley said, choosing not to comment on Jesper's search tactics, "but she didn't answer. I didn't think she would for me, but you should try."

Jesper nearly snapped his phone in half as he hastily fished it out of his pocket and flipped it open. His hands shook so hard he could barely press the buttons. He found Ally's name and waited. It rang. It rang. Riley watched the phone screen with the same amount of crushing anxiety. He kept pulling on his beanie.

It rang so long that a lady who was not his sister told him he had to disconnect.

"Try again," Riley said tightly.

He did. A third time. A fifth. Ten calls later and no Ally.

"Do you know where she would go?" Riley demanded, and the harsh edge to his voice made Jesper flinch, even though he felt the same desperation in his own bones. "Did she tell you where she hangs around?"

Jesper shook his head miserably. He'd never really asked. They'd had a lifetime of him letting her wander where she wanted, helping her feel like she had a semblance of freedom. Coming to a new place should've made him change the habit. It hadn't.

"It's dark out already," Riley said, "but maybe she didn't get far. I'm going to have a look around. Once the police station opens we can go talk to them too. Maybe they picked her up." He was out of the room before he finished talking, his voice echoing down the hallway. Jesper could hear him shaking H awake and filling her in.

Ally is gone.

Jesper couldn't think past those words. Brief flashes of his mother assaulted his brain as he lurched out of the room.

No, it couldn't end like that. Not again.

Jesper wouldn't survive the loss of his sister.

They all bundled up in coats—Jesper borrowed one of the extra Riley kept for anyone that needed one—and they headed out into the night. H surprised Jesper by coming with them. She'd made it clear she didn't care for Ally in the slightest. Jesper had come with her on several occasions to look for Kat, so maybe she felt like a debt was owed, but Jesper *liked* Kat. She was Jesper's friend too.

Jesper wondered if Riley made H come. The thought made him uncomfortable, but he didn't give himself the chance to find out. He just stared at his shoes instead of risking any glances at her face.

The freezing wind tore at them, somehow piercing through Jesper's coat and chilling his bones. That didn't deter him though, and thankfully it just spurred Riley on. They spent hours searching the couple blocks surrounding the apartment building, going in every direction. Then they came back to get Riley's car so they could drive farther out faster. Nobody spoke the entire time. Or, if they did, Jesper wasn't listening. Ally's name pounded in his mind like a headache.

The hours passed too quickly. It seemed to take ages just to get from one street to another. All too soon, the sun started cresting back up over the skyline, enveloping Jesper in a deeper dread.

Finally, Riley pulled over at the police station. "I'm going to check Crims," he said, his voice not betraying even a hint of exhaustion, as if it was his sister they were searching for. "I hope I'm wrong but we have to cross that off. You guys go see if the police have seen her. It's a good time to follow up on Kat again too."

Jesper couldn't fill his hands or feet when he got out of the car. He didn't look at H as they trudged up the stairs into the police department.

The woman at the front desk gave them a tired smile when they walked in and gestured for them to sit on the bench by the door. She picked up the phone and Jesper heard her speak quietly into it. "Those kids are back."

Jesper had only been in the police station once before a week earlier, and he didn't like it. Phones rang, papers shuffled, voices chattered over each other, and the TV volume stayed at least six notches too loud. It reeked of the desperation that came with constantly showing up too late.

They waited a few minutes before the woman directed them into an office. Chief Harbour, the man in charge of the entire police, sat behind a giant wooden desk. Jesper could've sworn he had even more wrinkles behind his overgrown beard than last week. He sighed when he saw them.

"No," he said, looking through a stack of papers. "I haven't found your friend."

H took that as an invitation to sit in one of the empty chairs across from Harbour, and Jesper followed her lead despite the man's unfriendly tone.

"It's been ten days," H said tightly, a folder clutched in her hands. "Ten."

Another sigh. "As I said before, Cheyenne has been a flight risk since the day she clawed her way out of her mother. Ten to one, she ran away."

H had practiced what she would say with Jesper last week so she would stay calm, but desperate rage took over her instead. "You don't know that! You have no idea what you're talking about! A girl is *missing* and you're sitting around here doing absolutely nothing! I know Kat. Better than anyone. I *know* that something is wrong."

Harbour glanced at the clock on his wall, drumming his fingers against his desk in a tuneless rhythm, then sighed again. This man sighed a lot.

"You have five minutes of my time."

Perking up, H took a breath and launched into her findings. "The last time I heard from Kat was last Thursday the twenty-eighth. She sent me a text around eleven in the morning and we went back and forth for about an hour."

She reached into her file—Jesper hadn't noticed she'd brought it with her—and pulled out what she called screenshots, showing their messages about a new music video that had been released that day. "She said she was doing an emergency vlog episode to talk about the video that dropped, which she did. The episode aired that night at six twenty-seven. She liked Kylie Jenner's pic at six forty-five, added a photo to her story about her makeup at quarter after seven. Then she responded to the comments on her vlog episode, the last one at eight thirty. And that's the last anyone has seen or heard from her."

"So eight thirty on a Thursday night," Harbour repeated, twirling a pen in his hand. "And you're sure she didn't just go out for the weekend?"

H huffed, straining for patience. "It's been ten days. I think she'd be back for the *weekend* by now. Check her social pages, her vlog account—she hasn't been active. She posts a vlog every Tuesday and she's always on commenting. But her accounts have been completely dead. Even her followers are noticing. And Riley's IT friends couldn't find anything either."

Harbour raised an eyebrow. He looked just as lost as Jesper felt whenever anyone started talking about online things. "You're basing this all on some face gram account?"

"No!" H's hands clenched into fists. "She *lives* with me! Not always, but usually. Or with Riley. We haven't seen her or heard from her in *ten days*. Yes, I know she's a flight risk and 'susceptible' to who knows what or whatever other garbage you want to throw at her. But this isn't her. She's gone and nobody is doing anything about it!" She shot him an accusing glare. "The first seventy-two hours are the most critical in a missing person investigation. If you don't get on it, you lose the trail, and then it's so much harder to pick up."

The first seventy-two hours. Jesper's stomach plummeted. How long had Ally been gone?

"And where did you hear all this? School?" Harbour glanced over her skeptically, as if even the thought of her still being in school was a stretch.

H scowled. "Unlike you, I educate myself. I keep tabs on the news, I read articles, I listen to podcasts. I make sure I'm not a complete *idiot*, so when a girl twenty years younger than me shows up in my office, she doesn't know how to do my job better than I do."

Tense silence leveled the room. Harbour tipped his head back against his chair, still playing with the pencil in his hands, and stared at the ceiling for a second. Then he dropped his pen, rubbed his face, and sighed.

"I'm sorry about your friend," he said, and for once Jesper felt like he might mean it. "I really am. You seem like a smart kid, so I'll be straight with you and tell you the facts. Cheyenne is eighteen. Legally she's free to go anywhere she wants. I can't do anything if she just picked up and decided to go somewhere."

H opened her mouth to cut him off, but he held up a hand and kept going. "I'm drowning in paperwork. I'm running dozens of homicide cases at once, Ricky is causing problems left and right, and Caleb's store got robbed *again*. Half my cops are dirty and the other half are so scared of Red and her new crazy prodigies that they'll barely leave the office and do their jobs. So when I tell you I just don't have the manpower to track down an eighteen-year-old likely runaway who doesn't want to be found, it's not me being a prick. I mean it."

"So that's it?" H demanded.

Another sigh. "I'll put a guy on it. Take a look around myself. One day is all I can really give you."

She looked like she was going to argue, then deflated. "Okay. We're here about something else too." Jesper felt her eyes shift to him.

He swallowed hard. "My-my sister."

The silence stretched out a little too long. "Your sister is missing too?" Harbour asked.

Jesper flinched. How many people would go missing in his life? Would he be the only one left, eventually?

When it became evident Jesper was too incapacitated to say anything else, H picked up the trail for him.

"She overdosed a few days ago. Riley brought her home from the hospital but she took off this morning. Won't answer her phone. We checked everywhere but we can't find her."

Harbour's bushy eyebrows furrowed. "I hate to say it, but did you check Crims?"

"Riley's there now. He didn't want us to see it."

He nodded. "That's good. Riley's a good one." Then he sighed. "Leave a description and your phone number with Ruby at the desk. No promises, but we'll keep an eye out."

"Tha-ank you, you sir," Jesper replied.

Harbour nodded back at him. Jesper straightened. "I'll call you if I find anything on either of them. Just…" Another sigh. Did he know how to breathe any other way? "I know it may be hard to hear, kid, but be ready for all answers. Including the one that Kat or your sister just didn't want to come back."

They walked back out to the desk and had to wait a moment while Ruby was on the phone. She handed them a pad of paper and pen. Jesper just stared at it. H took it and started writing, whispering to Jesper as she did.

"Ally…Lewis, right? White, blonde…eye color? Blue? Probably like five foot five or somethin'…"

She finished and handed it to Ruby just as she hung up the phone. The lady glanced over it routinely, then her eyes narrowed.

"Ally," she said, her voice tight. "Your sister?"

H jerked her thumb at Jesper. "His. And I forgot, she always wears this, like, goth cloak. It was pretty dirty when we saw her."

"Uh huh." Jesper could've sworn the lady was slowly getting paler. She swallowed hard, her mouth twitching into a frown. "Have a nice day."

When Jesper held the door open for H, he glanced back just in time to see Ruby rip the paper in half and toss it away like it had a disease. His shoulders sagged.

Riley hadn't come back yet, so they just started walking. It was all Jesper could do to not give into hysterical panic or traumatic memories. They didn't talk the whole way home.

To Jesper's surprise, Riley was home when they walked in. The hairs on the back of Jesper's neck stood on end when he saw Riley's face: red and puffy from crying.

Something was wrong.

Jesper's thoughts immediately jumped to the worst for Ally, but Riley's anguished gaze fell on H instead. She froze.

"Why are you looking at me like that?" she demanded, her voice rising. "Why are you looking at me like that? *Why* Riley?"

Riley stepped forward and took one of her hands in both of his, a single line of tears falling down his face.

"Bingo Night," Riley finally said. "Mama March was coming home and she…clean hit and run. A stolen car, most likely. It was empty when somebody finally got there. She died on impact."

And with that, Jesper saw the sky cave in on H's shoulders. She wasn't strong enough to carry it. And she snapped clean in half.

Both Riley and Jesper held her as she screamed until she lost her voice. Her body thrashed with gasping, rasping sobs. Was there no end to her pain? Could there be an end when she had just lost the last of her family? How could you possibly heal something like that?

When Jesper met Riley's eyes over H's head, he saw Riley crying too, mouthing something to himself.

What are we going to do?

Riley, who worked three jobs and went to school. Riley, who had given up a future to stay and help those who needed it. Riley, who had just lost the last functioning adult that helped him keep his makeshift family afloat.

Jesper tipped his head back just like he did the night his mother died, with Ally sobbing in his lap.

What are we going to do?

Just like all those years ago, the sky had no answer. Jesper and Ally had still been left all alone. And Mama March was still gone.

* * * * * * *

Ally sat sprawled out on the smelly couch, the red fabric long since torn and faded brown, with her head lolled back. Some part of her could feel her body firmly planted here on the couch; most of her had floated up, up, up, and only the ceiling kept her from drifting into the sky. The air pulsed around her, a living, breathing thing. She made herself take a gulp of it, and her nose wrinkled. Maybe the couch didn't smell. Maybe she did.

She'd woken from the car accident on an unfamiliar and unflattering brown couch with a massive headache and a sore shoulder. AJ had been so pathetically proud of himself that he'd been the one to pull her out of the car.

"I got a tip from a buddy of mine," he explained when she demanded to know how he found her. "He saw the wreck but nobody really reports those for a while in case Red set it up. He let me know he thought he saw you." Then he grinned at her. "A thank you would be nice."

Ally rolled her eyes despite how much it hurt her head. "Not likely."

The couch vibrated underneath her again. Ally sighed. It had been two days since she had broken herself out of Riley's apartment and stayed hidden in case he came looking again. Jesper had been texting her nonstop since. She had replied just once to say she was okay, then ignored the rest.

Truthfully, shame scalded her to the core. She couldn't face her brother again until she had something to offer back to him after all he'd done for her. She had to pay the blood debt.

"Debts are rarely settled as easily as we think."

The eerie voice came from behind the couch, and Ally closed her eyes so she didn't have to look at her mother's grotesque face. She hadn't left Ally alone for hours.

302

Ally reached blindly for the glass bottle on the coffee table in front of her, sloshing another swig of liquid down her throat. She didn't throw it up as much anymore. AJ had been impressed she could hold it so well. She said the talent ran in her family.

She hated them all.

The fire of the alcohol burned her painful thoughts away, or at least kept them at bay momentarily. AJ had told her he could get more pills for her if she wanted—for a price of course—but they both knew Ricky would have her head if he knew she was buying from somebody else. And she couldn't shake the look on Jesper's face.

Mom, you have to stop!

What a waste it all was.

Time dragged and lurched. AJ talked on his phone and ate some noodles out of a cup. She didn't care enough to listen to the conversation. Wasn't that the point anyway? Turning her brain into mud so she couldn't think about the truth.

So she couldn't remember that she still missed her mother even as the rage against her burned Ally to ash and her soulless eyes haunted her every step.

So she couldn't remember that her bones still ached to stab her father in his gut and watch the life slowly bleed out of his eyes.

So she couldn't remember that she had never once mattered at all.

The cushion underneath her started to buzz again.

"Your brother doesn't know when to quit, does he?" AJ muttered as he got up to throw away his empty cup.

Grumbling to herself, she dug her arm underneath the cushion and felt around until she found her phone. The screen blurred when she tried to look at it, but she finally managed to focus enough to see that she had over twenty missed calls. The first letter of the caller wasn't the 'J' that usually started her brother's name, but an 'R.' Right then, it started to ring again.

Ally groaned and swore under her breath before answering. "What?"

"Excuse me," Ricky snapped back, more irate than she'd ever heard him. "I'm looking for a rat I dragged out of the sewer and made my star employee. Can't seem to find her anywhere."

"I've been busy."

"Of course you have. But I don't care. I gave you an opportunity and you don't get the choice to leave it in the gutter."

"I'm not." Ally rubbed her burning eyes. "I'm still here."

"Then show up, love, or I'll send someone after you. And I won't bother to tell your brother where we left your pieces."

She wanted to ask who he would send, since Ally was the best he had, but the line went dead. She sighed and dropped her phone into her lap.

"You're getting soft," her father growled from the corner of the uncomfortably small room, "if you're letting Ricky threaten you. Weak."

Slowly, Ally pulled herself to her feet. AJ watched with a raised eyebrow.

"Gotta go to work," she said, pulling her muddy boots on.

"It's about time."

Ally glared daggers at him, and he had the good sense to lean away.

"Take it easy," he said, holding his hands up in surrender. "You've just been slummin' it on my couch for a bit, that's all. Not that I'm complaining. Just didn't think you were the type to sit around. You can barely make it through a stakeout without going berserk."

"Yeah, well people think a lot of things, don't they?"

They think things their whole lives and then those things turn out to be lies.

For once, Ricky wasn't smoking when Ally found him on his corner, sitting in the same camp chair. She could feel his gaze burning into her.

"You're late, chickadee. By about a week."

"I got here right when I wanted to," she snapped.

"You did, did you?" His usually foggy gray eyes were now crystal clear and it unnerved her. She shifted on her feet. He didn't look as crazy as usual. No talk of blue moons or talking trees. Just fury. For the first time, she had the thought to be afraid of him.

Finally, she had to break the silence. "What do you want?"

He barked a sharp laugh. "An employee, for one. Been payin' her but she hasn't shown up in a week."

"I told you. I've been busy."

"Busy? Ha!" He slapped his knee. "Busy cryin' yourself to sleep on your boyfriend's couch? What happened, little Ally, did your brother break your doll?"

Ally scowled. "I never had any dolls." No, she only had sticks and rocks that she had loved just as much.

Mommy, look. Look what I found.

Mommy, wake up. Don't leave me.

Mommy, come back. Did you ever love me at all?

"Wake up, love," Ricky snapped, jolting her back to the present. "Do you want to belong here or not? Because I'm just about ready to move on and set my wolves on you to clean up the mess. Not to mention you got pills from Pat, of all people. Don't look good, love."

"Stop acting like I sold you out." The words came out whinier than she intended, and she just hated herself more. "It's been a long week, okay? Besides, if I had asked you for vac you would've taken every cent I had."

He pursed his lips and looked at her for a long moment. "You take my stuff, love, and you won't quit. I promise you that."

Her mother appeared behind Ricky's chair and smiled at her, knife in hand. "He's right."

Ally shook her head to clear it. "And you'd want me to quit? That's funny, coming from the dealer."

"I'd want someone competent, at least. I thought you were a hidden gem I stumbled upon, but now I'm not so sure. Last we talked, we were thinkin' up a big merger with Red. Any progress on that? Or did you forget while you were gettin' pumped at the hospital?"

She gritted her teeth. "I'm working on it."

"Are you now? Tell me, love, how have you gotten this far in the first place?"

"What?"

"Duchess, AJ, Walrus, McKennis, heck even the police know about you. Not to mess with ya. How'd you get there?"

Instinctively, Ally's fingers brushed against the rock in her pocket. "I'm powerful," she said. "That's all you really need to know."

"Uh huh." He stared at her and itched under his beanie. It took all of Ally's concentration to hold his gaze instead of glance at the knife in her mother's hand. "I'll ask you again, chickadee: do you want to belong here or not?"

She hated herself when the word came out as a strained, desperate whisper. "Yes."

More than anything. More than everything.

She had nothing else.

"Then do your job."

Ally cleared her throat, trying to pull herself together for at least a moment. "Okay. What do you have for me?"

Ricky sat back in his seat. "Nothing. You missed it all."

Ally scowled. "You dragged me out here just to tell me that?"

"I dragged you out here because you needed to be dragged. So that you could get some real air and realize you need a shower. Bad."

"You're one to talk."

"I'm the crazy drug dealer that lives on the street corner in his camp chair. I can do whatever the devil I please."

Ally rolled her eyes. "You live here? On the street. And you're getting after me for staying at AJ's?"

"I've lived in places you can only dream about." A hint of bitterness slid into his voice. "It doesn't matter now. We gotta make do with what we have, and we have this place. I want you to talk to Red."

"About what?"

"Tell her I can move it for her for seventy-five percent of what she pays now and in half the time. We need to get this merger back on track before it goes stale."

"What is it?"

"If you needed to know, I would've told you."

She sighed in exasperation. "Fine. Anything else?"

"No. Except that I'm disappointed."

"I got that," Ally said flatly.

His eyes flashed, as if in challenge. "You know, chickadee, that first day when you and your scraggly brother moped past me, I had a feeling about you. I could sense it underneath your skin. That's why I brought you on when you asked. And you started so promising, you really did. Never been impressed as I was with you. But now it seems you're committing to staying exactly what you looked like: nothing."

You're nothing.

A stick to be buried.

Always have been.

She brought you into this world just so it could kill you.

"You've always looked like nothing to me."

Ally couldn't help jumping, and turned to see her father standing behind her. A wave of nausea threatened to make her sick.

Ricky cursed under his breath, and when she glanced back at him, he glared at her. "Payin' attention? Go find Red and see what real power looks like. Seems you forgot. Off with you, then."

The dismissal infuriated her more than anything else. Nobody ever told her when to come and go. Nobody dictated her life.

"A word of advice, love?" Ricky called after her, the edge still in his voice. Ally hated herself for stopping, but she couldn't risk making him angrier. She couldn't lose this job. She couldn't just be nothing. She couldn't let her brother down again. "Either go overdose and put yourself out of your misery, or clean yourself up. The wasted little girl act gets tired. You're no use to anyone like this."

A million snarky responses gathered in her mind like clouds, but in the end, she couldn't see through the storm. She chose silence and walked away.

The farther she got from Ricky—and closer to Red—the more his words sunk into her skin like shrapnel. She had never cared for how she looked, but she found herself trying to untangle her hair and wipe the grime from her face as she walked. It burned her pride to present herself to Red like this.

Is this who I am now? she thought. *This is who she was. This is the most she ever wanted me to be. Nothing.*

It left a worse taste in her mouth than the alcohol vomit.

This is my chance. I can still salvage this. She repeated the words to herself over and over, holding onto them like her last lifeline. If she could still secure the merger with Red, she'd be back in Ricky's good graces. She could ask Red for help in getting Jesper free from Riley. With the power of Red and Ricky behind her, Ally could make sure that her brother never wanted for anything ever again.

This is my chance. I can salvage this.

He'll be so proud of me.

Steeling herself, she finally reached Red's corner. The twin redhead guards were posted at the entrance of the gateway. Ignoring how hollow and pathetic she must look, Ally straightened her shoulders and glared evenly. "I need to talk to Red."

"You'll have to wait." The taller one said, jerking his thumb back. "Execution goin' on."

Ally peeked around his shoulder to see Red sitting on her makeshift fire escape throne, her crimson lips twisted into a snarl as she glared down at the man on his knees before her. Ally couldn't believe the sight. A grown man, about Monty's age, kneeling before Red.

He was crying. Begging.

"It was a misunderstanding," he sobbed. "That's all. That's all. I would never betray you to McClain."

"A misunderstanding?" Red repeated. The dangerous glint to her voice made Ally want to both go closer and run far away. "So you're telling me you were too stupid to understand what was happening. That's it?"

"No…no, I…I don't…no. No, I…no." He blubbered now, stuttering worse than Jesper.

"I was always taught that stupid people deserved to die," Red said. "A service to everyone else, honestly."

The man just cried harder. Even from here, Red's eyes blazed with fury. A grown man alone with her in an alley, and not only was she not afraid, but she held all the power. Nothing could take her down. Ally just stared in awe and longing.

What she wouldn't give for that security. To make someone like Monty beg Ally, instead of the other way around.

Red pulled a gun out of her jacket and the man screeched with panic. But when she pulled the trigger, nothing happened. Just an airless click.

The man sagged and broke into fresh tears of relief. Red frowned at her weapon, then shrugged and tossed it to the ground. "Guess it's your lucky day." She rose to her feet, descended the stairs, walked up to the man, and stabbed him in the chest. Once. Twice. Three times. Ally couldn't look away.

Red freed her wet blade and the body crumpled onto the ground. Crimson blood sloshed around her boots as she looked at the dead man with a bored kind of disgust, then yelled at the twins to get rid of the body.

"Floor's yours," the shorter twin muttered to Ally as he and his brother started for the body. "Good luck."

Ally took a deep breath, then followed. "What did he do?" she asked Red casually as the twins hauled the corpse between the two of them.

"Pissed me off," Red growled. "Honestly, what was he thinking? McClain? Idiots. I still have you to thank for snuffing that coup out for me." Then she gave Ally a slash of a smile, as if she'd used the same knife to cut her mouth open. "Since the kill really belongs to you, should I have cut off his head execution-style? Make you feel more at home?"

Ally managed a shrug. "You can do anything you want."

No threat is a match for you.

I'd give anything to have that.

Anything.

Red smirked as she wiped her blade off on her pants, leaving a dark smear along the black fabric. "So, you got off the couch to come see me, huh? Must be something important."

Aly flinched, shame scalding through her. She should've gotten something on AJ, something to use to buy his silence, even from Red. "AJ was just thrilled to have a girl in his apartment for once. I'm sure he oversold it all."

Red barked a laugh. "I didn't hear it from AJ—I have more eyes than just him."

AJ didn't tell Red? Why not? He always made a big deal about telling Red everything about her.

"So why are you here, Ally?"

"To deliver a message. From Ricky."

"I take it he won't be aligning with McClain?"

That felt like lifetimes ago, but it had been barely a week: Ally on her way to convince Ricky not to take the deal, so full of hope and strength. Feeling for the first time she was going to be okay. Safe.

"No, he won't be."

Red nodded. "I owe you for that then."

The words gave Ally confidence. She could salvage this. She could save her brother.

"Since he's not going with McClain, he wants to merge with you. Expand both of your empires and ensure that we won't ever have a problem with McClain or anyone else ever again. Ricky says he can move it for you for seventy-five percent of what you're paying in half the time."

Red backed up to lean against the pole of the fire escape. A black mass above shifted at the movement. Jabber, the massive dog. Only now, Ally noticed him sprawled out on the fire escape stairs above Red's head.

"Merger, huh?" She scoffed. "Ricky's been trying to do that for years. Smart to send you, but the answer is still no. I hate Ricky and I won't work with him, period. Ever. Even if he claims to see it in his smoky stars." She cocked her head. "You know, you'd be better off working for me, Ally. I thought that's why you were here."

"Ricky told me you're a monster," Ally said coolly, refusing to look too eager at the offer. "And I needed to get some personal things in order first."

Red laughed again. The sound could draw blood. "Of course he did. He's right, isn't he? Isn't everyone a monster?"

It takes a monster to hold back a monster, don't you think?

"He basically said Riley was a monster too."

The crimson smile stayed plastered to her ivory face, but the light in her eyes flickered out. She ran her tongue along her teeth. "Yeah, I'm sure goody-two-shoes Riley Hatton and the insane drug dealer are *best* friends. Probably have dates at Gordy's on the weekends." The sarcasm in her voice felt too barbed to land right. She quickly composed herself and breezed on. "I do owe you for ratting out McClain for me. If it takes a personal favor to get you on my side, then name it."

Ally couldn't help the flutter of excitement that went through her. This was what she'd been waiting months for. "I've infiltrated Riley's group. I know all about the operation he runs there and how it works. I've wanted to take him out for a long time now, but he has my brother. I want my brother back, and in exchange you give me the manpower to leave Riley in pieces. Then he won't be a problem for either of us anymore."

Red's mouth just twitched, making her smile look more like a scowl. The silence stretched on a second too long before she said, "That won't be necessary. I have that situation under control."

It took everything in Ally to hide the shock from her expression. She had the situation *under control?* Ally had actually been inside that situation, and Riley did whatever he wanted without consequence. He even recruited people away from Red and helped them escape their debts.

No, this didn't feel right. It didn't match with the puddle of the dead traitor's blood around Ally's feet.

"But Riley is actively *against* you. He takes people like my brother and brainwashes them, makes them think they are safe just so that he can get off running their lives. How is that any better than what McClain is trying to do?"

Red snapped her teeth together. "As I said: I have that situation under control. Drop it, or I'll assume you're a traitor too."

What? Ally blinked in shock. "But what about my brother? I want him back!"

"I can't make your brother stay away if he doesn't want to."

"Really?" Ally growled, kicking her boot through the puddle of blood. "Because it seems to me like you can make anyone do just about anything. I thought you ran this place."

Out of nowhere, Monty walked past Ally and inspected the fire escape with skeptical eyes, as if he was imagining how to easily bring it down with the flick of his wrist.

"She's weak," he scoffed. "Pathetic." For the first time in her life, Ally agreed with him.

I thought you were more than this, Red.

I thought nobody touched you.

But maybe somebody did. Maybe everyone had been so focused on Red's screaming blood fest that nobody thought twice about the ever quiet Riley on the other side of town.

His side of town.

No. This wasn't right.

Ally had to bend to a brutal and murderous man who breathed vicious violence.

Red bent to a twenty-something-year-old boy in a relationship with his computer.

All the power, all the admiration…all a lie.

Red's eyes narrowed and she straightened up, flexing her fingers around the knife still in her hand. "Look, little Ally, you're new here. There are rules and things that were set in stone long before you washed up. If that's disappointing, get over it. You're in over your head."

Alice laughed. Ally flinched and turned to see the black eye sockets staring at her. The knife glinted in the light. "What, did you expect something like Pepperjack? That you could come in here and offer your broken soul like your father did, and somehow make it all better? Nothing will ever fill up that hole inside you."

The Molds had been built on straightforward violence: an eye for an eye, blood for blood. She'd grown up in a land full of monsters who didn't pretend to be anything else.

But landing in Ducat had made her realize a painful truth, a lesson she should've learned long ago. From her mother. Her brother. Riley. Red.

Nobody was ever as they seemed.

"You really are stupid," her mother said. "Aren't you tired of being disappointed by people?"

"What are you looking at?" Red asked, stealing Ally's attention back.

Ally just glared at her, and Red bristled as the dog growled under his breath. "You really won't touch Riley to get my brother?"

Red met her gaze evenly. "No."

Without waiting for a dismissal, Ally turned on her heel and walked out to the street, feeling the point of Red's gaze like a dagger on her back. Her parents followed her.

"It's Riley," she muttered to herself. "Riley is the threat."

"And he has Jesper," Alice added, her blue lips twisting into a frown. "He'll never escape them."

"Nobody is going to help me. I'll have to do it myself." She nodded. She could do it. Jesper would do it for her. "I have the power anyway. I thought I needed somebody else but I don't."

Monty grunted in reply. "You don't need anyone."

I don't need anyone.

When she got back to AJ's apartment, she practically kicked the door down. He was sitting on the couch, his own fingertips stained with blood and a crooked smile on his face.

"Hey there, Als. Long day on the job?"

Ally just slammed the door shut and started pacing in front of the couch, too many ideas coursing through her to sit still.

AJ picked up a half empty bottle of alcohol she'd left behind. "Been awhile since you had a hit."

"I don't want it." The itch in her veins hadn't gone away—she knew it would take some time—but now it only repulsed her. The temptation was gone.

I don't need anyone or anything.

I'll do what my parents never could: I'll save Jesper on my own.

And I won't need Pepperjack or any stars-forsaken drugs to do it.

"Come on, don't you—"

"I don't want it!" she screamed at him. "Get rid of it!" He stiffened, gaze flicking to her hands, as if anticipating an attack. Then he offered her a slightly strained grin and set the bottle back on the floor.

Surrendering. Good.

"What's the deal with Riley?" Ally asked.

"Riley Hatton? Who cares?"

"I do."

AJ pursed his lips, clearly not thrilled she cared about Riley, and shrugged. "His uncle was part of a rival gang—can't remember whose now. King mowed them down. I think most of his cousins went down too. His dad pledged to King to save his life, but he bit the bullet for snitching years later. His mom is a basket case. I think she's downing antidepressants but I don't know where they get them from. Not any of my people anyway. A few years back, Riley had the chance to leave to WSU on scholarship. That doesn't happen to anyone around here, but the idiot didn't take it. Now he runs some kind of shelter for lost kittens and pretends to be better than the rest of us. Even back in high school he had that holier than thou thing." AJ rolled his eyes. "Not my favorite guy."

"But he's not affiliated." Ally knew that. None of Riley's pets were part of Red's gang.

"Red doesn't force draft into her ranks unless she requires their skills. As long as people follow her rules, she doesn't care if they wear her tattoo or not."

Ally gritted her teeth. "But Riley doesn't. He has his own territory. His own space. He is openly against Red, everyone knows it, but she doesn't do anything about it."

AJ watched her carefully for a moment. She could see him trying to build a lie behind his eyes. Her deadly expression made it clear that was a very bad idea.

He sighed and hung his head. "Look, anyone who asks Red about it gets shot, and the few people who have actually gone after Riley tend to disappear. I'm smart. I don't ask."

"And that doesn't bother you?" She knew AJ. She knew his need for attention, his jealous desire to be the favorite, to be stroked like a pet. "The pathetic computer nerd has more power in this place than you do. Red *gave* him that power. She let him take it. Has she ever given you that much?"

AJ stayed quiet, angry clouds gathering in his expression as he mulled over her words. "Of course it bothers me. I just never…look, I have no lost love for the guy. If you want to go after him, I won't stop you."

"Even if Red said not to?"

His eyebrows shot up. "She told you *not* to?"

"Yeah, she did."

"Well that doesn't…" he trailed off, his hands balling into fists.

"Make sense? I didn't think so either." Her cloak billowed behind her as she paced the small room. "I worked myself into the ground to be noticed by Red, and I don't care anymore. I don't need her. I'm going after Riley, I'm going to save my brother, and I will smother anyone that gets in my way." She stopped pacing and stared at him. "Are you going to be in my way?"

AJ barely took a minute to consider before shaking his head. She made a mental note of how quickly his allegiances had changed. He'd traded King for Red. Now Red for Ally. She'd have to watch for the moment, in days or weeks or months, when he traded her for someone else.

"You better watch yourself, Riley," she muttered. "I'm coming for you, and I'll leave you in pieces."

From across the apartment, Alice gave a razor-sharp smile. "That's my girl."

CHAPTER 9

OFF WITH THEIR HEADS

They found Kat's body two days later.

Harbour called H at one thirty in the morning. The ringing woke Jesper up first, who had been sleeping on the floor next to the couch. He raised his head as H groaned and swatted at her blinking phone. The ringing stopped. Jesper put his head back down.

A few minutes later, the door down the hallway opened and Riley padded out, his messy and notably beanie-less hair a stark contrast from his grave face. He had his cell phone at his ear. Jesper heard him mutter a response, then he dropped his phone onto the floor.

The clatter made Jesper flinch and H startle completely awake. Jesper pushed himself up on his elbows as Riley staggered up to the couch and collapsed onto his knees.

"They found her," he whispered, his wobbly voice hoarse. "She's…she…"

H let out a half sob, half scream. The sound punched Jesper in the gut.

"What?" He pushed himself up, his breaths coming out in gasps. "What?"

"Gone." Riley's voice cracked as his eyes filled with tears. "She's gone."

What do you mean gone? Jesper wanted to screech. *What do you mean?*

Kat had just been here. She had just been here with him, showing him how she applied her pink eyeshadow, detailing her favorite Meryl Streep scenes, praising the woman named Kim and her daughter.

"What?" Jesper gasped again. His mind tripped over itself, yet a deep emptiness echoed inside him.

Kat.

His friend.

Gone.

He didn't realize he was crying until the tears dropped onto his shirt. H fell from the couch to the floor sobbing, and Riley surged forward, making Jesper cringe back. But Riley just wrapped the two of them in a giant hug. There in the dark they all cried over their friend.

And Kat *had* been his friend. She had found him, brought him to Riley. She was the first to want to get to know him. The loudest person he'd ever met, but also the friendliest and most loyal. She stuck up for him, looked out for him. He had never had anyone like her before.

Was this what a family was supposed to feel like? So tangled up in each other, so emotionally dependent on each other, that the loss of one felt like a limb had just been ripped off?

Jesper knew his heart would have a Kat shaped hole for the rest of his life. She'd been his first friend, and his first true loss.

When the tears ran dry, Riley let them go. "They can't get a hold of Mary Ann," he explained. "They want me to go…to go identify her."

"I'll go with you!" H cried, her face swollen. "I want to see her!"

Riley let them come, but he wouldn't let them see her body. Jesper wondered if it was better that way, to only know Kat as the colorful person she was, or if they should know the truth of the horrors of the world. One was kinder; one was smarter.

"What did she look like?" H asked when Riley came out of the room that held her body.

It took Riley a moment to talk. His eyes glistened as he shook his head, then a small, sad smile splayed on his face. "Pink hair. Pink nails. Pink skirt. Still our Kat."

Afterward, Harbour sat them down in his office and explained that Kat's cell phone had been found in the same dumpster her body had in the next town over. Through it, they were able to piece together an idea of the last night of her life.

She had filmed her emergency vlog episode, just like H had said, in Riley's living room while H and Jesper were at work, Riley bought groceries, and Jenny slept. Then she went over to Miguel's where she put the episode together and uploaded it online. They placed her in Harriet's apartment at seven that night based on the picture she had uploaded to her story in the bathroom mirror. An event in her calendar she'd named 'TB' had been set for eight that night. Besides a few responses to comments at eight thirty, nobody else heard from her after that. The police inspecting Kat's body said they put time of death between ten and midnight.

So what happened in those four hours?

For a while, nobody had been sure. The first guess was a drug issue—H scoffed at that—but there weren't any drugs in her system. A random mugging, maybe? Harbour could only guess until one of his officers with Kat's phone opened up Puddles: a dating app she'd installed on her phone. She had dozens of chats on the app with dozens of different people, but after sorting through all of them, the officer found the one they were looking for. A man named Trevor Benson. They'd chatted for two weeks and had set up a first date for that night at eight, exactly like a dozen other dates Kat had set up in the app for the coming weeks.

The account he had used had since been deleted. The police had looked into possible 'Trevor Bensons' but there weren't any in the area.

Harbour called it catfishing.

He managed to keep his grim voice clear as he explained that Kat had been raped, strangled, then left in a dumpster. Like garbage. Like she wasn't a person at all.

The thought made Jesper start trembling so violently that he bit his tongue and blood coated his mouth. Ever since they landed in Ducat, he'd felt a duty to get home, but never before had he *wanted* to. Ducat had been grimy and violent, but it had never once seemed worse than the moldy misery Jesper had been raised in.

Because at least there it made sense. There were rules, awful rules, but everyone knew the game. An eye for an eye. Blood for blood. You knew the lines and you did not cross them. You knew your neighbors were monsters and they didn't pretend to be anything else. They didn't change their name to Trevor Benson just to gain a girl's trust and trick her out of her body and her life.

This was madness.

This was a nightmare.

The second they got back to Riley's place, Jesper staggered into the bathroom and threw up everything he'd eaten in the last few days. When the vomit filled his throat and he couldn't breathe, he thought of Kat and started sobbing.

Kat.

His friend.

Gone.

Please don't leave us here.

Jesper stayed on the bathroom floor for the rest of the day, dozing in and out. When night settled and he knew there was nothing left for him to throw up, he dragged himself into the living room. Riley and H sat on the couch in the dark, the pink blanket wrapped around their shoulders, watching Kat's vlog with swollen eyes.

They didn't even say anything. H just held her other arm
out and Jesper sat next to her. When she wrapped the end of
the blanket around his shoulder, covering them in the last
scraps of their friend, for a moment it felt like Kat was there
too. Bouncing in her seat, telling Jesper the entire plot of the
movie before they even turned it on. Saving him the last
marshmallow because she thought he deserved it. Constantly
reminding him that she was utterly shocked a guy as decent as
him still existed.

You were my first real friend, Jesper thought. *And now you're
gone.*

Jesper studied the girl on the screen, her blonde and pink
hair flipping around her shoulder as she demonstrated a new
style and talked about Meryl Streep's new movie. A girl who
covered herself in sparkles to hide the decay she came from.

With Kat's voice soft in the background, Jesper took out
his phone and typed a text to Ally. He'd been trying to call her
every day still. She'd answered just once a few days ago to tell
him that she was alive and okay. Still, he'd been so sick with
worry, desperately begging the stars that she'd come back to
him. That she wasn't already gone too.

* * * * * * *

Ally gulped down the rest of her lukewarm coffee, then
tossed the empty cup in the pile on the ground. Her eyes
burned from lack of sleep, but she kept them open wide as she
rifled through the papers scattered out all around her, each with
the same name printed on it.

Riley's current apartment.
Riley's childhood home.
Riley's family tree.
Riley's school transcripts.
Riley's clean record.
Riley.

Riley.

Riley.

Riley.

"Where are you?" Ally muttered under her breath. She knew the real Riley was buried somewhere in this pile of his life. "You're here. You're here, I know you're here. I just have to find you. And I'll find you."

She'd find the nasty truth she had always suspected and she'd show that truth to Jesper.

Her brother would be so grateful for her strength and smarts. He would abandon Riley and come back to Ally wholeheartedly.

She'd carve out a space for them in the world, and they would live the rest of their lives safe and protected.

Where are you Riley? She imagined the rabbit she had chased back in the Molds, lifetimes ago. Sure, Riley was faster than her and had the familiar land on his side, but Ally was smarter than him. Eventually he'd find himself in a hole.

And Ally would bury him alive.

"He has Jesper," her mother said, glancing over the papers. Ally had already yelled at her twice for staining the pages with her decaying fingers. In the corner, Monty sharpened his knife, as if preparing to go hunting. She kept a close eye on him, knowing any second, he could turn on her.

"He has Jesper," Ally agreed. "We'll make him regret taking my brother from me. I'll save you, Jes. I'll save you."

The front door opened and AJ walked in carrying—thank the stars—more coffee. Ally reached her hand out. He did his best not to step on any of the pages littering the floor as he made his way over and sat on the couch behind her, then gave her the cup. She felt him glance over at the pile of empty cups she'd made in the last two days. He didn't comment though. Smart of him.

"Find anything yet?" he asked instead.

"What do you get out of this?" She handed him a wad of papers as she took a drink, letting the warmth zing through her veins. It gave her energy and focus—the exact opposite of what the pills had. She tried to hone it on that, to forget the fact that part of her still ached for drugs and alcohol.

"My girl through and through," Monty growled. Ally glared at him.

AJ narrowed his eyes, as if eager to concentrate and prove himself, but he deflated after looking at the first paper. "They're just transcripts."

"Right." Ally didn't let her confidence slip. She recognized the letters, but couldn't make out most of what the papers said. Infuriating, but she would never let AJ know. "What do you think it means?"

"I think it means he's a cocky know-it-all."

Ally rolled her eyes, buying a second to cover herself. "I got that. Since you're a top informant, I thought you could give me something deeper."

AJ's mouth quirked to the side, but she saw the challenge glint in his eyes. She tried not to look too eager as he flipped through each page, going back and forth, taking a few minutes to study them all.

"Struggled in art class," he commented. "Above average in P.E., science, and literature. Terrible in creative writing. Best in math and computer science. To get grades like this, he'd have to lean heavy on analytical thinking and be pretty smart—or with a teacher." He smirked. "More interesting, but less likely. He was in a couple of geek freak clubs, but didn't do much else. Probably a smart alec too afraid of failure to try anything outside of his comfort zone." He glanced up at her. "I remember him. We were a year apart in school. Before I dropped out, anyway."

Ally kept her face passive, careful not to show any sign she was impressed. He got all of that out of a bunch of letters? "What was he like back then?"

AJ shrugged. "Scrawny. Quiet. Hardly even knew he was there. I forgot about him back then, really, until now."

Stupid Riley and his clean record. There had to be something she could pin on him. He had to mess up *sometime*.

"Nobody's hands are clean," Alice agreed.

"What about his mom?" Ally asked.

"Useless, as far as I can tell," he said. "If that was my old lady I would've kicked her out a long time ago."

"So maybe he's getting something from her?"

AJ smirked at the eagerness that slipped in her voice. "Pills, maybe. But I doubt it. She's much more strung out than he is. I still don't know where he gets her meds from. He doesn't have any prescription records, and people would notice if he was heading down to Crims on the regular."

Ally gritted her teeth and took another swig of coffee. Time to change topics. "You mentioned his dad earlier. King killed him, right?" She scoffed. "For being as annoying as his son?"

The smirk on his face melted into his regular crooked grin, his face lighting up. "I forget you aren't from here—it was a thing back in the day. Riley's dad was a member of the Black Cards. He snitched on King to the cops. And you know what snitches get."

"A bullet in the head?"

AJ laughed. "Close. Stitches, usually. At least, only when you actually survive being cut into pieces. Hatton Senior wasn't so lucky."

Chewing on her lip, Ally put down her precious coffee cup to sift through papers with both hands. She pulled out a picture of the family: Riley, about twelve years old, with his two parents. The three of them stood in front of a banner, huddled close, the kid holding up a piece of paper. An idea began forming as she stared at young Riley.

"You remember him in school?" Ally asked absently. The wheels started turning in her head, dredging up Kat's voice from her memories. "I thought King forced a bunch of kids into the Black Cards."

AJ nodded, pulling on the sleeve of his leather jacket to show her the black playing card tattoo on the inside of his wrist.

"Wouldn't Riley have been a part of that too?"

"Um, I guess?" AJ took a moment to count in his head, which annoyed Ally. They were only one year apart. How much counting was needed? "I don't know. I never really paid attention to him. If he was, I didn't know the details."

Had Riley been lying to them? Was he just as dirty as the rest of them? She thought back to every conversation with him, trying to picture his wrist, then realized he had always been wearing long sleeves. Like his stupid beanies.

"You didn't notice that before?" Monty asked, looking at her like she was something he'd stepped in and couldn't get off his shoe.

Ally growled. "Shut up! I'm trying to think."

"Jeez, Als," AJ muttered, "I didn't say anything."

"Stop talking!"

Caffeine sped her thoughts into a sprint, each idea coming faster and faster. Riley had been drafted into the Black Cards under King. Red killed King and took over, but left a chunk of Ducat to Riley to do whatever he wanted for no reason.

Except there *was* a reason. There had to be. Red wouldn't just give that up. She was smart and cruel and strong, and would only walk from a fight she thought she wouldn't win.

Maybe Riley wasn't an innocent boy taking in nobodies like he claimed. Maybe he was the most dangerous one of them all.

"I'll bet King gave him something," Ally thought out loud. "Some kind of secret job on his computer that made him less noticeable. A job that gave him skills and connections that anyone, even Red, would respect."

AJ nodded, surprise in his wide eyes as he took the string of ideas. "And then when King fell, Riley threatened Red. So they made a compromise. He gets his own square of town and she doesn't bother him."

A true member of the original Black Cards. Who would've guessed?

It seemed Ally was the only one. And what did that mean?

"It means Jesper is in the hands of the most dangerous person here," her mother said gravely.

Tossing the bundle of papers onto the ground, Ally lurched forward, snatched her phone up from among the mess, and dialed Jesper's number.

"He'll want proof," AJ drawled unhelpfully as the phone rang in Ally's ear. "He's been staying with them for months. You really think he'll just believe you?"

Of course he will, Ally wanted to snarl back. *I'm his sister. We only have each other.*

But when the phone rang and rang and rang, she started to wonder if AJ was right. Jesper had called her a million times in the last week. Why couldn't he answer *now?*

Scowling, she slammed her thumb down on the hang up button and typed out a text instead, careful to turn so AJ couldn't see how much she struggled forming words.

chek rily rist blak crd

"That's a start," she muttered.

"It's not good enough," Alice grumbled back.

"They have him. They have him, and if I don't set him free, nobody else will. He'll be lost." Take away the fact he was the only person in the world Ally had ever, or likely would ever, love—she owed him. He had helped her carry them out of the rotten Molds, and now that she had the strength, the power, she could pull him out of Riley's clutches. Not stand by drunk and watch as he destroyed himself.

Her mother had been the rotten core of their family. She had poisoned them all.

Ally wouldn't let anyone else poison Jesper's life again. She would be better than her mother.

She would save him. She would be the hero. And Riley would fall.

Ignoring AJ's dubious look, Ally grinned at her mother. "Are you proud of me now?"

* * * * * * *

H GMA BURY 2MOROW. WAIT 4FUNERAL L8R 4
BOTH. KAT GONE.

Riley had spent ages two nights ago convincing H they
needed to bury Mama March. She had drowned herself in
denial, Riley told him in private, and that kept her putting it off.
Denial and wanting Kat to be there. Denial and hoping that her
best friend hadn't left her like everyone else had.

But H hadn't wanted to do the memorial service yet, and
Riley finally agreed to the compromise. They would bury her
now and do a memorial service later. Jesper had been touched
when they both invited him. Monty had burned Alice's body
and taken the ashes somewhere—Ally and Jesper never really
said goodbye. He'd never been to a burial before.

H decided she wanted to have a joint memorial service.
Mama March had always welcomed Kat into her home and
heart with open arms, and Kat would've been honored to share
a day with her. Plus, H had added when explaining her decision
to Riley and Jesper, it meant only one hard goodbye for them.

They had spent the last two days preparing, while Jesper
worked at Miguel's almost non-stop, picking up all of H's
shifts. Miguel came in to give him the money he'd earned in the
last week—nearly triple what he usually got—and it felt heavy
in his pocket as he made his way back home. Well, Riley's
apartment. He wasn't sure what rules there were about making
a home. He wasn't related to any of them.

Home.

Elaria. The Molds. Monty.

The money weighed heavier with each step. He had to get
back.

But how could he leave?

But how could he stay?

Ally would never understand it, even now that she knew
everything, and maybe nobody would, but Jesper knew he
wouldn't be able to live with himself if he never went back to
Monty. The guilt would eat him up. He'd never rest. He'd never

breathe. Despite everything they'd been through, leaving Monty would feel like the ultimate betrayal.

Would Ally come with him? Would she want to? He had to believe that whatever had broken between them would mend. It would take time. It would take work. But especially after what had happened to Kat, he was willing to do it. And when she was ready, when she had time to accept the truth of their parents, they'd find a way to return to Elaria. He'd get her away from the influence of drugs and alcohol so she didn't end up like their mother. Unless taking her back to their home would just trigger the resemblance faster.

She was his everything. She could make it.

And he would do anything for her to make sure she did.

Jesper refused to think about what it would be like to leave Riley and H. Some part of him thought it would never happen, that he could just stay with them forever. And, stars, he wanted to. But would he ever be able to rest?

And the cycle of thoughts repeated, swirling into a constant storm.

The stairs in the apartment building were harder to climb these days, as if his feet were made of stone. He hoped footsteps were loud enough for a warning of his arrival. The other night when he came back from work, he walked in on some kind of conversation between Riley and Jenny. It wasn't a fight, really, or even a conversation since Riley was the only one talking.

"We're on our own now!" he nearly shouted. Jesper thought he might be crying. "Do you understand that? It's just us. We are all that's left. Can you at least talk to me? I'm scared, Mom. I'm scared!"

Jesper had been mortified when he didn't have time to vanish before Riley saw him. Riley played it off well and was careful to smile at Jesper more, but it didn't fool him. Jesper knew what it was to live in a house as it started to crumble.

Thankfully, when he pushed himself inside the apartment, he found it empty, the lights off, the air stale. He didn't need the light to find his way into the kitchen and drink a glass of water. The liquid sloshed down his throat, and his empty stomach garbled. Despite Riley telling him otherwise over and over, Jesper never felt he was allowed to find food on his own—someone had to give it to him, and even then, he still felt bad for eating it. Unless it was spaghetti. Then he only felt a little bad.

Leaving his cup in the sink, Jesper trekked through the quiet apartment, looking for H. She'd eaten much less than he had in the last two weeks. If anything, she was the one who needed food. But the kitchen and living room were both empty. So was his room. Jenny's door was shut, as normal, and no light came from Riley's room. Jesper poked his head in anyway to see if she had fallen asleep on Riley's bed instead of her usual place on the couch.

"Hey."

The voice out of the dark made Jesper jump back against the doorframe.

"Sorry," Riley said from somewhere in the space, his voice small and scratchy. "Didn't mean to scare you."

Jesper shifted on his feet, unsure what to do in this situation. Ally would want to be left alone, but he'd learned a long time ago that Ally and Riley weren't the same.

"Um, are you...are you okay?"

A soft, lifeless laugh echoed. "Yeah. Just having a good cry."

Jesper blinked in surprise. For a moment, he wondered if he'd heard right.

Shut up! Monty roared in his head. *A real man doesn't cry, Jes. A real man doesn't let his weakness get the best of him.*

Why would Riley just admit he had been *crying*? Weren't you not supposed to do that? He didn't seem ashamed at all.

"You can come in, if you want," Riley went on after a few seconds of Jesper's confused silence. "I think I'm done now."

Not knowing what else to do, Jesper stepped slowly into the room as his eyes finally adjusted to the dark. Riley's small space was a surprising mess of clothes and books, and Jesper had to step carefully around the desk to get to where Riley sat on the floor, his back against his bed. Jesper stood there awkwardly for a moment until Riley patted the space next to him. Jesper sat.

"They had an assembly at the high school for Kat today," Riley told him softly. "H arranged it. She's still over there. It's pretty cool what she's been able to do there. Kat was always so ashamed she came from here, but her story is really shining a light on how easy it is to forget girls in her situation. I hope…" He sighed sadly. "I hope maybe it can keep someone from ending up the same way."

Jesper shifted to sit like Riley: back against the bed, knees up, arms around his legs. He felt small, even in the tiny space.

"Memorial service for both of them is tomorrow morning." Riley glanced sideways at him. "I hope it goes without saying that you're invited."

H had already said so as well, and Jesper had been touched. Monty had burned Alice's body and taken the ashes somewhere—Ally and Jesper never really said goodbye. He'd never been to a burial before.

"I've, um, never been to one. Is there something…I should do? Say?"

"What do they do where you're from?"

Jesper shrugged. "I don't know. I never…I never, um…knew." He cleared his throat, then winced as the sound ripped through the delicate atmosphere and lowered his voice even more. "Have, um, you been? To one?"

"Yeah." Riley let out a sigh that could've been a laugh. "Far too many, I think."

So he was an expert? "How many?"

"Um, well…"

In the dark, Jesper felt his face get hot. Was that the wrong question? "Sorry, I—"

"No, no it's okay. I guess it's just a lot to count. Gets overwhelming sometimes." He paused for a minute, and Jesper's muscles clenched with tension that he did the wrong thing. "Six cousins. My aunt and uncle. My grandfather.

Probably at least a dozen friends and classmates." He hesitated a second between the last two, his voice getting progressively quieter. "A baby sister. And, um, my dad." He took a breath. "Makes you start to wonder if you're the problem, you know? If you're the common denominator. If someday you might be left all alone."

"That's a lot," Jesper murmured. It had just been him, Ally, and Monty for so long. He couldn't imagine that much loss. "And you...you still let people in here. How? Aren't you...scared? Of losing more?"

Out of the corner of his eye, Jesper saw Riley nod slowly. "Terrified. Every time. But I have to. I know it sounds crazy, but I…I just have to. Even if everyone who walks through that door is cursed. Even if everyone in this city is cursed and there's nothing I can do about it. I just…I have to try. No matter what it does to me."

They sat in silence for a few moments before Jesper reached into his pocket and pulled out a bundle of money Miguel had just paid him. He didn't count it before he offered it to Riley. "Here."

Riley stared at it in awe, like he'd never once seen money before. He shook his head. "I...thank you, but I can't take that from you. You've worked so hard to save up."

"You let u-us stay here. Gave us, gave us food." Jesper shrugged. "Where I come from, I would be, I would be dead now, dead, for taking all this without pay-payment. I owe you mo-ore, really."

"No, no of course you don't owe me. I don't—"

"Just take it. Please."

Riley gave a faint smile and took the money. "Thank you. Really. Now that...now that Mama March is gone, there's a lot...well I've just been scared. Of how we could all survive just on...just on me." He gestured to the money. "This will help. Thank you."

"Why do you do it?" Jesper asked. "Did anyone tell you to?"

"No, not really." Riley shook his head thoughtfully. "I think you and I are built the same in some ways. For whatever reason, we were built as givers living in a world of takers. Everyone and everything just takes and takes and takes—and we want them to, we don't ask them to stop. And we give and give and give every ounce of ourselves. We'd bleed ourselves dry for anyone. And it looks crazy. But we still do it, because it feels like maybe if we gave enough, then someday the world would be filled. Someday it would be okay. And somehow, for us, that would be worth losing ourselves in the process.

"It's not noble. It's not even healthy, really. Nobody ever told us to. Nobody ever taught us. We just are. And we can't seem to change." He shrugged. "If we did, then who are we, you know?"

Jesper nodded slowly, taking time to process each word. "I only ever wanted to protect Ally. I never cared what happened to me. Now she doesn't talk to me. And *I* don't even know me."

"Family can be hard. Even when you love each other, it's still hard. And if you base your whole identity on them and then one day they're gone? Then you don't know who you are. It's scary. I'm sure for you too. But, if I've learned anything over the years, it's that it's not just about blood, you know? Family is also who you pick up along the way. And despite how painful it can be, we need people. People to help us be something more. We need something to hold onto."

Then Riley let out a long breath. "Anyway, you heard from Ally yet?"

Jesper sunk into himself and shook his head. Suddenly exhausted, he sighed and rested his forehead on his knees. "I lied to her. About our mother. Our whole lives. I thought I was…protecting her. I lied to her and she found out and got angry."

There it was, the truth laid out. He hadn't said the words out loud since the dreaded phone call with Ally.

"I think…I think I'm afraid," he admitted, out loud and to himself. "After the…when she…she…I mean, she texted me she was okay, but if she started...she started..." The words scalded his mouth. "Started drugs. I'm afraid of her ending up just like her."

"Just like your mom, you mean? Did she use drugs too?"

Jesper pressed his forehead harder against his knees. He felt the urge to scrub his face. "Yes. Overdose."

"I'm so sorry, Jesper." After a few moments, he asked, "You don't talk about this a lot, do you?"

Jesper shook his head. "Never."

"Thank you. For trusting me with it."

The response was so surprising, so foreign, that Jesper's head snapped up, as if he could see the lie written on Riley's face. But it wasn't there. No sneer, no mocking, no anger. No jabs about being a 'real man' or pointed glances at every mistake. The judgments of Monty that Jesper had grown so accustomed to.

"I don't want to be him," Jesper blurted, thinking of his father, the eyes that he saw every time he looked in the mirror after trying to scrub himself clean. "I want to be just like you."

Riley's eyebrows bunched together underneath the line of his hat, and he gave a sad laugh. "I don't know if that's something to wish for."

A buzzing sounded, and Jesper stiffened when he felt his phone start to vibrate in his pocket. Could Riley hear it too? He had gotten after H and Kat many times for pulling out their phone during what he called a 'real conversation.' Jesper would never want to disrespect Riley. Especially right now.

A few seconds passed with tense indecision before Riley said, "You can answer that, if you want. I don't mind."

Deflating in relief, Jesper pulled out his phone just as it stopped ringing. His heart stuttered at the contact of the missed call.

"It's Ally," he whispered in awe, more to himself.

Riley straightened. "What?"

"It's Ally." After so long without her reaching back to him, Jesper was suddenly paralyzed. Did she call just to yell at him?

To say she'd changed her mind and she really did blame him for everything?

Where were you to stop us from falling?

"Call her back!" Riley exclaimed, but before Jesper could do it, a text message popped up.

chek rily rist blak crd

"Um…" Jesper turned the phone to Riley. "What's this mean?"

Riley squinted against the harsh brightness of the screen, his face wrinkled in concentration. Jesper watched the shapes reflected in his glasses for a minute while Riley slowly repeated the phrase three times in confusion.

After the fourth, his expression crumpled. He slowly lowered his arm to place the phone on the floor, creating a blob of light on the ceiling.

"Ah," was all he said.

Anxiety built in Jesper's gut. Had somebody else died? "What's wrong?"

Riley closed his eyes and tipped his head back against his mattress. "She'll probably tell you anyway, won't she?" His voice had a dark edge to it that Jesper had never heard in him before. It scared him.

"Te-ell me what?"

With a grim set to his jaw, Riley opened his eyes and pushed his right sleeve up, displaying a black square on his wrist.

Jesper recognized the symbol from others' wrists: Red, the redhead twins, the men that had mugged him.

The symbol of the Black Cards.

"I knew she didn't like me," Riley muttered. "Should've guessed she would start digging."

Everything in Jesper told him to run, the alarm bells going off in his head screaming that this was exactly how it started, how life ended up in pieces. But either fear or exhaustion or curiosity kept him in place.

"Ally likes to dig," he finally said. His voice must've reflected his newfound fear because Riley frowned.

"Is it that you think I lied to you? Or I'm possibly a monster?"

Jesper took a few deep breaths in an effort to clear his mind. To separate past from present, Molds from Ducat, Monty from Riley.

"My father was soft. Kind. The most I have ever known. And now he's the scariest monster I've ever met." Jesper nodded at Riley's wrist. "It started with something like that."

Riley tipped his head back and closed his eyes for a long time. It was probably only a minute, but it felt like hours. "She'll tell you about it, won't she?"

"Ally won't stop." One of the few things Jesper knew for sure. "She doesn't know how."

With a sigh, Riley opened his eyes again, his voice drifting far away. "My dad's family got mixed up with gangs early on. His brother, sister-in-law, and nephews all died because of it. He swore he'd keep me out of it. But when King rose to power, he drafted everyone. Including us. Draft or die. So I went in. My dad took the bloodiest street jobs as a trade with King, so I could work from the safety of our apartment on my computer."

He sighed. "I won't lie and say I didn't do bad stuff. Because I did. I was thirteen years old and knew it was wrong, but I knew I had people to protect too. And I knew what happened to my cousins, my friends. So I did it anyway. And, honestly, as much as I hate to say it, I'd do it again. If I had to. If it came down to H's life. If I could bring them all back."

Jesper's throat had started closing up, but he had to ask. He had to. He had to know that there wasn't just one ending to this kind of story. "What happened to your dad?"

Riley winced and took a shuddering breath. "I rarely...I've only talked about that day once. It's...well, if she finds out anyway, might as well make sure you heard it from me first."

It took a few moments for Riley to prepare himself. Jesper's body started to ache, but the pounding of his heart drowned it out.

"I understood the back side of things," he finally started. "Computers, accounts, money, hacking. That was my thing. It was hard for me to grasp the street side of it. School was easy for me; I stayed home and acted on King's instructions and looked after my pregnant mom. I had a frie…" He hesitated for a second. "I'd heard that King had set up my dad for a bad job. I still don't know why or if it was on purpose. I panicked and called the cops. When they got there, my dad had been shot. They took him to the hospital an hour after I'd arrived with my mom after her water broke in the kitchen. I left her for a minute to go see my dad, but the doctors wouldn't let me in his room yet. When I came back, my mom had…my mom…" His voice trembled. "She'd delivered a stillborn. And in between her hysterics, we find out that my dad's doctor was a Black Card. Let King right into the room so he could cut him up in his bed."

Riley stopped for a tense moment. Jesper closed his eyes against the horror.

"I pretty much lost both of them that day. My mom, as you probably have noticed, never recovered. It takes bottles of meds just to keep her alive. To this day, she still doesn't know I'm the one that called the cops. King never did either. They thought my dad had snitched and he…he died for it." He took a shaky breath. "So I got out. Got beat up a lot for it, but I did it. Eventually I made the right friends, and the wrong people stopped bothering me. But that didn't…I mean, bad things still happened, all around me, every day. Just because they weren't happening to *me* anymore didn't mean anything. I couldn't live with myself just standing by. So I started taking people in, helping them out, trying to set them straight. It's the only thing that keeps me alive."

The room fell silent. Riley took a few ragged breaths until he evened out, and slowly the tension started to loosen in Jesper's limbs as he took in the story.

"So you made a choice," Jesper whispered. "You chose to be different. And it worked."

Riley glanced at him for the first time since telling him the truth. "You say your father's a monster. That doesn't make you one."

That doesn't make you one.

Was that possible? Jesper considered the people he had met since leaving his father's prison.

Duffer, the man who risked his own life to help lead them through the In Between.

Arlo, the man who chose music and love over expectations and rules.

Riley, the man who traded his life and soul to save those who couldn't save themselves.

It could be Jesper, the child of the Molds who rinsed off the decay he'd been raised in and chose a different path.

And Jesper was so relieved by the possibility, he started crying.

"I don't want to be like my…like him. I did once, but I…not anymore. I can't." Jesper covered his face with his hands. "I can't forget. I can never forget. Everyone forgot except me. And it's so heavy. I don't…I don't want it anymore."

Riley put his hand on Jesper's shuddering shoulder, and the simple contact felt like a lifeline. If Jesper didn't take it, he would drown.

Thankfully, he didn't cry for very long, and once he started to dry his tears, the sting of shame never came. It shocked him to find he wasn't embarrassed about his show of weakness at all.

Riley handed him a tissue. "I know you haven't been here very long, really, but it feels like a long time. And I'm really glad you found us Jesper."

The words washed over Jesper, soothing as it went, leaving him feeling clean, for the moment. Calm.

"There," Riley said with a faint, sad smile once Jesper had wiped his nose. "Nothing bonds two souls like a good cry. Let's just hang on to that for now, okay?"

A memory flashed through Jesper's mind: of Duffer explaining the symbol tattooed on his face as he led them through the monster-filled land.

As long as you're anchored to what matters, no matter how dark the journey may be, you'll always find your way back home.

And so Jesper grabbed onto the shards of good he'd been given and refused to let them go.

* * * * * * *

NOT WAT U THINK. FOONRAL 2DAY COME 2 TALK. PLEASE.

Ally scowled at the message Jesper sent back in the early morning, several hours after she'd sent the warning text about Riley. It looked like he had tried to call her back right after, but she'd been too wrapped up in her research and didn't notice.

Another buzz. She glanced at the screen.

IM SORRY ALLY. EVERYTHING. JUST WANT 2 TALK FACE2FACE.

Hissing in frustration, Ally threw her phone across the room. It nearly hit Monty, still sharpening his knife in the corner, and he growled at her. She snarled back.

"You failed to convince him again," Alice said, her eyeless gaze no less judgmental. "Didn't you?"

"I told Jes about Riley. He said it's not what I think, which means Riley already told him lies about what really happened." Ally clenched her jaw. "He believes him over me."

Alice shook her head. "It's worse than I thought. You need to talk to him. Set him straight."

"But I…" Ally glanced over the papers all around, none of them holding the proof she needed. "I don't know if he'll believe me. "I need proof. If the Black Card tattoo wasn't enough, then I need something bigger. Something Riley can't spin for his own benefit." She tapped her fingers against the couch in an angry rhythm. "Jes mentioned there was a funeral today—probably for the stray cat. And Riley is probably going. I can go to his apartment while everyone is gone and find what I need."

She craned her neck around toward the bedroom door, ready to yell for AJ, but she stopped when she saw him standing in the doorframe. Eyes wide, face pale, eyes on her.

"What's his problem?" Monty muttered.

"I'm going to—"

"Break into Riley's apartment?" AJ asked, his voice slightly strained and void of its usual cockiness. "I heard."

Ally frowned. He was eavesdropping? "Can you get me the time and place of the funeral?"

He hesitated. "I don't know…I got a lot of stuff going on today."

"Like what?" she demanded, and he stiffened. "What could possibly be more important?"

"Well, I…I mean, I have a job, Als."

Her eyes narrowed as she stood, sliding her hand into her pocket. "You mean for Red?"

Monty scoffed. "Pathetic."

It only took a few steps for her to cross the room and get to him, and she picked up the gun from where he'd left it on the table the night before. He took a small step back. The rush of power it gave Ally was more intoxicating than any drug.

"He's beneath you," Alice hissed from behind. "Make sure he knows it."

"Look, Als, I have other obligations to Red that—"

"Stop talking!" She barely had to think of wrapping her fingers around the rock in her pocket before a burst slammed AJ back into the doorframe. He gasped as the breath was knocked out of him, his eyes on the gun that she kept loosely trained on his chest. "You help me get into Riley's today or I'll put you next on my list."

"You could rip him apart," Monty grumbled.

"I could," Ally agreed, "but he could still be useful."

"Maybe you should anyway."

"Maybe."

"Fine!" AJ exclaimed, raising his hands. "I'll help you break into Riley's, all right? Just quit the freaky stuff."

Ally practically bared her teeth at him. "I don't need your *help*," she spat. "Send me the information when you get it, and make yourself useful. Or you'll regret it." Then she sauntered out of the apartment, slamming the door behind her.

Pulling her cloak tight around her shoulders to shield from the biting cold, Ally stowed the gun in her other pocket as she walked and stopped to get a huge coffee on her way. Even at nearly six in the morning, she found Ricky sitting in his chair on the vacant corner. How had AJ never seen him here? He literally never left.

"I need information," Ally told him without greeting. "What do you want for it?"

"Mornin' chickadee," he drawled, puffing out smoke as thick as the clouds in the sky. Ally wondered how he hadn't choked and died on it yet—there was always so much. Part of her wished he would. "Someone's up and at 'em."

"What do you want?"

"Depends on what you're asking for, love."

"How long have you been working this street corner?"

Ricky paused his puffing and raised an eyebrow. "You're asking about *me*?"

"Yes."

He regarded her for a long moment with narrowed eyes, a clarity in them she'd never seen before. He almost looked sane.

"You didn't go narc on me, did you, love?" he finally asked.

Ally rolled her eyes. "Yes, because working for the police is *exactly* what I'd love to do."

The corner of Ricky's mouth pulled up slightly. "Nah, you don't belong in the light. I meant Red. You trade me for her that fast?"

"No." Ally gritted her teeth. "Red means nothing to me. Are you going to answer or not?"

"I've been doing this forever. As long as anyone can remember, I've been on this corner." He finally puffed out smoke. "Where did you say you were from?"

"I didn't," Ally said curtly. Next to her, Monty chuckled. "So you were here when King was in charge?"

"No something for nothing, love, remember?" He sucked in a drag. "Truth for truth."

Ally scowled and crossed her arms over her chest. "Far from here. Different country. Were you here when he was in charge?"

"Of course I was."

"And were you a Black Card?"

Keeping his pipe tight between his lips, he reached up to pull on the right sleeve of his dirty blue jacket, barely exposing the black tattoo. "We all were, love." He put his sleeve back. "Dark time around here. Owe my life to a few people, in fact."

"And Riley was too. Which you didn't tell me." Her anger barely simmered under the surface of her tone.

"Didn't ask."

"I asked about him *all the time*!" Ally exploded. "You said you didn't know anything! That you 'didn't talk to him much.'" When Ricky just shrugged and puffed, she forced herself to take a breath. "What did he do for King?"

"Truth for truth. How did you get here?"

"I walked across the ocean," Ally snapped impatiently. "It was a trip. What did he do?"

Ricky leaned back and crossed his legs, his gaze trained on her. "Interesting. Riley was a pro at flyin' under the radar. His dad helped with that. Few people knew he was a Card at all. King had him working at home on the computer, transferring money, taking out security footage. Stuff like that. You walked across the ocean?"

"Across the bottom of it. Goes on forever." She was starting to run out of truths she was willing to give—she had to choose questions carefully. Two more. "Is there any proof of what he did? Anything to show what he really was?"

"Careful, love. People often have more than two faces."

"Well?"

Another puff. "Doubt it. Riley would be smart enough to cover his tracks. I'm sure any record of his nefarious dealings has been conveniently misplaced. What country did you come from?"

A half scream of frustration escaped her. "None of them. I'm a rat born in the middle of nothing and left to survive on its own. What's the connection between Riley and Red?"

His bushy gray eyebrows pulled down. "Does that answer really count? At least tell me what the bottom of the ocean is like."

Ally didn't care to revisit her time in the In Between—if she thought too long about it, she couldn't breathe right. "Dark. Endless. Frustrating. Like a cave without a ceiling that never ends."

Taking the pipe out of his mouth, Ricky pursed his lips and looked her over again. She didn't like it. He needed to get high again now. "I don't have details on any alleged connection between Riley and Red. I know they were a year apart in school, they were both members of the Black Cards, and both had a personal bone to pick with their bloodthirsty overlord King." He shrugged. "They had that in common with hundreds of other kids their age."

Ally shook her head in frustration. "No, there has to be more. There has to be something. He *did* something, I know it. Why else would he have the standing he does?"

"I think the better question, love, is why does she give it to him? The entire city in her pocket after she took on the deadliest man it's ever seen. What is she hiding?"

"I never liked her," Alice said, jerking her chin out as she brandished her knife. "She's hiding something."

"Something to do with Riley," Ally muttered. "But she shouldn't be afraid of Riley. She shouldn't be afraid of *anyone*."

A small smile played on Ricky's face as he stuck his pipe back in his mouth. "Maybe she's not quite who you thought, love. Dunno if she's worth your undying respect. Might be better off sticking with people you *know* will give you power."

Monty shook his head. "Nobody is worth your respect. You have to do things yourself."

Ally glanced at him and nodded. "I have to do this myself. I have to save him myself."

Ricky's eyebrows quirked up. "Save who, chickadee?"

Ally didn't bother to answer. She turned on her heel and walked away, barely noticing when her parents followed again.

"You're welcome, love!" Ricky called after her.

"You'll be thanking me," Ally said as she strode down the street. "You'll be thanking me when you're all safe from him."

Her mind reeled while she walked, working to wrap around the new idea. Riley wasn't the center of this. Red was. Red did something, screwed up big time, Riley got pissed, and the only way to keep him at bay was to leave him and his people alone.

Red was weak and pathetic, and would be easy to expose quickly.

But Riley had her brother. And even the queen of Ducat wouldn't cross him.

She had to save Jesper before it was too late.

She hadn't received any information from AJ yet, so Ally went to Gordy's to eat a free breakfast and load up on coffee while she thought out her options.

When both plates she ordered were empty and she signaled Wanda to fill her coffee cup for the third time, her phone rang.

"What?" she answered, tapping her fingers against the table in a fast, violent rhythm.

"Funeral is at ten," AJ started without his usual preamble. "Riley and his clan will likely leave the apartment between nine fifteen and nine thirty. I've got people watching the apartment, his car, and the funeral home."

Ally's eyes narrowed. "You mean you have Red's people on this?"

"Loosely speaking, yes, but I prefer to call these guys 'my people.' I told them your theory on Riley and Red. Turns out it's been bugging people for a long time. Nobody has been brave enough to say it." He cleared his throat. "They won't say anything."

"Have them watch the apartment until Riley moves out. I want him followed. Once it's clear, I'll sneak in and look around for evidence. And make sure everyone keeps me updated."

Hanging up the phone, Ally snagged another cup of coffee and headed for the police station. Ruby the secretary scowled when she walked in, but gave her what she wanted: the police report of Riley's dad's death.

The file was sparse and only gave a few details that she didn't already know: King had set up Riley's dad for a job that night, the doctor was a Card, Riley's mom was in labor at the same hospital. The crime scene photos made Ally's coffee-filled stomach squirm a little.

Now it was almost nine. She sent a text to AJ—just a question mark—and he responded within a minute.

No

Getting antsy, Ally dumped the file back on Ruby's desk. What else could she look at while waiting for Riley to leave?

"Did you work here back when King died?" she asked the secretary.

Ruby's green eyes burned with contempt, but she answered, much to Ally's delight. "I've been here almost twenty years."

"So that's a yes?" Ally bounced on her feet and patted her leg, unable to be still. "What do you remember about that night?"

Ruby just pursed her lips and clutched the chain around her neck. A cross. "I think she's a devil. And I think you might be one too."

Ally gave a sly smirk, checking her phone again. "Well you're not wrong."

Nine fifteen. Riley had to be leaving soon. No way he'd be late for this.

"Your brother was looking for you," Ruby said. Ally's head snapped up, and her mother hissed under her breath. At their reaction, Ruby's lips pressed together. "So you do have a brother."

"He came here?" Ally demanded. "To ask about me?"

"With the March girl. They were here about her friend again. Before they left, she asked about you."

Monty shook his head, his fists clenching. "Using Jesper as bait."

"It's a trap," Alice agreed.

Ally glowered at Ruby, and the woman at least had the good sense to look frightened. "Don't. Talk. About. My. Brother."

Suddenly the small, pathetic building felt too claustrophobic. Before the walls could close in around her, Ally lurched outside and paced in front of the doors.

At nine forty-five, she called AJ. "What's happening?"

"He hasn't left yet, Als," he answered, a slight edge to his voice. "I don't know what's up."

"The funeral starts in fifteen minutes! He's going to be late."

"Just tellin' ya what I see."

Ally gritted her teeth. "You don't think *he's* watching *us*, do you?"

The line went silent for a second. "No, that's not likely."

"But possible?"

"I—" AJ cut himself off. "We got eyes. Riley's leaving the apartment with the March girl and your brother. They don't look happy."

Ally scowled at the mention of Jesper. She was so close to freeing him.

She waited on the line until AJ told her the coast was clear, then she started for the apartment.

* * * * * * * *

The burial ended up being a quiet, short event. Only Riley, Jesper, and H were there—as Jenny couldn't be convinced to come—and a handful of old strangers. They buried both Mama March and Kat next to Arlo and H's father. After they'd lowered the box into the ground, the group broke their solemn silence, chattering softly amongst themselves and apologizing to H again and again. He wondered if she even heard them. Her eyes looked so far away.

They had done the burial first to try and escape the forecasted rain. Huge gray clouds hung overhead, heavy and ready to burst any moment. Soon, the small group would move to the mortuary building in town, where they would have a memorial service for both women.

Riley kept checking his phone, clearly distracted. They'd almost been late because he had spent so long practically begging his mother to get out of bed and come. Jesper couldn't stand to listen; he had stepped outside.

He'd almost texted Ally again, to ask her to come. Now, though, despite the ache in his gut for his sister, he admitted it was probably for the best. Ally and H clearly didn't get along, and neither of them needed the extra pressure that the other would bring.

After the funeral, though, he would find his sister. He wouldn't stop looking until he did. Even if she didn't want to see him, he would beg her to talk with him. So he could explain. So he could let her know that he was there for her, and hope that she could be there for him too. Maybe, with the support of each other, they could choose another life, another path. Be anything they wanted to be.

348

Jesper didn't know exactly what that was yet, but, stars, he wanted to try. He didn't want to waste any more time. Life was truly too short.

He stood off to the side, watching the small group slowly start heading for their cars to go to the mortuary. Riley said something to H before coming up to Jesper.

"I'm going to go check on my mom," he said, his voice hoarse with unshed tears. "I'll be back in time for the service. I gave H my keys, I'll meet you there."

As Jesper watched him leave, H stumbled over to Jesper and took his hand, grasping it wildly as if she would freefall otherwise. She trembled so hard, he wondered if she would break.

"Do you believe in something after?" she asked. "Like after we die."

Ever since Ally's overdose, Jesper had retreated into himself. He'd largely ignored H, sidestepping the strange bond they had with each other unless she was devastatingly emotional and needed something. In this moment, he realized he'd been scared of it. The feeling of friendship, comradery, support was all unfamiliar. The overdose had shoved him back in time to a small and scared Jesper who tried to force himself into the tiniest space possible. Who knew it was up to him and him alone to save what was left of their family.

But even though the silent, suffering solitude was more comfortable, he realized he'd grown out of it, like old shoes. He could spend the rest of his life trying to force his grown feet into them, and maybe they would still fit, but he'd never walk like he used to.

Maybe he didn't want to.

Maybe it was worth building a life that mattered when it ended. Worth having people to know the real you, to support you, as you were, enough that they missed you when you were gone.

So he mustered every tiny bit of courage left inside of him, and forced himself to meet H's eyes.

"I, I…thought I'd gone…there once," he answered, remembering how Ally's voice had echoed through the In Between. *Is this what happens to people? What a waste.* A waste of what, he never asked. Maybe he was afraid of the answer, for himself too. "But now, now I…I know it, um, wasn't."

Squeezing his eyes shut, he thought back before it all. Before the In Between, before The Day, before the Molds. Before Ally, even. It put too much pressure in his head to go back that far, like a giant hand would crush his skull. But he did it anyway, careful to avoid falling into a hole. And he found himself in his father's lap.

"My…my dad said…once…that there is someone in the stars. He said everyone had, um, they had forgotten her na-ame. But his, his grandfather would tell him sto-ories about, about the lady in the stars that, that…she watched over everyone. And when they passed o-on, she brought them home. To her."

He opened his eyes, back in the present again. H had tipped her head back to look up, so he did too, pleased when a slight break in the clouds allowed them a rare peek at the gray-blue sky.

"You…you think they're up there?" H asked softly.

Jesper didn't know for sure, but he nodded anyway. They all needed something to hang on to.

A sob broke from H's chest. "I miss you," she murmured. Then she buried her face in Jesper's shoulder and started crying.

With his arm around H, Jesper kept watching the sky. Did the dead really find a home in the stars? Despite the tragic scene of the cemetery, he found a stillness here, a presence. Here, it was easier to believe that Harriet, Kat, Arlo, and H's father were not gone. He found himself hoping they were up there. They could watch over H. Maybe, if they weren't too busy, he could ask them to watch over him too.

Was his mother up there? He wondered if he could bear the thought. Had she found peace? Remorse, even? Grief, for getting so lost and not living long enough to find her way back?

For whatever it's worth, Jesper thought as the clouds slowly started to cover the patch of sky, *wherever you are, I hope that you're okay.*

For the first time in his life, he really did.

* * * * * * *

The second Ally picked the lock and walked into the apartment, she realized what had made Riley late: his mom's bedroom door was closed as usual, meaning she was asleep inside.

"Does Riley drug her?" she wondered. "Is that how he keeps power over her?" Maybe his mother would also thank Ally for exposing her deceitful son.

"She'll be grateful to be put out of that misery," Alice said, perched on the couch. Bits of dead skin fell off of her with every movement, littering all over the furniture like ashes. "Few things in life are more disappointing than children."

Ally scowled at her. Across the room, Monty had been going through the kitchen cabinets, and he glared back at Ally.

"You won't find what you're looking for in there," she muttered.

Her phone buzzed, slicing through the still apartment, and she swore under her breath.

r is here

Turning her phone on silent and keeping her steps just as quiet, Ally did a quick sweep of the kitchen and living room, noting the dirty dishes on the counter and blankets strewn out all over the couch.

"We need to get Jesper out of here," Alice said, wrinkling her nose in distaste. "He's not safe with them."

"I'm trying."

She'd never been in Riley's room before, and she found it
to be disappointing: a tiny desk crammed next to a tiny bed
took up most of the space. Ally sat down at the desk and
started digging through the notebooks and textbooks.

From what she could tell, most of it looked like
schoolwork—she recognized the strange symbols from when
Riley would work at the kitchen table while failing to teach her
to read. That wouldn't help her.

As small as the place was, it took her almost an hour to find
what she was looking for. On her fourth inspection of his
closet, Ally finally found the tiniest fissure in the back wall that
ran a little differently than the other cracks. She had to probe it
a bit, but eventually it opened.

A secret cupboard to hide his laptop. Interesting.

She opened it up, but a screen popped up asking for what
she guessed was some kind of code to get in. Between her and
AJ, they should know someone who could break in. Or maybe
the rock could do it for her.

"And then all your secrets will be out."

Monty nodded in approval. "Burn him to the ground."

Before she closed the hidden compartment, she felt her
hand around inside in case anything else was in there. The first
pass left her hand empty. And the second. On the third, her
fingers found an uneven groove. When she pried it with a
fingernail, it opened as well.

"You just keep going, don't you?" Ally muttered. She
pulled out a thin black binder and set it on her lap. It held a
thick pile of paper, all covered in writing—some looked like
more homework, others were typed, but most were
handwritten. Dated too. A journal, maybe? A ledger?

She squinted her eyes, trying to concentrate on the words,
testing the letters out in her mind. Lots of the letter 'R.' That
would make sense for Riley, but it seemed another name
showed up even more. Rose? Like the flower?

It must've been code for a secret plot or meeting place
because that's all he seemed to reference in the handwritten
pages. The homework pages had both Riley and Rose written

on it. Maybe not homework then. Formulas for drugs? Did he make his own drugs for his mom? AJ still hadn't figured out where Riley got the supply. Rose could be the codename for it. He was clearly obsessed.

Ally realized she had gotten lost in the words. She took a few of the pages with formulas out of the binder, then hid it back in the secret space. Obviously, Riley would notice his laptop was missing, and hopefully that would distract him from noticing the missing pages. She could come back for the rest later if she ever needed it.

Securing the laptop underneath her arm, Ally pushed the chair back under the desk and crept out of the apartment, shutting the door behind her. She practically bounced down the stairs. Victory was close and she could taste it.

As she reached the sidewalk, she pulled out her phone to update AJ. Her feet stumbled when she saw the dozens of text messages and missed calls.

he's coming!!!!!!!! get out on my way

Sucking in a sharp breath, Ally glanced up and looked around as she automatically lurched for the first alleyway. Just as she rounded the corner, she locked eyes with someone halfway down the block.

Riley.

It was too late. She knew he'd seen her.

Coming from his apartment.

Carrying his laptop.

She didn't have time to run before he walked into the alley in a battered black suit like he had all the time in the world. He stopped two feet in front of her, gaze zeroing in on the laptop, then let out a tired sigh.

"If I tell you the real story, will you just leave it alone?" he asked. "I came clean to your brother."

"You lied to him." Ally was certain. She used one arm to clutch the laptop to her chest while the other slid discreetly into her cloak pocket. "If you had told the whole truth, he wouldn't still be here."

Riley sighed again and glanced up at the cloudy sky. "Look, just come back to the funeral with me, okay? Spend some time with your brother. He's had a rough couple weeks, and he misses you. He's really worried about you. I don't think he's even slept. Come see him, then tonight we can talk all together."

"It's a trap," Monty barked. "Don't listen to him."

"I don't know how you convinced all of them," Ally said. "I really don't. But I'm smarter, smarter than you, and you'll never *ever* get me."

His eyebrows furrowed under his black beanie. "Get you? I've been *worried* about you, Ally, worried sick. I'm not—"

Alice scoffed. "Worried? Jesper is the only one who cares if you live or die, and you let him down."

"Shut up!" Ally's hand closed around the weapon in her pocket, and it shook as she pointed it at Riley. "Just shut up!" She'd chosen the gun so that he would recognize it, respect it, realize that he was in over his head up against her.

But Riley didn't cower like Ally had been expecting. Hoping. He stiffened slightly, then the corner of his mouth pulled up in a sad half smile. Her thoughts must've shown on her face because he said, "You think you're the first to pull a gun on me? Come on, Ally, think through this. You're obviously upset. You don't have to go to extremes."

"Yes I do," she hissed through her teeth. "You *made* me. You gave me no choice. You're the enemy and you took my brother. I have to protect Jesper from you. He's *mine*."

"I didn't take him." Riley shook his head. "I would never hurt either of you. I think you know that."

"Of course he would," Monty growled. "You're stupid to think he wouldn't."

Ally glared at her father. "I'm not stupid! Be quiet!"

"Ally..." Riley's eyebrows furrowed as he watched her. "Are you okay?"

She turned her attention back to him. "Shut up! I'm in charge here, not you!" All that coffee was starting to feel like a bad idea. Her thoughts were moving so fast she could barely keep up. "I know something happened between you and Red. An alliance or fallout or something. It doesn't add up."

"There isn't—"

"I know there is! Tell me." She tried to even out her shaking hand, grasping for control.

"I can't help you if you're set on things that aren't real. Red is a stranger to me, all right? I don't know why you're so stuck on this. She's the girl that lives in an alley down the street with that scary dog and knifes people whenever she wants to. I have never spoken to that girl. And I don't want to," he added, a bitter note in his tone.

"To *that* girl," Ally repeated. The specific phrasing jogged something in her head.

Ricky's words from this morning: *Careful, love. People often have more than two faces.*

Red, the cruel Queen of Ducat. Red, the painter of secret murals to beautify her city. Red, the sharp-toothed wolf.

Except before she was the wolf, she'd just been a girl hiding under a hood.

"You knew her before, didn't you?" Ally said as the truth dawned on her. "You knew her before she became King's. You're about the same age. Went to the same school."

Riley kept his face passive, but his body went so still she wondered if he stopped breathing. After a long moment, he asked, "Did she put you up to this?"

She pursed her lips, not wanting the indecision to show in her expression. "Would that change your answer?"

The sky thundered overhead, as if it would split apart. A single drop of rain splashed against Ally's nose.

"It's going to rain," Riley finally said. "Let's go inside." He started to turn to go, as if she didn't matter, as if she wasn't a threat. And even though Riley leaving would be the best thing for her in this scenario, she found fury shooting through her veins. How dare he just turn his back on her? She was *more* than that.

"I know what happened that night!" she called out on an impulse. It was a wild bluff, but a smart one—everyone had a night they'd rather stay buried.

As she hoped, it made Riley stop. Slowly, he turned back to face her, eyes narrowed slightly.

"What night?" he asked.

It was a gamble on which one would keep him more interested, but she guessed she had a fifty-fifty shot: either the night his dad died or the night King died.

She settled for vague, hoping to trap him so he'd reveal it for her. "The night he died."

He raised an eyebrow—he didn't fall for it. "The night who died?"

A handful of raindrops splattered on her face. A leap. This was a leap. If she guessed wrong, she'd lose him. Even though the night his dad died would probably be more personal to Riley, Ally didn't have as much information about it. On the other hand, she only knew what Red had told her about the night that King died, but maybe it was enough to trip Riley up.

"It wasn't just King, was it? Red murdered someone else that night too. She murdered her father."

That reeled him back in, brought him a step closer. Ally reaffirmed her holds on the laptop and the gun as the rain picked up speed.

Riley didn't seem to notice, though. He just stared at her for a long moment. "How did you find out? Did...did she tell you?"

"Yes. She told me everything."

"Why? She would barely even tell me. Why tell you after all these years?"

"I'm sure she has her reasons."

It was pouring rain now. Water dripped from Riley's glasses as he rubbed his face, his shoulders sagging. "It was never supposed to happen that way," he said softly, barely audible over the sound of the rain. "I could've gotten her out of there, out of that apartment with him. I tried to...I tried...but now..."

Hair plastered to her forehead, Ally bounced on her toes, eager to finally watch the unraveling of Riley Hatton. But he just bit his lip, took a breath, and pulled himself back together.

"None of that matters now anyway. It's all in the past. We're talking about you. You don't have to end up like her. There are other ways, and your brother is learning that too." He met her gaze. "Look, Ally, I know about the...situation with your parents. Jes told me about your mom. I know that's probably a lot to come to terms with..."

Alice screamed. A blood curdling screech of rage that made Ally flinch. Her mouth opened so wide that it seemed her rotting jaw would split apart. The scream never ended.

Riley kept talking, but Ally zoned out, her focus on those six words.

Jes told me about your mom.
Jes.
Told.
Me.
About.
Your.
Mom.

"Why would he tell you?" Ally exploded, desperately trying to drown out her mother's shrieking. She shook the gun at him, her wet finger slipping against the trigger. "What did you do to him?"

Riley held his hands up, eyes on the gun. "Nothing! Hey, nothing, all right? Jesper told me because he wanted to, okay? I'm just trying to help."

"Jesper's always been weak!" Monty yelled, punching the wall in fury. "I wish he was dead, I wish you were both dead!"

"Help is for the weak," she snarled. "You have to do it on your own. I'm doing this on my own! *I'm* doing it, I'm saving us. I can't trust anyone. I have to do it alone."

Riley's face fell, and Ally realized he feared the gun in her hand but he didn't fear her. More than anything, he felt bad for her.

"No," he said softly. "You don't."

Ally screamed alongside her mother and pulled the trigger.

She didn't realize it until after: after the shock hit her hand, the sound burst in her ears, the vibration traveled up her arm. She didn't realize what she had done until Riley's eyes went wide, his hands found his bleeding stomach, and he collapsed in a puddle of red rainwater.

Then it hit her.

"I just shot him."

"About time," Monty retorted. Alice still hadn't stopped screaming.

"I just killed someone." She shook her head. "I was saving my brother. I had to save him."

"Ally?"

Ally started at the shout, the movement jolting her back into reality as AJ and a handful of others ran up to her, all of them soaked to the bone. She recognized most from her time spent with AJ or her own snooping, but couldn't dredge up a single name from her memory over the sound of the screams.

"I heard the shot," AJ said, his eyes glancing over her and the laptop dropped on the cement at her feet, forgotten. "What happened?"

A girl with cropped hair wearing a million rings was the first to see it. She gasped and pointed at Riley's body, then snapped a picture with her phone. Murmurs erupted from the rest of her group.

"Is that Hatton?"

"Hatton's dead?"

"About freakin' time."

"Hated that guy. So high and mighty."

"Got what he deserved."

AJ's eyes widened in genuine surprise when he saw. He glanced at Ally with a mix of shock and respect. "You did that?"

She could barely hear them all. Her father yelling and her mother screaming, and somewhere in the distance she could hear the cries of her younger self.

"SHUT UP!" she shouted at her mother, nearly smacking her own head with the gun as she pulled at her hair in a frenzy. "Shut up shut up shut up shut up!"

"She's crazy, AJ," one of the boys muttered. "You sure you just don't wanna get rid of her?"

Ally shrieked and narrowed her rage on him as she reached for her rock. Instantly a burst more powerful than ever before surged around her. AJ and his people smacked against the wall with painful cracks. Riley's corpse blew back into the alleyway, out of sight. The boy who threatened her contorted violently, his neck snapping with ease. When his dead body hit the ground, Alice *finally* stopped screaming.

They all stared at it, then at her, with wide, panicked eyes. The blood drained out of AJ's face.

"What are you?" he whispered.

Ally just glared at them. "Find. My. Brother."

CHAPTER 10

WE'RE ALL MAD HERE

The heavy rain drowned out the music that still played from the mortuary as Jesper and H stepped outside to go back home. A recording of Arlo's sax music, H had told him earlier when the music started to play next to the gravesite, a mix of Kat and Mama March's favorite songs of his. Once again, Jesper found himself wishing he'd known the man. And once again, he felt a little grateful that he hadn't. Saying these goodbyes was hard enough.

H's mouth pressed into a hard line, her eyes glaring at the sidewalk as they trudged down the street to where Riley's car was parked. She didn't seem to care about getting soaked. Jesper didn't either, but he had borrowed one of Riley's suits and was worried about getting it wet. He didn't dare mention that to H, though. She probably was purposely getting his suit soaked for that very reason.

Riley never came back to the memorial service, and H was furious.

"She must've been pretty bad," H muttered as they walked, a harsh edge to her voice, "if he didn't come back or even answer his freakin' phone." She didn't sound very understanding.

Jesper hoped the drive home would cool H off, but when she went to her grandma's empty apartment instead of Riley's, he knew that wouldn't come anytime soon. She parked without a word and got out, and he followed.

Her phone must've buzzed because she reached into the pocket of her black jeans to pull it out, not even bothering to shield it against the rain. The water gathering on her screen made Jesper nervous, and he was just about to warn her about the dangers to her phone when she tripped over her own feet and skidded to a stop in the middle of the sidewalk.

It took Jesper a step to realize she'd stopped. He turned around to see her sopping hair dropping around her face, eyes wide with horror, mouth open, as she stared at her phone.

Panic seared his veins, so frigid cold it hurt. "What's wro-ong?" he choked out. That seemed to be the only question he asked these days.

H shuddered and blinked, as if she could blink an imagined image away. Her lips trembled as she read, "Ding dong, the bi—the...the…" She gulped and her voice dropped to a whisper. "He's dead."

Jesper shook his head rapidly, flicking rain in his face. No more dead. No more.

"Who?" he croaked, terrified of the answer. Terrified he already knew it.

H angled her rain smeared phone so they both could see the message. It had been sent to a large group—at least twenty different numbers. A grainy image took up the space under the line of words. An image of a body crumpled face first on the cement smeared with blood, wearing a soggy black suit and beanie.

Jesper couldn't breathe. The image sucked all the air out of his lungs. He clutched his chest and wheezed as he stared at her phone, his brain scrambling to find some other meaning. Some other answer.

His knees buckled and he almost fell to the ground, but something new caught his eye, freezing the entire world. There, in the top right corner of the awful picture, was the tip of a shoulder and stringy blonde hair.

Jesper would recognize that cloak anywhere.

A new message popped up under the picture. His mind was too scrambled to read the words, but he recognized his sister's name.

H swore again and again as sobs started to overtake her. Jesper sunk to his knees.

Ally murdered Riley.

Ally murdered Riley.

Ally murdered Riley.

My sister murdered my best friend.

My best friend murdered a stranger.

My sister is a murderer.

How had it come to this? When? How had he let her fall this far?

Rain splattered against his face. His clothes were so soaked he started to worry they would unravel. No, not *his* clothes. Riley's borrowed suit.

Jesper had been nervous this morning for a dozen reasons, one of them being what clothes he should wear to the funeral. He only had the handful of pants and shirts he'd picked out with H at a thrift store. He didn't know if there were certain rules, and he really didn't want to break them.

But he hadn't wanted to bother anyone. Especially right before the funeral. Thankfully, Riley saved him, as he usually did. He'd walked in with this suit and tie with a soft smile and said, "I think this'll fit you."

"What about you?" Jesper had asked, hesitating to fall into relief just yet.

"I have an old one of my dad's I can wear."

"Are you sure?"

Riley had nodded, coming out ten minutes later in a faded suit similar to Jesper's.

The suit of his dead father.

The suit he had died in.

A fresh sob worked its way up through Jesper's chest, and he choked as he swallowed it back down.

This couldn't be real.

Somehow they stumbled into the apartment. Jesper couldn't remember walking up the stairs. The second the front door shut, H started hyperventilating.

"What do we do?" she whispered again and again, sinking to the floor. "What do we do what do we do what do we do what do we do." Her voice broke. "Riley."

Jesper opened his mouth—for what? To apologize? Beg forgiveness? Scream?—but a soft sound from the hallway caught his attention.

He barely saw the glint of the knife in time.

Stumbling backward, Jesper pushed a chair to the ground just as a young man with purple hair rushed out from the hallway. The man tripped over the chair, nearly dropping the knife in his hand, and H screamed when he recovered quickly. With murder in his eyes, he lunged for her.

Jesper didn't think. He just threw his body over H and closed his eyes.

Instead of a blade, he felt a hand grab his ankle and yank him back. The man shoved him off of H and she scrambled away, but he made no move to hurt Jesper. His sight was set on her.

Jesper tackled him, wincing when his elbow hit the ground hard. They both rolled into the couch. The man held Jesper down with his knees and glanced up, looking for H. Suddenly, he jerked violently and H screamed again. For a moment, Jesper feared the worst. Then the pressure lifted off of him and he clambered to his feet.

By the time he stood, it was already over.

H cowered in the corner with fresh sobs breaking between the hands she held tight over her mouth. The man with the knife lay crumpled on the floor, a thin bloody line on his neck.

Standing over the purple-haired victim was another man, maybe thirty-five, with a short, neat beard and piercings in his eyebrows. A man much bigger than Jesper.

The man saluted at both of them, as if he hadn't just killed somebody. "Mr. Lewis. Miss March. I have instructions to safely escort you from the premises."

H lurched forward and grabbed onto Jesper, clutching the sleeves of his borrowed suit in her fists. He stepped in front of her, eyes on the stranger.

When a full minute passed and nobody said anything—and he didn't try to kill them—the man just saluted again.

"Mr. Lewis. Miss March. I have instructions to safely escort you from the premises."

Jesper's eyebrows furrowed. "Instructions?" he asked hoarsely. "From who?" They had nobody left.

"Sir, with respect, we are still in a dangerous situation in regard to the hit on Miss March's life and I don't feel it's a good idea to answer you right now, sir. For safety."

"What?" H gasped. "A hit on me?"

"Hit?" Jesper didn't understand what that meant. "Somebody…somebody wants to…to kill her?"

The man nodded. "Miss Ally Lewis."

Jesper nearly collapsed right then, and H swore under her breath. "But…but…but…" Jesper stammered. "But that…she wouldn't. She…"

Wouldn't she?

"Are you working for her?" H asked, distrust rising in her tone. "Are you here to kill me too?"

"No ma'am. I have different orders, ma'am. Escort you to safety."

"You're going to make us go with you no matter what, aren't you?"

"With respect, ma'am, yes I am. I got orders, ma'am." He saluted again. "Lieutenant Dodo at your service, sir and ma'am." He looked at Jesper, who still felt he might faint. "With respect, sir, we need to leave now."

Jesper shook his head. "Wait. Just wait. I need to…I need to call her. Talk to Ally. There has to be…"

Lieutenant Dodo nodded once. "I understand, sir. I can safely recommend that we stay here for another three to six minutes. After that, sir, I must insist we get moving."

Taking a shaky breath, Jesper ducked into the hallway for a bit of privacy, careful to position himself so he could still watch H with the stranger there. Then he pulled out his phone and dialed his sister's number, begging the stars that there had been some kind of mistake.

* * * * * * *

When her phone rang and Ally recognized the name on her screen, the first bit of true peace she'd felt in weeks washed over her.

"With any luck," Alice said, peering over her shoulder with empty eyes, "the girl is dead by now. Our Jesper is free."

Monty pressed his fist against the brick wall. "It's about time."

Barely an hour had passed since she'd killed Riley and put a hit out on H. She'd sent AJ and his crew out to the streets to get the word out and watch for Jesper to emerge. They'd all been too terrified to do anything but comply. In the meantime she'd climbed to the roof of Riley's building to watch for anyone coming back with the good news that the brat was dead.

And now, here, finally, Jesper was calling her. He'd probably heard by now, maybe even had made the connection that it was his sister who had set him free. Her debt paid. A future for the both of them.

She'd waited her whole life for this.

Alice nodded in agreement. "He's going to be so proud. So grateful to have a sister like you."

A giant, genuine smile spread on her face as she answered the phone, bouncing on her heels in excitement to give her brother such a gift. "Jes! I—"

A dry, broken sob burst through the speaker. "Tell me it isn't true. Please."

The sound jarred her out of her celebration like the snap of a twig. She turned away from the street, pacing toward the center of the rooftop as her parents eyed her. "Jes? What are you talking about?"

"Did you…did you…kill…him?"

She blinked, confused. This wasn't what she had imagined. "Oh, Riley? Yes, I did."

Jesper sucked in a sharp breath as if she'd punched him. It sent Ally on the defensive, desperate to prove herself to her brother. To still have their winning moment.

"He was a gang member, Jes. Did he tell you that?"

"He didn't—"

"Yes he did! He was a Black Card, just like everybody else. He tricked you. He wasn't what he pretended to be."

"Pretended to be?"

"He was dangerous. He worked for King. Why can't you see this?"

"No." Jesper's voice trembled. "He told me. He told me what really happened."

Ally gritted her teeth. He still believed Riley over her? "Yeah? Did he tell you what awful things he did, he *lied about*, to get what he wanted?"

He shocked her by yelling through the phone. Had he ever yelled at her before? "He did that to save his family!"

Her eyes fell on the two people watching her intently. "And who does that sound like?" she shouted back. "Huh? I just saved us all from a monster! He's gone now. He can't hurt us."

"Riley would *never* hurt us!"

"Really? Do you know that? Didn't you used to think that about our *father*?" She spat the word at Monty and he glared at her. "Mom? You can never really know that. It's stupid to think you can. Now we *know*. We'll be safe. Nobody will ever hurt us again."

Silence.

It was settling in. Jesper was realizing she was right.

Ally gave a small smile, some of her old excitement returning. She couldn't wait for him to say it—after all this time, she couldn't wait to hear it. She had to ask. "Aren't you proud of me?"

A choked breath of disbelief came from her brother. "*Proud* of you? You just killed somebody! You just *murdered* my best friend! How could I possibly be proud of you?"

Ally drew back as if he'd slapped her. It took a moment for the words to sink in, and they slashed like knives down to her core.

You just murdered my best friend.

"But…" she whispered, voice shaking. "But *I'm* your best friend. I love you the most. I…I did this for you. For us. After everything you did for me…it's my turn now. To give something back. You're mine, and I love you the most."

But Jesper took her offering and crushed it in his hand to toss like garbage. "That's not love, Ally. You did this for yourself. You murdered him."

"But I…" She took a shuddering breath, her mind struggling to fix what should've been the happiest moment of her life. She could fix it. She had to fix it. "But I didn't. It was self-defense. He attacked me. He was angry I told you about his tattoo. He said nobody was ever supposed to know what happened to his dad."

That struck something in Jesper, she could tell. He went quiet and she could sense the doubt there, his mind at war with itself. She teetered on the balls of her feet. She had him. He'd come back to her.

"I found out about his dad, that he snitched on King. Riley was mad that I had dug that up. We argued about it, and he came at me. I didn't mean to do it. I was just trying to protect myself. Wouldn't you want me to protect myself, Jes? Since you weren't there to do it?"

She heard him open his mouth, then close it. Again. A painful breath escaped him, like he was being ripped in two. But he would believe her. He had to. She was his *sister.* It had only been the two of them for so long. Why would he abandon that now?

"I'm not lying," she said, both to her brother and herself, strongly enough that she believed it. "That's what I had to do."

A moment of heavy silence passed. "Were you always this?" he whispered. "Or did you turn into it when I wasn't looking?"

Ally took an unsteady breath. Why was he being like this? "I found my strength. I can protect us now. Why can't you see that?"

"This is madness!" he yelled back at her. "Why can't *you* see that? I would have...stars, Ally, I would have done *anything* for you. I would have...I..."

Why did she feel something in her heart cracking? "You don't have to anymore. I've done it for us. It's my turn to protect us now. You've done enough."

I did it for you.

I love you the most.

You're mine.

"No, Ally, no. I don't want it. Whatever you think you can give me. I don't want it. Not like this."

I don't want it.

Alice started shrieking, pulling at her rotting skin in a frenzy.

I. Don't. Want. It.

Monty slammed his fist against the wall. "Traitor! I knew he wasn't worth anything!"

I

Don't

Want

It

With those words, something inside Ally broke. Snapped clean in half. Fractured into pieces. The cold she'd felt in her bones since shooting Riley thawed out. Rage, scalding white rage, boiled under her skin, consuming everything she had ever been.

"You don't want it!" she exploded, pacing around in a frenzy. "You don't *want it*? I have given *everything* for you! I have done everything to keep you safe. To give us the life we deserve. And *you don't want it?*" she shrieked.

Jesper said something else, but she couldn't hear him over the sound of her and Alice screaming.

"It doesn't matter!" Ally yelled over her brother. "It doesn't matter! Riley is dead, and soon H will be too. They won't be able to confuse you anymore and brainwash you against me. You might not want what I've given you now, but you will. I'll make sure you have nowhere else to go."

"Call it off," Jesper demanded hoarsely. "Call it off now and leave her alone."

"No," Ally said coldly. "She'll turn you into Monty. Don't you see that? I have the whole city looking for her with a price for her death. I hope whoever gets it makes her scream. I hope her last thought was that she regretted ever trying to take you from me." She took an unsteady breath. "You don't need anyone. You're just mine."

"It doesn't have to be this way," Jesper pleaded. "It doesn't. If you keep hunting her I will just stay hidden with her. There's nothing you can do about that."

Ally bared her teeth. "Then I will burn this city to the ground to find you."

* * * * * * *

You're just mine.

H clutched his hand as they followed the stranger down the stairs, waiting behind a corner while he checked to see if the coast was clear. They saw no other option than to follow. Where else could they really go? Jesper almost felt too empty, gutted, to really care.

I will burn this city to the ground to find you.

As he walked next to H, Jesper dug deep inside himself and found a scrap of courage to say the words pressing down on his lungs.

"I'm sorry," he whispered to H. "I'm so sorry."

I'm sorry about my sister. I'm sorry we invaded your life and your family and your job. I'm sorry about your grandma. I'm sorry about Riley.

No, sorry didn't even cover it.

H didn't respond. She wouldn't look at him, but she gripped his hand like a lifeline, as if she had no one else. And she didn't. It made him ache all over.

What have I done?

At Lieutenant's signal, they ducked out from the cover of the apartment building and kept a quick pace down the street. Jesper didn't bother to try and keep track of where they were going. He didn't know how long he could. The guilt would drag him down. The sorrow would drown him.

"Hey!" The shout sent a spasm of terror through Jesper. "There she is!"

He barely turned around to see who was shouting, when a shot rang out much too close. Both Jesper and H yelped and fell to the ground.

"Let's keep it moving, sir," Lieutenant said, pulling Jesper up with one hand as he held his gun in the other. A crumpled body lay in a bloody heap just yards away.

Madness.

Ally what have you become?

Jesper kept his grip on H's shoulder as Lieutenant dragged them around the corner. "With respect, ma'am and sir," he said, stopping next to a big metal circle in the road, "can I request your assistance with this?"

It took all three of them to lift the metal circle, and Lieutenant had H go down first, helping her find her footing on the ladder. Jesper gulped as she disappeared into darkness. Why did he always find himself falling into dark places?

He made himself go down anyway, and tried not to shudder as Lieutenant stepped down after him and dragged the metal circle slowly back into place with a grunt. Thankfully, he had a flashlight.

"This way, please." Instead of plunging into the murky water like Jesper feared, he went behind the ladder, and the flashlight illuminated a steel door in the brick wall. It looked like it had been rusted shut years ago, but he typed a code into a hidden keypad and it opened right up.

Lieutenant gestured for them to go in. "In here please, ma'am and sir. Boss is waiting to see you. Someone else too."

Jesper wanted to know who his boss was—who did they have to worry about *now?*—but it seemed pointless. They were already here. They were alive. Onto the next thing. He glanced at H, and she pursed her lips but nodded. No other choice she could see either.

Hesitantly, Jesper stepped inside, H squaring her shoulders and following. The space was about the size of the coffee shop and made into some kind of storage area. Rows of metal shelves held all kinds of crates and bottles. Lieutenant shut the door and led them between the shelves until it opened up. Two figures were waiting for them: one sprawled in a chair, the other curled up on a rickety cot.

Jesper froze, heart stuttering in his chest. H choked on a gasp and lurched forward, yanking Jesper along with her, then dropped his hand just as she collapsed on her knees in front of the cot. Fresh tears streamed down her face.

"Hey," Riley croaked. His voice sounded like it had been run over repeatedly and left in the street. His pale and sunken face only looked grimmer underneath his blood-stained dress shirt and pants. Underneath the shirt, Jesper could see a thick bandage wound around him.

Jesper slowly sunk to his knees, leaning against the cot for support. His eyes raked over Riley's battered form over and over, unable to believe it.

"Riley," H sobbed, clutching his hands in her own and holding them to her chest. "Riley Riley Riley Riley Riley."

"It's okay." He winced as he said it, but he was alive to say it. "It's okay, H. I'm here."

The voice that came from Jesper didn't sound like him at all: hoarse and withered and choked. A shell of himself.

"Was it...was it really...her?"

Riley looked at him for the first time. Pursing his lips, he gave the slightest nod. "She broke in to get my laptop. I saw her in the alley. I tried to talk her down, but..."

Jesper flinched. Whatever had been holding him together started to unravel.

"Either she thought I was dead or didn't want to finish it," Riley went on. "I got lucky."

"No," a voice piped up from behind. "You got *me*."

Jesper and H whirled around to see Lieutenant had left the three of them with the man in the chair. He wore an oversized blue hooded jacket with a silver beanie, and a pipe shoved between his lips. It took a minute for Jesper to place him: the first day in Ducat, they'd walked by him on the street, asking people if they wanted to see crazy places. He'd been high, and Jesper had wanted to get away from him as quickly as possible. But he had never seen him around since.

"Ricky?" H looked between the drugged man and injured boy, two puzzle pieces that did not connect to each other. A hint of her old fire returned to her voice. Protective of Riley. "What's he doing here?"

Ricky held his hand against his chest in feigned offense. "Look, here, chickadee, this is my place. You're guests of mine, understand? The real question is what are you doin' here?"

Riley sighed. It sounded like that time the car engine died on Kat. "My dad did him a favor back in the day. After he died, Ricky watched out for us. He helped me get out of the Black Cards."

"That's right," Ricky said, sounding awfully proud of himself. "I'm not one to forget a debt. Helped Riley get Jenny's pills for cheap so they didn't have to go back to that hospital." He shrugged. "I know, I know, I'm a saint."

H glanced back at Riley. "Jenny? Does she know you're okay?"

Very slowly, Riley closed his eyes until they were squeezed shut tight. Lines spread across his face, caverns so deep, and Jesper wondered if he would crumble into bits.

"She's dead," Riley breathed.

The room went still. Ricky, for all his shame, had the decency to lower his head while H and Jesper just stared blankly.

"Are you sure?" H finally whispered.

Riley took a shuddering, painful breath. Ricky answered for him.

"Sanctioned hit." When they continued to stare blankly, he clarified. "Means someone went in to kill her. Likely to bury the Hatton trail for good. Leave no room for retaliation."

Jesper's shoulders caved in, realizing what he meant.

Ally had Jenny killed too.

Ricky straightened, as if the moment was over. "Down to business, kiddos. There are people stationed at every exit point in the city, and they're all lookin' out for the two of you. Not to mention Riley here is supposed to be dead and not doin' too good of a job of it." He looked at H. "The price is high, love. Everyone's goin' to be itchin' to shoot ya. And I take it none of you have a place to go?"

H's lips trembled as they pressed together into a harsh line. Riley still had his eyes closed, a single tear trickling from one, and didn't answer. As if he'd lost all hope. It made something crack in Jesper's chest.

Ricky glanced at Jesper now and puffed out smoke. "Be honest, kid," he said, sucking on his pipe. "Where you from?"

Jesper blinked. That was the very last thing he could think about. "It's, uh, it's…it's not around here."

"Uh huh. I'm familiar with the concept. Where? Seattle? LA? Jersey? Somethin' crazier, Canada?" The way his gray eyes probed at him unsettled Jesper. "How'd you get here? Long walk across the bottom of the ocean?"

With a start, Jesper's eyebrows furrowed. "What?"

"I don't got all day, kid. Where you from?"

"Um, it's called Elaria." He felt stupid saying it out loud again, after so long of everyone pretending it didn't exist. Maybe it hadn't. Maybe Jesper had made it up. Or maybe Ducat had been one giant nightmare.

Did it matter which was the nightmare?

Ricky's eyes widened, so big they nearly popped out of his head. "Elaria?" Then he started to laugh, a deep laugh that made him double over. "You gotta be kidding me. You gotta be *kidding* me. It all makes sense now. Elaria."

"Ricky," Riley said, as if in warning, flicking a worried glance at Jesper.

But Ricky just laughed and shook his head, then wiped his eye with his finger. "Tell me, kid, is King Asher still runnin' that place into the ground or what?"

* * * * * * * *

After Jesper hung up on her, Ally's veins pulsed with wrath, a living, breathing thing inside of her that demanded to be let out. Violent chaos swirled in her mind, yet she knew her path was sure.

Taking a few breaths, Ally yanked her phone out and dialed AJ. He answered on the third ring.

"Set up checkpoints," she barked before he could say anything. "Nobody in or out of the city without me saying so. And double the price on H's head. She doesn't live to see tomorrow morning."

"Done," AJ said, a little too quickly. "Whatever you want. Heads up, I heard Red's looking for you. She's mobilizing her own people, but from what I've heard, she's lost a lot of them to you. Or people are choosing to wait on the sidelines and see who is left."

White edged around her vision. Ally's teeth snapped together. "Shoot anyone who doesn't swear to me and track down the people you know won't leave her side. I will not let them get in my way."

AJ hesitated and Ally screamed, "Are you going to get in my way? Because I *will* find you."

"No, no," he said. "I will make sure everybody knows you're in charge tonight."

"Good." Ally snapped her phone shut and stowed it in her pocket, then curled the rock in her hand. Instantly, power rose up to meet her fingertips. It crackled with electricity—so much more satisfying than the cold metal of the gun. She kept the weapon in her other hand though, just in case.

She was going hunting.

With her parents trailing behind her, Ally stormed down the street, heading for the apartment H shared with her grandmother. AJ had told her where it was once, weeks ago, when she'd found out Jesper had spent time there. She burst through the door only to find a dead body. Not H.

In a rage, Ally tore the place apart with Alice, both of them shrieking as picture frames and lamps and vases shattered on the floor. Monty just kept checking the cupboards and cursing when he couldn't find any alcohol, and Ally would scream at him to be quiet. They had much more important things to worry about.

Fuming that H had already escaped, she decided to go back to Riley's. With the cat dead and the grandma's apartment empty, there wasn't anywhere else Jesper or H had to go.

She strode back down the street, keeping to the shadows, her cloak billowing behind her as the rain continued to pour. For a rare moment, the sun poked out from behind a heavy rain cloud. Ally glowered at it, demanding more, just as she'd done for years in the Molds. And rather than beat down on her, beat her into submission like everything else, for the first time the sun retreated. The cloud swallowed it back up again. Ally smirked.

Yes, today was her day.

Her bones shuddered when Riley's building came into view again. A tiny part of her, a part that felt like a ghost of Jesper, waited for shame to flood those shaking bones. Regret. Guilt. But nothing came. She'd done the right thing after all.

Dashing up the stairs, she stepped inside and ducked out the rain. She couldn't help but think of the first time she'd done that, months ago, hair dripping and throat sore and mouth full of questions.

If she'd only known.

Ally didn't hesitate when she got to the door and found it unlocked. She waltzed inside like she'd done a million times before, like she owned the place. And now she did, really.

She had a moment to register the absolute silence echoing throughout the room. Deep and impenetrable and everlasting. Like a tomb. Maybe Jesper hadn't come back here after all.

Then she heard the faint sound of a door clicking, of a dog growling, of quick footsteps.

Red appeared through the hallway, Jabber baring his teeth at her heels. Her eyes were a torrent of emotion, a violent storm that didn't match the hard set to her mouth. In her hands she clutched one of Riley's beanies. The crimson paint on her lips had smudged; she was bleeding just like this city.

"You killed him," she said, her voice somehow full of rage and empty of life at the same time.

Ally smiled. "You heard the news then."

Red's eyes narrowed, emotion gushing out of them. "What do you think you're doing, Ally?"

"Taking back what's mine."

"And what did Riley have to do with that?"

"He had *everything* to do with it!" Ally felt the hysteria rising up in her. "He pretty much owned half the city and you didn't do anything about it. He had my brother, and not even you, ruthless queen of it all, would do anything about it!" She took an unsteady breath. "I did what I had to do. What nobody else would do."

Red clenched her teeth. "You're even crazier than AJ said." Violence rolled off her in waves, and Jabber growled at Ally. "You made a mistake. And you'll pay for it." She raised her arm, revealing the gun she had hid underneath the beanie. Ally barely had time to blink before the shot fired.

A flash of desperation coursed through her, pushing into the rock. She felt the power rise up, could sense the buzz of it in the air, like lightning in the storm. Both she and Red watched as the bullet sped toward Ally, then bounced off some invisible wall just inches from her head. It clattered to the floor and rolled away.

Red's lips parted in shock, the most unguarded Ally had ever seen her face. Taking her own surprise in stride, Ally gave her a sly smirk. "You were saying?"

She forced herself not to flinch as Red tried to shoot another time, then a third. Nothing touched her. Ally's smile grew.

Red took an unsteady step back, her eyes wide. "What are you?" she murmured.

A thrill went through Ally, as intoxicating as the power in her veins. "I'm the wolf your mother warned you about, Little Red."

Red flinched back so hard, she smacked into the wall behind her. Pathetic. Ally took advantage of her brief distraction to raise her own gun and let out three shots: one for the dog, one for Red's shoulder, and one for her knee.

A scream tore out of Red's throat, raw and savage, but her eyes were on the dog's crumpled body, as if she didn't even feel her own bullet wounds. She'd dropped her gun, and Ally strode forward to kick it out of her reach.

But Red didn't protest. Didn't cry. She just settled her lethal gaze on Ally, ignoring the way she bled scarlet all over the floor.

"You've made a huge mistake," Red said, only a hint of strain in her voice. "You'll regret this."

Ally screamed in frustration. Even here, standing over her, clearly *winning*, Red still looked at her like a kid. Someone not worthy of her concern. Ally wanted to smash through that composure. She wanted to *prove* she was better than this pathetic girl in front of her.

Monty scoffed as he rifled through the cupboards. Alice laughed. "She's really nothing in the end, isn't she?"

Ally glared at her mother. "You weren't anything either. But not me—"

"You're still nothing!" Monty growled.

"Shut up!" Ally shrieked. "Shut up! You don't talk over me! Not anymore." Then she glared at Red. "You promised me strength and you couldn't even get my brother back for me. You. Are. Weak. And I am not."

Ally tightened her grip on the rock in her pocket, feeding it the bloodlust in her veins. Then with another shriek, Ally zeroed her focus on Red. The girl's body spasmed and contorted violently, muscles tearing and bones cracking. Finally, a cry of pain escaped her crimson lips.

Scowling, Ally used the power to drag Red along on an invisible leash, the girl moaning in protest and leaving a smear of blood behind as they went.

There were only a few people on the street and she felt their stares as she passed, dragging their old queen behind her like yesterday's garbage. Several audible gasps sounded. Whispered murmurs. They followed behind her, the group growing the farther she went.

When she reached the alleyway, she found AJ there along with twenty others. Eight of them were kneeling on the ground with guns at their heads. Loyalists then.

Not for much longer.

AJ sucked in a surprised breath when he saw her pulling Red along. Ally relished in the sound. All of the attention. This was exactly the spectacle she needed to solidify herself.

She dumped Red's crumpled form on the ground, her blood running freely over the stains of past executions. Red stared up at the sky, letting the rain wash over her, before resting her gaze on Ally again. Too calm with icy rage. Not enough begging for mercy.

Fine. If she was going to try and take Ally's satisfaction from her, then Ally would take something right back.

Steps slow, so every person could mark the movement, so Red could *feel* every crunch of Ally's soggy boots, Ally climbed the metal steps of the fire escape and lowered herself into the makeshift seat. The throne.

Her throne.

From up here, the world stretched on for ages. From up here, Ally could see a life, the life the Molds had tried to take from her, the life she had sacrificed to make for herself. She sucked in the scene like a drug, more exhilarating than any high: an army bowing before her. The enemy, bloody and helpless on the ground. Her parents, cowed to submission behind her. A throne, a power, that protected her, that ensured she would never be the one bloody and helpless on the ground ever *ever* again.

At the prodding of the frightened girl standing behind him, AJ stepped forward, his head slightly bowed in reverence. He flinched slightly when his eyes fell on Red. "What do you want to do with her, boss?" He threw the last word in there desperately, a lifeline to keep himself afloat amidst the storm of Ally.

Red spared no glance for AJ or the followers that still swore to her—the ones everyone probably guessed would die next. She just stared at Ally, no trace of pain or fear in her expression except the tension in her jaw. Just sharp hatred and steely resolve.

"To make it feel more like home," Ally answered, echoing words from a lifetime ago, when the roles had been switched, "we'll do it like they do where I'm from." For a moment, she could've sworn she saw a flicker of relief pass in Red's face. Relief for what, she'd never find out. Nobody would.

Ally held her gaze, baring her teeth in a wicked grin. "Off with her head."

* * * * * * *

"What?" Jesper gaped at Ricky from his spot on the ground, sure that he had heard wrong. The grief and terror of everything had gotten to him. He was hearing crazy things. "What did you say?"

Ricky leaned forward with his pipe sticking out of his mouth, making his chair groan through the quiet. "King Asher, yeah? Queen Sarafina? Their little rat of a son…I forget what they were going to name him."

Riley moaned softly as he lifted his head, H still clutching his hands. "Ricky, don't—"

"I'm not, kid. Elaria is a real place. I've seen it."

Jesper shook his head to clear it. Hearing the words spoken out loud by someone besides Ally made him feel both more and less crazy. This couldn't be happening. Could it? "You have? But how?"

"Long walk on the bottom of the ocean," he answered. "Least that's how your sister described it. I think it was more cave-like. Less ocean-y. Packed with monsters too, to be sure. Nasty place." He shuddered softly. "What part of Elaria you come from?"

"The Molds." When Ricky's bushy eyebrows pulled down in confusion, Jesper clarified. "The Jacklands."

"Ah. So Pepperjack's still large and in charge, huh?"

"Um, he was. He died right before we left."

Ricky blinked, and his pipe almost fell out of his mouth. "Jack is dead?"

Jesper just nodded. He couldn't believe this conversation was happening.

"It's been a long time," Ricky said, more to himself as he sat back, lost in thought. "A long time."

The door flew open and Lieutenant Dodo came back in, rain dripping from his beard. "There's been a development, sir," he said, chest heaving and eyes wide. "It's big, sir."

"They got a patrol set up, don't they?" Ricky asked with a glance at H. "They'll be lookin' for you, love."

Lieutenant nodded. "Yes, sir. The whole city is crawlin' with them."

"See, now—"

"But there's something else, sir," Lieutenant interrupted.

Ricky glared at him. "Well out with it."

He opened his mouth, but it took a second for the words to come out. As if he himself couldn't believe them.

"Red is dead, sir."

Ricky sat back, chewing on his pipe. H gasped and Jesper stared, dumbfounded. A cry of pain came from Riley as he forced himself up to a sitting position on the cot.

"Hey," Ricky said, "careful there—"

"Are you sure?" Riley demanded, his voice hoarse and eyes on Lieutenant. "Are you *sure*?"

Lieutenant nodded again. "Yes, sir. I saw it myself, sir."

Riley stared in horror, agony etched on his face. H glanced over him, clearly confused by his reaction, and asked, "How did it happen?"

Jesper didn't want to know, but Lieutenant Dodo told him anyway.

"Ally Lewis, ma'am. Decapitation."

A cold silence settled. Jesper's shoulders crumbled and he held his face in his hands, remembering his sister's words.

Where we're from, the crown usually chops people's heads off.

It took a few minutes for H's whisper to break the stillness. "She killed Red?"

"Yes ma'am. Most Black Cards have joined her cause. The few who didn't were also decapitated. It's unclear if Red—"

"Rose." Riley sat slumped in defeat on the cot, his voice haunted. "Her name was Rose."

"Well sizzle my britches and call me Cassidy!" Ricky exclaimed, looking at Riley in a way that made him curl further down on the cot. "All these years, Red was that girl you were in lo—"

"Not now," Riley murmured. He sounded so fragile. So defeated. "Please, just not now."

Jesper glanced at H. She shrugged. She didn't know Rose either.

Ally what have you done?

"Well now," Ricky said, slapping his knee. "What a day. I never dreamed she'd go that far. Yes, siree, what a day. Solves most of my problems." Then he turned to Lieutenant. "We've got a lot to do, and we gotta do it fast. The city will be in chaos. Ally won't know what comes next." Jesper stiffened at his sister's name. "I'll give the chickadee a moment to bask in her glory before callin' her in. It'll bite all our butts, but the key will be to grovel a bit. She's comfortable with our system. Trusts me more than anyone, that's for sure. We shouldn't have an issue fallin' in line—"

"What?" Jesper cut in after the words had sunk in. "What are you doing with my sister?"

Ricky turned his gaze to him, unimpressed. "Well Ally *is* my protegee, so to speak."

"No." Jesper shook his head. He didn't understand that word, but he knew it was wrong. "Ally had nothing to do with you or your system. She works at a gas station."

Ricky barked a laugh that made Jesper feel two inches tall. "A gas station, huh? That's a good one. Girl is more than I bargained for, that's for darn sure." When Jesper just stared blankly at him, he pulled his pipe from his mouth. "Chickadee was lyin' to ya, kid. Ally's been mine for a while now."

"And you told her to do *this*?"

"You mean take off Red's head? No, I didn't tell her to do nothin'. She's a smart, paranoid girl who wanted something more. That kid AJ knows power when he sees it—he traded King for Red in a heartbeat—so I knew he'd be drawn to her if they spent time together. I put her on the path. She chose to walk it. I didn't know how far she'd make it, especially after her little drug lapse, but she's done good."

"Done good?" Jesper repeated, an unknown rage filling up the empty spaces inside of him. "Done *good?*"

Riley sighed, and it sounded hundreds of years old. "Ricky, what did you do?"

Ricky just shrugged. "King knew I had a gift, didn't question why vac was better than anything he could think up. I was his main supplier until that red girl kicked me out for reasons I can't explain. I was top of the world, you understand? I've been trying to get back in with her for years. But now, Red's gone and Ally's *my* girl. She won't trust none of Red's people. With her in charge, she'll turn to me, and I'll get all my business back."

H gaped. "You mean you let all this happen just so you could sell more vac?"

The question rattled something deep inside Jesper's brain that he'd long since buried in a deep hole. *King didn't question why vac was better than anything here. Because vac isn't* from *here.*

"Vacara," Jesper breathed, the word scalding his throat on the way out. "You sell vacara here?"

Ricky grinned at the recognition, straightening with pride. "Vacara is the best leaf in Elaria, and I managed to bring it here. Takes a lot to grow it, and it ain't as powerful, but for the folks here?" Ricky whistled, then winked, as if they were both part of some sick inside joke. "It's outta this world."

A surge of hatred overtook Jesper and he clenched his fists. For the first time in his life, he wanted to hit someone. To rip them to pieces. "Vacara murdered my mother. We would've been okay if she had never touched vacara." His body started shaking so violently he thought he might explode. "Vacara *ruined* us. And you used my *sister* to help you sell more of it? Is that how you're controlling her? Is that what you did to her?"

Ricky just shrugged, indifferent. "I didn't do nothin', kid. Like I said, I showed her the path, but she walked it. The girl out there murderin' folks to get what she wants—that's your real sister." He whistled again. "Must make those family reunions tough, huh?"

That's your real sister. The rage simmered into despair. He'd seen that fire in his sister since coming here, and consciously or not, he had chosen to ignore it. To pretend it could get better. To hope that he could protect her from everything, but also from herself. Jesper slumped over, the weight of it all too much to carry.

"How could you do this?" H demanded, getting to her feet. "Look at what you've caused!"

Ricky leaned back in his chair without a care. "Now, look, I'm sorry you got in the line of fire, chickadee, but that's not my fault or my problem. You *should* be more worried about survivin' the night. If Ally sees you or Riley, it's over, and she's got people watchin' everywhere. You'll never get out of Ducat on your own."

"But we will with you?" H shot back in disgust. "What's your price, huh?"

He raised his hands, as if bestowing a great gift of charity. It made Jesper want to punch him again. "Free of charge, for your trouble." Then he flicked his gaze to Jesper. "I know the portal outta here, and I know the one to get you back to Elaria. It's your safest way out."

Jesper couldn't believe it. All these months trying to get home, and he could've just asked the dealer on the corner. He narrowed his eyes. "Why have you never gone back? If Red took all your business, why didn't you go somewhere else?"

For the first time, Ricky's bravado deflated slightly. He took a long drag of smoke as he considered, his gray eyes worlds away. "I would've, back in the day. I've been everywhere. I've seen things…" he trailed off in wonder, and Jesper realized that all those places he'd rambled on about were actually real. How many portals had been in the In Between? Dozens? Hundreds? It had been so hard to tell in the dark.

Ricky sighed. "While you wandered, you ever meet the Banished?"

Riley opened his mouth, as if to protest, but Ricky shushed him. Jesper nodded. "A settlement of people. All of them said they couldn't leave the In Between."

"It's a nasty fate," Ricky said, his voice grave. "Stuck in that darkness forever. Could drive a man mad. And it should've been me, banished in there. I managed to escape—and don't get me wrong, kid, this dump of a city is still better than that wasteland—but, you see, now I'm kinda reversed banished."

Jesper watched him for a minute, letting the meaning of the words sink in. "You can't leave here."

He shook his head, and he looked truly devastated. "This world is a fading ember compared to ones I've seen. But I can't go through another portal." Then he cleared his throat, and his expression hardened. "This place is what I got now. I make it mine, in my way. And I will mow down anyone that tries to stop me."

The air crackled with electricity, flooding Jesper with a sensation he hadn't felt in a long time. His jaw fell open when he recognized the presence of magic. Elarian magic, not the internet they had here. Ricky's gaze bore into Jesper, an unspoken threat that nobody else noticed.

H just hissed in frustration. "You're talking crazy! You should be helping us *stop this,* not just get us out of the way so you can get what you want."

"Look, love," Ricky said coolly, not an ounce of remorse in his tone. "I want what I want. You either go with the flow or drown. Your call."

"I'll take her with me," Jesper thought aloud. "I'll take Ally home with me, and you can do whatever you want here."

Ricky laughed. "You know her better than me, kid, but I'm thinkin' there's no way she leaves this behind. She wants this. And I'm happy to give her the spotlight and all the heavy work so long as I get my money back."

She'll pick me. Jesper and Ally had alway been a team, the two of them against the world. Nothing could tear them apart. He had to believe that. *She'll pick me.*

"Let me talk to her," Jesper said. "In person. If she sees me, she'll come to her senses, I know it. I'll take her back with me, and you can take over from there. Either way, you get what you want."

Ricky just shrugged. "Your funeral, kid. If you don't come back I ain't wastin' the resources to get you back. You accept those terms?"

Jesper nodded and gestured to Riley and H. "As long as you make sure they are safe."

"I mean, I'll do my best kid, but my gut says they won't survive the In Between without you."

"They won't have to."

Chewing on his pipe, Ricky weighed the options in his head. "Fine, but mostly 'cause I'm curious. Lieutenant, here, will show you out and a quick escape through the sewer if you decide to cut your losses and come back before she cuts off your head too."

Jesper recoiled at the thought, but didn't hesitate to follow Lieutenant back out the door they came through. He couldn't bring himself to give one last glance to Riley or H.

He could fix this. He had to.

She'll pick me. Jesper and Ally had always been a team, the two of them against the world. Nothing could tear them apart. He had to believe that. *She's hurting and confused, but when it comes down to it, she'll pick me.*

He listened half-heartedly as Lieutenant led him through a tunnel and pointed to a ladder, explaining that this grate was light enough to lift on his own and Ricky would have his head if anyone followed him back down here.

Jesper winced at the expression. Lieutenant had the decency to lower his head in apology.

"If I may speak out of turn, sir," he said, "I hope you get your sister back."

Get her back. Because Jesper hadn't realized that he'd lost her until it was too late.

No, not too late. She'll pick me.

Jesper nodded. "Thank you." Then he climbed the ladder and pushed himself back up and onto the street deep down an alley. Nothing had changed, but everything looked so different. The same bones of the city but painted over and unrecognizable.

For a disorienting moment, Jesper realized he didn't know where to even look for Ally, but then he remembered the sobering news and shuddered. If she'd killed Red in her own alley, maybe she was still there. A part of him hoped he was wrong.

Lieutenant must've been thinking the same thing, though, because when he walked out of the alley and into the street, he found himself less than three blocks from Red's old throne. Not even a minute passed before somebody shouted his name.

A young man with intricately buzzed hair ran toward him, grabbing his forearm roughly, almost desperately, then let him go. His eyes were wide and jumpy. He jerked his head to look back over his shoulder like something was watching him, then took Jesper's forearm again and started pulling him down the street.

"She's been looking for you," he muttered under his breath. "Maybe now this insanity can be over."

Jesper opened his mouth, a million questions prepped to flood out of him, but they all dried up into dust when they rounded the corner.

Blood.

So much blood.

Jesper couldn't even see a clear spot of pavement.

His stomach rolled at the stench of the massacre, then heaved at the object hanging from the fire escape like the freshener in Riley's car.

Red's head.

Next to it, her signature black jacket hung, though it was drenched in so much blood it was hardly recognizable if not for the threaded rose peeking out from the sleeve.

And sitting on top of the makeshift metal throne was Ally.

She didn't look like his sister anymore.

Like the city, the bare bones of her were the same, but Jesper did not recognize the distorted mania painted on her face. The same stringy blonde hair, but now so dirty it was browner and missing in small patches. The same narrowed eyes, but now tinged with something wild. The same sly mouth, but stretched into a razor sharp, bloodstained smile.

"What have you done?" Jesper breathed. The young man who had dragged him here glanced over, then swallowed hard and turned back to Ally.

"I found him. Looked like he was on his way here."

Ally laughed in delight when she saw Jesper, but for once, the sound grated on his ears. "AJ, clear the area. I want everyone gone. This is just for us."

AJ nodded, looking a bit too eager as he fled the alleyway, and Jesper heard him call out to others and repeat the order.

Ally said something about not trusting anyone to eavesdrop, but her head was turned at an odd angle, as if talking to somebody over her shoulder. But she sat alone.

"Jes!" she exclaimed, bouncing in excitement as she pulled herself to her feet and practically leapt down the stairs. There was a lilting kind of unsteadiness to her movements that made his eyebrows furrow. When her boots hit the ground, the pool of blood actually splattered, and he flinched away from it.

"Are you drunk?" he blurted. He hoped she said yes. He hoped she was on heavy drugs and once he could flush them out of her system, she would be his sister once more.

She laughed again, and it was a thousand needlepoints against his skin. The scene didn't match. The sound didn't go with the dried blood on her face.

"If you mean drunk on power, then yes! I did it!" Then her face dropped into a deadly scowl, the whiplash nearly breaking Jesper's neck. She turned slightly over her shoulder again and screamed, "I'm better than you! I don't need it anymore! I have everything you never did!"

Jesper swallowed hard. Was she talking to…Red's severed head?

Then she turned back to him, smiling bright. "I'm so happy you came. I knew you would, I just knew it. *Some* people," she rolled her eyes and glanced behind her again, "doubted, especially after our sad little phone call, but I always knew we would end up together again. You were just confused. Now you're free. We both are!"

"Ally." Even to him, his voice sounded old and defeated. The words sliced right through Ally's excitement, cutting it in half and leaving the corpse on the ground in the puddle of blood. "Stop. You need to stop this madness and come home."

"Shut up!" Ally shouted, but she threw the words over her shoulder like a grenade. When she looked at Jesper again, her expression had shifted to offense. "Home? *Home*? Where's home, Jes, huh? Let me tell you since you keep forgetting: We. Don't. Have. One. We've *never* had anything to go back to, and I never planned on going back. That hellhole was not a home. I'm *making* one. We never had a real home, not one we were safe in. Now we do. Because of me!"

Jesper struggled to follow that line of logic. "How can you…how can you think that? How is this making a home? How does cutting people's heads off seem like the right thing to do?" Even just saying the words out loud made him recoil. "How does it make sense to choose this over me?"

Ally hissed. "You mean like you chose Riley? That stupid blob of hair and dirty cat? Don't talk to me about choosing. I'm giving you a place to come back to even after you left me for them. I love you the most, and this is how I prove it. I forgive you for that. I give this to you. This is what I do for us, to keep us safe."

Then she turned over her shoulder again. "No," she said coldly, "because you never did."

"I never did what?" Jesper asked, dread creeping up his spine at the certainty in her words, the crazed way she flipped back and forth to talk to the wall. "What should I have done? I'm just…I've only ever tried to protect you."

She sighed in exasperation. "We don't need protection anymore. Don't you get it? I've made it so nobody can ever *ever* hurt you again. Nobody can hold power over us if we have it all. There is not a single person in this city that won't answer to me. This place is ours."

I did this for you, she had kept saying on the phone, as if bestowing a great gift. Jesper had always wanted that for her too. To be safe, whole, happy. But not like this. Never like this.

The haunted words slipped from his mouth before he could trap them. "I thought you could take care of yourself. I left you alone in this place and then…I was so afraid—*so afraid*—that you would turn into Mom. Instead you've turned into Dad."

And in that moment, Jesper had a bolt of clarity shake him.

A real man would take care of his family no matter what, Monty would say, when their world teetered on the balance of staying sane and falling apart. Back then he said it like a prayer. Later, he would hurl the words at Jesper like knives. But maybe the blades had never been meant for Jesper in the first place— maybe Monty had cut himself on them instead.

For the first time, instead of feeling unrelenting guilt when it came to his father, Jesper understood him.

A real man would take care of his family no matter what. Maybe that's what Monty had tried to do all along, what Alice had hoped she could do someday. Maybe that's what Ally was trying to do now. But they all got lost. Lost in the sorrow, lost in the fear, lost in the madness. It would be so easy for Jesper to get lost too. And maybe he had been, for a while, for years. But now he had found good. He had found good worth hanging onto, good worth protecting.

Ally's jaw snapped shut with an audible crack. A snarl came from her throat and her whole body trembled with fury in a way that Jesper had never seen. Her eyes widened as if in response to something, and in one move, she twisted on the heel of her boot, yanked a gun from her cloak pocket, and shot three times.

"Shut up!" she shrieked. "Shut up shut up shut up!"

The bullets lodged into the brick wall in a haphazard triangle. Jesper couldn't help an unsteady step backward when Ally turned her frenzied gaze back on him.

"How dare you?" she shouted, smacking her head with the gun as she ripped some of her hair out in her fists. "I am nothing like him. Do you hear me? I am *nothing like him!*" She took a breath that did little to settle her. "I'm doing what it takes to protect us. There is so much bad and I'm doing what it takes to keep us safe. Does that sound like our father?" She spat on the ground toward the bullet filled wall.

"There is a lot of bad," Jesper said softly. "But Ally there is good too. Good things that give you strength. That protect you just as much as your gun does. Better than your gun."

Friendship and coffee and good movies and a soft bed. The list Jesper had made of good things in the last few months was nearly endless. Did they really protect against the darkness in the house he'd lived in, in this world that was so corrupt and bleak?

Riley was good. He chose to be good, despite everything. A bright spot in the dark sky. And he'd shown Jesper that he could choose to be something good too.

"Yeah, really?" Ally laughed, but now it was fast and sharp. "And does it make it worth it, Jes, when all that fake good turns on you? When you realize there *is* no good in this world, when that pathetic safety net is all just a lie?"

Jesper thought of Kat, if the pain of losing her was worth the joy of knowing her, even for a short time. "Yes. It's worth it."

And now, looking at her, seeing her utterly and completely lost, he knew. He knew what he would turn into if he let go. He knew he had to hang onto that good, to walk toward the light, claw his own way out of the darkness.

Even if his mother hadn't been able to.

Even if his father didn't have the chance.

Even if his sister wouldn't follow.

"This conversation is ridiculous." Ally's voice hardened. "It's all over now anyways." She gestured to Red's head with the gun. "It's already mine. You'll see, eventually. It'll take time, but you'll be grateful to me someday. My debt will be paid, and you'll be proud."

Jesper shook his head slowly, and his voice cracked. "Ally. Ally I would've...I would've done *anything*."

A flash of a memory came: baby Ally, crying in his lap, clinging to his shirt.

Will you leave me too? she had cried. *Will you leave me like Mommy did?*

And I promised her I wouldn't. Tears filled Jesper's eyes as he realized what breaking that promise would mean, the guilt and anguish threatening to overwhelm him. *I promised I would never leave her.*

You didn't. The thought came soft and simple. *You were always there for her. You killed yourself over again and again for her. You never left her. She left you.*

A sob worked through Jesper and he closed his eyes, tears falling down his face, as his words split his chest in half. A wound he knew he would never fully recover from for the rest of his life. "Where you're going," he whispered, "I can't follow. I won't follow. This is it, Ally. Come back with me. Please."

His whole world teetered on the balance right then and there. Just a handful of seconds, frozen, suspended, as Jesper watched their entire life play out before his eyes. Every painful, misguided, and hopeless step that had brought them here, on opposite sides, instead of fighting with each other. Fighting *for* each other.

Then Ally took a shaky breath and time moved again. She stared at him with a deep-rooted resolve, sealed with the blood at her feet. "You're wrong. And you'll see. You'll all see. I'm right."

The breath got knocked out of Jesper with the rest of his hope.

It was over. He'd lost her.

"I still love you, Ally," he told her. "I always will."

For the first time, her voice wavered with uncertainty. "Don't say it like you're saying goodbye."

"The day you were born was the happiest day of my life. I don't think I ever told you that. Part of me...part of me loved it, just a little, when Mom went off the deep end because taking care of you was my favorite thing. We were a team."

She shook her head, and it might've been the reflection of streetlight, but he thought he saw a glimmer of tears in her eyes. "Stop."

"You...you were my reason. You always have been." He took a breath, hearing baby Ally call to him in his mind, cry out for him, hug him. "I'll remember you like that: the little girl who loved to collect rocks and play with sticks and held my pinky in her fist when she was scared."

"You can't leave. I've got people everywhere. I won't let you."

Jesper just shook his head. "I won't follow."

Ally started to hyperventilate, her voice growing louder with each word. "So what? What's your plan, then, huh? You have *nobody left!* Nobody left but *me,* your sister! You don't have anywhere else to go!"

Then she whipped around and shot the same wall again. "He's mine! He's always been mine!"

When she faced him again, all the shreds of his sister were gone. Her eyes seemed to shine with mania, and she shrieked so loud that the sound bounced off the walls, splitting Jesper's ears.

"You think I will let you just *walk away*? After everything I've done for you? No! No, no, no, no, no! You're mine!" Then she raised the gun, pointing it squarely at Jesper's chest.

Jesper's heart stopped. His gaze dropped to the gun, and he raised his hands automatically. "Ally—"

"No! You've made your choice and I've made mine. If I can't have you to myself, then nobody can have you at all. I love you the very most."

"I love you too," he choked out. Slowly he took a step back. "I always have." Another step back. "I always will."

"Stop!" Tears streamed down her face now, the two wet lines the last dregs of any humanity left inside her. She reaffirmed her hold on the gun and forced the words through her teeth. "Don't move or I will shoot."

But Jesper kept backing up. She wouldn't shoot him. Somewhere inside, somewhere deep, she wasn't so far gone that she would take the shot.

Wasn't she?

Another step. Another. Just two more and he was out.

Just two more and she was gone forever.

You have nowhere else to go. His steps faltered.

"Jesper!" Ally screeched, her sobs starting to overtake her. "Jesper, no! I will do it! You're only mine!" The arm holding the gun kept bending and straightening violently, as if trying to force herself to shoot.

She wouldn't bring herself to pull the trigger. She couldn't.

"Goodbye, Ally," he whispered. He took one last glance of the deranged, blood-soaked girl that used to be his, then shifted on his feet, preparing to run. The second he did, the moment he turned the corner, he heard the shot ring out.

The sound was deafening. The air scalded his face as the bullet whizzed by, barely missing him.

Jesper ran.

Jesper ran like he never had before, and in his wake, Ally's scream shattered the sky.

* * * * * * *

When Jesper was safe underground again, he unraveled. He collapsed against the metal ladder, his chest torn open, a part of him cut off and gone forever. He cried for all of them, for everything. For Alice and her daughter, who had fallen into holes so deep they could only see darkness. For Monty and his son, who had lost themselves trying to pull them out. For Riley and H, who gave everything they had to being a dim light in the void. For Kat and Mama March, who were taken by the darkness anyways.

You have nowhere else to go. He had only known the darkness for so long. Would he ever belong in the light? Could he ever live without her?

The agony of the next steps nearly crumbled all his resolve. Go back. Face the home that had been his prison. Leave the girl who had been his home.

He took a shuddering breath and would've screamed if he had the will do to even that. For a wild moment, he wondered if death would be the only release from this anguish. If so, he would welcome it.

A real man would take care of his family no matter what. It was the first time in years that his father's voice brought him…maybe not peace, but stillness. Enough clarity to bury the torment in his heart for a moment longer, to live another day if only to prove this sacrifice wasn't for nothing.

So Jesper took a deep breath, wincing as it seemed to puncture his lungs like a million knives, and tried to set his emotion aside and focus. He knew now without a doubt that Ally would have Riley and H killed the moment she found out they were alive. And she would never stop looking for Jesper, even if they managed to escape the city limits by some miracle. Where would he go? He knew so little of this world outside of Ducat. How could he possibly hope to survive?

And that was even if they could leave this hideout. Jesper knew he didn't have much of a choice, not really. Ricky wouldn't have told them so much about who he was if he planned on them sticking around in this world. If they refused him, Jesper would be no match for his magic, and Riley and H were already weakened. One way or another, Ricky would get rid of them.

Jesper swallowed and forced his wilting body to straighten, his numb limbs to move. One foot in front of the other.

A real man would take care of his family.

The three of them must've been arguing while he was gone: H had her fists raised and was breathing hard, and Ricky had lines of impatience running across his forehead. They all fell silent and looked at him. Riley let out a long sigh and H's shoulders slumped when they saw the look on his face.

"Yeah, didn't think so," Ricky muttered.

Jesper ignored him, walking straight up to H and Riley and kneeling in front of the cot. H gave him a measured look, as if conflicted; Riley's eyes were just lifeless and tired. Jesper's chest wound throbbed, but he understood their distance. He wouldn't blame them if they never wanted to see him again.

"I brought this to you," he choked out. "I didn't mean to, I...I never would. You welcomed us and we...we...I am so *sorry*." His tears overtook his voice for a moment. "I know...I know that can't...it can't make up for it. It doesn't matter. But I am so sorry. And I understand if you hate me for it. That's okay."

He swallowed hard, fighting for composure. "But my dad told me to always protect your family. And you can hate me, but I...you are the family I found. And if you'll let me, I'll do everything I can to get you out of here safely. I can't...I can't promise much, but I can...I can promise something."

Bracing himself, Jesper waited for their scorn and bitterness, for them to cast him out of their lives.

With a grunt of pain, Riley reached his hand over and placed it on Jesper's shoulder. "You aren't your sister, Jesper," he said softly and Jesper nearly crumbled with relief. "We're grateful for everything you've done." He flicked his gaze to Ricky. "I just...I'm not sure if...that's the best idea."

"What other option you got, kid?" Ricky asked. "Get your head outta your computer and try belief for a change."

H rubbed her face and looked at Jesper. "A portal to another world? And it works?"

Jesper nodded softly, aching for her approval again, her friendship.

She glanced over him once, twice, thinking hard. Then she sighed. "It's like that freakin' Amy Adams movie Kat loved."

Through his tears, Jesper grinned faintly. "This is the reprise. You've got about thirty seconds to decide if you're in or out. Then the show must go on."

H gave him a small smile. "She would kill me if I said no, and I don't really want anyone else to kill me either. I guess I'm in."

"Alright then." Ricky stood from his chair, joints popping, and turned to Lieutenant Dodo, still standing at attention. "Long journey home for these kids. Get them whatever the boy wants and be ready to move out in twenty."

Looking at Ricky too long made Jesper's blood start to boil again, so he turned to Lieutenant. "Food, water, flashlights, batteries, rope, and any weapons you can spare. Nothing that makes noise."

He nodded and headed for the shelves. While he gathered supplies, H went to the bathroom and Ricky checked on Riley's wound. Jesper was shocked to learn that Ricky had used *magic* to save Riley from the bullet.

"How?" Jesper asked. "I haven't seen any of that magic here."

"It's dull, kid," Ricky answered. "I'm a shadow of my former self. There are roots of magic here that I can pick at, but nothing flourishes. It's why I keep to the sidelines." He nodded at Riley. "I've done what I can, but you'll want to get him to a doctor ASAP."

Jesper glanced sideways at him. "Why not just kill us now? Why go through the trouble of getting us out?"

"Three reasons," Ricky said as if they were talking about the weather and not about murder. He pulled up Riley's shirt to inspect the angry red wound while he listed them off. "One, I keep to my debts. I'm a man of my word when my word seems fit to keep. I promised Riley's old man I would help him, and I will do just that. Second, I don't like dealing with bodies if I don't have to. They're gross and smell bad. And third, I don't need the fallout. If your sister ever found out somehow, I don't need her goin' crazy on me and cutting *my* head off."

Jesper flinched. "But what if she finds out you snuck us out? What if someone sees us?"

"She won't." Ricky winked at him, which made Jesper very uncomfortable. "Why do you think you've only seen me once in all the months you've lived here? And how has Riley and the little lost animals he adopted stayed safe from Red with targets on their backs? I still got enough magic for survival. I only get seen by those who want to find me. And who *I* want to find me, mind you. Nobody will see us."

Riley, having been unconscious when Ricky first used magic on him, gave them both a skeptical look. That quickly melted from his face when Ricky passed his hand over the bullet wound. A slight buzz filled the air, and the redness went down ever so slightly. The edges of the wound pulled closed, barely, and it didn't look like it would hold for very long, but at least it was something.

"I think I'm still in shock," Riley said as Ricky taped up his stomach with bandages. "That's it. I'm still in shock."

Ricky chuckled. "Wish I could be there to see your face, kid."

The next half hour passed in a dream-like blur. Jesper floated above his body, numb to the world, in a determined daze. If he stopped for more than a second, he heard Ally's voice in his head. Yelling. Empty. Crying. He had a feeling he wouldn't stop hearing her voice for a long time. He probably deserved to.

He helped Lieutenant Dodo go through the shelves and pack supplies into three bags. Jesper took all the flashlights, candles, and lighters he could find. Dried food, bottles of water, first aid kits, coils of rope. He accepted two lightweight bed rolls, for H and Riley. He knew Riley would insist on carrying something, so Jesper would give him the rolls and carry two packs.

As he arranged everything in the sturdy black backpacks Lieutenant had produced—these shelves had stockpiles of everything from giant bags of pistachios to a dozen air filters—Ricky came up to him. The man had abandoned his pipe for the time being, but the stench of smoke still stuck to him. In the short time Jesper had spent with him, Ricky had his mouth set, his eyes focused, his expression arrogant. But now he had his lips pursed and his eyes on the ground. Unsure of himself, for the first time.

"I made a copy of this," he said, clutching a folded paper in his hands. "I first made it, oh I dunno, at least twenty-somethin' years ago when I started workin' on it. Maybe more. Hard to say." He hesitated before offering the folded paper to Jesper. "It's a map. Of the In Between. Tough to really get it to scale, but I tried to measure with footsteps best I could."

Jesper watched him warily before taking the paper and opening it up. It wasn't as much a map as instructions. A circled ink blot showed where they would end up in the In Between after going through the portal. Lots of words and numbers and lines filled it up, but Jesper recognized the destination: Elaria.

"It's not the full one, of course," Ricky went on. "Didn't have time to put all the details in it. But that can help you get where you need to go. Just…" He leaned toward Jesper, and Jesper did his best not to lean away. "Be careful who you show that to, you hear me? Not everyone is friendly in there. They'd sooner skin ya for the pelt and map than point you in the right direction."

Jesper just nodded blankly and tucked the map in his bag. Ricky huffed to himself, then ushered them on, back to business. "Alrighty you folks, let's get going. I gotta make the trip myself to get you there, and I want to get back before anyone misses me." They all knew he meant Ally; nobody said it.

Lieutenant Dodo helped Jesper hoist Riley to his feet. The blood drained from Riley's face and he swayed, but managed to keep himself upright. With a tight nod, he urged them forward with H at Jesper's side.

Ricky led them through the sewer tunnels, keeping a brisk pace despite the slight limp that Jesper just noticed he had. Riley trembled as he walked, and Jesper broke into a sweat under his weight, but he kept pressing forward, Ally's voice chasing him through the empty space.

Jesper didn't know what to expect, so he was surprised when Ricky finally led them up a flight of crumbling stairs and straight onto a dock. The fresh night air seemed to slap Jesper's face, waking him up a little. He watched as Ricky held up his hands and a ripple of electricity went through the air. Shielding them. Jesper couldn't see the invisible wall, but he noticed the way Ricky's shoulders slumped and his limp grew more pronounced afterward. Using magic really did take its toll here.

A medium-sized white boat awaited them at the end of the dock. Lieutenant helped Jesper get Riley inside, then Jesper reached back to help H step down too, only to find she'd already done it herself. She gave him a nod; Jesper hoped it meant something encouraging.

From the dock, Jesper hadn't been able to see much of the ocean in the dark. The second the boat pushed off, though, he knew it was a bad night for a water ride. The boat lilted to the side roughly, then back again, as the waves slammed into it again and again. Unlike the last time he'd attempted this though, the boat was just big enough to stay upright.

The last time was with me, Ally's voice snapped in his head. *You almost drowned me that night, and now you're leaving me behind.*

Shaking the memory out of his head, Jesper sat on the bench and let H clutch his hand. The waves or the rain or both had already drenched them, and both H and Riley shivered on either side of him. Jesper couldn't even feel the cold. He watched as Ricky commanded the boat with ease, barking orders at Lieutenant every once in a while. He steered with one hand and held a compass in the other. Taking him home. Jesper still couldn't wrap his mind around it.

How long had they been in the boat? Twenty minutes? An hour? Jesper knew it was just the beginning of wondering the time, of going mad about it. When he truly thought of returning to the In Between, his stomach lurched. Could he really do it again? Especially without Ally by his side?

"Alrighty folks!" Ricky yelled over the raging waves, turning to shine a flashlight on the water. "Here's your stop."

"What are you talking about?" H shouted back. "We could drown out here!"

Ricky just shrugged, giving Jesper a knowing grin. "This is where you get off."

Riley's eyes were wide with disbelief behind his dripping glasses. "You're insane. We can't just jump into the ocean."

"How'd you get here, kid?" Ricky asked Jesper, pointing with his flashlight again. "Look familiar?"

Clinging to the side of the boat, Jesper stood and peeked over to where Ricky's light hit the ocean. At first, he thought it was a trick of the light, but then he saw it: a strange spot where the water seemed to cave in on itself somehow. As if there were a mirror there instead, reflecting the wave back to itself.

"That's the portal point," Ricky explained. "You see where the magic cuts in? Dunno why it's here, just know it is."

Jesper remembered the lake in the Molds, how Ally had dived down to get a stick or rock or something. She'd been so set on having it. And Jesper hadn't seen the strange pattern of the water until too late. Until they fell down into oblivion. And now here it was again.

Both H and Riley muttered something under their breath when they noticed the irregularity in the water too. Jesper's instinct was to hesitate, to question, to fear. But now he had no time for that. He had people to take care of, and he got the feeling that if they didn't go on their own soon, Ricky would just push them overboard. Might as well go when it was his choice.

Jesper secured his packs on his back and tied the straps around his waist, then turned to H and Riley and helped them do the same. Riley kept trying to tell Ricky to take them back. When Jesper glanced at H, she bit her lip as water ran down her face, her fear written out all over her. But when Jesper offered her his hand, she took it. The simple act gave him strength. He would protect his family. Even if it killed him.

Not allowing room for any rational thought, Jesper took Riley's hand too. Then he nodded at Ricky. A flicker of anger simmered when he thought of everything Ricky had done, but he let it pass. He'd already held on to too much in his life. Ricky tipped his head back at him, then Jesper jumped right into the raging ocean, pulling H and Riley with him.

He heard H scream right before they hit the water. The ruthless waves tossed them around as if they were nothing, sucking them under, under, under. Jesper's lungs ached, then screamed, then threatened to burst. His body begged him to give up. But he refused to unclench his hands to let go.

For a second, he wondered if he'd made a mistake. If he had made the entire thing up in his head. If he had just murdered them as Ally would've.

But then the bright white hit. The water drained away, air filled his lungs, and he collapsed onto a lumpy ground. When he could sit up and open his eyes, he found himself in the vast darkness of the In Between. The sour smell that tainted the musty air nearly made him vomit.

Still holding hands, H gasped as she slicked her hair back from her face and looked around. Riley had gone utterly still and even swore under his breath.

"What is this?" Riley asked in a daze. "Did we drown?"

Ally had wondered the same thing when they got here the first time. *Do you think we're dead?* she'd asked. *Is this what happens to people? What a waste.*

If he thought too much about her, especially here, especially now, he knew he would tumble into a dark hole and never be able to climb back out. He couldn't fall apart now.

As they caught their breaths and collected themselves, Jesper told them everything about his time here. The monsters called vrykol, the banished settlement, the other beings that Ricky had alluded to.

"This is how I got here," he said. "We fell into a portal by accident. We wandered for a while before we found Astrid and Duffer. Then when we were under attack, we jumped into another portal to save ourselves."

"And that brought you to Ducat?" H asked in awe. She listened to him as if he wove some magnificent fairytale. Riley just stared silently at him as if he were sprouting three heads.

"Yeah," Jesper finished. "I don't know how it works. I just know it does."

When Riley felt well enough to stand, they took out a flashlight and started walking. Jesper recognized all of it and none of it. There was nothing here. Endless nothing.

He answered their whispered questions as they walked. What the vrykol looked like, the legend of how they came to be, the way they hated light. He told them about the candles in their backpacks, and to light them if they needed to fight. He showed them Ricky's map, which ended up being only mildly helpful—they had no idea which direction to go, and the compass Jesper had taken from Ricky's supplies didn't work. It just turned again and again, aimlessly. As lost as they were.

When Riley couldn't walk anymore, Jesper settled him on the bedrolls as comfortably as possible. Then he pulled out a coil of rope and started to tie one end around his own ankle and the other around H's.

"What are you doing?" She stared at him with wide eyes, but this entire misadventure had brought some of the spark back to them. Or at least distracted her from her pain for a little while. Despite hating this place, Jesper found himself grateful to it for giving her a small break.

"I'm scouting out ahead," he explained. He pointed his pathetic attempt at a knot in the rope. "This will keep us from getting separated. If we run out, I'll stop and come back."

"At least let me do it," she said. "Those knots look like they're gonna unravel in seconds."

Jesper watched in awe as she expertly weaved an intricate knot around his ankle, then her own, and pulled them tightly. When she saw his expression, she just shrugged. "I read a lot, okay? And if I don't know something I read, I look it up. I'd say don't tell anyone so I'm not ridiculed as some nerd kid, but I guess it doesn't really matter anymore."

He grabbed another flashlight from his backpack so H could keep the one she had. Then he paused, taking in her disheveled hair and Riley nearly unconscious on the ground. "Will you be okay?"

H nodded, so fast Jesper wondered if she was also trying to convince herself. But she didn't hesitate. He admired her bravery. "I'll get us out of here," he said with more conviction than he felt. He only felt desperate. "I promise."

She shocked him by stepping forward and giving him a hug. Even now, all these months later, it surprised him. Such a simple way to heal people, even just a tiny bit. If Ally had been hugged more, would things have turned out differently?

You're kidding, right? Ally's voice scoffed in his head. *What in the skies have these people done to you?*

"Be careful," H whispered. The words gave him strength. He didn't flinch or hesitate as he turned and walked into the darkness alone. After all, he had wandered in darkness for a long time. He knew now that he could find his way, and the weight of the rope on his ankle gave him the resolve to keep going.

Time meant nothing in the In Between. He tried to keep it anyways, counting each beat of his bleeding heart. Each step toward his friends and each step away from them. Each time he heard a monster hissing in the distance, waiting to drag him under. And each time he used the light to drive them back again. Sometimes it barely worked, and he had a moment of thinking that he would die right there. Other times he heard Ally screaming in his head and nearly threw his light to the ground, begging for the monsters to put him out of his misery. But despite the vrykol's claws and close calls, Jesper managed to keep hold of the light, and as long as he held on it always drove the monsters back. Again and again.

By his best guess, it took them nearly two days to find the settlement. Jesper was shocked to find Astrid and Duffer recognized him the second they saw him. He gave the barest explanation of his journey. They helped him bring H and Riley in. He divided out their food, water, weapons, and lights to share with the people. Ricky's warning echoed in the back of his mind, but Jesper ignored it and gave Astrid the map he had, in exchange for helping them get to Elaria. She showed him the map she'd been working on herself, but admitted it didn't have as much detail as this one did and thanked him for it.

H was the one who pointed out Jesper's face, once she finally got a good look at him after their harrowing travels. In the chaos of it all, he hadn't paid attention to the painful stinging sensation of a fresh red spot high on his cheekbone, underneath his eye. The slightest burn from a bullet that had just barely grazed him. The bullet his sister had fired.

He couldn't bring himself to explain, and H, thankfully, let it go.

When they had all settled down, Riley's wounds tended to and food passed out, Astrid finally asked about the gaping wound in Jesper's chest.

"Where's your sister?"

A lump formed in Jesper's throat. He stared at the dried apple in his hand as Ally's voice shrieked at him. "She…she got lost."

Astrid nodded tightly, always the grieving soldier. Duffer gave Jesper a sympathetic smile, clapped him on the shoulder, and repeated the words he'd once said lifetimes ago.

"As long as you're anchored to what matters, no matter how dark the journey may be, you'll always find your way back home."

* * * * * * *

The weeds and gravel crunched underneath Jesper's feet as he made the long walk. After the endless silence of the In Between, the sound was utterly deafening.

Sweat dripped down his back as the sun beat down on him from a cloudless sky. The air was thicker here, somehow, harder to breathe. Filthier. It burned Jesper's nose and made him long for a good rainstorm to come wash the hazy air clean.

No, he hadn't missed the Molds at all.

Using the map from Ricky, Astrid and Duffer were able to get them to the Elarian portal. Riley had held up the best he could, but the trip through had nearly overwhelmed him. He'd collapsed by the lake they came out of, next to the rabbit hole Ally had been so obsessed with. H had stayed with him while Jesper went to get help.

Despite the ear-splitting sound of his footsteps, everything was quieter than he remembered. No screams of pain or wails of punishment sounded in the distance. Just empty. Jesper could hear every thunderous footstep, hear his sputtering heart as it started to beat faster and faster with every passing second.

Every second closer.

He hadn't been sure what he'd find. He didn't know what he *wanted* to find. Everything just as it was? All of it burnt to the ground? What would satisfy the ache in his limbs, the frantic buzzing in his mind? *Could* anything put it to rest if she wasn't by his side?

Jesper nearly doubled over at the thought. When he glanced down, he saw a pair of eyes staring at him from a hole in the earth. It made him stop in disbelief. Sure enough, the rabbit scampered out of the hole and sat there watching him, its nose twitching.

Could it be the same one? Had it managed to survive all this time? The burn under his eye seemed to flare.

After he recovered from the surprise, Jesper kept walking. The rabbit followed him for a while, but one time he looked back to see it had disappeared again.

A painful jolt shuddered through him when their crumbling house came into view. It definitely looked worse than when he'd left that morning: more holes in the walls, a caved in roof, cobwebs everywhere. Jesper had to rub his eyes. Somehow he couldn't reconcile this place with his house. He felt he was an outsider now, an audience member, seeing this tragedy from a different, distant lens.

Jesper had been right, both to his immense relief and crushing shame: he had grown, and he didn't quite fit here anymore.

Based on the state of the shack, he guessed there was little chance of anyone being inside. But despite knowing that, despite how every nerve prickled, Jesper put his hand on the knob and softly turned it. He had to take four breaths before he could get himself to step inside.

The inside matched the outside—an absolute wreck. Every piece of furniture broken, every cupboard door hanging off its hinges, every surviving window smashed to bits. His eyes tracked the trail of destruction until he saw the lump in the corner.

Jesper's heart stopped. Every muscle in him froze. Ally snarled in his mind as he realized the lump was his father. His beard was now completely white, his eyes bloodshot, his blistered skin cracked and ridden with purple veins. Monty had always been a solid wall of a man, standing firm and strong. But he'd been knocked down, finally destroyed beyond repair. Huddled in the corner like an animal, strung out and slowly starving to death.

"Jes?" Monty croaked, his unbelievably gaunt cheeks flapping with the movement. "Jes, you're alive?"

Jesper flinched at hearing his name in that voice. Part of him wanted to run, part of him wanted to hide, part of him wanted to break down crying, and part of him even wanted a slap across the face just for something familiar, for something easier.

There were a million things he could say. A million ways to attack, a million ways to hurt him. Nasty words describing horrific moments. Anger. Blame. Hatred. A punishing blow for everything he'd endured, especially while Monty was so weak. And yet, though a small part of him yearned for some kind of revenge, he had an overwhelming urge to drop his eyes. Duck his head. Retreat back into the holes in his mind.

Falling into the holes was so much easier than climbing out.

But Jesper couldn't ignore that he'd seen it firsthand. He knew how things started, how they got lost. He knew there had been a time when Monty picked him up and hugged him and told him stories about his day, and things were good. He knew his father loved him then. He knew that their mother had problems, that she didn't always respond right, that she couldn't seem to get the help she needed. He knew that things changed when they got here and Pepperjack took hold of their lives like they were just puppets on a string. Because Monty had been a solid wall of gentle goodness. And Pepperjack had seen that and done what he could to destroy it.

There was a day when Monty came home smeared in blood and locked himself in his room, and Jesper overheard him sobbing, "That poor girl," again and again. *What did he do to her?* Jesper had wondered, but he had an idea. *Something awful.*

Jesper knew that Monty never looked at Ally after that day. That they lost their father that day.

And he was *so tired* of carrying that. So tired of the endless cycle that had claimed his parents. Claimed his sister. He wouldn't let it claim him too.

It might kill him, but he was climbing out of this hole.

No excuses. No blame. Just the truth.

So instead of cowering in front of Monty or screaming at him like he shamefully still wanted to, Jesper met his father's gaze for the first time in years.

"I remember," Jesper said quietly. "I remember all of it."

Nobody meant for this to happen.

But it did.

And it ends now.

His father's once blue eyes had almost turned completely gray. No longer the gray of harsh steel, but the gray of wet rot on spoiled bread. The latest victim of the Molds. Those eyes stared into Jesper's as years of history played out silently between them. Monty's hand twitched, but for the first time in a long time, Jesper wasn't afraid of him.

Because Monty had been hired by Pepperjack for his skill in blacksmith magic. Monty was a fortress of a magician. And yet, he never once used magic on his children. Every time Ally and Jesper would slam the door between them and their father, they knew it didn't mean much: Monty could blow it right off its hinges with barely a thought. Some part of him, however buried, did not want to hurt them.

Not an excuse. Just the truth.

I can love you and I can hate you. I can want to be better than you. I can remember you as you were. And I can let you go.

"My friend needs help," Jesper went on, still unable to raise his voice more than a whisper. "Help me help him. Then we are leaving. We're getting out of the Molds and turning ourselves in. I'll tell my side of the story, that we were roped in by Pepperjack. I'll help you explain and find help. But we are leaving here. And we aren't coming back. I'm not coming back."

I'm not coming back home to you. I'm not yours anymore. The invisible rope that had tied Jesper to his father, that had forced him to return home instead of leave, that had choked him with guilt for the last years, was finally cut free.

Jesper had a gaping wound in his chest and a head full of ghosts, but he was free. And even if his limbs shook and his heart nearly gave out, he was going to climb out of this hole.

Monty took a deep, shuddering breath that seemed to rock the very core of him. Years of regret glistened in his lifeless eyes as he nodded once. Accepting defeat. Confirming to Jesper that Monty had already planned to die. He didn't want to think about what must've happened here in the last months to reduce Monty to this.

His nerves screamed at him, but Jesper held his hand out to Monty, if only because he knew it was what Riley would have done. He gritted his teeth as he helped his once powerful father struggle to his feet.

"You talk normal now," Monty stated gruffly, his voice as threadbare as his stained shirt. Then he gestured for Jesper to lead the way, and they stepped out into the blinding sun.

* * * * * * * *

Dear Ally,

Today marks two months since I last saw you. I miss you so much that I just decided to start writing this letter. I know you won't really get it, especially since I destroyed the portal, so it's kind of stupid, but it's also cool that I can write at all. Riley has been teaching me using a magic dictionary: I can say the word I'm looking for out loud, and it will automatically appear on the page so I can copy it down. You should've seen Riley's face the first time we used it. He's getting better at expecting it, but magic still shocks him every day.

I guess this whole time Riley actually thought we were crazy. Can you believe that Ally? When we first got to Ducat and said we were from Elaria and Riley couldn't find it and we acted weird, he thought we were patients that had escaped from a hospital. He thought that and still helped us out while he tried to track down any psych ward named Elaria or something like it.

I'm not sure if it's funny, exactly, but it's something.

The first thing I did here was take care of Dad. We just finished up his trial, and he's in prison now for all the things he did. But he won't be executed. I made sure of that. In a few years, he'll get a chance for probation if he wants it, part of a deal made for those trapped in Pepperjack's web. I'm not sure what I think about it yet.

I can't believe I did that without you. ~~You should've been with me.~~

Anyway, when we made it back to Elaria, the first person we ran into was Sterling Corona. I've never met him before, I just knew Dad didn't like him. I guess he started doing routine checks on the Molds after Pepperjack died to try and stop some of the faction wars going on. He found us and took us in and helped heal Riley. He reminds me of Riley a lot, like a grown-up Riley. I don't know why, but I felt like I could trust him. So I told him everything. He's the only one that knows our entire story.

When I told him I destroyed the portal, he said that was the right thing to do, and that we should keep it between us. I was so relieved. Then

413

he introduced us to his family. His daughter, Rosalind, started a relief fund for Pepperjack's victims and has been helping all the survivors. I don't know why she cares so much, but I'm very glad she does. Without her, we would probably be dead. She's given us a place to stay, food to eat, and a job to help us get back on our feet. She's quiet and really nice. I like her a lot. I don't know if you guys would get along, but I hope so.

It's been a huge adjustment for Riley and H, obviously. She jokes about being as dumb as I was when we first got to Ducat. She's doing okay, I think, as much as she can be. Rosalind has found a lot of people who were stolen and sold, many of them meeting fates like Kat. H talks to the survivors a lot. I think it gives her a piece of her best friend to hang onto.

Riley has just been lost. He doesn't have a purpose and he spirals without one. And since I don't really have any stability or life in Elaria, I've been worried about where we should go or what we should do now that the trial is over and Riley is better, you know? ~~*You were right: I have nowhere to go.*~~ *Just sitting around forever in someone else's house doesn't sound like a good idea.*

I've been thinking about it a lot as I've worked in the gardens with the Coronas' friend Gothel (he's quieter than Rosalind and a bit less nice, but H likes him. I do too). Anyway, one night H pulled out her cell phone, thinking it was just me and Riley. But Rosalind and Gothel walked in and saw it too.

I tried to cover it up, but it was too late. I was afraid of what they would think or what would happen if the story got out, because both Sterling and I thought it would be bad. Especially when Sterling confirmed my suspicion that cell phones and similar technology are illegal in Elaria and we should destroy everything we had. So far, it's the only promise I've made to him that I haven't kept. I feel really guilty about that.

I was afraid they were going to get mad at us or tell Sterling. But Rosalind and Gothel got very serious looks on their faces and had a whole secret conversation without talking. You could just tell. And then Gothel showed us his watch.

Not a magic watch. A regular watch. The kind you would find in Ducat.

Rosalind told us to keep it quiet, even from her parents, but she and Gothel had been looking into this kind of technology. She knows it's illegal—and that she would be in major trouble if she was caught—but she wants to change that. To bring more equality in Elaria. I thought that was pretty cool coming from her since she's supposed to be a very powerful magician.

They told us about this new pirate that's starting to make a name for themselves. This pirate deals in illegal technology and is slowly making waves throughout the kingdom. H is up for adventure and Riley is dying for a purpose, so we are heading out tomorrow to find this pirate and see if they can point us in the right direction.

I have no idea what's going to happen or where we will end up. I have no idea how I got here at all, really. And I don't know what I'm supposed to do. I guess now I just keep going. Funny how that feels like the strangest thing now. How do you manage to count the days you didn't think you'd ever have?

Elaria really is a beautiful place once you get out of the Molds, but I do miss the rain. It doesn't rain as much here. I miss it.

I miss you, Ally. I have nightmares about you. I love you and I'm scared of you and I feel like I let you down. I hear your voice all the time but you aren't actually there. It still breaks my heart every time.

H says your choices aren't my fault and I have to let it go, but I just have to ask.

When was the moment you chose that path? Was I with you? Could I have stopped it? If I loved you more, protected you better, would you be back here with me now?

Maybe you don't even know the answers. Maybe we both have to live with not knowing them.

I know it might not mean anything, but I have to tell you this before I go try to make this new life without you.

I love you. I hate what you turned into and I will carry that for the rest of my life. But I will always love you. You'll always be my little sister. And if you ever get tired of being a monster and know we are safe from Dad, I would take you. If you wanted to change, I would help you.

We fell into a deep dark hole, Ally. And I don't know how, I only know it's the hardest thing I've ever done, but I'm climbing out. If you ever decide you want to, you just have to reach out your hand. I'll always be there to pull you out.

No matter what happens, you can always come back home. You said we don't have one, but we do. Our home is each other.

And, no matter what, you'll always be my little sister.

* * * * * * *

Look at this! I went out and bought myself a nice new phone, and look what I found. I can talk to it and it will type everything I say. Can you believe Riley wasted so much of my time trying to teach me to write?

Ha!

I hate Riley! I hate him so much! What a stars-forsaken idiot.

I'm so happy I murdered him.

Today marks two months since I've seen you.

No. Since you left me.

And that's what you did, didn't you? It took me so long to figure it out. I had spies set up all over the city. I had eyes everywhere. Everywhere! Everybody was looking for you and that little blob. You've never been a good runner, and you disappeared off the street almost out of thin air. Then the days passed and you were just gone. Vanished.

Like magic, right?

Ha!

I know you went back to Elaria. I don't know how, but I know you did. It explains what you said to me, to come back with you. You found a way back and you took her and left me.

You left me.

You left me!

I still can't believe you left me.

I was so angry, I painted Ducat red. You know, I always always appreciated what you did for me growing up, the sacrifices you made. I did! I really did. And here I do all this for you, to keep you safe, and what do you do? You throw it away for some scrappy nobodies. How is that fair? How is that even fair?

It's not!

You threw me away like garbage!

But I realized I don't need you. You just held me back. Ricky and I have turned this place upside down. I'm the best leader there has ever been

416

in Ducat. Nobody dares question me and I want for nothing, while you're back in that wasteland hunting dead rabbits.

Ha! I bet you regret it now, don't you?

I wonder if some part of you is proud of me, even if your brainwashed mind can't admit it. What I've done is amazing. Someday you'll see that. You'll regret you didn't see it sooner. We could've had such an amazing life here together.

Your loss.

Enjoy Elaria while you can, I guess, if you can enjoy that dump of a place. Because I have a secret too.

I have magic. You know that rock that we found, the rock that brought us here, to my destiny? It's magic. It's made me the most powerful person in Ducat and I get better at using it every day.

So I'll find you. It might take me months. It might take me years. But I will find you someday, when my kingdom has turned into a massive empire. When you won't be able to doubt me. When you finally finally realize everything I did for us.

I'll see you again, Jes. You can count on it.

And you'll see me as I was always meant to be, with control, power, loyalty, and magic. With hundreds—no, thousands—that will kneel in front of me and protect my life with theirs.

I am queen of their hearts, queen of this wonderland.

This is the home I've always deserved. I built it myself from the ground up.

And I will never let it go.

Emilee King is the author of the Arie's Story survival series and the Elarian Chronicles. She loves fairy tales, superheroes, and murder mysteries, and is constantly on the hunt for good stories. When she's not writing, you can find her reorganizing her bookshelves, eating food, beating the high score on Galaga, or spending time with her family.

@emtheauthor

www.emileeking.com